The Branch and the Vine

900 Days Riding with Forrest

Confederate Reunion
Little Rock, Ark., May, 1911

GEN. THOMAS J. ("STONEWALL") JACKSON.

By

Richard Ledbetter

Twisted Pines Publishing
Post Office Box 677
4-Dice, Arkansas 71742
Phone: 870-352-2922

"I thoroughly enjoyed the read." Dr. Bill Gurley M.D.: Professor Of Pharmacology, Univ. of Arkansas School of Medical Sciences / author & co-editor of "I Acted from Principle", 2002 U.A. Press

"I was amazed at the expert writing, such a distinguished book. It should receive an award!" Barbara Meeker: Editor, ARC Press of Cane Hill

"General Forrest was no doubt the greatest cavalry commander of the war. To ride with him must have been a life's experience. The description of the sword fight in the preface immediately plunges the reader into the story. I could hardly wait to turn the page." Gov. Sidney McMath: Brigadier-General U.S.M.C., retired / two term Democratic Governor of Arkansas / thrice published Historian

"The Branch and the Vine" is an interesting, well-written story based on fact and dramatically fleshed out with amusing dialog. It commands the reader's attention at once and never lets up." Agnes Wynne Phillips: Dallas County Museum Founder & Director / Fordyce News Advocate History Editor

"Hard to put down once started, it should appeal to many readers and would readily make a great movie. It even includes a visit to a Memphis bordello, a subject seldom found in Civil War narratives." Dr. Bob Nunnally M.D.: The Parham Report Book Editor

"Thanks. It blew my mind!" Steve Earle: songwriter / musician / author of "Doghouse Roses", 2001 Houghton Mifflin

"On a level, perhaps, akin to such classics as "The Red Badge of Courage" and "Cold Mountain." Betsy Meador: Editor / Journalist

"It makes you feel like you're right on the battlefield!" J.C. Patterson: WLBT-TV3 Host, Jackson, MS. / author of "Big Easy Dreamin'" 2001 Pelican Press

"You're given many vivid word pictures of the grinding monotony and heart pounding energy of war." The Pine Bluff Commercial

The Author, Richard Ledbetter

9-20-2003

For Dennis Bownes,

I'm very happy to meet you and glad to meet a fellow Forrest student. Enjoy the read!

Thank You

I wish to express my humble appreciation to Betsy Lowe Meador, gratefully acknowledging all her diligent efforts and helpful suggestions during the final editing of this manuscript.

I also wish to thank four fellow descendants of the story's main character, cousin Sam Ledbetter, who originally suggested I investigate and document the saga, along with Charles E. Ledbetter, Donna Lyon and Billy Evans for sharing with me their insightful knowledge of family events.

Copyright 2002

Published by:
Twisted Pines Publishing Co.
P.O. Box 677
Fordyce, Arkansas 71742

2003 Revised Second Edition

For additional copies or to comment/receive information pertaining to Twisted Pines Recording and Publishing Services, call 870-352-2922 from Monday through Friday 8:00 A.M. to 4:3O P.M. Central Time. Also e-mail: rled@ipa.net

Cover art courtesy of Kim Allen
Twisted Pines ISBN #: 0-9720389-0-6

Acknowledgement

I would like to express my sincere gratitude to all the individuals who thanklessly labor within the historic societies and organizations that shine a bright light on the events of our national past, by preserving for proceeding generations the relics, documents and locations where our heritage was born. Through their efforts, ceaselessly opposing the unrelenting forces of decay and "progress," those who wish, may yet share a kinship of spirit with our ancestors, provided to us through a brief glimpse into their former ways of living and dying, momentarily suspending time when sharing the same unchanged spaces they trod and methods to which they were accustomed. The vigilance of these historians helped make this interpretation possible.

Thanks to:

Arkansas History Commission Archives
  Little Rock, Arkansas
Brice's Crossroads Battlefield Park
  Baldwin, Mississippi
Beauvoir Museum and Presidential Library
  Biloxi, Mississippi
Bradley County Genealogical Society
  Warren, Arkansas
Carter House Museum
  Franklin, Tennessee
City Park-Union Ave.
  Memphis, Tennessee
Chickamauga National Military Park
  La Fayette, Georgia
Confederate Hall Museum
  New Orleans, Louisiana
Corinth Historical Interpretive Center
  Corinth, Mississippi
Dallas County Public Library
& Dallas County Museum
  Fordyce, Arkansas
DeSoto Historical Society
  Hernando, Mississippi
Delta Cultural Center
  Helena, Arkansas
Fayetteville Confederate Cemetery
  Fayetteville, Arkansas
Fort Pillow State Park & Battleground
  Fulton, Tennessee
Gayoso House Hotel
  Memphis, Tennessee
Headquarters House Museum
  Fayetteville, Arkansas
The Heritage Museum
  Hermitage, Tennessee
Hernando Museum
  Hernando, Mississippi
Historic Arkansas Museum
  Little Rock, Arkansas
Lake Catherine State Park
  Hot Springs, Arkansas

Pine Bluff / Jefferson Co., AR. Museum
MacArthur Museum of Arkansas Military
History
  Little Rock, Arkansas
McCulloch / Chidester House Museum
  Camden, Arkansas
Museum of Natural Resources
  Stephens, Arkansas
Moro Bay State Park
  Jersey, Arkansas
Okalona Confederate Cemetery
  Okalona, Mississippi
Old Courthouse Museum
  Vicksburg, Mississippi
Ouachita County Public Library
& Ouachita County Genealogical Society
  Camden, Arkansas
Oxford County Courthouse
  Oxford, Mississippi
Pea Ridge National Military Park
  Garfield, Arkansas
Pink Palace Museum
  Memphis, Tennessee
Point Park
  Lookout Mountain, Georgia
Prairie Grove State Park
  Prairie Grove, Arkansas
Shiloh National Military Park
  Shiloh, Tennessee
The Old State House Museum
  Little Rock, Arkansas
Tennessee State Library and Archives
& Tennessee State Museum
  Nashville, Tennessee
Tupelo National Historic Site
  Tupelo, Mississippi
White Oak Lake State Park
  Bluff City, Arkansas
Wilson's Creek National Military Park
  Liberty, Missouri

For my family

Dedication

This book is lovingly dedicated to the memory of fellow Civil War historian and re-creator, Dr. James Walter O'Dell, without whose vast resource library I'd have too often been lost.

Foreword

This story concerns 900 days and nights spent by a pair of my ancestors in the Confederate mounted service, from enlistment February 22, 1862 until returning home September 4, 1864. In addition, it explores the workings of the old homestead farm located in lower Arkansas, granted to our family in 1855. It is recalled by Private John Riley Ledbetter, years after the fact and told from the comfort of his rural south Arkansas home to my grandfather Charles Polk Ledbetter, John's grandson, over a period from 1908, when C.P. was but a lad of nine, until just before the 75-year-old John's passing on Saint Patty's Day, 1911. It explores how two brothers found their way into Major General of Cavalry Nathan Bedford Forrest's personal escort.

I believe one of the most important elements in the research of history is an ability to read between the lines. When pursuing a paper trail of official, antiquated documents, interpretation of what sterilized governmental papers are actually trying to tell us becomes essential in order to connect all the dots into a sequential narrative. In my investigation of old Union and Confederate, state and county records held in the historical archives of Arkansas, Mississippi and Tennessee, I happily found an abundance of information about my great-great-grandfather and his elder brother William Edwin, whose military careers were spent mostly together in the Confederate mounted service. Many of those documents are replicated and contained herein at the end of the chapters to which they pertain.

In addition, I had passed-down verbal histories to draw on, gathered from various descendants of the characters whose lives during and after the American Civil War I've attempted to herein portray. Further, I read and plundered extensively from the many histories written about the units in which the two men served through the conflict.

I would also submit to you the importance of noting that this is no cloistered academic investigation alone. I walked or rode over the very grounds and waters where the described actions occurred those many years ago.

Thus, although dramatized, the story unfailingly follows the written and oral accounts of their service and much of our family's history in the Americas, striving to verify oral history from written records wherever possible. Drawing from the various sources of historical fact, I fashioned an anatomically correct skeleton of accuracy over which to lay the flesh of the story as I envisioned it while retracing their journey through the various lands they crossed and commands they came under. What I discovered over the course of my research was a story I felt well worth telling. Although it strictly follows the document trail as I found it, dialog was added to flesh out the characters and give them greater identity.

This manuscript is thus the result of combining scholarship, serendipity and tales learned from loved ones both living and long since dead, hopefully revealing a brief glimpse into the lives of our elders and betters, if often sad, also joyous, interesting and at times profound.

It is not merely a "family" history, but rather an excerpt from our national chronicles as observed by one bright eyewitness. It also concerns the unswerving spiritual journey of an old farmer, a nurturer by trade, long tortured by memories of his time as a warrior, hiding from the wider world a secret, until eventually purging his soul of its haunting demons and coming at last to terms with his lingering guilt when coaxed by his two grandsons to share with them the unromantic realities of war.

Like our Lord on Calvary, the Southern horse soldiers found trial and suffering through their baptisms of blood and fire. And as is so often the case, they witnessed too many generals of both sides attempting unsuccessfully to re-fight the last war, ignoring the technological advances of the age that rendered so many of their former tactics obsolete. But, to their benefit and that of we their descendants, who would never have come to life as such had not the two brothers survived the war in order to sire our forbearers, the pair were fortunate to find service in the personal escort of one of the most gifted officers who ever led mounted men in combat, Major General of Cavalry, Nathan Bedford Forrest.

For any student of Memphian N.B. Forrest, this work gives fresh, front row insight into the workings of the man, while carefully retracing the path he followed in the western Confederacy and the many acts of war he waged there against the perceived enemies of his fledgling nation. At the same time, it also attempts to reveal something of the private feelings held by soldiers caught up in events beyond their control, trying just to survive the turbulent period when neutrality was impossible. True, the General had his personal faults as attended by the subjects of this work. He suffered from terrible fits of rage and did many things "in a temper" that he often later regretted. He was difficult and demanding and many men and animals fell while riding by his side. But when left to his-own devices and not subjected to the command of inferior tacticians, those who did fall were not needlessly wasted as useless sacrifice, gaining nothing for their cause, or comrades. His legendary ruthlessness probably saved more lives by rapidly deciding engagements as often by intimidation as by violence, frequently forestalling or even averting protracted bloodshed altogether.

Encounter after encounter, almost without fail, his commands drove their adversaries before them, even when odds were greatly stacked against them, turning the enemy's line with sweeping flank movements and daring frontal assaults that were rarely stalled. They had an effect far out of proportion to their numbers and man for man, inflicted many more casualties than their enemies ever could. This then is a first hand account given of those bloody days when the whole country became inflamed with blood and plunder, told by the very men who lived and survived them. It is also a bold testament to the unfathomable power of determination and courage and what together they can accomplish. The intent of this manuscript is to reveal to both Northerner and Southerner alike, of every race, a brief glimpse back into a terrible time in our collective history that changed forever the lives of all who since have called themselves Americans and propelled our yet young country from backwater frontier to great, continental nation.

I consider my cousins and I, from whom I gleaned many of the passed-down accounts, fortunate to have had ample opportunity to sit at our grandparents' feet and listen to their tales of bygone days, much as they had heard many of the same stories at the feet of their grandparents before them. Those oft repeated oral accounts are the inspiration and primary basis for this work. The entire tale related herein, is presented as a recounting by my paternal grandfather of the stories presented to him, when he was but yet a lad, by his then elderly paternal grandfather.

Coming from mostly rural stock, those of our family derived benefit and experience of the old ways, as witnessed about the farms where we spent much of our youth. What we experienced there gave us a solid connection to the land and our heritage and a keen sense of family and place, things now so sadly lacking in this advanced age, and helped enrich our lives immeasurably. It is that bright spirit of hardihood, independence and respect for the Earth that I've tried to capture.

The language of Americans has also changed dramatically since those early years of settlement. In pouring over many volumes of accounts from the period, I rediscovered a richness of long forgotten words and colloquialisms that have largely disappeared from our modern dialect, most likely resultant of mass media's advent and the propagation of rapid transit. Once isolated regions became evermore connected to the "global village," sharing in and assimilated by the "melting pot" culture of the shrinking planet. But back when the written and spoken word were all there were and newspapers were largely local affairs, English flourished in a more eloquent manner that most of us have long since forgotten. It is this use of arcane words and flowing run-on sentences common of the time that I've also attempted to accurately recreate.

Last but by no means least, this manuscript is a testament to the absolute waste of all war, squandering precious resources, both natural and human, with no real winners remaining in the final analysis, save perhaps munitions manufacturers alone. But even they, in the end, pay the insurmountable costs associated with the waging of war. I sincerely hope the awful sum of sorrows resultant of the many sad acts and events recounted herein, will not have gone for naught, but may help reveal to readers the true, inglorious nature of armed conflict, causing you, like me, to abhor the very thought, devoutly dedicated, wherever possible, to the resolution of even the most opposing viewpoints without the employment of force or violence.

"THOSE HOOFBEATS DIE NOT UPON FAME'S CRIMSONED SOD,
BUT WILL RING THROUGH HER SONG AND HER STORY.
HE FOUGHT LIKE A TITAN AND STRUCK LIKE A GOD
AND HIS DUST IS OUR ASHES OF GLORY!"

Virginia Frazer Boyle

From the base of General Forrest's equestrian statue in City Park, Memphis, Tennessee

CONTENTS

****

PREFACE

Forshadowing—(page 1-4)

CHAPTER I

Brave Men, Brave Horses

CHAPTER II

The Furies

CHAPTER III

Bridge of Time

CHAPTER IV

Remembrances

CHAPTER V

The Crossroads

CHAPTER VI

Again to Storm the Heights

CHAPTER VII

The Letter

CHAPTER VIII

Mars' Spawn

CHAPTER IX

The Tempest Renewed

CHAPTER X

Came the Horsemen

Spring of 1864 — Approach and attack on Fort Pillow, Tn. — Visit to Covington, Tn. — Return to Headquarters in Jackson, Tn. (pages 301-325)

CHAPTER XI

Homeward Leg

May 1864 to 1866 — Execution of a Mississippi private — Battle of Brice's Crossroads, Ms. — Raid on Memphis, Tn. — John seperated from detachment and seriously wounded — Swimming the Mississippi on horseback— Journey home through war ravished eastern Arkansas — Homecoming — John marries T. A. Atkinson's widow — Post war and Reconstruction (pages 326-368)

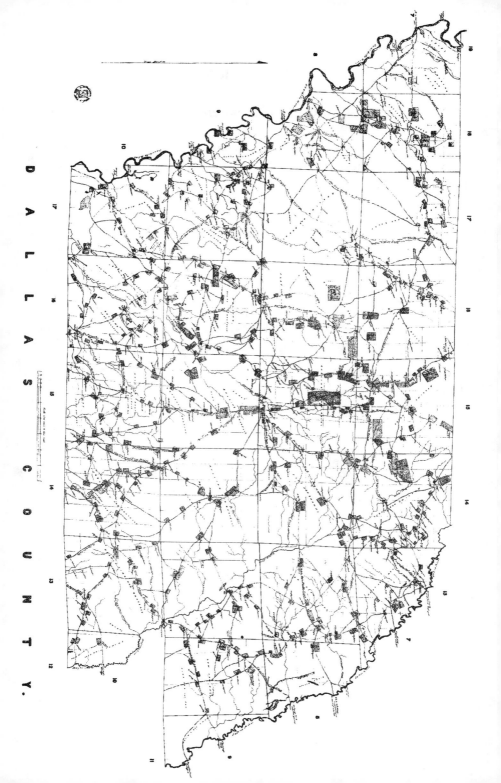

DALLAS COUNTY.

Preface

During the initial approach and attack of the Federal position, the Confederate forces suffered mightily at the hands of the deadly enemy gunners. Now fate had brought the young Rebel private to stand with his long cavalry sword drawn and held above the head of the Yankee artillery commander. In the next instant it flashed like lightning, cleaving the smoky air with two quick brandishes that challenged the surprised adversary before him. The saber of his opponent, the Federal artillery officer, quickly appeared in response, held erect in his steady hands. In the next seconds the sound of clashing steel rang out over the other noises of the battle surrounding the two men as they wheeled and parried. The heavy air came alive with the first flurry of blows, all well met with agile prowess as they sized each other up. The Federal landed the last strike against the Rebel private's counter before they each stepped back a pace, circling, nostrils flared and sweat running in streams from beneath their wool caps. Then with a grunt of fury, the Yankee renewed the attack with a series of bone-jarring blows, wheeling his sword again and again against the young private, who somehow miraculously managed to ward off the vicious blade with equally matched strength. Then with blood chilling savagery, the young Rebel expelled a high shriek and delivered repeated quick, powerful lashes with his own sword, each one coming an instant closer to out maneuvering the Yank's defense. Then, after the latter of several blows thrown by the Confederate and blocked by the Federal, the Yankee officer brought his saber up in a swift climbing movement over his head before again bringing it back down with all his might, putting the private once more on the defensive. The Yank persisted in his newly merited offensive position with a barrage of quick and assorted, if however, mild thrusts, trying to force his adversary to fall back into a trapped position against the earthen wall of the fortress within which they were met. Then the Reb's only retreat would be to awkwardly back his way up the incline of the surrounding embankment. Sensing his opponent's intentions, the agile young man flowed with the

1

movement more easily than should have naturally been expected. The officer continued to maneuver his blade in a manner designed to herd the private in the direction he so desired.

Then, suddenly and without warning, while yet several steps from the base of the approaching earthen wall behind him, the Confederate wheeled and ran headlong for the terrace, scaling and gaining its height. He spun around grinning, sword at the ready, standing a head higher than the level where the Yank yet stood surprised by the agile move. Atop the wall with feet placed well apart for balance, the private stood in this manner for a long moment as the two faced each other with panting breaths. Then the Rebel leapt, muttering an indistinct curse, back to the lower level. The Federal officer stepped back to avoid the fatal steel of the renewed onslaught. The leap carried the young private's sword forward with terrible force, striking the upraised weapon of his opponent. The impact of the attack drove both men to their knees, the defender rolling backward and the aggressor tumbling forward. As each man scrambled in the dust, the private swung his blade along the ground to strike at the officer's feet.

No yelp was heard to issue from the Yank, but precious blood began to usher forth from the slice in the sole of his left boot, darkly staining the ground beneath him. Seeing his advantage regained, the private struggled quickly back to his feet and pressed hard against the gallant defense of the downed officer who now found himself in desperate straights. The private struck fiercely at the hilt of the officer's sword, severing the right hand that had held his blade. The hand fell palm up, quivering on the ground, as the sword dropped harmlessly away. It was the same hand and sword that had ordered the destruction of his fellows by shot and shell.

Their eyes then met for an instant, piercing deeply one into the others. In the last seconds of his life, the Yank officer seemed to take on an inexplicable serenity as he looked steadily upon his executioner. Remembering the ragged, bloody bodies of his comrades destroyed under the Yankee guns, the Rebel raised his mighty blade, hesitating but a brief moment, face taut, jaw clenched, lips pressed firmly together, then drove the long, sharp edge down through the left shoulder of the waiting Yank, cleaving his heart asunder.

2

With that, the old man sat bolt upright, emerging from his recurring dream and the sweat-soaked sheets of his featherbed. The memory brought him full awake there in his dark, quiet room. The clock on the mantle made the only sound as it ticked away the passing moments. Regaining his composure after a short spell, he came to realize it was only an old, familiar nightmare returned from oblivion to yet again haunt his restless sleep. He swung his feet to the old floorboards, sitting motionless for a time on the edge of the bed remembering. He recalled how the splattered blood of the Yankee officer had run down his own cheek and onto his lips. He could still taste the salty, acrid flavor of the warm, thick liquid as he licked it away. Then, after withdrawing his sword from the fresh made corpse, he'd wiped the dripping blade on an unstained portion of his felled enemy's garment. He'd then given the shiny blade one last inspection before replacing it in its scabbard until again needed. It is, he was reminded, a terrible thing to take away a man's life.

After sitting there steadying himself a little while, he pulled open the drawer of his bedside table and brought out the tin of tobacco and a leaf of rolling paper. There alone in the predawn darkness, he rolled a smoke and lit it with a match as he thought of his older brother William and the many experiences of war they together had shared. He dearly missed his now-passed sibling and longed for the consoling visits they once shared after returning home from that long-distant conflict commonly called the Civil War, though civility had little to do with it.

Like so many veterans, he could not readily bring himself to speak of those years with anyone else other than the one soul who had ridden with him through it all and it was a matter neither ever discoursed outside their own company. Who else could ever understand the real nature of something so horrible without actual experience of it? Left feeling as hard and empty as an old hollow oak from his unpleasant memories, he lifted up a silent prayer for some form of relief, if even death, from their unrelenting torture. If only, he thought, there was someone else like Will, that he could now share some of the great burden with. But who, he puzzled, could that ever be? He knew full well he could only play out the hand that was dealt him, however the cards might fall.

3

As he drew in a deep breath of the calming smoke, the red coal of his cigarette glowed like some mad, lone firefly on a moonless night, dimly illuminating the clock face while the chime struck four.

Brave Men, Brave Horses

I set forth herein to give an accounting of the experiences related to me by my grandfather, lovingly known to our family as "Pappy." He was John Riley Ledbetter, my father's father. I am Charles Polk, the middle son of his only child, Charles Edwin. I have condensed many piecemeal tellings, as shared with me by Pappy over the course of time, into a complete sequential narrative of the events that transpired in our family from before 1860 to around 1866. He rode for nine hundred dark days, at the height of the war, with the several cavalry regiments commanded at the time by Nathan Bedford Forrest, barely living to tell of it while sharing in all the hardships and privation common of the Confederate soldier through the long struggle.

Although initially reluctant to ever speak of those bygone days, the old fellow eventually came to address me, starting in 1908 when I was only nine, with his many tales of wonder and adventure from that earlier time. He had been witness to various acts of both bravery and great treachery during the War of the Rebellion and afterward in the Reconstruction.

I spent untold hours sitting in his corner bedroom as a child, listening to the hiss and crackle of the glowing hearth and to Pappy's well told accounts of his and his comrades' actions through trial and fire. The narrative, with the change of season, would relocate from before the fireplace in his bedroom, to the shade of the tool shed out beneath the great oak tree. On warm summer days we would often sat in store-bought, steel chairs while he steadily swatted pesky flies, keeping a running tally of that day's kill. Often, when the score neared a hundred, he claimed to have killed as many flies in one day as he'd killed Yanks during the whole of the war.

In the cool of summer evenings, we sat on the broad front porch of his hewn-log home, listening to frogs croaking and crickets noisily chirping amidst the lonesome calls of the whippoorwill and the occasional screech or hoot of an old owl. Through the course of our many visits, Pappy revealed to me much about our family's history. It is widely held how his grandfather James Heath Ledbetter, a tinsmith and pewter maker by trade, along with his elder brother, the right Reverend Russell Ledbetter, who was himself an itinerate Methodist Episcopal preacher, were the first two of our line to arrive together on American shores from the old country. Being not much welcomed then back in Ireland, due mostly to the strong prejudice held by pure blooded Catholic Irishmen toward our Protestant Black-Irish ancestors, young Scotch-Irishmen such as they, commonly left their childhood homes in the northern counties of the Emerald Isle, seeking passage out from Dublin, looking for a better life among the varied opportunities awaiting them in the American colonies. Arriving in Virginia around 1773, the two brothers settled for a time in that fair, coastal colony, just prior to the outbreak of the War for Independence from England.

Pappy explained how our name, Ledbetter, was said to derive from our Scotch ancestors being pewter makers of great renown. "Their trade secret," he told me, "was said to be that they used a higher than average percentage of lead in their mixture of it with nickel, to make their pewter superior to all other's. The lead made it better, thus, Lead-better. Our branch of the family then dropped the 'a' at some point along the line, becoming Ledbetter! "

After a brief pause, speaking in an almost conspiratorial tone, he shared an alternative version of our surname's origin.

"There's another explanation of our family name, going much further back in time to our Celtic ancestors in Europe. You see," he began before pausing briefly to glance about the room, "both the Scotch and Irish are Celts, who migrated from the Continent to the Isles long ago. Our clansmen, like most Celts, were warriors by nature.

"Polk," he said to me, "I was told by my grandfather, your Great-great-grandfather, James Heath, that our name was originally derived from the Gallic French term for, 'the person who is the beast,' on account of an unusually fierce-natured ancestor of ours. If'n I'm to understand it correctly, 'le' is Francaise for 'the.' 'Bete' is the Frenchy term for 'beast' and when you add 'eur' to the end of their words, it means, 'the person who is.' Put all together, you have L-E-B-E-T-E-U-R... pronounced, Lay-bet-air, translated as 'the beast person.' This then, so I was told by Grand-pappy James, later evolved into its present form of Ledbetter."

He went on to explain how once James had established himself over here as a tin-knocker and before the revolt broke out, he sent to Ireland for his bride to be, Miss Nancy Moore. They were married soon after her arrival in Virginia and to their union were born three fine children. The oldest of these was my great-grandfather, Pappy's father, John Ledbetter Sr., born in 1804. He had two younger brothers, Ozias and James.

The family, like so many of the time, made numerous moves, ever searching for the promise of a life they had hoped to find in this new land. And, too, the primary cash crops raised by these early cultivators were corn and cotton, which rapidly depleted the soil in a time before commercial fertilizers. Because of this they were required to find new ground to clear and plant at least every few years or so when the worn-out earth could no longer sustain their efforts. They went first from Virginia to North Carolina, where my Great-grandfather John Sr. (Pappy's father), wed Miss Elizabeth Yarber. The family grew rapidly around the hearthside with the preceding years, seeing the delivery of several children to the second American born generation.

Along with John Sr.'s parents, my Great-great-grandfather James and Great-great-grandmother Nancy, they all moved on for a spell to Cannon County in middle Tennessee, before shortly again relocating, this time further west to Madison County, Tennessee. Then they moved much further west to Springfield, Missouri. During that eight-year period as they moved from place to place, John Sr. and Elizabeth were blessed first with Pappy's older brother William Edwin in 1831, then elder sister Mary in 1833, next my Grandfather "Pappy" (John Riley) on November fourteenth, 1835 and finally baby brother James Andrew in 1838. The family was blessed in a time of high mortality, to remain mostly intact through all their hardship and toil, when roads were few and rugged and fraught with peril. Only the requisite, occasional infant Ledbetter was left behind in now long lost graves, forever forgotten to family history.

They moved yet again, for reasons now unknown, after less than two years, from central Missouri back to the Volunteer State of Tennessee. They eventually came to settle in Tipton County, with its western boundary reaching clear to the muddy banks of the Mississippi, in the rich, rolling agricultural country surrounding the village of Covington, lying but a short train ride north of the teeming Memphis markets. There they joined a community of other farmers, peacefully comprised at the time of roughly equal numbers of both Irish Catholics and Scotch-Irish Protestants.

There my Great-grandfather John Sr. and Great-grandmother Elizabeth saw the further addition to their household of little sister Martha in 1850, followed finally by baby sister Cynthia Louise in 1853.

Eventually, the ancient, inevitable Catholic/Protestant religious intolerances, long held by both Irish and Black-Irish alike, began to reemerge, creating thereafter an ever-increasing atmosphere of tension in and around Covington that became evermore insurmountable with the further passage of time. So, by the spring of 1855, in company of several other strictly Protestant, Scotch-Irish families from their west Tennessee farming community and a few other like-minded kinsfolk coming to join them from up near Dyersburg, three whole generations of the Ledbetter household decided to once more load all they owned onto wagons and again set out to relocate on new ground, this time in south-central Arkansas, just east of the Saline River, in what was then newly formed Dallas County. The Ledbetters homesteaded a tract just south of the county line in what was still a portion of Bradley County in her original form, while the larger part of their neighbors situated their new homes further north along the crest of the low lying, red-clay ridge that gave the new community its name of Redlands. The vast majority of the early white population in the region resided in what was then still the eastern most part of early Dallas County. Pappy was age twenty when they moved.

That part of old Dallas County where their first neighbors could then be found, along with the large, northern portion of early Bradley County containing the Ledbetter place, were both later cut off and ceded in 1873 to make up newly formed Dorsey County. The fellow Dorsey, who was the original namesake of their now common county, was a most unpopular, post-war Republican carpetbagger come down from the North. So amid much ongoing controversy over the following years among the mostly white, Democratic residents, the new county was later renamed as Cleveland in 1888 for then popular Democratic President Grover Cleveland.

The Caddo Indians had called the place "Arkatha Cohasset"..."land between the waters." Following the lead of their red-skinned predecessors, the new pioneers settled on the fertile ground that lies between winding Moro Creek to the west and the Saline River on the east. The Black-Irish settlers called their two new communities Redlands Township and Saline Township respectively, after the long, red clay ridge and the neighboring river, both gently angling southeasterly through the district. They were joined in the first wave of early settlers to occupy the new land by many other Protestant, Democrat, Scotch-Irishmen and their families such as the Atkinsons, the Adams, the Attwoods, the Barnetts, the Baggetts, the Bridges, the Burfords, the Carmichels, the Carpenters, the Davises, the Garners, the Kilpatricks, the Kennedys, the McMurtreys, the McCaskills and the Mitchells to name but a few.

That period of American history is widely known as "the age of the common man." Our family, like their neighbors, was strongly Methodist in their religion and practitioners of lively Democratic politics. They worked, like their fellow settlers, almost ceaselessly on their hardscrabble farm of eighty acres, clearing and planting, year in, year out. They gained more acreage and mostly prospered during those early years, living and dressing simply in homespun and buckskins, while raising cash crops and a surplus of food, along with large families and similarly numerous livestock herds. Being of proud Black-Irish descent, the farmers of the new, little communities were no slavers. Too well the elders could remember the heavy heel of Lords of the Manor back in the old country and would not be party to the subjugation of other men for their own leisure and gain. They sired and reared strong sons and daughters and toiled shoulder to shoulder with them in the fields to produce the good crops that the fertile bottomlands brought forth at their callused hands.

The colorful, rawboned, yeomen knew horseflesh, breeding and training some of the finest stock to then be found anywhere in the district. They hewed homes and raised barns from the great cypress, pine and oak timbers then still so prominent in the yet virgin land. Pappy would often say when surveying the farm, "I can well remember when all this was trees three men couldn't reach around."

In due time, they built Camp Springs Methodist Episcopal Church near the spot where the original settlers first found a good spring and high, solid ground when they arrived in the area and where the initial casualties of frontier hardships were laid to rest. This was where the newcomers first thanked Providence when they arrived safely in their new home, and where the community still comes together to give thanks for God's abundance.

Near the end of their days, when both were in their late nineties, the Patriarch and Matriarch of our clan, Irish emigres Great-great-grandfather James Heath and Great-great-grandmother Nancy, with whose names the original 1855 land grant was attended, traveled to the county seat of Warren in Bradley County. There, on the fourth day of September 1860, they appeared before Justice of the Peace John S. Daniel and in their heavy Irish brogues, dictated their final wishes, gifting to the Trustees of Camp Springs Methodist Episcopal Church and Cemetery, the land that became the first public burying ground for early settlers in these parts and where the first permanent church house was built in the 1850's. The old couple was soon after laid there in eternal rest.

The 1860 Census showed no slaves or free Negroes present in the communities. The vast majority of all their collective personal property was fine horseflesh

According to the census for that year in Dallas County, Arkansas, Great-grandfather John Sr. was fifty-one and Great-grandmother Elizabeth was forty-eight. Their real estate was

11

valued at $2500, with personal property worth $1230. All their children still resided at home, with the one exception of eldest son William Edwin, then age twenty-nine, who was married to Susan Ledbetter, age twenty-seven. They already had two youngsters, Galacia and Gideon Machai. He was a blacksmith by trade, a profession no doubt passed down to him from his metalworking grandfather James. William showed to own no real estate and held $400 in personal property.

Grandfather John R., "Pappy," was twenty-four, owned $800 worth of real estate and $300 in personal property. He remained yet single.

On August first, 1860, youngest brother James Andrew, age twenty-two, wed Miss Caroline Miller, age nineteen, of Toledo, Arkansas, near present day Rison. They soon went to live with her family in Toledo. Later that same year, they were blessed with the birth of their first daughter. They named her Mahulda. By 1881, Caroline would give birth to two more daughters and four sons. They were Nancy, born 1863, Jessie Andrew in 1866, Melinda in 1873, William in 1876, Frank in 1878 and finally Charles in 1881.

I spent half my young life on Pappy's farm just down the neighborhood dirt road from my own immediate family's spread, so through prolonged exposure to one another, the old man and I became fast friends despite the great gap in our ages. We, like all those before us, shared our spread with chickens, cows, horses, mules, hogs, cats, sheep and dogs. Away from the ways of town-folk, I learned from my elders, by necessity, the ways of the farm and a keen sense of self-sufficient, economical, practical independence.

Of the many tales of life and family history related to me by Pappy, the saga I most often recall stands as clear in my mind's eye today as I imagined it those many years ago while sitting listening at his feet. You may now only imagine the numerous and vivid scenes conjured up by his words in the mind of a mere lad, bored so as I then was with all the many mundane chores of a farmhand. His narrative was related to me over many sittings, with favorite parts occasionally repeated upon request. But, as previously stated, he was initially quite hesitant, like most veterans, to recant his sad memories or share with anyone such weighty stuff as the cruel realities of war as he'd known them, much less with one yet so young as I.

But eventually, at my urging, he began relating the story to me one cool, late-fall evening while we sat together in the warm glow of his bedroom hearth, awaiting our supper. Watching the old man carefully, I learned how to properly place a backlog and manipulate the wood and coals of an open fireplace with practiced artistry. The year was 1908 and I was then but nine.

We sat staring together into the bright embers beneath the heavy dog-irons. He was leaning forward, fire-poker held in his right hand, elbows resting on his knees. I sat upright, boot heels hooked over the wooden stays of the straight-backed wicker chair I occupied. He regularly stirred the logs with his long, iron poker, ever adjusting them to produce the maximum heat. The red bricks beneath our feet were stained with spit, his dark from tobacco juice and the phlegm of wasted lungs, mine still clear as innocence.

"Pappy, would you tell me about the war, were you a hero?" I first asked.

The old man, recently turned 73, wearing his full head of white hair and a thick white beard, never looked up from the fire, but only stirred the red embers as he drew up those painful recollections from a time that had purged our nation with blood and fire, a time of war that claimed both fools and wise men alike.

Up until then, he'd never before, to my knowledge, spoken to anyone of his experiences as a trooper. "It's done, not much to be said," he always replied curtly whenever someone might occasionally ask. Yet it was indelibly etched in his memory. The fact of the matter was he had long held a secret that made him reluctant to ever broach the subject aloud. After much brave service to the Cause, doing his duty with distinction on every occasion, he'd repaid the government a hundred fold for the initial expense of his military training. So the time eventually came when his war waging began to near its end, many months before the Southern government could finally admit its own inevitable defeat.

13

The war by then was already long lost, it only remaining to be proven out to some, the final result being sadly written with the blood of many an ignorant innocent.

Soon however, I began to learn from him more and more about how he'd miraculously managed to return home, changed forever in ways unfathomable, to find his precious mother near death from the hands of their own Southern people. White-trash "Jayhawkers" marauded in those dark days throughout the local countryside, defiling and robbing loyal Confederate families at will, operating under the full sanction of the invading, Federal, military government, then garrisoned less than forty miles to the northeast, on the Arkansas River at nearby Pine Bluff. It was because of his and his brother's service in the Confederate Army, that these reprobate scallywags received carte blanche to wreak the havoc that left his mother but a shell of the gracious Southern lady he'd bid farewell two and a half years prior.

President Davis and the Southern Congress, in all their wisdom, had left our home environs unprotected from the threats of local and foreign ravishers when all Arkansas men-at-arms, including Pappy and his brothers, were ordered transferred in 1862 from the Trans-Mississippi District, across the Great Muddy, to the so-called Western Theatre, then made up of Mississippi, Kentucky and Tennessee.

After two and a half years of hard, faithful service, he found himself cut off from his detachment, gut shot and left for dead late in August of 1864, while participating in a cavalry raid against the Federal garrison at Memphis. He and his trusty mount escaped capture by traversing first the treacherous currents of the wide Mississippi, then the equally dangerous Arkansas River, while traveling west in late August and early September. After stealthily crossing a dozen other Arkansas rivers and counties, severely wounded and at times only half conscious, he managed against great odds to again reach home, only to find all that a generation of backbreaking labors, along with everything they had held precious enough to fight for, nearly vanished by the hand of traitorous, thieving "Jayhawkers." His place he felt by then was clearly at his

14

ill mother's side, regardless of military protocol. So he spent the next several months safely hidden within the log walls of his regained home, cared for and caring for his failing parent, assisted by one Widow Atkinson, who was acting as nurse to his mother at his unexpected return. With each day back he grew stronger, as his mother's strength steadily ebbed away resultant of the treatment she'd received at the hands of the black-hearts come plundering through their neighborhood. T'was as if she ceded her life to him, that he might again flourish. But with her waning, so too his heart, for he knew no other cared for him as did she. Fathers are naturally hard taskmasters, especially on a farm, while mothers are often doting, earning a tender spot in the hearts of their children.

He'd lost many messmates and comrades-in-arms, but was naught by comparison when she departed. He thought at the time that he cared for nothing of this Earth. Not his brothers, yet away at war. Not his fellows, who so recently ranked greater than even life itself by his own estimation. Not the good horses he'd had the pleasure to serve with. Not the Cause, for which he and they performed so gallantly on all occasions when duty called. Not the elegant ladies who'd comforted him at times so well. Not even the home he'd so pined for in his long, distant absence, nor his sisters and father who were as dashed as he by their mother and wife's rapid decline.

So, with the help of a few close neighbors, they soon buried her among the crape myrtles, cedar trees and leaning stones of Camp Springs, late in '64 before war's end, with two sons yet away and unaccounted for. A large chunk of petrified wood marked her grave, for they were far too poor during the war and afterwards in Reconstruction, to afford any store-bought marker.

Pappy puffed on his pipe, recalling all this before he finally responded to my request. "About the War of the Sesech' you ask… what do you know of the war, boy?"

"Well sir, only that it was and you was in it!"

Looking off thoughtfully before eyeing me wryly, he began for the first time to share the secrets of his past that he'd so long held only to himself. "About the war," he said again, as if not knowing just where to start describing an elephant, "I reckon at nine, you're about old enough now to begin hearing of it.

"Well son, I was a full-growed lad of twenty-five whenever it all begun, a farm boy, reared in me pappy's shadow. I'd plowed, picked, dug, or hauled somethin' 'bout this here place every day of my yet young life, 'cept'n the Sabbath, since I could recollect. I helped provide for the family's well being, just like everyone else in the household did and just as you now do Polk.

"Word come 'round 'bout the Lincolnites figurin' to come off down here and make us into such as them and we weren't gonna' have none of it, nary a soul!

"I'd never seen a slave before my twelfth birthday. They come through in a cart that cool November morn, traveling on the Old Military Road. Say's they's taken 'em to sell at a market in Pine Bluff. Though I seen 'em only less than half an hour, still struck me odd, men, women and children bein' for sale. Even bein's they's darkees, somehow didn't seem right to my way of thinkin.' My granddaddy didn't take to it none neither," he said, referring to his Grandfather James, " 'Nigras is nigras,' he'd say, 'they works the same as anyone else if'n they're worth their salt. If not, be shed of 'em quick. But to trade 'em away like an old saddle, just don't rightly fit by my estimation.' More than once't I heared him say, 'When I left the old country, I swore I'd be no man's slave, nor any man's master.'

"We never give darkees a thought in our figurin' to jine up. Brother Will and I was caught in the same throws of mass delirium that infected most everyone else at the time, just a'wishin' to have us a taste of Yankee killin' too, afore the party was all done, just cause it seemed like such a rare and fine opportunity, legal killin' and what. We looked on Lincolnites, forcing their tariffs on us and invadin' our homeland, with far less regard than coloreds. Jining the fight was a choice we never thought otherwise to make.

"Well, we later come to learn those mini-balls flew both ways. I dare say our early enthusiasm withered right quickly under the heat of canister and lead, to a more recognizable form of worry. Some of us earliest volunteers soon come to mourn the departure of numerous others in such sad places as Corinth, Mississippi and Murfreesboro, Tennessee.

"With time, the initial small skirmishes turned into pitched battles as more regulars jined the ranks of both flags, swelling the number of targets afield, until right smart dead and dying lay under foot. I remember my tall boot tops stained dark with their scarlet blood from wading through the midst of fallen friend and foe alike."

The old man paused in his recital, puffing at his cold pipe before checking and tapping out the bowl on the top of a dog-iron, ashes drifting down into the glowing embers. He left the tale hanging like the smoke in midair, while refilling and tamping his pipe from out a flat, red tin with a silver flip-top. Then, plucking a broom-straw and touching it to the flames to rekindle the renewed bowl, he again turned his vision inward and back in time to memories for a while gladly forgotten.

He continued to relate a story I believe he soon became compelled to share with his grandson, lest it be lost, with no account given of how our branch of the family conducted the war. I think too, he hoped to perhaps save me with the knowledge he shared, from the vainglory of war that overtook so many in that turbulent time. And perhaps not the least of his considerations, was to make sure I got the "straight story," lest I someday hear some inaccurate gossip's version of his ending up "away without leave" and think him no better than a coward and deserter.

"Although I am now old and worn, 'gone to seed' you might say, I recall with great satisfaction much of mine and my comrades conduct. We rarely had occasion to shoot one of our own for cowardice. Not that we weren't plenty scared, plenty often, but we were local boys, especially early in the conflict. We wouldn't have any of our family names disgraced by poor accounts from a neighbor boy returning home with a bad report. We'd rather have died, or been maimed, than fold in the face of the hated foe. We stood together in the mouth of the tiger unlike a few others we witnessed crumble like sandcastles rolled under by the tide.

"We come to be right proud and confident in our pluck and skill. We learned through tireless drilling as recruits and by countless experience as veterans, that our greatest strength lay in our unity, unshakable even in the worst of spots. We learned well the merit of focusing on offense, even when in a defensive position. Stand together in the thick of it and always return fire as rapidly and as accurately as possible. When your messmates fall from the ranks, close up the gaps, brush elbows and move ever forward, like an unbroken chain, sweeping across the new ground, cutting away the last stubble of cleared woodland. That new earth grew richer by the blood of Yank and Reb alike, oozing away from fallen soldiers, to pay a sacrificial price for a new nation being born in a land yet little changed from how God first created it."

It was clear from his speech, that though he'd not before spoken of it, he'd thought much on the subject, trying in his own mind to bring some order to the chaotic events of those long past years. It was then that I first realized how often old codgers can be full of surprises. It seemed now the floodgates were finally opened and there was no stemming the tide of pent up emotions that had lain so long dormant within his breast.

I noticed how, at certain points in his telling of the stories, there was a perceptible change in his speech, when his eyes were once more lit with the ardor of battle, as if it were no longer simply the old man I'd until then known only as my grand-pappy, telling of long past events, but instead the young warrior again stirred back to life. The teller was somehow instantly changed before my eyes, revealing one much more eloquent, philosophical and worldly than the simple, elderly farmer I'd before known, speaking at great length in lofty tones and phrases less common, often sounding to me more like the written word than the mere spoken.

"Dominance of spirit, we learnt from our commander General Forrest, is the key to success in any competition between men or even when men pit themselves against beasts. 'He can conquer who believes he can,' the General would oft say.

"In sport, well as battle, a continence of extreme menace can oft overwhelm the resolve of an opponent. Confidence, built on a sound footing of training and experience, instills the spirit with an expectation of success and a nearly invincible ability to achieve any and all objectives, even against the worst of odds!"

I stole a quick glance to insure myself that it was indeed my old grand-pappy speaking in this unusual, new fashion. My surprise would be compounded many times over as he proceeded.

"Nathan Bedford once't told us, 'When ever ye' meet the enemy, no matter how many of them, or few a you, always show plenty fight!'

'Fear profits no man,' the old warhorse would remind us, 'you must first face ye' fears, going right on into the fight. Ye'll git ye' courage afterwards when all's said and done.' 'Ten can chase a hunert if'n they's properly armed with an attitude of menace.' 'When all seems lost,' he'd add, 'with little sign of hope left, then ye' simply gits downright mean! But don't never give up!'

"We oft overwhelmed our foe simply by charging headlong, brandishing sword and pistol, without ever strikin' a blow or firin' even a single shot, cause 'hunert-day warriors' would simply collapse at the mere threat of our unbridled violence. That's the very point of a cavalry charge you know... to shock and frighten a surprised opponent!

"Knowing this, it becomes somewhat less difficult to stand up steady when on the receiving end of a massed attack, for one recognizes how thin the veil of confidence held by charging troops when met with properly delivered defensive fire. Assaults are broken, as well as made, from shock. Even the bravest and most determined ones are cut down in heaps, wrecked and broken, scattered like flotsam before a well-rendered, fiery steel wind. And what a terrible sight it is to behold, retreating through the torn pieces of your fellows, looking down where they lie staining the ground that unmistakable, sanguinary color, all amidst the constant oppressive smells of death, choking powder smoke and burnt flesh. Those awful sights and scents are yet to leave me, even after nearly fifty years.

"Some say there's no glory without clamor, bloodshed or destruction. I say, 'hogwash!' A field hospital will alter any reasonable person. The sight, sound and smell resultant from the wreckage of so many mere mortals under and around one canvas roof, where unimaginably maimed soldiers surrender their fates to sawbones surgeons and swarming flies, too frightened and too weak to do otherwise. But that I could somehow imprint such visions on the minds of men from all social ranks, then war would surely be of little attraction when seen for its true unsavory nature and must thus become a less popular course of action. Only by such memories will men finally relent of their infernal war waging.

"There will no doubt be other wars if history teaches us much, equally terrible, likely even in your generation. Men have been a'killin' one another since the time of Cain and it appears to be naught God can do to stop us, save return with an army of angels to put away our warring with an even greater force-of-arms of His own. We all too often seem to prefer sorrow over joy and war to peace. But mark me words lad, a day of reckoning will surely come in our Maker's own good time. Only then will men share an understanding about the qualities inspired in us by martial conduct, both noble and horrible, perhaps learning at long last that nobility may be better found without such destruction. But for now at least, that's a lesson not readily concluded without personal experience of all its rage and horror."

With that, he fell again silent, stirring the embers with the poker before stoking his pipe. He looked sidelong at me briefly, checking my reaction to such weighty words.

I stared into the flames, pretending not to notice his inquiring glance as I wondered silently at his speech. But his words were not then so really odd to me, coming from the man I loved perhaps even greater than my own father. His words seemed somehow familiar, as if I knew of the experiences about which he spoke and too wholly agreed! That subtle sensation of understanding was quickly lost on a young boy of nine and only now gains its truer meaning, remembered back across sixty years of my own experience, when I am now the same age as he when he first began to tell me the stories.

Just then, our visit was interrupted by the welcome rattling of plates, the clatter of pan lids and the sound of cabinet doors slamming, all coming from Mammy's kitchen, followed by her cheerful call, "Supper boys!" It was my grandmother and we could but obey her summons, which I always did with great relish. Although Pappy's appetite was no longer equal to my own, he always enjoyed watching a growing lad wolf down good vittles and admonished me to eat hardy, for with age, he said, all the sensual pleasures subside. I never disappointed him in that respect.

As we sat at table, Pappy rejoined his account along a less disturbing line of thought. "When there were plenty of victuals, I became right accustomed to field meals, a piece of meat, salt pork mostly, or jerky and the occasional fresh beef or chicken when we were the first 'liberators' into a district. Bread, too, when we had it, 'wet shuck' mostly and often tatters or fried hominy to go with it and even on occasion, early in the war, some carrots and apples."

"What's a 'wet shuck,' Pappy?" I asked around a mouth full of Mammy's good cooking.

Smiling at my innocent ignorance, he explained, "More oft as not, being a cavalry unit constantly on the move, carrying only what our individual horses could manage in addition to saber, Bowie knife, a pair of pistols, rifle and bedroll, there weren't too much room left for carrying the niceties of proper cooking utensils. So, when we found ourselves fortunate enough to have flour or cornmeal, we'd roll it up in a damp corn shuck or large wet leaf and cook our bread right in the fire." Grinning at Mammy, he added, "Weren't no way comparable with your grandma's biscuits, but to a hungry man, near starved as we often were, it was mighty good!"

Mammy only raised an eyebrow and gave a brief glance in noting Pappy's newfound animation about those long lost times.

"Another means we used to roast flour into bread was to mix dough and roll it out into the shape of a snake, wind it around a stick or a musket ramrod and cook it over an open flame."

"Huh!" I exclaimed with amazement between bites, picturing the process in my mind. Mammy then interrupted Pappy's recitation, asking after some detail of a financial account, changing the conversation to the necessities of household life. My mind turned then from their routine discussion and the kitchen where we sat, back to thoughts of camp life, fully intending to try my hand at some "wet shuck" bread on my next camp out.

After supper I helped Mammy clear the dirty dishes from the table. She then covered the bowls of leftovers with a red-checkered tablecloth before Pappy and I retired back to his fireplace.

As so often before, we sat silent for a long spell, digesting our supper and using a broom straw for a toothpick, while basking in the warmth and glow of the cheery fire. After a spell, Pappy freshened his pipe as I fetched and placed new logs from the wood box atop the burned-down embers. Using his poker, Pappy carefully arranged each piece just so on the dog-irons. After awhile sitting still in my seat staring into the dancing flames, I interrupted the silence. "Will you tell me more Pappy?"

This must have disturbed his revelries, for he had yet to kindle the tobacco in his renewed bowl, so lost in thought was he. He turned his attention on me. Our eyes met, still filled with the glow of the hearth. Somehow we both understood we were safe here for now from the dangers of the world. He reached over and tousled my hair gently with his left hand, smiling around the pipe clutched in his teeth and softly chuckled. After a moment of my smiling up at him in return, he first, then I too, turned our gaze again to the hypnotic fire, finding great comfort in its warmth and each other's company.

Continuing in the lighter vain of the topic of conversation we'd shared with Mammy at the diner table, he began, "The campfire is to outdoor life what the hearth fire is to domestic life. This time of evening in camp, when the meals were done and all the mundane chores of the day were completed, animals tended and the night sentries posted, we'd gather together around the light and warmth of a roaring blaze. Just the mention of it now stirs my memory to again smell the sweat, leather and unwashed uniforms, mixed with gun oil, spent powder and the smoke of the cook fires.

T'was there I first learned the simple pleasure of an after diner pipe, lounging amongst me fellows.

"We'd spin yarns and recollect about home and family. Some would share news of kin in recent letters from home. We'd listen to the reels and jigs of the many fiddlers as they traded tunes. Though they came from every region of the South, their rural melodies shared similarities, bein's they generally originated from common Irish ancestry. But common origin aside, they were still quite different despite the similarities. Since their transplantation into various hills and hollers across the South, they'd taken on the flavor of that soil in which they took root.

"With no formal training, garnering instead their talent from kin, or frien', past down from generation to generation, the backwater fiddlers brought an individual mark to the music as unique as the weavers hand shows in a piece of homespun cloth. One good thing I can say about the war is, when all the far-flung fiddlers were gathered together in the Corps of both armies, the music achieved a newness that I theretofore only seen amongst the Gypsy violinist, that used to wander often through these parts. They, like the warrior musicians, garnered tunes and snippets from all the stops along their travels, to incorporate them into their own ethnic, ancestral melodies, thus creating a wholly original theme all their own."

He once again stirred the coals, sending a flurry of crackling sparks rushing up the chimney. We stared endlessly on the blazing hearth throughout his recitations, somehow more easily capturing in our mind's eye, the scenes from the faded past, while gazing deep within the yellow, red and orange combustions.

"Yes sir, there were some good things that come out of it all," he began again. "People put away for awhile their petty, personal concerns when faced with the implications of what war meant to the lives of the entire citizenry. We were but plowboys from hardscrabble farms, living our whole lives up 'til then as simple cultivators, suddenly summoned, then cast into a war of great brutality, horror and fear. We were made to face a degree of reality concerning the worth and meaning of life that our hard working, family lives had before isolated us from. We were called on to give even our own lives upon the alter of self-sacrifice for our fellows and honor. No greater love could ever be taught by circumstances.

"That ole' war simplified our generation's quest for satisfaction in life. It provided an escape from the tedium of family, chores, church and schoolmasters. The politicians regularly liked to remind us, 'T'is a virtuous path to glory for God and your country.' As young men in our prime, we faced the clear choice to fight the good fight, or not. It turned out not to be so simple after all."

He once more stirred the embers, readjusting the burning wood, then sat listening to the hiss of steam escaping as it cooked out of the still green sticks that he'd taught me to intentionally mix in with the dry. Glancing up at him, I caught a dark, grave look settling over his features. He grew quickly pale with the power of some new memory come calling from the forgotten past. I knew he pondered some loathsome, buried event from those bygone days. I felt meek in the presence of such powerful emotions. He drew himself up, looking on the fire from under the furrowed brow of his bowed head, until slowly raising his chin from his chest.

"There's a code, son," he stated, rejoining the saga, "that men live and die by. That code of honor still abides in the hearts of righteous men. In war, we met men from all walks of life, thrown into all types of service. Generally, the officers were either planters, aristocrats, or educated city folk, the later of which often being doctors or lawyers in their civilian walks. On the whole, they were mostly gentlemen, displaying the greater characteristics of forbearance, generosity and mercy. In battle, the best of 'em showed real dash and courage. They lived valorously, preferring to forfeit life before honor, for what is life without honor? Many of 'em died by 'the code,' rather than shirk the responsibility of personally leading their men in line of battle. In the infantry, your better commanders, oft as not, rode horses at the head of their marching boys, sitting well above the ranks, so as to be seen by and inspire their lads by their own example of courage. I rarely saw southern men, especially Arkansans, not give a good accounting of ourselves when our officers were present, guiding us steady on. But a mounted officer, sitting high above his unmounted command, makes an ideal target for every line soldier and sharpshooter alike. I saw many a good man fall in that manner and many brave horses dedicated to the same code as their riders, died beneath them as well. But I reckon it's kindly like billiards, if'n ye' don't play by gentlemen's rules, what's the challenge or pleasure?

"Others did occasionally shirk, officers and enlisted alike. Their messmates and mine died from their dishonor, whilst many of those cowards yet live. God knows the really good ones always did their part and many of them would yet be amongst the living had a few others done their's. I actually pity the sad survivors who folded under pressure, living still with the shame of their past, wishing only to have it to do over again," he said, almost spitting the words out with disgust. Then he did spit, as if in their eye, raising a tiny cloud of steam from the red embers and leaving a cooled, dark spot where it hit. "Do you know what courage is boy?" he asked. Shocked by the unexpected question, I couldn't immediately manage a reply. "It's fear that's said its prayers," he said, in answer to his own query.

"The enlisted came mostly from frontier farm families, 'plain folk' like our own. Most had been Arkansans for less than a generation, come into the service from a land still mostly frontier. Their families had homesteaded or bought smallholdings and without slaves, managed to carve new lives from an uncivilized wilderness. We were the backbone of America, the sons of the middle-class. In general, we country boys may not at first have been as sharp as most of them fellers from larger population centers like Tulip or the big land holdings over in Drew County, who were generally wealthier, more educated and readily adept at social graces. But that is not to say some of us didn't soon learn from our exposure to culture and become ourselves more gracious and somewhat keener. The competition for attention and the embarrassing ridicule of one's ignorance, often found in your larger gatherings of folk, requires that you so adapt.

"Yet in all, ignorant as we were, we were seldom lacking in our adherence to and understanding about the code of honor. As men, both classes desired to live by it or die by it and most did with distinction. Not to say that war, in all its forms, is not the most horrible common human experience imaginable, but there is something noble about the human spirit that allows us to perform our duty unflinchingly even when confronted with such trial. Stripped under fire of all pretense, we grimly immersed ourselves in our common task. And in truth, it weren't nearly as much out of patriotism, as some would have us believe, as out of love for and dedication to our close associates. Far too many didn't outlast the experience, called early as they were, to the last muster."

He paused a spell and checked his pipe. He stirred the bowl with a broom straw, only to find no worthy remnant of Prince Albert yet deserving to be re-fired, so he again tapped out the ashes on the top of a dog-iron and turned in his chair to his nearby desk, setting the pipe there in its stand. Turning back to the fireplace, he went in his hip pocket and brought out his Schrade folding knife. Then he reached back around to his desk drawer with his right hand, retrieving from it a plug of Bull of the Woods chewing tobacco. Opening the blade on the Schrade and peeling back the wax paper wrapper on the chaw, he sliced off a medium size plug. Holding it between his thumb and the knife blade, he deposited it in his jaw and worked it around in his mouth until he was satisfied with its size and position. This done he returned the knife and plug back from where they came and resituated himself comfortably in his chair, facing again the fire. From the size of the piece he'd cut off, I knew it would yet be a little spell before he called lights out. Even so, I could hear Mammy in her adjoining bedroom, for they no longer shared the same bed, preparing to take her evening's rest, because tomorrow would bring, for her as well as me, another long day's tasks again at hand.

We would rise early on the morrow, before the rooster crowed. Mammy would begin our day for us with a good country breakfast of pan-fried sliced ham, redeye gravy, fried eggs and her delicious biscuits, fresh rolled and cut out to the ideal size with the lip of an empty Clabber Girl can. On those floury delights, we'd spread her homemade jams and fresh churned butter. I would wash it all down with a tall glass of Bessie's fresh milk, while Pappy sipped hot coffee from a saucer. I never saw him use a cup for his coffee. It being boiled atop the wood stove and piping hot, the steaming saucer allowed it to cool faster than would a cup.

Then I would be out into the first light of day, regardless of the season, to gather the eggs from the hen house. The chickens were mostly still at their leisure, snoozing comfortably in their nests, so I would have to slightly disturb their slumber. I gently eased them to one side with the back of my hand while my fingers felt for the newly laid eggs snug beneath their warm feathers. On cold winter morns, this would help return some sensation to my frigid digits. Once located, I'd palm the eggs and slide my hand from under the now softly clucking hen. This gentleness was not only out of consideration for the chickens' rest, but also helped prevent from having the back of my hand painfully pecked, usually to the point of drawing blood, by a startled pullet.

Then I'd head out for the pigpen to slop the hogs with table scraps and a bucket of shucked corn that had soaked overnight in limewater. After that, I'd climb through the small entrance to the corncrib built from notched and stacked pine poles. After skinning back the husks so the cows and one old mule could more easily get at the exposed, dried kernels, I tossed them out into the barnyard through the not too widely spaced openings left in construction between the logs. In the winter, which it then was, I would next be up into the barn loft to fork down hay down into the manger for the cattle. Bessie had her own private stall, away from the other heifers, where I would lead her with another bucket of shucked, water-softened corn. Pouring her feed into the trough made from a half section of a hollow log, I'd then fetch the short, three-legged milking stool from where it hung on the wall and with the freshly scrubbed milk pail, position myself to her right side nearer the business end, to begin artfully working her udders. My cold hands on her teats always seemed to startle her a bit, but then, as they quickly warmed, the thick white liquid began to shoot out in a stream that rang against the side of the shiny tin pail.

Returning to the house with milk bucket in one hand and egg basket in the other, I gave these over to Mammy and bid Pappy a good day before setting out to begin my work in earnest. The time of year determined what the day would hold for me from this point on. In the spring, it would be plowing and planting, in the mid summer tilling and hoeing, late summer gathering and storing. With the autumn, came again plowing and planting for winter crops. In the winter months, besides attending school, it was clearing brush, dragging and piling fallen limbs from around field edges and cutting up firewood. Whichever task it was, it usually meant catching the mule, Old Tobe and fixing him in harness before leading him off to hitch to whatever implement the job required.

Only the old man was free from labors, his usefulness for such things mostly spent by that point in his life.

But, for the moment, that was all yet the other side of night and we still sat in the glow of the evening's fire. I patiently waited, studying the change in color of the flames as gases escaped from the burning wood stacked atop the matched dog-irons. Pappy worked up his first mouthful of tobacco juice. That goal at last achieved, he sent a dark stream of liquid from between his teeth sizzling onto the embers with a noisy report of smoke and steam. This done, he again took up his thoughts on war.

"After some forty-odd years, they some nights still yet disturb my slumber, the rider-less horses, veering through the stacks of bodies piled about the field, terror in their eyes, smoke in their flaring nostrils. From their distorted faces comes the word 'nightmare.'

"Even in time of peace do those horses ride through the dreams of survivors, in and out of sight amongst the drifting clouds of smoke and dust, forever anguished and spooked. They wear the same look I've seen on the faces of routed men, fleeing from the point of contact, nerve and will broken in the presence of the enemy and death.

"The scene after a battle is one unreal in its aspects of grotesque human postures. They lie entwined in knots in their prone repose, their blue and gray uniforms intermingled with fallen horses of every color. They fought to remain separate and dominant, but the irony of fate brought them together in the same tangled heap, their blood mingling in pools where it ran. They were conquered by and united in death. How must their spirits have proceeded to the next world, so many enemies departing together from the same time and place, meeting in the air, en route together to the beyond, their war at last forever finished."

He spat again upon the hearth and wiped a remnant of juice from the white of his beard.

"The real trick to behaving with honor in the very thick of it is something green troops seldom have and comes only from experience after meeting the elephant a time or two."

"What elephant?" I piped up .

He chuckled at this rare interruption by me and explained. "That's what the boys used to call going into battle, especially for the first time, 'meeting the elephant.'"

"Oh," I said, still a bit puzzled with the term and the image it inspired in my mind.

He continued, "Yep, only by experiencing combat do you come to learn how you'll react and begin to gain some confidence in your own abilities and those of your comrades. There develops a bond through this shared experience, that makes ya' fear lettin' down your messmates more'n even death, or maiming."

He again fell silent, listening to the hiss and crackle of the fire and creaking of the old log timbers as the house settled in the cold night air. The sounds reminded me of the ghosts of his fallen comrades that Pappy spoke of, called back from beyond the grave by his mention of their sad plight.

He again spat and went on, opening for the first time old wounds, to drain away the festering fragments that had long done injury his soul as well as flesh. "In each of us is a beast, like an ole' bar that's been a'sleepin' through the long winter. You've gained some sense of the 'beast' within ye' when out a'huntin'," he said looking me straight in the eyes for a brief instant, referring to my love of being afield with dog and gun.

"A predator, cunning and patient, he is, stealthy on the trail, yet fierce at the moment of the kill. But the truest sense of the beast coming back awake in spring, only really comes in heated combat. Much like the ole' bar cornered in its lair, coming to from a long rest, hungry, with only one way out, that through the adversary.

"Man's ancient respect for the bar, comes as much from recognition of ourselves in that terrible visage, as from the threat of its giant hulk slashing and smashing down on us.

"Only when witnessing the mystery of death, whilst holding in your arms a dearest comrade whom you would have died for, as the color flows from his face and the spirit slips away from the flesh before your very eyes and is gone, then may the beast of battle be again for a while rendered dormant. The uselessness of killing seems so plain at those times, that one wonders why it isn't immediately so evident to each and all. But more oft as not, our resulting despondency is intentionally replaced with a more tolerable anger and a need to act, to avenge, to again stir and set loose the beast against like beast in our opponent's breast. There is relief from anguish in action, acting in vengeful violence as a balm to our crippling grief. Killing again becomes easy as we discover how to call out at will the 'bar' within, to do one's dirty work with adeptness. Then, when fighting is again for a while done with, the time comes to once more put away in its lair, that entirely different critter from our civilized selves.

"We need the 'bar' within to save us from danger, when we alone could not have saved ourselves without him. But when called on too often, as in war, we become ever more saturated by the bar's base personality, becoming ourselves beasts at last.

"It's like when the air, hydropsical with moisture, reaches its dew point and water settles out of it onto the leaves and blades of grass. So too are we similarly changed. But dew settles on dung as well as roses. And like the dew marks the approaching dawn of another day, each one different, yet the same, we find ourselves forever altered in spirit, though our flesh seem little changed.

"The knowledge of the beast within alters us in ways more insulated persons, who haven't become hunters, or prey, of one kind or other and haven't had cause to call on their animal instincts to survive, may not yet be aware of. But still he's there, within even the meekest breast, an animal who's only instinct is to live.

"He too, like the 'nightmares,' visits my dreams from time to time, striking again at dreaded foe, reaping death in his awful wake.

"Sometimes it's months without a single visit, then, with startling clarity and unexpected battle rage, I'm jolted awake by the smell of spent powder riding on the winds of my unconscious, reminded again of former combat, where not even with darkness upon the field, does death cease from his busy harvest. Respite from that dreamscape of my memories comes only with the dawn."

With that he spat and stirred the logs atop the irons, sending a rush of noisy sparks up the flue, like the flurry of burning memories rushing back on Pappy.

"I don't often like to think on some of the things I've done and seen," he rejoined.

In the course of telling his story, describing the heat of conflict, he often changed the tense, from past to present, no longer looking back on former experience, but with eyes glazed, he actually somehow was briefly transported back, reliving those bygone days anew. So deeply etched on his heart were those times that his narrative occasionally came to be related to me as if he were speaking in real time.

He grimaced at the sound of flying shrapnel and the whiz of bullets that again filled the air of his thoughts.

When he next spoke, it was with a distant look upon his face, "The same air, bearing now only black and gray smoke further aloft, was but a short while ago filled with flesh shredding missiles of every size, shape and composition. Had I then been standing amidst the debris strewn at my feet, I too would have been torn apart but moments before, left as mere pieces of my original form.

"The sound of sure death ripping through the air never leaves you, unseen but for its effect at meeting flesh, bone, wood, or stone. But, as horrible as that is, it's no less terrifying than a hand-to-hand, face-to-face encounter with the enemy. The smell of the soured sweat of fear, mixed with the hot breath of your attacker, whilst slashing, kicking and biting, tasting his blood in your mouth and feeling his flesh ground between your teeth. You look into his eyes, as you struggle with your every ounce of strength to plunge your blade deep into his breast and watch the light of life flicker and extinguish from his eyes, as his blood seeps through your fingers."

The fire made a loud pop as a green stick expelled a pocket of hot gas and a piece of bark flew away. It was again as if some old ghost was trying to make its presence known. Pappy was startled back into the present, returned to the bedroom where we sat.

He spat at the spot from where the pop had come, as if to chase away the ghost. The tobacco juice boiled and rose with the smoke, hurrying away like the moment now past. With that he stretched and yawned, before removing the well-spent plug from his mouth, committing it, too, to the flames.

"It's past our bedtime young feller," he spoke.

"Yes sir," I replied.

I looked over at him, as he seemed to study my face for some reaction to what had only just transpired. Trying to reassure him, I smiled and said, "Thank you Pappy for sharing all that with me."

"Polk," he said to me, "I didn't mean to frighten you, boy."

Plucking up my bravest face, I said, "You didn't scare me none Pappy, I'm a chip off the old block!"

He again smiled his familiar smile and rubbed my curly hair, "Goodnight then son, I'll see you in the morning. Say your prayers, and say one for me."

"Yes sir," I again answered, now heading for the bedroom door with flickering lamp in hand, to make my way to my own bed, whose covers Mammy had earlier turned back for me. I stopped at the door and turned once more to this man who had revealed depths of himself this day, that I'd never before dreamed existed and said before leaving, " Don't let the 'nightmares' bother you, sir."

He grinned sheepishly at me from his chair, perhaps a little surprised and embarrassed at the depth of emotion and secrets he'd shown, being no way able to genuinely promise me his rest would not be again disturbed. He said instead only, "Goodnight boy."

I lay in the front bedroom, listening for a long spell to the wind as it rose in the darkness outside, imagining the many ghosts of local boys who had gone off to serve in those once renowned, now forgotten regiments to such sacrifice. Sleep came fitfully that night, haunted as it was by the visions of rattling bones in ragged uniforms, rising from their shallow graves up and down the long war road.

He would tell me much more as the next few years progressed.

UNITED STATES
TO
JAMES LEDBETTER.
THE UNITED STATES OF AMERICA.
TO ALL TO WHOM THESE PRESENTS SHALL COME...GREETING:
WHEREAS, In pursuance of the Act of Congress, approved March, 3, 1855, entitled, "An Act in addition to certain Acts granting Bounty Land to certain Officers and Soldiers, who have been engaged in the Military Service of the United States," there has been deposited in the General Land Office, Warrant No. 43618 for 80 acres, in favor of James Ledbetter, Private Captain Delong'd Company, Tennessee Militia, War 1812, with evidence that the same has been duly located upon the West half of the Southeast quarter of Section Four in Township Ten, South of Range Twelve West in the District of Lands subject to sale at Little Rock, Arkansas, containing eighty acres, according to the Official Plat of the Survey of said Lands, returned to the General Land Office by the Surveyor General the said tract having been located by th said James Ledbetter.
NOW KNOW YE, That there is therefore granted by the United States unto the said James Ledbetter, as assignee as aforesaid and to his heirs and assigns forever:
IN TESTIMONY WHEREOF, I, James Buchanan, President of the United States of America have caused these Letters to be made Patent and the Seal of the General Land Office to be hereunto affixed.
GIVEN under my hand at the City of Washington, the First day of October in the year of our Lord one thousand eight hundred and sixty, and of the Independence of the United States the eighty fifth.
By The President; James Buchanan.
By J.A.B.Leonard, Sec'y.
718621.
I.N.Granger, Recorder of the General Land Office.

1855 Dallas County Land Grant

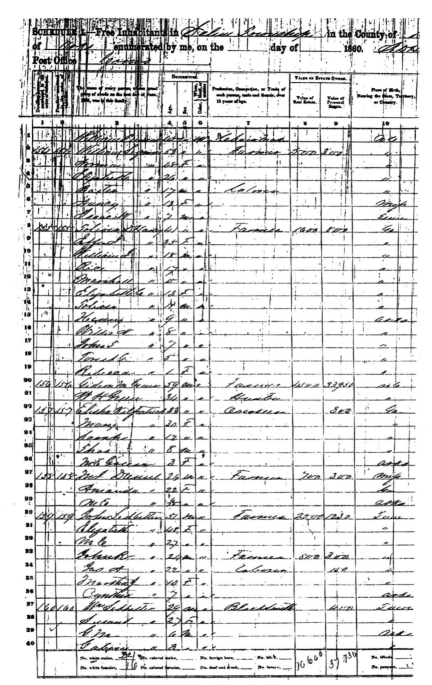

1860 Dallas County Census

34

Bk 1, Page 353 & 354,

Bradley County, Arkansas
September 4, 1860 continued

In testimony whereof we have
hereunto affixed our hands and
seals the day and date above
written : L_____ Childers
Mary E. Ledbetter
              James Ledbetter   (seal)
              Nancy   _ Ledbetter (seal)

State of Arkansas
County of Bradley
                On this the 4 day of
September in the year of our Lord
one thousand eight hundred and sixty-
before me John S. Daniel an acting
and duly commissioned Justice of
the peace within and for the county
of Bradley in the state of Arkansas
appeared in person James Ledbetter
to me personally well known as the
person whose name appears upon
the within and foregoing Deed of

Conveyance as one of the parties
Grantors and stated that he had
executed the same for the
consideration and purposes
therein mentioned and set forth
and I do hereby so certify.

And I further certify
that on this day voluntarily
appeared before me Nancy Ledbetter
wife to the James Ledbetter to me
well known to be the person whose
names appears upon the within
and foregoing Deed and in the
absence of her said husband
declared that she had of her own
free will signed and sealed the
relinquishment of dower therein
expressed for the purposes therein
contained and set forth without
compulsion or under influence of
her said husband. In testimony
whereof I have hereunto set my
hand as such Justice of the Peace
at the county of Bradley on the

4th day of September 1860.
    John S. Daniel J. P.

State of Arkansas
County of Bradley   I Charles N
Seay Clerk of Circuit Court and
Ex-officio Recorder in and for
said County do hereby certify
that the annexed and foregoing
instrument of writing was
filed for record in my office on
the 10 day of October A D 1860
and the same is now duly
recorded in Record Book E,
page 34.

    In testimony whereof I
have hereunto set my hand as
Clerk and affixed the seal of my
office this 10 day of October,
1860.

    Charles N. Seay, Clerk

Camp Springs Church and Cemetery

The Furies

I thought much on my grandfather's tales while toiling away at my many chores. I was responsible for helping out on the old couple's farm, as well as at home on our own place that lay just down the road and around the curve. This added duty made for long hours and often as not, left little time for our undisturbed visits. Only then would he open up to reveal the dark recesses of a bloody past.

I longed for the quiet moments, unencumbered by tasks and need, when I could ask specific questions, closing gaps in my understanding of his epic. In good time, opportunity would always come. This day, it found us on the wide porch of his old log home. We rested from summer toil in rockers with our feet propped on the pine-pole railing nailed up between the cedar roof-support posts that lined the perimeter of the wide front stoop. The smooth-worn, round rails stretched, with the exception of the front steps, the entire length of the covered veranda, safely enclosing the three-foot high plank floor that reached the breadth of Pappy and Mammy's roughhewn home. Our boots were perched comfortably upon the weathered gray rail that had, like the rest of the house, never known paint. Here we enjoyed the breeze that preceded the coming summer squall, while the sun yet burnt brightly on the pastured slopes out beyond the shade of the porch and trees.

"I've oft watched the approach, awaitin' the onset of a thunderstorm," he began "and I've noticed a remarkable resemblance to that of the air of a'comin' battle. A placid patch of Earth is overrun by the flash and noise of meteoric origin, much in the same manner the war swept 'round abouts. Each succeeding line of clouds rolls across the heavens, bringin' ever more fury whilst further darkening the sky, until the final ranks turn the firmament from gray to pitch black, wholly blotting out the sun.

"And much liken to the most severe storms that occasionally blow over the Redlands, looking for a spot to touch down, the unkind actions of men are akin to cyclones, spinning ever faster, until they too become receding spirals of destruction. They go round and around in increasingly tighter and quicker rotations, carrying all in their path in the same dizzying pattern. Up and up go everything the whirlwinds swallow, until the flotsam is spit out at the height of the vortex, freed to tumble back to Earth, but a broken relic of its former self.

"One may always thank God to witness and survive either a battle or a twister. A near lightning strike tests nerves much as exploding artillery shells do, whilst distant ones are but a flashing spectacle, followed by echoing report. In either case there is a special quality left in their wake, both frightening and inspiring. Perhaps men draw on the primal strength developed over the ages in the face of God's wrath to deal with that of war.

"I've heard some say you can make rain with gunpowder. It's true enough that a toad stranglin' downpour generally followed every major engagement. The good Earth would wash away all the blood, sweat and tears and drowned out the weeping and moaning of the stricken."

He sat again silent for a while, listening to the distant rumble of thunder, yet some piece out beyond the big creek we called the Moro, approaching, like most summer storms, from the southwest.

After a spell I asked, "Pappy, tell me how you came to enlist, please sir?"

"Well Polk," he said, pausing briefly to recall just how it had begun, his war, so many years before. "It'll have been forty-six years on the twenty-second of this month (February, 1862) that your Uncle Will and I jined up. At first, most folks round here figured it'd be done afore we could make that first year's crop. The war was still a long ways off back in '61. Unlike so many others, caught up in their first flush of patriotic excitement, I felt right certain it weren't all goin' to be done within a mere six months.

"I was the only one yet unmarried of we three brothers, a trait, I'd been tolt', that made for better soldiers. I reckon I owe that, in part, to the deep regard with which I held my mother, your Great-grandmother Elizabeth. She and I had a special bond that made it more difficult to find a girl of a caliber that I figured I could make a permanent life with.

"We made both our summer and winter crops in '61, as the struggle in the east grew more furious, building in intensity and creeping ever nearer with every passin' week. A second state wide call-to-arms went out again from Governor Henry Rector in Little Rock, asking for more brave southern boys to jine with the ranks of other Arkies like the Capital Guards, who'd already gone east the previous year to fight the Yank invaders, so's to stop 'em over yonder afore they could march on our homes here abouts.

"Both Texas infantry and cavalry, along with Injun horse soldiers from out the Nations, were already on northwest Arkansas sod by the outset of '62, under command of Texas Brigadier General Benjamin McCulloch. He was mustering an army in that vicinage of our state to meet the Federal threat coming from out the Missouris. Them and General Sterling Price's Arkansans had already whooped 'em once't the year before up in southern Missouri at a little battle near Wilson's Creek. It all went for naught however, because they was unable to consolidate any of the gains the victory offered, due mostly to the number of casualties the fledgling band suffered during the engagement. They therefore could not, as desired, pursue the enemy all the way back to their St. Louie stronghold. Word was though, next time, with a larger, better trained, better equipped force, our generals intended to meet Billy Yank again in the Ozark hills and this time drive him all the way back to St. Louis in hot pursuit. Once't there, McCulloch and his army of Texicans, along with Price's Arkansawyers, and any Missourians recruited along the way, would take that major river port away from the Feds, denyin' 'em any further use of the upper Mississippi. Any rocking chair general could see how this was bound to turn events in our favor and hasten the satisfactory outcome of the conflict. So, with all that in mind, I began figurin' to do a hitch to help bring the thing to a conclusion and get a little Yankee blood on me knife. When I spoke to brother Will about it, he said I wasn't gonna have all the fun without him. It's odd to look back on it, knowing what we now know and wonder how we could've ever been so naïve.

"It was about that time one Major T. J. Reid come into our country, back in February of '62, recruitin' for the Second Arkansas Cavalry. He set up his enlistment station over at Mount Elba on the riverside. We made up our minds to do a hitch and tolt' all the family so. Little brother James Andrew had a brand new wife and baby, with another'n already on the way, so we all thought it best he remain home to watch over his new fold and to look in from time to time on Ma, Pa, our sisters and Will's girls. We were able to go away with much less trepidation, knowing we weren't abandoning them, with none of the brother's left to keep an eye out. He wrote us at regular intervals, although mail delivery to a mobile cavalry unit was right irregular. His letters, along with others from Ma, our sisters and Will's gals, helped to keep us appraised as to the state of affairs back home, least ways up until Lil' Brother's correspondence ceased with his conscription. Despite all James Andrew's best efforts to remain with the family on the home front, the Congress of the Confederation passed the Conscription Act on the sixteenth of April 1862. By February first of '63, under martial law declared by the Confederate commander of the district General Henry Hineman, our kid brother was drafted into Confederate service with Hardy's Nineteenth Arkansas Infantry, just less than a year after Will and I rode off to capture our own glory on the fields of combat.

"Mine and Will's enlistment day came on the twenty-second of February, 1862. Lil' Brother Andrew had ridden into the farm on horseback the evening before to spend the night and bid us farewell next morning, leaving Caroline and the baby back in Toledo with her folks. Big brother Will rode in same evenin' by wagon with his wife Susan and their two younguns, who were by then ages eight and five, sitting all together snuggly up front on the springboard seat.

"We spent supper that evening around the long table, shoulder to shoulder on the old slab benches. Sister-in-law Susan was quieter than usual, perhaps saving her goodbyes for later during her last few hours alone with Brother. Our three sisters talked and laughed. They prodded and teased us to relieve some of the anxiety that was so prominent in our moods that night, despite everyone's best efforts to be cheerful."

The old fellow twisted around in the wicker-backed rocker, repositioning himself more comfortably, before continuing his saga. "I was the one going away with no wife or child left behind and I wasn't sure I could have done what Will was about to do. But each man must decide on his own.

"There was not all that much, to my thinkin', to hold me here at twenty-six. As much as I loved Ma, I longed to be free from the restraints of living up under she and Pa, to be my own man, proving my worth to others and myself by my own actions. Not to be judged by my family name or reputation and to kick up my heels without rebuke from the parson, far from the watchful eyes of home. And not least of my considerations, was to get out from behind the ass-end of a mule team and away from the never-ending cycle of work on the farm. There was a wider world awaitin'! I think maybe brother Will might have considered the same, though we never discussed it. I reckon he surely didn't mind a break from a house full of females and the backache associated with his hard trade of blacksmithing.

"The next morning, before daylight, we were shuffling around this old log home," he said referring to the very house on whose porch we then sat, "preparing to ride out at first light. Our pa made sure Will and I rode off on good mounts. Mine was a blaze-faced, chestnut gelding, called Prince after bonnie Prince Charles of old. Will, being the elder, got the black stallion with the four white stockinged feet, that Pa had named Fury.

"Our father took us aside as he led out the two fine animals and handed us their bridle reins. Standing close-by, he told us how, in former times, our Scottish forefathers were widely known for their skill with horses, when even the rankest peasant amongst them rode some sort of pony. After being treacherously betrayed by the English monarchy, they were exiled to Ireland from their ancestral homes amongst the wastelands of the southern Scottish border country and forced to become, for a time, mere vassals and bondservants, looked down on by their new Irish masters. By his father's time, whilst still residing in Ireland and even since coming to America, during first the Revolutionary War and again in 1812, only gentry and landholders were allowed to fight mounted in the regular army, leaving the lower classes to make up the vast ranks of infantry. He said that now that we'd come to settle in Arkansas, we too were at last again landholders and if'n he had any say in the matter, we would go to war astride fine animals like our proud Scotch fathers had done three hunert years earlier!

"The Black-Irishmen, as the refugee Scots had come to be known, eventually came to settle here, bringing with them from the old country their love and knowledge of horseflesh. We boasted some of the finest animals anywhere around, least ways afore the Yanks stole everything we'd formerly treasured. In those earlier days before the war, planters come for miles from their fine homes and large holdings over in the Delta, to our two little communities of Redlands and Saline Township, to purchase and trade for stallions and mares that were raised and trained by our neighbors and us. It was this love and knowledge of horses and our possession of premium animals that first brought Major Reid into the lower Saline district looking to recruit horse soldiers and warhorses. And that same love and knowledge sealed Will's and my fate as cavalrymen for the following years.

"Martha, Mary Louise and Cynthia each presented Will and me with mementos of the occasion. They had knitted us two new pair of good, warm, wool socks apiece and also provided another set of long-john underwear and an extra quilt to pack in our bedrolls.

"Ma had us a basket filled with enough good vittles to tide us over for several days, if'n gov'ment issue rations turned out to be short. They each hugged our necks and gave us a peck on the cheek, trying to be brave for us. Even so, we all had to blink the mist from our eyes, for we knew it would be the longest and probably the most distant separation our little clan had ever known.

"Brother Andrew brought out a kerchief wrapped around a pair of long objects and unwrapped two Bowie knives, sheathed in black leather scabbards. 'I heard back in Toledo, that these here are sort of a trademark of Arkansas soldiers,' he said holding one of the foot long implements in each hand. Grasping them by the tip of their sheathed blades, he extended them to us wooden handle first. We each took one. 'I figured you boys oughta' have a couple of 'em. They should come in right handy for pickin' your teeth after you've polished off that basket of grub Ma fixed ya'll.'

"We unsnapped the straps that held them in their black leather holsters, to remove and examine the menacing instruments. It gave me a chill when I first held mine in my hands as if I somehow sensed the destruction I was to do with it ere I returned this way again.

"In turn, first we each shook his hand, then bar hugged our little brother, thanking him appropriately. I spoke into his ear whilst in my embrace, to 'watch your corn' and take good care of all in our absence."

"What'd you mean, 'watch your corn,' Pappy?" I asked him.

"Well Polk," he replied to my question, "that means watch your head, or keep your head down. We used to say it in the war when the bullets were flyin', to remind a feller not to stick his head up above the trench line, else he might get his ears clipped off, or worse."

"Oh," I said, again falling quiet while listening intently.

"Then, I bent to bid our old hound Buster a fond adieu with a pat on his head. With that, we swung up into our saddles and touched our spurs to the animal's sides. James Andrew held Buster as we rode off around the bend in the road, looking back together for one last time, at a life we would never see in the same way again. They were all standing tight together, arms entwined around one another, waving and sobbing, when we disappeared from view. I could still hear Buster barking for a good spell after we rode out of sight. Brother and I proceeded in silence for a good piece, neither one looking at the other, to hide the tears that streamed down both our cheeks." Pappy cleared his throat, as if choking down the lump that recalling the sad day had again put in his craw. He spat the offensive thought out into the dust of the yard and went on with his account.

"It was a ten mile ride over to Mount Elba. Along the route we met up with other neighborhood boys with the same purpose in mind that day as ourselves. In the group of horsemen that rode into the recruitment camp with Will and me was Manuel Davis, who was a good ten years older than myself. We were also in company of three James's: James Tolson, along with James McCaskill and James Bridges. Two of the James, McCaskill and Bridges, later became Judges after the war.

"When we arrived, we saw other neighbors already milling around amongst their horses and about the tables set up in anticipation of our coming. I saw present from our immediate neighborhood, in company of their own fine animals, John Stewart, George Marks, George England and James Hopson. All told, there were a little better than three hunert lads and accompanying mounts. A finer stock of horses ye' never saw, whilst the men weren't so bad neither. We were quickly formed into three companies of roughly a hunert or better each, designated as B, D and G.

"Major Reid stood on a stump and made a little speech to the gathering, explaining how he was looking for brave men and brave horses to fill the ranks of his regiment and he'd come expecting no less from us tough, skilled frontiersmen and our racehorse stock.

"After his talk, Will, Manuel and me were directed down the way along the river bank. It was just beginning to show the first real signs of spring. The robins were back from their migration and they tweetered and flitted amongst the bare branches over our heads. When we came to the place where we'd been instructed, we found the various men and mounts that were to make up Company D of the Second Arkansas Cavalry. Some we knew and some we didn't yet know. We soon came to know them all well over the following weeks.

"We tied off our animals and formed two lines in front of one of the cloth covered tables. We were proud horsemen and our spurs jingled at every step. We took a turn each standing in front of a uniformed officer, giving our names to the soldier seated before us. As we waited turn in line, Manuel Davis suggested I keep quiet about knowing my letters else they'd make me into a clerk like one of them fellers seated behind the tables, then, he said, I'd never get the chance to see combat. By the time we got up to the table, Major Reid had taken up position behind it and proceeded to muster us in, asking what skills, besides horsemanship, we brought to the service of the Cause. I was behind Manual Davis and directly in line ahead of Will, so they both heard when I told the Major I had skills as a blacksmith. I was about to pipe up that all the boys in our family had learned metal working from our pa and grandpa and that my brother here was a smithy by trade, when Will kicked my anklebone to shut me up. I immediately came to the painful realization that he did not wish to be put right back to the job he was jining up to escape from, so I kept silent about his trade and thusly he avoided, for the duration, a return to horseshoeing on a daily basis. I, on the other hand, was immediately detailed as a blacksmith.

"Though the work was hard, it served me well through the conflict on more than one occasion. I missed a few hard fights during our many campaigns because of working at the forge. And in the cold of winter, it was the warmest job around, not to mention that in the heat of summer, it was much like the sunny side of hell."

We sat in the shade of the porch fanning and listened to the grumbling of the gathering clouds, as they built in the west. The sky was darkening and the wind kicked up occasional dust devils out in the road. A neighbor hurried by on horseback, trying to beat the storm home. His hat was pulled down low, to keep it from being blown off his head in the strong gusts that threatened to drive our visitation together indoors. But, for the moment, he resumed his story where we sat.

"So, as Will and I stood before him, we each told Major Reid our names, which he promptly misspelled whilst settling our respective fates on the spot. Somehow we all knew it was so and steeled our souls to the dark purpose. His adding of the letter 'a' back to our last names, worked out in my favor when I later finally ended up away without leave. When occasionally asked by several nosy busy bodies for years after war's end if it was indeed my name on some Confederate roll or other, I could honestly answer 'no!' The misspelling begun that day on the banks of the Saline as L-E-A-D-B-E-T-T-E-R, followed us through all our various, subsequent service records.

"The morning was two hours past when we stepped to the Quartermaster's table to receive our mustering in pay. We didn't know it at the time, but it was the most prompt pay we would ever receive during our service. Thereafter, we would go long spells between full receipts of payroll.

"Each man received an initial payment for a one week period, at $24.80 a day for horse and rider. We kept ownership of our mounts, unlike our Yankee counterparts in the Federal cavalry, who we came to learn, were paid $150.00 up front for title to their horses when they jined up, with fodder provided thereafter by their gov'ment. We, on the other-hand, were responsible for the board, care and feeding of our own animals and ourselves from the allotted daily allowance given us by our gov'ment. We were also paid another dollar a month for provision of each of our own weapons, if approved after inspection by the enlisting officer. With two good pistols and a shotgun between us, Will and I split the three dollars down the middle, taking pay for one barrel each of the scattergun.

"Quartermaster W. D. Leiper counted out $175.10 in crisp new Confederate coin and bill, before handing over to me more cash money than I'd ever before held in my hand. I fairly radiated with glee as I stepped away from the pay table in the mid-afternoon sun. All present were equally pleased and mighty fascinated with the new currency.

"By the time all the boys received their mustering in pay, the late winter sun was rapidly receding toward the western horizon. So we bivouacked by the riverside that night, gathering around campfires in the cool evening air, displaying weapons brought from home of all sort and vintage. There were many an 'Arkansas toothpick' amongst the ranks, which made me hope they would get us in contact with the enemy right soon, lest these fellers decide to test 'em out on one another first. As a mustering in bonus, a ration of whiskey was distributed, supplemented by other jugs brought from home, ensuring the disturbance of the usual evening's quiet on the normally placid riverbank. I was reminded of my mother's admonitions before leaving home, that 'liquor on an empty stomach killed more men than ever bullets had.' I thought to slightly amend her pronouncement to include 'liquor and Bowie knives.'

"Next dawn found us being unpleasantly rousted out for the first time by bugle call, a sound I would come to hate during the next couple years. The bright morning sun found us with only minor cuts and bruises inflicted amongst the troops. After brewing coffee brought from home and dipping our clouded heads in the icy water of the stream we'd slept beside, we rolled up our beds, watered and fed our mounts and saddled up for the long trek ahead. We hoisted our headaches into the saddle and at Major Reid's command, rode out along the riverbank in a column two abreast, headed east. The crisp air and sunshine soon restored our vigor.

"Between us, Will, our horses and I carried a saddle and saddle blanket a piece, two bridles, a curry-comb and horse brush each, two pairs of spurs, two wide-brim felt hats, one medium-size coffee pot and in two large linen sacks slung across our pommels: oats, a twenty-pound smoked ham, a hunert biscuits, a hunert corn dodgers, five pounds of coffee beans, two pounds of sugar and five more pounds of 'Lot's wife,' as salt was called in the parlance of the age. In addition, we either wore, crammed into two bulging sets of saddlebags, or strapped to every remaining conceivable space, two large pound cakes, six shirts, eight pair of socks, six pair of drawers, four pair of pants, two jackets, two pair of heavy mud boots, two pair of leather teamster's gloves, a pair of Navy Colt revolvers, two Bowie knives, a double-barrel, ten-gauge shotgun, two powder horns, two ammunition pouches, two canteens, four wool blankets and a lariat apiece; amongst divers and a'sundry other trinkets and small artifacts bestowed upon us by family and friends, including two compact Bibles given us by our mother. As the other troops were similarly furnished, we appeared to my eye, more like a wandering Gypsy caravan than an army setting out on spring campaign.

"Any thought of adding fresh venison to our larder with a hapless deer that might wander out along our trail in front of the sights of the various marksmen in our midst, was quickly forgotten. Every deer within two miles fled long before our arrival, forewarned of our approach by the clamor and clatter of pots and tins, rattling against one another where they were strung and tied to our saddles of every description.

"Our hats were tilted forward to shade our eyes as we rode into the still rising sun. We spent all that day and the next, in the saddle, riding southeast on the River Road along the east bank of the Saline. I admired the stark beauty of the winter river bottom landscape. There was hardly any noticeable rise in the contour of the dark, leaf-covered soil. Great, bare trees, older than any man, or even many countries, towered over the flat terrain. The road roughly followed the curve of the river, bypassing some of the tighter bends, only shortly ever out of sight of the gentle winding stream. I was reminded of how there are not many things more pleasurable than riding a fine horse through fresh country in good company.

"We were to follow the Saline to its confluence with the Ouachita River. We would then again make camp there for the night before striking out downstream next morning for Moro Landing. There, we were told, we would be loaded along with our animals aboard packet steamers to begin our journey downriver to where the Ouachita flowed through the railroad junction town of Monroe, Louisiana.

"When I asked why we took such a circuitous route, rather than riding more directly overland to the northwest, I was informed that they didn't wish to wear out our horses marching them up and down hills, when they expected to commit them and us to combat shortly after disembarkation at Van Buren. And, too, I was told, it was a fur piece yet from the river port that we were making for, to the ground where we would most likely meet the enemy, at the end of a trail winding through more rugged hill country than either we or our animals were accustomed to. For that leg of the journey, that they said could not be crossed by river or rail, we would need to save all our stamina.

"So on our third day in the service, we loaded on the boats at Moro Bay. As you can imagine, this was no simple task for men and animals who'd never walked up a gang plank 'afore." He chuckled softly, recalling to himself some of the comic incidents that took place between men and beasts that day on the banks of the Ouachita. Then after a brief interlude, he again picked up the story.

"It's hard to imagine now, what with the advent of the railroad in these parts, but way back then, we knew we were headin' places. Will and I had seen both the Mississippi and Arkansas Rivers when we were still just boys your age Polk, when the family relocated from Tennessee to Arkansas. Several others amongst us had made the same move when they were about your age or a little younger, but none of us had seen those places since and they were but a vague memory now to the younger ones of us. Upon first seeing those paddle wheelers tied up at the landing on the Ouachita, we knowed we was doin' somethin' excitin', whilst all at the gov'ment's expense. Then, once to Monroe, seeing the railcars and smoking steam engines for the first time, we could only imagine what we might yet see ere we passed this way again.

"We offloaded the boats and climbed aboard the waiting boxcars leaving behind the Ouachita River for an eighty mile rail ride due east through northeast Louisiana. We rode the track as far as it went to where it ended on the west bank of the Mighty Mississippi, just across the wide river from Vicksburg on the further shore. Once we reached the Big Muddy, we again boarded much larger paddle wheelers than what we'd ridden to Monroe and whilst seeing Vicksburg from no nearer than a boat deck in midstream, turned our bows north against the current and proceeded aboard the steamers toward the expansive mouth of the Arkansas River.

"Once reached, after traveling many upstream miles, we then continued on in a northwesterly fashion up the Arkansas, finding ourselves once't more within the confines of our own home state. We journeyed fur upriver, through Little Rock where we saw our white-columned Statehouse restin' on the high bluff above.

"As we plodded on against the steady current, our early excitement faded with each passing day aboard the boats between Vicksburg and our final objective of Van Buren. Aside from sightseein', the trip was crowded, long and boring, with only the care of horses, occasional card or dice games, checkers and the odd bottle brung from home or procured at some port-a-call along our route, to help pass the time. Many a sharpie had already fleeced green recruits out of all their mustering in pay, as well as their cooking utensils and most anything else they had of value before even we reached the confluence of the Arkansas with the Mississippi. We were a fortnight, all told, on horseback, rail, or aboard the cramped steamers en route far upstream to Camp Van Buren. Several took ill from the cramped, unventilated confines below decks and the damp, chill air above. Will caught a cough along the way that would prove his near undoing before it was all said and done.

"Just short of where the great river flowed out of the Indian Nations, we finally reached the Confederate encampment at Van Buren, Arkansas, disembarking there on the north shore.

"As it turned out, we'd have probably done better by riding our animals overland north, rather than the long way around we took by boat, for we arrived too late to accomplish our originally stated objective. It was March tenth before finally we reached Camp Van Buren, where we were greeted by the news that the Union push had come south sooner than had been hoped for, preventing us from arriving in time to jine in the fray.

"The Confederate Army of the Trans-Mississippi, it turned out, camped out north of Fayetteville, met the approaching Union Army on March seventh at Elkhorn Tavern, a stage stop near the community of Pea Ridge just south of the border with Missouri. Jeff Davis, it seems, had relieved both Texas General Ben McColloch and Arkansas General Sterling Price from overall command of their respective armies, by making them subordinate to the supreme command of a West Point classmate of Davis's and fellow Mississippian, Earl Van Dorn. On the second morning of the ruckus, Ole' General Van Dorn ended up quitting the field with his undefeated army after having discovered he'd failed to bring up his reserve ammo wagons during the night. Without fresh powder and ball to renew their spent reserves, our lads couldn't sustain the good fight they'd made during the first day's engagement. Fightin' Ben McColloch had been mistakenly fired on and killed by his own boys during the early fighting of day one, or he'd likely have prevented such an incredibly expensive oversight that not only cost us the much-needed victory, but ultimately, probably resulted in our loss of the Mississippi and as a result, the entire struggle.

"By the time we arrived in Camp Van Buren, there were some south Arkansas boys already back from the fight, who had come up with the Twentieth and Nineteenth Arkansas Infantries at about the same time we of the Second Cav. were loading on the boats at Moro Bay. They'd been held in reserve during the engagement, a few miles south of Elkhorn Tavern, at Camp Cove Creek in Cross Hollows. They were such fresh and untrained recruits, with little or no weaponry and in many cases not even shoes on their feet, that it was felt best not to commit them to the fight unless absolutely necessary. Their proximity, south of the battleground and thusly south of General Curtis's Union Army, made them the first ones back to Van Buren after the fray. Most of the balance of the Confederates had to straggle back south the long way around through the mountains, because after the battle's end, the Federals sat astride our force's immediate line of retreat.

"Some of our boys had kin amongst the Nineteenth and Twentieth and once't we were settled into camp, sought them out. They were informed by the un-blooded veterans, how our boys had given the Yanks the worst of it, only to have Van Dorn out-general his own army. According to them, nobody beat us at Elkhorn but Van Dorn. Sentiment in the camp was not running high for our new theatre commander at that time and only got worse with experience of his imperial character.

"Within a few days of the failed Confederate campaign in the Ozarks, President Davis ordered General's Van Dorn and Price to transfer their armies out of Arkansas, abandoning the Trans-Mississippi District for the time being, to concentrate east of the river in north-central Mississippi at the vital rail juncture of Corinth. We were to reinforce General Alfred Sidney Johnson in the defense of that rail crossroads so vital to transportation in the middle South.

"It's fair to say that there were quite a few amongst our ranks that didn't cotton to this sudden turn of events nary a bit. You see, back then we were so isolated in our little burgs that we didn't feel any real connection to far-off places such as the state of Mississippi. To a man, we had jined up to defend our homes from the bloodthirsty northern invaders and frankly, we didn't give a hoot, nor holler for what problems they might have way over in Mississippi. We pretty much figured on handling the Yank in Arkansas and we were content to let them Mississippians deal with there own version of the war. But Ole' Jeff Davis, being a Mississippi planter himself, must have figured his boys was gonna' need some real fighters from over our way to help tip the odds in his favor.

"Regardless of what we thought, or how we felt about it, there weren't much else we could do at the point 'cept desert and that was said to be plumb unhealthy for a feller if'n they caught you, which they was bound to do sooner or later. So, even though most of us talked about it for a spell, nobody that I know of, from our outfit, Company D, actually high tailed it back home. We'd signed up for at least a year of loyal service to the Confederacy and even though we'd been somewhat hoodwinked into believing we were to defend our own soil, we were now committed to go where they sent us. And, after all, as I heard one officer explain it, in the wider scope of things, technically speaking, Mississippi was in fact 'our soil.' I'd liked for him to have known where I thought he should pound that soil too!

"Camp Van Buren was soon evacuated and we found ourselves temporarily relocated back down the Arkansas, then up the White River, further to the northeast, at the port town of Dardenelle, Arkansas. It was here in our new camp that we first began to face the formidable task of converting plowhands into warriors and saddle ponies into warhorses. The task of taking our personal riding horses and teaching them to charge gallantly into battle, rather than follow instinct and run from it, was no small feat. That challenge presented itself not only to mounts, but to their riders as well, green as we were to combat.

"The primary reason so many cavalry and mounted rifle regiments were dismounted in those first two years of the war, is because it was easier for the average officer to make foot soldiers of plowhands, than it was to make warhorses out of jug-heads, that too and the fact that many of those other soon dismounted units had enlisted with mules rather than horses. Not the least of such reasons was also most generals of the time didn't yet know how to properly employ cavalry by that stage of the war. Still, they figured they'd need us to counteract any Union cavalry we might meet up with. Only three men, Nathan Bedford Forrest, Fightin' Joe Wheeler and John Hunt Morgan provided any examples of the proper, effective use of mounted troops at that time and to our good fortune, we soon found ourselves under the command of two of those three gifted horsemen.

"Due to the integrity of our animals and our ability to train them, we, unlike so many other Arkansas units, remained mounted for the duration, except when temporarily dismounting to engage in the occasional battle or skirmish. Our hard working and hard sporting lives up 'til then had physically prepared us for what we faced. But nothing prepared us emotionally for what was to come in our first test at Shiloh.

"Will and I were born to the saddle and weaned on saddle leather. We proudly declared the Scotch in our Scotch-Irish bloodline had come from the sixteenth century Border Reavers, long riders who plundered and raided for cattle on horseback through the disputed Borderlands, from Scotland into England and back again. They stole women as well as cattle, thus helping first bring the civilizing English and Christian influences to our ancient pagan culture. And, like us, they picked and bred their horses for stamina and speed and were rarely caught up with by their pursuers for that reason. According to my Grand-pappy James, a couple thousand of these Reavers were enlisted because of their superb mounted fighting skills, some three hunert years ago, as King Henry the VIII's first light-cavalry regiment. They were swift, light-horsemen, armed with the long lance, short sword and dagger, wearing a bonnet of steel atop their crown, whilst wielding a handgun with deadly precision, being masters of cut and run tactics, who, like us, reckoned it a disgrace to hafta' go anywhere afoot. They were a tough, quarrelsome and crafty peoples, who, when once't committed to a pitched battle, were unswerving unto its final conclusion for as long as axe and sword would endure. It was their dash and daring that set the mold for all future cavalry. When not employing their mobile fighting skills on some expedition in either service to the King or for plunderous self-profit, our ancestors honed a sharp eye and the exacting judgement of horse traders and stockmen, passing the gifts along down the generations.

"I got my first set of saddlebags at age six, with 'John' stenciled on either flap. I begun ridin' solo from a tender age, first on a Welch pony, but soon on my own full-growed mount. Will and I had great fun riding side-by-side, across country, from west Tennessee to south Arkansas driving the herd of horses and stock we brung here with us in '55. And most all the other boys were reared in like manner. It wasn't too very long afore we'd sharply honed our natural instincts, shaping men and animals into a single cohesive fighting force.

"One old Irishman's trick we used to groom our animals into fighting mounts had to do with teaching our horses to first trust in us absolutely. I've showed it to ye' afore," he said reminding me of the time which he spoke. "You run your lariat from around a front ankle, up over the top of his neck, then use it to lift one of the animal's forelegs off the ground until you can easily unbalance and tip him over from his three-legged position. Once you've got him down on his side on the ground, you gently rub and pet him all over for a long while. You set on his side and neck whilst stroking him 'til he's completely gentled. From this exercise you prove to him who's the boss, whilst at the same time showing him you mean no harm. From that he then comes to understand you're the master, but also that you can be fully trusted. Once accomplished, all other tasks become much easier lessons for him. Unfortunately, far too many horses found out the hard way that trusting their safety to soldiers in combat is a dangerous proposition.

"We practiced and drilled daily, Sundays included, until we could perform the many precise formation maneuvers of General Phillip St. George Cook's Manual of Cavalry Tactics. As per Major Reid's original plan, we became the crack shock troops that Arkansas had to offer. We were horsemen par excellence, even before we came into the service. After electing company's officers and being instructed in the ways of conducting mounted warfare, we became a force the Yankees would soon have to reckon with.

"Shortly, the three Dallas and Bradley County cavalry companies of B, D and G were again loaded, like cattle, aboard packet boats and shipped back down stream to the Great Muddy. We were directly set ashore in Memphis, then, almost immediately, rail freighted to our sister state of Mississippi and deposited in its upper regions at Corinth.

"I tell you now son," he said, turning to meet my eyes with his own, "Mississippi is a pretty enough place when ye' first lay eyes on it, but now days, I'm always a little unsettled by the memories of my grizzly service there."

He returned his gaze back to the approaching clouds and continued. "Not all of the Second Cav. were immediately transported to the east due to logistical restrictions. In fact, only B, D and G companies made the trip when we did, because of the urgent demand for paddleboats elsewhere.

"It must have quickly become obvious to command that the balance of the Arkansas cavalry units weren't gonna' be brought up to the front anytime soon, for within a week of our arrival, we of D, along with companies B and G were 'temporarily' assigned to various units of Tennessee Cavalry. It was better than a month before the other Second Cav. companies or any other Arkansas Cavalry outfits made the crossing to the east. Besides our three companies, only a few unmounted Arkansas units, including the entire Second Arkansas Mounted Rifles Regiment, went east to Corinth at about the same time as did we. Unlike us however, the Mounted Rifles made the trip without their mounts, for they were permanently dismounted whilst back with us at Camp Dardenelle. Unlike us of the Second Cav., mounted rifle units were designated as dragoons, foot soldiers mounted only for the express purpose of moving rapidly from one point to another on horseback, to then fight only dismounted as infantry rather than mounted like we of the cavalry. Even so, all southern cavalry were eventually required to become at times dragoons long before war's end, being flexible enough to regularly employ dismounted tactics as the situation might require, as well as in an effort to help preserve our ever more precious mounts from the hazards to them associated with mounted combat. I reckon too, the Second Mounted Rifles were unsaddled because most likely that ragged passel of mules and poor ole' plow horses they enlisted with was right suited and more needed for pullin' wagons than for any cavalry charges. We joshed 'em quite a bit over the course of our service together about their bein' 'unmuled.' But, the truth was, they made as fine an infantry outfit as ever there was, serving with distinction from Shiloh to Appomatox.

"When the western army of the Confederacy was consolidating in and around Corinth, it was like one big cotillion, with one soiree after another in town and the surrounding countryside nearly as often as the days of the week. Everyday was like a holiday, but for the military demands made on us by our officers. The drilling we complained of then was later appreciated when we faced both the elephant and the tiger.

"Corinth was the first place I ever saw billiards, they having a regular pool hall there with eight tables. I saw far too many Arkansas toothpicks flash from their scabbards within the walls of that little establishment. It became pretty evident that if'n we didn't jine with the enemy pretty soon, we'd whittle each other down right considerable afore the Yanks had a chance to do it for us. We were like scorpions in a bottle, slowly devouring our own."

The wind was whipping up smartly by now, so we decided we'd best move indoors before the bottom dropped out and we became soaked by the rain blowing horizontally in under the porch roof. He tossed his used-up chaw out into the dusty yard where the first raindrops were just kicking up little clouds of dust. We stopped at the drinking pail by the door and each dipped a good long draught of cool, freshly-drawn well water. After I'd finished with it, he took the dipper and rinsed the tobacco juice out of his mouth, spitting his first mouthful of water into the dust. We went to his bedroom and took our respective chairs before the now cold hearth. The wind whistled in the chimney and moaned in the attic rafters as the old house creaked in the mounting fury of the storm.

"Corinth is a pretty little town with its fine, old, brick and frame homes and broad shady streets. It reminded me a lot of Camden back before the war, or what Fordyce is like now," he said comparing it to local towns that had existed before, or grown up since in our region. "Its quiet, brick-paved streets didn't give the slightest hint to the danger lurking in the water supplies. With so many crowded into the hilly country surrounding the town and without proper sanitation, many a lad fell victim to dysentery or cholera long before we ever saw the first Yank. Of the better than three-hunert troopers in companies B, D and G that transferred to Mississippi in late March, near a third were unfit for duty when we set out for Pittsburg Landing in mid April. Amongst those on sick call was Brother Will, left back at Corinth in hospital, fightin' the pneumonia that he'd first caught aboard boat on our long voyage from Moro Bay to Van Buren. Also on sick leave was my gelding Prince who'd stepped in a hole during an exercise just the day before we were to march north against the Federals. It looked for a while like I might not make the sortie either until I went to visit Will in hospital. When I told him what had happened to Prince, he first asked after him. When I explained to him that his leg wasn't broke and that he'd be fully recovered by the time Will was, he then offered me the use of Fury to ride to Shiloh. I declined at first, knowing full well the risk and not wanting to be responsible in the case that something happened to that spirited, fine black beauty, that Will was so proud of. But Will insisted, saying that Fury didn't want to miss the fracas any more than did I. He was mighty right. Being unbloodied and having heard what a big push this campaign was intended to be, I was anxious to get me some. It didn't take Will all that long to convince me once't he'd assured me he knew Fury would be as well looked after by me, as by him. When he put it that way, I couldn't refuse his charity. So, when the time came to saddle up, I put mine on one of the best looking mounts in the bunch.

"Corinth boasted not just one, but two different railroad lines running through it. T'was these rail lines that made it the transportation hub of the entire South. The Memphis and Charleston ran roughly northwest by southeast, whilst the Mobile and Ohio ran nearly due north/south. The Yanks, freed by their victory at Pea Ridge from holding a large number of troops in Missouri to protect St. Louie against the threat of invasion by a Confederate army marching north out of Arkansas, began using the port city as a staging platform to swarm into the South via our many navigable waterways, thus beginning their invasion in earnest. The Confederate fort at New Madrid, on the Mississippi River just above the Arkansas/ Missouri line, fell to them on March thirteenth of that year. Too, the commanders of Forts Henry and Donaldson had surrendered them without much of a fight on February sixth and sixteenth respectively.

"We had to wonder at times if'n the gov'ment was in fact fighting the same war as us. Command wasn't always blessed with some of the brightest stars in the southern constellation. Those dunderheads at Donaldson had called a council of war after only the first day of the siege and decided to surrender to Grant, even after the defenders under their command had successfully and thoroughly driven off the initial probes of the overland attackers. I heard one eyewitness say that the first day's battle in the rifle pits outside the fort, resulted in the most thoroughly whipped bunch of Yanks he ever did see. The main threat to the fort however, came not from the army of Union infantry assaulting the outlying defenses, but from the menacing iron-clads stationed out on the river, systematically reducing any target with their heavy naval guns. Even so, our emplaced artillery had knocked out or driven them off during the first day's engagement.

"With the sole exception of Forrest's Cavalry and a couple-hunert infantrymen who braved waist deep, icy waters in their flight, the entire command was surrendered to Grant en masse by Confederate Generals Floyd, Buckner and Pillow. The loss to the Confederacy was something approaching thirteen thousand irreplaceable men and accompanying arms, along with herds of horses and mules, many of both having come out of Arkansas. Ole' Nathan Bedford, bein' the fighter that he was and refusing to capitulate, stormed out of the war council and against orders, took his troopers out through the bitter cold with their horses by way of a partially flooded river road that the Yanks left unguarded. According to the boys I served with in the Tennessee Cav. who road out of Donaldson with him, they could have took out most, if not all the rest of the command with 'em, without ever havin' surrendered a soul. Those that did escape the Yank prisons, numbered about four thousand, some seven hunert of which were Forrest's Cavalry.

"The same Federal army under Grant's command, fresh from their uncontested victories at Henry and Donaldson, began massing during early March in vast camps at Pittsburg Landing on the Tennessee River, just a short thirty mile march north of Corinth in south central Tennessee. In just two days, April the sixth and seventh, the fates of both the last river stronghold above Memphis, located on Island Ten and the vital rail-hub in Corinth, were decided.

"Corinth was oft called 'The backbone of the South,' as indeed it was, much as the rivers were the lifeblood. Its geographic locale would soon make it even more vital to Southern transport and communication with the impending fall of our extensive river networks into the control of the approaching Union gunboats. If Corinth also fell to the Federals, the only remaining all-weather supply line from east to west in the upper South would be severed. The Confederacy would suffer as surely as one with a fractured spine. Thus, everybody was ordered to the defense of Corinth, all other fronts being abandoned to rush any and all available men and horses to the Crossroads of the South," he said before pausing to listen to the rising pitch of the wind.

The rain outside now pounded the old cypress-shake roof, calling to mind the drumming of the enemy, forming to march against that far-off town in north Mississippi. He sat quietly for a spell, considering perhaps opportunities lost those many years past. A few drops of rain dripped down the chimney onto the hearth bricks, clean of ashes as they were in the middle of summer.

"Not more than a week before the spring Confederate offensive began in earnest, our three Arkansas companies of now crack cavalry, were consolidated into the Eighth Tennessee Cavalry. For the occasion, we were presented with well-used, passed down sabers. Our Tennessee colonel wasn't gonna' have us Arkansas boys spoiling the overall look and effect of his Tennessee horse warriors, who handed their battle tempered weapons on to us after receiving shiny new ones. Thomas Griswald and Company of New Orleans had made the blades we were given. I considered they'd be fine instruments, being fashioned as they were by an Irishman. The Tennessee veterans cautioned us that they had nicknamed the weapons 'old wrist breakers' due to their heavy, cumbersome weight.

"These were instruments of war that we were pretty much unfamiliar with the use of 'til then. The long, awkward blades were clumsy to wear, noisy and often irritating. But, the feel of one in your hands, especially when atop a horse, which is what they were made for, is magnificent. We didn't like walking around with them on, but then we weren't that fond of walking anyway. But on a horse, they were fine. A sword gave you a menacing feel, which added to the overall effectiveness of a shock-trooper.

"We were instructed, as novices, to hold the blade resting against the shoulder of the arm we carried it with whilst charging, so as not to accidentally stab ourselves when bouncing in the saddle. Then, upon overtaking our prey, to extend the blade at arms length with the tip aimed at our target. We practiced running the long blade through dummies, then smoothly withdrawing it as we galloped past the wood and straw victims. We were instructed on the fine points of utilizing the curve of the blade to achieve this without jerking our arm out of socket with a hand hung in the hilt of a stuck saber, or leave the sword behind sticking out of the straw stuffed bodies. Nothing would get you razed so much as leaving your sword in a training dummy. On occasion, Old N.B. Forrest himself would demonstrate the proper technique for employing a saber on horseback. One of the first things I noticed about him was how he wielded the weapon left handed, whilst holding the bridle reins with his right. He was a southpaw.

"In no time we became attached to our new badges of merit, as proud of our swords as any officer was his. Cavalry privates were the only enlisted men with sabers and we could tell it didn't sit well with many of the infantry line officers. But, we weren't under their command and there weren't much they could do about it 'cept scowl at us. The issuance of sabers amongst our enlisted did incalculable good for unit morale. Right then and there, I developed an abiding respect for our commander, Major General Nathan Bedford Forrest, still only a colonel then, because of his willingness to take care and provide for, to the best of his ability, all the men of his command. Only later did I come to know a much darker side of him, blacker than the skin of the nigras he so hounded."

He paused to consider some yet unrevealed portion of the past, perhaps remembering the feel of the saber in his hand. "That's the same sword that's now in the old chest out in the dogtrot," he told me, in reference to the shiny sword whose blade showed several nicks that I'd often marveled at since my earliest recollection.

I asked with wide-eyed amazement, "Did you run many Yanks through with it?"

"Don't get ahead of the story, Polk," he reprimanded me gently.

"Yes sir," I replied.

"Two days before the Battle of Shiloh," he went on, "we rode out of Corinth with the mounted troops of the Eighth Tennessee Cavalry, in the command of one of the finest cavalry generals I ever had the honor to serve under, General Forrest. At that time though, like I said before, he was still only a colonel, over only one brigade of about five-hunert men and horses.

"The plan conceived by headquarters for the spring offensive, was to catch the Union troops gathering at Pittsburg Landing by complete surprise before they had consolidated all their forces. Hemmed up against the Tennessee River as they were, camped in unfortified open fields, we hoped to drive them back to water's edge, where they would have no where to retreat, then decimate the better part of the army of invaders before they were even sure what had hit them. I read in my Bible that Ma gave me, where, in the Book of Judges, chapter twenty-one, a civil war amongst the Hebrews was finally settled at a place called Shiloh and peace was again restored to the twelve tribes. I prayed the upcoming encounter might too conclude the war that we were now engaged in.

"We attacked roughly sixty-five thousand Federals, with less than forty-eight thousand men of our own. Surprise was our biggest tactical advantage. For we green troops, the hope was that our first battle would be so decisive, that it would also be our last battle. As it turned out for far too many, it was just that, though not the last battle of the war. Our first taste of combat was a larger portion than most of us would have cared for.

"We could not have had a finer overall commander of the Army for the job, General Albert Sidney Johnson. But, much of the individual planning was left to his subordinates. Thanks to these lesser officers, our infantry arrived on the Plains of Shiloh dog tired from two days forced march, with no provisions left and no time to rest before being thrown into the waiting meat grinder.

"We cavalry were more fortunate. We also left for Shiloh two days prior to the battle, on the fourth, but riding is much less tiring and quicker than marching with all your gear on your back.

64

Anyone who doesn't appreciate riding a good mount, never had to walk in the dust kicked up and the droppings left behind by a passing cavalry unit.

"I've always admired the lay of the land and the roll of the hills. The country from Corinth to Shiloh was fine, with gentle, steady-rolling ground, covered with fresh-budding hardwood timber. The roads were fair, passing by occasional newly plowed fields of dark earth. The smell of turned over dirt reminded me of home and what I'd be doin' if'n I were still back there. I didn't miss the work, or the tedium, always worrying about too much rain, or not enough and I enjoyed the ride in the clear spring air, remembering from my youth the country we rode through. The only complaint I could muster at the time, was that we'd left Corinth with two days cooked rations and they had already long since disappeared.

"The evening prior to the first major engagement ever fought between two great armies south of the Mason/Dixon Line was one I guess I'll always remember. It made quite the spectacle, tens of thousands of men confined in such a small area as the night's camp. Unlike our camps back in Corinth, or even at Dardenelle, it was very quiet. We knew that on the morrow we would be committed into the jaws of death and who would not return to camp at the next sunset?

"We were drawn up for battle in the coolness of the predawn. I recall hearing turkeys gobbling at first light and hearing their wings rattle in the tree branches as they flew down from the roost to begin their day. How I longed to break ranks and go find some fowl afoot to ease the gnawing in my stomach. I said as much to the feller next to me in line. How well I remember his reply. He spat his tobacco juice into the dust between us, missing my stirrup and boot a mere inch and looked from beneath the wide brim of his hat, his face in shadow. He was a gent from the neighborhood back home, about my own age, named J. J. Mitchell.

"Musterin' up his most solemn face, he said, 'Son, we ain't lost nothin' yet, but some sleep and our bellies full. There's pert near a hunert thousand who's done pledged their lives in this here rebellion.'

"I couldn't help but feel a little sheepish at that moment, ashamed for complaining of a little hunger when faced with the plain spoken truth so well stated.

"Soon the coolness of the dawn gave way to the heat of the day, as we sat mounted, without benefit of shade, except for our wide-brimmed hats, waiting in reserve for the issuance of the command to move up. We sat in the heat and flies, swatting and sweating, silent and solemn. We knew that the end to our present discomfort would come in the form of enemy contact.

"In battle line you feel both alone and connected at the same time. No other could know one's feelings about family and home so far away. Yet, we each shared such thoughts in silence whilst standing in our long rows, knowing from previous training that our only chance lay in holding together as a unit. Each one depended upon all the rest. Everyone focused on his individual assignment, parts operating as a whole.

"Right there that day, in our loneliness and silence, missing our loved ones, we began to grow relationships with one another beyond normal human experience. It is a pure brotherhood-in-arms, like good steel, refined through fire. You learn to respect a man for the mettle he's made of and not the social rank or stature of wealth he was born to.

"As a result, when a member of the unit is slain, as will happen in combat, it is an overwhelming loss, even though some we knew but for a little season. That loss comes home to each man in his reflections, with the knowledge that we all die alone, no matter whom or how many are around. It is another great irony taught by war, similar to the fact that there is no greater sense of being alive as when so near death. I remember how vivid the spring colors and odors were to me at that final instant just before our charge.

"That day and many others to come, we saw men die in vain, wasted due to inept military leadership, both on the field and in Richmond. This too, added to our feelings of being alone and connected at the same time. We stood alone as a unit, even when the companies around us disintegrated, depending on our abilities, regardless of how badly command might squander us, or other companies might falter on our flanks. We were like a family. But the living, by definition, must learn how to live with the loss of the dead. That is what soldiers do and civilians as well. That is what it means to be mortal."

The storm seemed at its height as he began the final description of the events that transpired on those three spring days in '62, unlike anything in the way of carnage that ours, or any other nation had ever before witnessed.

"We were held in reserve that dawn, whilst most everyone else charged down on a surprised foe. We heard the big guns open up down the line to our left and right, followed by the crack of massed musket fire all along our front. The minutes dragged into hours as the crescendo of battle rose ever louder, then died away again and again. We were held back all through the morning and on into the afternoon. From my vantage, I could see Colonel Forrest impatiently pacing his horse back and forth at the crest of the hill that blocked our view of the engagement. Both he and his fine looking steed seemed to be chomping at the bit to jine in the fracas. From time to time he'd gallop down the slope, his aides in tow, to ride up and down our line inspecting and encouraging his boys.

"In turns of four each, he let troopers break ranks and ride up near the top of the hill, just far enough to peek dismounted over the crest and view the sight of the now distant battle, whilst holding our horses reins as they grazed on fresh grass. When it came my turn, along with J. J. Mitchell, Manuel Davis and another feller, we trotted up near the hill's crest and dismounted so's to walk up to a vantage point that allowed us to watch without bein' easily observed in return. What we saw there still brings cold chills to me even now on this hot summer day and made me proud that I was a horse soldier and not infantry. It was the devil's own work that we witnessed.

"The field was already littered with our dead and wounded from the previous advances. Still, the line officers were aligning the boys for another go. The bugle sounded the familiar note and they advanced in lockstep. The Federal line glinted with sunlight off shiny bayonets, but no fire yet issued from their muzzles. The Arkansas and Louisiana regimental colors snapped crisply in the breeze that blew in their faces. The bright red tunics of the New Orleans Zouaves stood out in vivid contrast, by comparison to the dull gray and butternut of mostly homespun and home-dyed flannel, worn by the Arkansans. They marched ever forward in an unbroken line."

"At half the distance to the enemy's front, they came upon the fallen from the previous attempts to rout the stubborn blue line. I watched as they stepped over the prone bodies left by the former assaults, the wounded grabbing at the pant legs of the fresh attackers. Their pallid faces starkly contrasted the Zouaves bright-blue trousers. They both warned of impending doom ahead and sought mercy and aid in their shock and terror. On went the line, ever nearer their objective. The officers shouted the order to double-quick and the line broke into a trot, maintaining their alignment well. Such a scream of defiance as then burst from the throats of the charging men, I'd never before heard. You would have thought we were at the gates of hell, listening to the damned rattling at their bonds.

"As they closed within mere yards of the enemy, I saw a blue-uniformed officer in the opposing line, drop his sword with the command to fire. Two thousand rifles and half a dozen cannon opened on the brave, but stunned lads. In an instant, they were stretched out in their gore, writhing, entire brigades dropping in their tracks under the hail of rifle and canister fire. Then the smoke from the enemy guns rolled over the reduced, but yet advancing gray lines, obscuring our view. Anxiously we watched, as did Colonel Forrest, listening to consecutive volleys that only thickened the smoke screen upon the field. The Rebel yell faded with the preceding volleys, until it was replaced by a more distant cheering of the Yankee Dutch. With that, we knew the attack had again failed. Momentarily our presumption was borne out by the figures straggling back through the ground haze, clutching at their heads and wounded limbs or limping with their muskets used as crutches. Before ordering us from our viewpoint, back into line, I heard the Colonel fairly spit out the words, 'Our boys are fallin' like rows of corn whilst we set here guardin' a damn crick!' He then wheeled his mount and rode off toward Generals Breckenridge and Cheatham. His dander was up and we were about to end our long wait.

"When he returned from his visit with the Generals, he drew up his mount in front of Fury and me, admiring the tall, black, stocking-footed stallion and commenting to me his pleasure at having such a fine lookin' animal under his command. He said he hoped I's as good a soldier as Fury was a handsome specimen. I thanked the colonel for his compliment to my brother's horse and with a hint of braggadocio, asked him to turn us loose and I'd be obliged to demonstrate our fightin' ability for him. 'Patience young feller,' was his reply, snorted out in a tone that betrayed his own impatience. He would later remember me, even without Fury beneath my saddle. That fact, along with a couple others, enabled me to stay with his command even after massive reorganizational consolidations scattered most of the various companies of the original Second Arkansas Cav. to augment other under strength Arkansas regiments as they arrived in Corinth from the Trans-Mississippi. Once we arrived back in Corinth after the Battle at Shiloh Church, there was soon nothing left of the Second Cav. Battalion, once't all the siphoning off of men and horsepower was done. But, we ain't yet to that part of the story."

"Don't get ahead of yourself," I said with my most devilish grin.

He inspected my expression for an instant, before replying deadpan, "Don't be a smart-aleck."

Even though he displayed no sign of amusement, I knew he appreciated my quip.

"Finally," he said, after my brief interruption, "in mid-afternoon on that first day, our company's captain, James Portis, came down the line with word we were about to attack. Every man silently and deliberately prepared for the terrible moment, readying to meet his fate, each in his own way. With the order to advance, we spurred our mounts with a mighty shout. We had lain in cover behind the rolling hills at the center of our lines, to mask our presence from the enemy prior to the assault. When we broke over the top of the rise, we saw the Yanks milling about in some confusion at the far edge of a wide cotton patch. They had continually repulsed every Rebel infantry attack, four in all, that Cheatham had thrown at them and must have thought we'd given up after such bloody losses. They initially had no idea they were under attack by cavalry. It didn't take 'em long however to figure it out though, when they looked up at the sound of thundering hooves, blood curdling screams and the crack of the few long-range rifles then in our possession.

"At first the Yanks laid down a concentrated fire from both rifle and cannon. I, along with the rest of the Arkansans riding in the column, had never experienced anything of the sort. Great blossoms of dirt sprouted out of the ground, showering us with dust and debris. I clearly recall my horror at feeling Fury's hooves striking the soft flesh of our dead and wounded men on the field and seeing horses stumble over their bodies as we charged. We rode in columns four abreast, leaping over the fallen infantrymen in our path. Through some miracle of Providence, the riders at the head of each column managed to weave a path through the hail of bullets and shot whilst the rest of us followed in tow. I was told later they had simply been trying to avoid trampling our fallen boys by winding a path where they were least concentrated. When I thought on it, I wondered if maybe that's not what saved us from their big, bronze guns, because the downed Confederates marked where the Yank cannon fire was most concentrated and those were the very spots we avoided.

"We bore down on their front ranks, swords a'gleamin', belching death from our pistols and shotguns. They stood so thick together you couldn't help but hit somethin' with every shot! Then, the blue line that had already turned back four previous assaults, finally broke. They scattered before us like dry leaves before the wind. We were hardly able to close with them near enough to use our swords.

"Our first taste of battle was sweet, seein' 'em drop everything and run and it was a hurdle crossed. We chased 'em until they hid like rabbits in the thickets to their rear. We were unable to continue the pursuit once't they reached the cover of the brambles, because it was too thick for our horses. I'd have loved to've seen 'em when they come out the other side. They's bound to a'been a mighty scraped up mess from the briars and brambles cuttin' at their bare arms and faces as they high tailed it.

"We were unable to drive the Yanks into the river that first day because the initial attack stalled all along the line, mainly because our poor, hungry lads had stopped their initial advance to fill their empty bellies with the Yank's breakfast left cooking on the abandoned campfires when we caught 'em so totally by surprise. The officers were eventually able to drive our weary boys back into line of battle, but the benefits of momentum and shock were lost when the hungry lads had stopped to gorge themselves.

"Whilst our boys were relishing the much needed sustenance, most of the weaponless, demoralized Yanks fell back and took cover huddling together like sheep below the lip of the bluff next to the boat landing, trapped between us and the swollen tide of the Tennessee.

"As the afternoon dragged on, the next big push bogged down with a fierce firefight in a peach orchard that we came to call 'the Hornet's Nest.' It was near a sharp bend in a sunken wagon road that bordered the orchard. Late in the day, the Loyalist Missouri Infantry and Ohio Artillery lodged in the Hornet's Nest, under the command of Yankee General Prentiss, were finally cut off and overrun by Arkansas and Louisiana infantry. But it was too late in the day to complete our victory and drive the remaining Yanks into the river. During the multiple delays in our advance, Sherman had managed to organize the Federal artillery atop of the bluff near the river so as to stem the tide of our final assault with their massed fire. So much Union artillery, concentrated as it was, delivered a withering fire against all our subsequent, attempted advances. We were so short of good long-range rifles or sufficient cannon, there was little we could do to dual with them, or pick off their gunners at the distance to which the Federal fire would allow us to close. Then, just before sunset, the Arkansas boys of the Nineteenth Infantry moved up on the Federal left near where it rested against the river bluff, in a valiant effort to flank the massed artillery. They were, however, driven off by the confounded Union gunboats Lexington and Tyler, settin' out on the river heavin' their explosive rounds at 'em. So ended the first day of the Battle of Shiloh, or Pittsburg Landing as the Yanks call it.

"At the end of that first day we knew we had whipped 'em on every front. If'n it weren't for the blood-engorged waters of the Tennessee, I doubt they'd ever have let up their egress 'til they was all the way back to Warshin'ton. Ole' Butcher Grant had his nose bloodied and any other self respecting general would have quit the field and skedaddled on that moonless night. That's exactly what we expected to find come mornin'.

"That theory about gunpowder bringing rain, may well have originated that night, for it came a terrible storm shortly after sundown. Ambulance wagons moved about the wrecked bodies strewn across the muddy, shell-plowed fields, picking up dead and wounded. Their coal oil lanterns cast an eerie glow through the sheets of rain. Mostly, the boys slept on their arms in line of battle, miserable in the cold, wet night, awaiting the morrow, when the fate of the Federals would be decided. Several of our Company D lads found a couple of abandoned Federal tents near an out-of-the-way spring, where we took shelter for the night. We slept as only worn out nature can.

"We were up well before first light, preparing for the final push. Venturing down to the spring in the fresh rain-washed air of the new morning, I found a small Injun stone adze at the base of an old oak, pushed up out of the earth by the spreading roots. I marveled at the handiwork of a people long removed from this place that was once so long their home. I stuck it in my saddlebags and hurried to the call of the bugle and the 'long roll' of the drum.

"All through the previous night, coming from the river landing we could hear the steamers goin' to and fro. Their plumes of dark smoke showed in the lightning and rain, above the blaze of their stacks, as the firemen over stoked their boilers to gain any additional haste, we thought, to aid their escape from the pinned-up position they held, backed against the river as they were.

"Were we ever surprised when first light broke over the Plains of Shiloh, to see their front fairly glistening with bayonets and bright new blue uniforms. The sons-a-bitches weren't retreatin' at all, they'd been reinforcing all night. Instead of haulin' 'em away, steamers had been haulin' 'em in. This here battle weren't yet done.

"In the melee that ensued on the dawn, I had opportunity to draw aim on more than one hapless fellow. During the night, we'd distributed the stands of arms abandoned by our retreating foe and now we had far better weapons than on the previous day. I soon put mine to good use. The second day we were dismounted and advanced on foot for a period late in the morning.

"One bearded fellow came rushing at my position wielding a bright new bayonet, with the evident intention of disemboweling me. I drew down on him, but missed my mark in the center of his chest. Instead, I nearly severed his right arm as the ball tore through just below the shoulder. He collapsed in a heap, his weapon clattering harmlessly to the ground. I rushed forward to return the favor with my own new bayonet. With his remaining good arm, he shielded himself from my onslaught, saying only, 'Oh mercy!'

"I drew up short, standing there over the bearded feller, momentarily shaken from the blood lust of battle rage that settles over one in such circumstances.

"As the hubbub of racket and confusion from the confrontation continued around us, I was seemingly aware of only we two men there in the midst of it all. I lowered my bayonet and knelt, holding my rifle in my right hand, its muzzle pointed at the sky and its butt set firmly in the torn, muddy soil. With my left hand, I reached toward the shrinking figure whose blood was rapidly spreading in a puddle by his side. I grabbed his canteen and rested my gun against my raised knee, freeing my right hand to uncork it. I raised his head with my other hand and poured the water into his open mouth. He propped himself up on his one good elbow, whilst his other arm dangled by a shear shred of flesh, blood pumping from the severed artery with each weakening beat of his heart. Some water spilled over his lips and mingled with his blood, but he managed to swallow one good gulp. When I released his head to re-cork his canteen, he collapsed from his good elbow onto his back. A vacant look glazed over his eyes as his pupils turned from me to fix on some far distant point in the now clear sky above. Then, as I looked upon his face, the pupils of his eyes grew ever larger 'til they covered the whole iris, hiding the bright blueness of them that had been there but the moment before, like a cloud blocking out the light of the sun.

"Sorry Yank,' was all I could manage as I gathered myself up to rejine the Confederate advance, the momentum of which had by then carried it yards beyond us. I moved out, looking back only once't to see the poor fellow fully in his death throws. I expected to again see the pale, bloodless corpse, dead eyes staring toward heaven, when we retraced our steps sometime later that day, en route to our night's encampment. But, the tide of battle would instead engulf us before the sun again set."

The summer storm was now passed over and the humidity left in its wake began to make the air of the bedroom feel oppressive. So, we again adjourned to the porch, stopping by the door to enjoy another cool drink from the wooden pail. We repositioned ourselves in the rockers, again comfortably propping our feet on the now damp porch rail.

The air, though heavy with moisture, was clean, refreshed and a good ten degrees cooler than before. Water dripped from the house eaves and leaves of the front yard shade trees into muddy puddles. The clumps of daylilies scattered about the yard within its waist high board fence, raised their drooping heads, sending forth their abundant fragrance, as if in gratitude for the drink from heaven.

As usual, Pappy didn't take up the story immediately when we moved to the new location. We both sat listening to the chirp of tree frogs and the chorus of birds sounding out their joy at the respite from the summer's heat. Even the chickens cackled and the cows lowed their appreciation for the much needed shower. The sun yet hid behind the overcast.

"This orta' make them crops jump now," he said, reminding me of the additional work that meant for brother Johnny and me, come harvest. At my young age, the philosophy I held was, 'if'n ye' don't make the crop, ye' don't have to put it up.' But I knew too, without it, we'd suffer other hardships.

Wishing to take my mind off hard toil soon to come, I asked Pappy, "So, what else happened that second day at Shiloh?"

He sat silent for a long moment, himself glad to forget unpleasant thoughts for a bit, but then honored my request to hear more, knowing he could really do but else.

"General Alfred Sidney Johnson, by all accounts, was as fine a field commander as the South ever produced. Had he lived, perhaps things would have turned out differently on that seventh day of April in 1862. Unfortunately for the South, he had fallen the day before whilst tryin' to urge on the Ninth Arkansas troops that were assaulting the Hornet's Nest. We affectionately referred to the Ninth Arkansas Infantry as 'the Parson's Regiment,' since they had more'n forty preachers all told enlisted amongst their ranks. I figured, if'n it t'weren't for so many of 'em being ushered into eternity from that slaughter pen we call the 'Hornets Nest,' there'd likely be several more varieties of Christian denominations 'round today. But they couldn't rightly refuse the appeal of their valiant general, sitting up on his horse where bullets buzzed all around like mad hornets, wielding Yankee General Sherman's captured tin coffee cup, that he claimed as 'his share of the booty.' He said to them, 'Men of Arkansas, they say you boast of your prowess with the Bowie knife. Today you wield a much nobler weapon – the bayonet. Employ it well!' And they did, with a savagery that defied reason. Infuriated by the hail of steel balls spewing from the rifled bronze guns, they charged into the very mouths of the flamin' cannon, being cut down like rows of grain, before finally, fighting tooth and nail, they swept over Yankee General Prentiss and his bloody boys in blue, killin', or capturin' the lot.

"The story I heared 'bout how General Johnson bought the farm went like this. Whilst advancing to the position where he got shot, he and his staff had come across some wounded Federals, abandoned by their own fleeing comrades. He, ever a gallant gentleman, ordered his staff surgeon, Dr. David W. Yandell, who was then the Medical Director of the Department of the West, to dismount and attend to the downed enemy until an ambulance came to relieve him. This being strictly against protocol, the sawbones objected, only to have his objections overruled by his commander. The General continued to ride on forward to the sound of the thickest fighting. Whilst riding amongst the badly repulsed Confederates of 'the Parson's Regiment,' in his successful attempt to rally them for another attack, he caught a mini-ball in his left leg, midway between the ankle and knee, just below his black boot top. He felt the blow of the small caliber round, but in the excitement and fury of the battle raging around him, he thought it only a flesh wound and barely paused to look down at the annoyance. With little regard for his own safety, he continued to rally the faltering Confederate advance to final success, until, weakened by a loss of blood from his severed artery, he toppled to the ground from atop his horse 'Fire-eater.' His nearest aide rushed to General Johnson's side, at first unable to ascertain the extent of the General's wounds. Finally, after examining his commander all over, he pulled off his left boot only to have blood pour from it. The slight wound had struck an artery and because the aide didn't know how to properly administer a tourniquet, the General soon bled out and expired on the spot. In all likelihood, but for his gallantry at leaving his surgeon Dr. Yandell behind with the wounded Yanks, General Johnson would have lived to fight another day.

"As it was, command fell to his second, 'the Creole,' General Pierre Gustave Toutant Beauregard, the chief engineer responsible for the ring of earthwork defenses and rifle-pits surrounding

Corinth, known to all as 'the Beauregard Line.' He was a fair enough general, but I don't think he appreciated, as had Johnson, the overall importance hinging on the result of that day's battle to the final outcome of the war. It was intended to be a knock out punch, bold and daring, to divide and destroy piecemeal the divisions of Buell, Grant and Wallace. In all fairness to 'the Ole Creole' though, the first part of the plan was already lost by the morning of the seventh. During the night, the three Federal divisions had united and were no longer 'piecemeal' outfits, but one immense army, a third again larger than our own battle and road weary band.

"Whilst some of our company slept in relative comfort in the captured Yankee tents, others of Forrest's Regiment were donning captured blue uniforms and scouting right up to and even behind the enemy's picket lines. What they discovered, hours before any of the rest of us knew it, was that the Yank divisions were, in fact, consolidating on the west bank of the Tennessee and forming above the river bluff for a counter attack at dawn.

"When the scouts returned to Forrest with the news, he tried to inform Beauregard, but couldn't locate him. It appears the new overall theatre commander had retired for the evening in Union General Sherman's captured tent, located somewhere out on our left, without informing anyone of his whereabouts. When Forrest, in his frustration couldn't locate 'the Creole,' he passed the information on to Brigade Commanders Breckinridge and Hardee. They simply told him to maintain outposts and continue to report enemy activity.

"What difference, if any, that news would have made in Beauregard's hands, I do not know, a night attack perhaps. But, as I've already said, with the first light we saw that we were facing, not the same demoralized, blue-clad veterans of the previous day, but two more divisions of fresh reinforcements. The task at hand, proved more than either we, or our leaders were up to. The Federals counterattacked soon after first light, driving down on us with a fury unseen the twenty-four hours before. We stood our ground and the waves of blue and butternut clad men washed back and forth across the plains and through the scrub oaks of Shiloh. Finally, by four in the afternoon, the superior numbers of fresher troops won the day, taking back all the territory we'd seized from them the day before. Even though our retrograde maneuver was made in good order, taking time to load captured wagons with the material that we'd gleaned from the Feds, it was most disheartening to file back past the little log Shiloh Methodist Episcopal Church that we'd so boldly ridden past two days hence. Most of our boys, who'd fought so valiantly at such cost, were raw levies, volunteers not conscripts, ignorant of discipline and drill and poorly provisioned and armed. They were wore slap out from two days hard marching followed by two days of ferocious fighting, with little or no sleep for that entire period. I saw many in the retreat marching asleep on their feet. Their sacrifice had earned two things, several thousand stands of badly needed small arms and supplies, scrounged from the Feds and an immortal reputation for the Confederate soldier of unyielding valor and cool, steady courage. But, our main objective, the destruction and repulsion of 'those people,' was not achieved.

"Forrest's Battalion of Tennessee Cavalry was given rearguard duty, with orders to delay any pursuit by the Yanks. The fair roads, that seemed so pleasant just some sixty or seventy hours before, were now mired with the tracks of weary, dejected soldiers and wagons full of the groaning wounded. In our retreat, we'd abandoned most of our dead and many injured, left behind on the field of battle for the Federals to tend to, or dispose of. Many a friend and brother were laid in mass graves, dug by the freed nigras of the area, forced at gunpoint by their liberators, to drag the torn bodies and shovel the dirt.

"All through the night and the next day, in a renewed, cold spring rain, the long line of human misery wound back south through the hills and hollers. Bone-tired foot soldiers, who'd barely slept or even paused to rest for nearly five days, dragged themselves on, ankle deep in the mired roads, seeking safety back at Corinth behind the protection of 'the Beauregard Line.'

"At first there was no sign of pursuit, the Yanks seeming content to have taken back all our gains and to have maintained their tenuous foothold on Tennessee soil. And besides, the churned-up roads we traveled back over, didn't facilitate any sort of rapid pursuit, especially by artillery caissons. But, finally at noon on the eighth, Sherman's forces came upon the tail end of our column, at a point about half way back to Corinth just north of Mickey's Crossroads.

"Company D was on down the line, guarding against a flank attack on the column where two side roads merged with the main road. We sat on our mounts, rain running off our wide brimmed hats. Some sought shelter inside and under the porch of Mickey's little country store that the crossroads took its name from.

"Shortly before twelve noon, we heard sporadic shots from the rear of the counter march and a galloper rode up, splattering mud in his wake. He had urgent orders from Colonel Forrest to beat it back to the rear with all haste. The Federals had overtook us!

"We quickly formed up in column, two by two and trotted against the flow of men and material pouring south. We soon came upon the ambulance train, bringing up the rear of the column, followed by its own swarm of flies. It was quite the contrast between our light horse cavalry and the lumbering wagons. They were filled to overflowing with the wretched, bloody casualties, dazed and bouncing away from the enemy, compared to the dashing figures astride warhorses marching to the sound of the fray.

"Our cavalry commander was never one to shirk a fight. That's one of the things I respected and liked most about him. He was a firm believer that a good offense is the best defense. When we passed the last ambulance, we soon came upon the Colonel at the lip of a ravine we later came to call Fallen Timbers, named so for the felled trees, abandoned in a prewar logging project. He was directing his fewer than three hunert men into skirmish line to stem the advance of the Feds. This caused the pursuing blue column to themselves spread out in line of skirmish, across't the ravine on the far lip, whilst beginin' a slow advance down the slope, through the tangle of felled treetops and crisscrossed trunks. When we rode up, he immediately ordered us to prepare to charge the enemy. In his haste, he didn't consider a couple of what I thought very important factors. First, we, the troopers he was ordering to prepare to charge, were the newest recruits to the Eighth Tennessee. We had thus far participated in only one mounted charge against an enemy and that whilst following in column behind seasoned veterans. Secondly, in the narrow path of the road, we could not spread out to counter the effect of the Yank fire coming from their dispersed positions where they hid within the cover of the felled trees on either side of the muddy lane. We would be easy targets for their concentrated crossfire. All this ran through my mind in an instant upon hearing and realizing his command to charge was directed to we mud-splattered Arkansans, just arriving on the scene.

"The Colonel reared his gray steed in the middle of the muddy thoroughfare, spinning him around in the midst of flying lead, preparing to lead the charge himself, perhaps sensing a reluctance on our part from some of the surprised looks on our faces.

"Come on you brave Arkansas boys,' he shouted, I suppose realizing for the first time to whom he'd issued the command to charge the throats of the guns, 'Follow me! Let's see ya' use them sabers I give ye!'

"By this time, the Federals had brought into position and unlimbered their cannon in the roadway and were releasing their first rounds, seeking the range. They fell short of our position. The rain impeded their fire, for they had to be cautious not to wet their powder, but they soon got off another volley, this time throwing up mud and water all around Colonel Forrest and us. In the confusion, we tried to form in a column, four abreast for the attack, which was all the road width would allow.

"Impatient as always to jine with the enemy, the Colonel drew his pistol and his sword, one in each hand and spurred his horse forward, right out in front of us, calling back over his shoulder, 'You boys better come on, the next volley will be right in amongst ye!' Without ever again looking back, he sped out before us, splashing mud, down the middle of the road into the ravine, straight toward the foe on the far side of the swag.

"With the head of our column barely started in pursuit of our leader, the Yanks let go another fusillade that sailed over Colonel Forrest's head and true to his prediction, landed right in our midst, knocking men and beast to the ground and splattering Fury and me with mud and blood. The shell bursts scattered the mounted troops and further delayed our pursuit of the Colonel. Getting Fury again under control, I looked up to see our commander fifty yards out ahead of the rest of the column, all alone, riding at full gallop toward the Federals, apparently unaware he was not yet being followed. I could imagine him being shot, or dragged out of the saddle, surrounded by the Yankee Dutch. In my fright at the thought of loosing yet another fine leader, I forgot about my own and Fury's safety and put the spurs to his side. I shouted to the others, 'Come on boys, the Colonel needs us!'

"Whether in response to my plea, or in an effort to escape the next artillery barrage, now that the Yanks had found the range, the others fell in behind me in pursuit of our lone commander.

"Before we could close the gap between us and Colonel Forrest, he was amongst the Yanks. There was nothing we could do but ride on in pursuit, for to fire at the enemy would have been to chance shooting the Colonel. We watched helplessly, driving our mounts on, as a crowd of swarming blue uniforms engulfed him. But, never under estimate the ferocity of a fine warhorse in the proper hands. Just as quickly as he'd disappeared amongst the unmounted soldiers, he reemerged, slashing and firing at his attackers and spurring his mount in rapid retreat. My heart soared within my breast to see him break free, only to drop again as I witnessed a Federal soldier leap from the brush at the road's edge, to run up and stick the muzzle of his weapon right in the Colonel's side before pulling the trigger. With the noise of the wind in my ears and the rain on my hat, mixed with the firing of guns all around, I couldn't hear the report of the Yankee's carbine, but I saw the smoke discharge from the muzzle and watched the Colonel rise well out of his saddle. At that instant I checked at the corner of my eye to assure myself I, too, weren't riding alone. I was glad to see other forms rushing to his aid. I imagined riding up to the crumpled figure in the mud and reaching down to drag him up on Fury behind me. I could only hope we would then be able to escape the hail of gunfire that was sure to follow after us.

"But, in the next instant, to my amazement, I saw the Colonel land back in his saddle and continue to beat his retreat toward our lines. Again my heart leapt with renewed joy!

"After riding only a few more yards, another Yank rushed out of the underbrush toward the Colonel and his horse. Again hope seemed to fade as I thought he was surely a goner this time. We were still a good seventy-five yards out from his position with nothing to be done but race on. What happened next, I wouldn't have believed if'n I hadn't seen it with me own eyes. Colonel Forrest, in one smooth motion, severely wounded as he was, reached down with his right arm to the lone Yankee infantryman and snatched him up on the horse behind him to serve as a shield against being shot in the back as he rode away from their skirmish line. At seeing that incredible sight, I couldn't help but laugh out loud, even in the midst of all the rifle fire being directed down on us."

His voice seemed to betray just the slightest hint of emotion before he fell momentarily silent and cleared his throat. I looked up at him, to see him blink several times and reach reflexively for the corner of his eye. I caught myself looking closer at his reaction, almost staring, to try to determine what was happening with him, though his tight-lipped grin revealed little. Without ever looking directly at me, after recovering his composure, he went on with his story.

"When we closed with the Colonel, I wore a broad grin as we met and splashed passed each other in the muddy road. His brightly flushed face was etched with a look of grim determination that marked his record to the very end of the war. We rode on another dozen yards toward the enemy, discharging our pistols and covering Ole' Forrest's escape, before reining our mounts around to follow the Colonel back to the relative safety of our own lines.

As I spun Fury in the road, the blasted Yanks loosed another rifle volley. A ball clipped the heel of my boot and ricocheted off, without cutting the leather or breaking my skin. It had ripped off my boot heel, but left me with no more than a badly bruised heel bone that made walking difficult for a good week. Fury, on the other hand was not so lucky. After striking my heel, the bullet went into the stallion's middle and lodged against a right-side rib bone, though at that moment, I hadn't yet realized that he was hit.

"As we sped back to our lines, again pursuing the Colonel, I saw him fling the unarmed, unharmed Yank off the rear of his horse. The poor, frightened fellow went sprawling in the quagmire of the lane. It was quite comical to watch him slipping and a'sliding as he struggled to his feet, only to be knocked ass over teakettle by our pursuing horses. The amazed Yankee private managed to escape relatively intact, if stunned, back through the crossfire of the ravine, to the company of his fellows.

"Once't we'd found cover behind our own troops, we realized not one horse returned from the foray without his rider, though that was not to say all were uninjured. Before the attack ever began, a solid shot had gone straight through two horses and their riders, killing them all in an instant, before plowing a furrow another thirty yards down the middle of the road. The disemboweled horses still lay where they fell, their dead riders dragged away to cover. There was blood, guts and dung splattered another twenty yards down the muddy road beyond the end of the shell furrow.

"Another trooper, seeing the running blood on Fury's side, asked if I were wounded? Climbing down on my tender foot to inspect the damage, I found the horse's wound. This brought tears immediately to my eyes, feeling both for the horse and Brother Will, who dearly loved the bold animal. I hadn't stopped long enough yet to consider my own fortune.

"As it turned out, both Fury and Colonel Forrest survived their wounds. The General, as we soon took to callin' him, was no way subdued by his close call and went on to fight many more engagements, having twenty-nine mounts shot from beneath him before war's end. Fury, on the contrary, was never again the ferocious fighter he had proved to be for me during those three fateful days in early April.

"Our outfit continued on rearguard duty the rest of the trip, but heard no more out of the Yanks. The display of apparently insane bravery, shown by our colonel and us when we charged at them down the narrow, muddy lane, was lesson enough to convince them to let us go about our business unperturbed.

"Staying with our battalion, Colonel Forrest, Fury and I, along with others of our riding wounded, moved with the best speed we could muster, back to Corinth for medical treatment. As we trudged on through the drizzle and the muck of the highway, I watched the Colonel pull on a bottle he occasionally produced from inside his coat. This, of course, was done to help reduce the pain of his injury, there being no other anesthetic available. From time to time, he'd pass the Tennessee whiskey over to me for a draw. In the course of the long journey back to Corinth, his mood swung from one dark, to one more cheerful, as did my own. By journey's end, the Colonel had invited me to jine him on an upcoming reconnoiter of Memphis, provided the Yanks didn't attack Corinth first, for his upcoming forty-first birthday party and to do some local recruiting to boost the battalion's fighting strength. Not having as serious an injury as my commander, I didn't pull as hard at the bottle as he. Because of that and the fact he took about three drinks for each of my own, I suspected the good Colonel might not recollect his invitation of a mere private to accompany him to his hometown when the time arrived.

"The inspiration I received from observing Ole' Forrest ride stoically on, with a bullet lodged against his spine, until we could reach hospital in Corinth, would serve me well when it later came my turn to stay long in the saddle after being grievously wounded.

"That same day, a couple hunert miles northwest of us, Island Ten fell, surrendered to the enemy before it disappeared beneath the rising river, or was reduced to a smoldering ruin by the incessant bombardment from mortar barges and gunboats. When we arrived back in Corinth on the ninth, we were greeted with the news that seven thousand Confederates, with their accompanying precious small arms and better than a hunert pieces of all size artillery, had been captured by Yankee General John Pope and his boys, when the island fortress finally capitulated." *II.*

I cut in, asking, "Is that Polk, like my name?"

"No son, it's Pope, P-O-P-E. You were named after one of our fine Southern generals, Leonidas Polk."

"I was huh?" I said to the new revelation. As I pondered this previously unknown fact and before I could ask more, he continued his summation of the state of the Confederacy at that stage of the conflict.

"The war news seemed to indicate that what we'd so recently expected to be a rapid conclusion to hostilities, was now going to be anything but. There was yet a long war road left to travel.

"General Johnson's body was laid in state at Rose Cottage across the street from the finest brick Methodist church I'd ever yet seen. The house had served as his headquarters before the battle and now served his remains as a funeral parlor.

"Nearly every other structure in town, including the Methodist church, all other churches and public buildings and practically every home and stable, became hospital wards. Corinth was one vast camp of sick and injured. The continuing lack of sanitation added to the ranks of wounded, with many suffering from dysentery, typhoid fever and measles. When I hobbled in to visit Will shortly after my return, he'd been moved from a comfortable, indoor bed, to a blanket on the cold, damp ground, exposed to the chill wind and hydropsical early spring air. His bed had been taken over by a far worse case than his own. After limping through hospital tents and makeshift wards all over one side of town, I finally located his whereabouts, to find him much improved since we'd last visited just before my departure to Shiloh. But, within the week, surrounded by so many ill and dying and deprived of the comforts of home and the ministrations of a loving family, he took a relapse that carried him nearer yet to death's dark door.

"The one saving grace that preserved both him and myself was, that as youngsters, we'd both had the measles. Because of that, we were spared the pitiable condition brought on to the thousands killed and made so ill by the epidemic that swept the camps. Will was amongst what I've heard was eighteen thousand soldiers on the sick list by the end of April. That's not counting the eight out of ten amputees who'd already succumbed to shock, tetanus and other infections. The wonder was, with no suitable food or water and little affective medicine, that any survived. All told, according to reports, Confederate losses were a thousand seven hunert twenty-three killed in action, eight thousand and twelve wounded and another nine hunert and fifty-nine missing, most of these but a short time in the service. I heard from our brigade commander that it was estimated the Union suffered similar losses, but with better than twice as many captured. Out of the roughly one hunert some odd thousand of both armies that participated in the Battle of Shiloh, nearly a fourth were either killed, wounded or captured. All present had a rough three days!

"To top off so much good news, we were fully expecting the Federals to begin their big push for the railroad junction at Corinth any day. In anticipation of such, all able-bodied infantrymen, not on hospital, or mess duty, were either kept busy digging graves, or digging and fortifying entrenchments. Still others within cavalry units were kept on constant patrol, scouting the position and dispositions of our approaching enemy. One piece of good news they were able to report back to headquarters, was that the Yanks certainly weren't getting in any hurry on their southerly march. They spent every afternoon throughout the month of May, after making only a short morning's march, entrenching to defend the evening's camp, perhaps still remembering the crazed cavalry charge that stopped their pursuit at Mickey's Crossroads.

"That, at least, was some encouragement to counterbalance all the abundant bad news. There were two other pieces of favorable news that came in May to offset all the setbacks of April. Because of his successful showing at Shiloh and afterward on the retreat, Ole'Forrest soon made the rank of Brigadier General. His promotion only awaited the final approval of the Southern Congress, which was expected to come on July twenty-first. The other good news was the eventual arrival by mid-May of our twenty-two thousand other Arkansas cavalry and infantry comrades from the Trans-Mississippi District, under the joint-command of the failed 'heroes' of Pea Ridge, Ole' Van Dorn and his new side-kick, General Sterling Price.

"In an effort to bolster the sagging morale of our defeated troops, the new commander of the Western Theatre, 'the Creole,' issued this proclamation, 'Soldiers,' he said, 'I assume this day the command of the Army of Mississippi, for the defense of our homes and liberties and to resist the subjugation, spoliation and dishonor of our people. Our mothers and wives, our sisters and children expect us to do our duty even to the sacrifice of our own lives. Our Cause is as just and sacred as ever animated men to take up arms and if we are true to it and to ourselves, with the continued protection of the Almighty, we must and shall triumph!" Pappy paused briefly, still wondering at the power those words once held, while I marveled at his unstammering recitation of a speech he'd heard so long ago. Then he proceeded.

"As a result of our satisfactory performance at Shiloh and then again at Fallen Timber Holler, some select members of Companies B, D and G were drafted as part of a special battle group on May fifteenth, under the command of soon to be Brigadier General Nathan Bedford Forrest, within his Eighth Tennessee Cav. A ballot was held in the new Company D of the Eighth Tennessee and field officers were elected that same day. Due to our being incorporated with an existing unit of Tennessee Cav., the larger number of Dekalb and Wilson County Tennesseeans in the outfit carried the vote for their fellow Tennesseean, Captain James M. Phillips, who was reelected as their and thus our company commander. Other officers elected or reelected were Colonel Baxter Smith, Lieutenant Colonel Paul F. Anderson and Major Willis S. Bledsoe.

"Because of Forrest commandeering our three companies into his, by then, regimental-size command, the recently arrived balance of the Second Arkansas was fully three hunert men under strength. So, the remainder of the recently arrived Second Cav. Regiment, had to be consolidated into Phifer's Sixth Arkansas Cavalry Battalion and another under strength unit, Slemon's

Fourth Arkansas Cavalry Regiment, to bring both up to regulation strength of five hunert and a thousand men and horses respectively. Whilst we remained in camp at Corinth, we kept in touch with our fellow Arkies and so were apprised of the results of their new officer elections. Posted in their May fifteenth vote were Major Thomas Jefferson Reid, who'd first enlisted Will, me and all the other local boys into the original Second Arkansas Cavalry. Also posted were Major William J. Somerall and Lieutenant Colonels H. R. Withers and Thomas M. Cochran. Thomas Garrison was Adjutant, Wesley D. Leiper was Quartermaster and Watt Strong served as Commissary officer.

"Our now being battle-hardened veterans, the new boys from home naturally looked up to us and wanted to hear all about the Shiloh campaign. They too were much improved as horse soldiers since last we saw 'em, having been extensively drilled on the parade grounds of Dardenelle and having ridden many patrols of those environs, raiding well into southern Missouri.

"The arrival of the Arkansas and Texas boys brought our operational strength at Corinth up to approximately fifty-one thousand seven hunert by the end of May.

"I was kept busy blacksmithing for my new comrade's horses. In a cavalry outfit, the farrier's work is never done. My heel hardly bothered me by then, so I spent long hours keeping the company mounts well shod. I was boarding in the stables with our horses and spent the whole of my days stirring amongst the animals. With the help of our company commander, I managed to get Brother Will released from hospital and into my more attentive care. That done and with hot, nutritious food and a good cot provided for his comfort, as opposed to the rancid rations and cold earth where he had bunked since the army's return from Shiloh, his health soon again improved. Will was always thereafter very grateful for my efforts on his behalf back then.

"Also, during this busy period from mid April through the middle of May, I learned new skills in how to heat up a sword edge and draw out nicks in the blade face by hammering it between an anvil and a two pound hand-sledge. The old smithy that shared that knowledge with me was Herman Culpepper from over near Raul. He is the one who first told me the old blacksmith's axiom, 'You'll go to hell for workin' cold steel!' We developed a strong friendship working together during those hectic weeks. It was Herman, in fact, who, not knowing any better, first honed a razor edge the full length of an officer's saber, rather than the cavalry manual's recommendation of only four inches of the tip. When the subordinate showed the modified cutting blade to Old Forrest, the Colonel liked it so well he had his own blade sharpened to length and soon after ordered all regimental sabers honed from hilt to tip. This would prove to be a deadly innovation to our cavalry ordinance.

"All the strenuous labor during that time wasn't so bad though, because war can make you appreciate such simple pleasures as a hard job well done. And too, it gave me ample opportunity to tend to Fury's wounded side, Prince's injured leg and Will's wasting lungs. They all progressed nicely under my care, though Will noticed Fury wasn't as apt as he had once been to attempt to tear down the barn wall when I had him and Prince in adjoining stalls, with the purpose in mind of getting at my horse for a contest of strength. Stallions are normally just naturally high strung that way, but Fury had mellowed considerably since being shot, no longer as keen for a confrontation.

"Our patrols informed us the Federals were inching ever closer with each passing day. We expected their final assault to come sometime around the first of June. As a result of their slow progress toward our well-defended position, Colonel Forrest was granted a brief leave to visit his home and family in Memphis, whilst recuperating from the surgery that had removed the Yank bullet from next to his spine. Much to my surprise and delight, a messenger found me one sunny afternoon laboring with a particularly cantankerous jug-head that wouldn't stand still long enough for me to replace his worn-out shoes. During the ensuing struggle, he jerked a still protruding nail that I'd only just driven through his hoof, right through the heel of my right hand. In a fit of resultant anger, I thoroughly cold-cocked him right between the eyes with my trimming tongs. Needless to say, that finally got his attention.

"The messenger, his presence on the scene unbeknownst to me before then, commented from his point of view behind us, that he could certainly see where the Colonel's apparent fondness for me came from, the two of us sharing such like temperament as we did.

"Startled by the surprise of having an audience during my little fit, I swung abruptly around, tongs still in hand, to find a staff Lieutenant stepping quickly back out of my reach. Seeing the uniform and epaulets of his rank, I dropped the tongs and snapped to attention, stammering out a hurried apology for my actions, as I saluted, blood dripping from my raised right hand. I felt certain I was in for it for abusing military property. Seeing the offending tongs drop harmlessly to the ground, a grin spread across his face and he visibly relaxed.

"At ease soldier,' he said in a deep, southern Mississippi drawl. 'I've got an invitation here for you from Colonel Forrest.' He handed me a folded note, which I promptly dripped blood on whilst unfolding it in my excitement, hoping perhaps the Colonel wasn't as drunk on our return from Shiloh as I'd first feared. It read, 'Your presence is requested on the front steps of the Tishomingo Hotel, at oh seven-hunert hours on the morrow, to accompany Colonel Nathan Bedford Forrest, by rail, on a reconnoiter and recruitment foray into Memphis and the environs thereof. You will need to bring your mount and provisions enough for said animal, for the one-day rail trip. Your commander and host will thereafter furnish provisions for the each of you. Expect a heap of fun!' It was signed, 'N. B. Forrest, Commanding Officer, Forrest's Regiment, C.S.A."

He arose, stretching himself, then carefully eyed and gingerly negotiated the wet wooden steps, holding tight the handrail, stepping off the porch and into the puddled yard. He said only, "But that's a story for another day."

The storm clouds were now rumbling on to the east, allowing the setting sun to burst forth brightly from beneath the trailing western edge of the cloudbank. He reached in the breast pocket of his old bib overalls and pulled out his well-used pipe, clenching it cold and unfilled between his teeth. I followed him away from the setting sun, past the daylilies and around to the east side of the old house, where we were greeted by a wondrous sight as we stood together, he resting his hand on my shoulder. The evening rays coming from the receding sun behind us, rushed at low angles from beneath the clouds, illuminating the rise of landscape across the fields to the east. Below the dark pall, in the shadow of the rapidly moving storm's footprint, the trees at field's edge flashed bright with the reflected light streaming suddenly from the west. Then, just as suddenly, a rainbow appeared within the thinning ranks of receding clouds. It quickly brightened, becoming more defined. Then another began to form above it, the second multicolored arch becoming clearer until completing its curve across the entire breadth of the eastern sky, opposite the twilight of the disappearing evening sun. For a brief moment we stood silently together, awed by the unexpected spectacle. Then, just as suddenly as they'd appeared, the two rainbows vanished before our very sight, as the sun dropped behind the western horizon. The storm, the rainbows and the setting sun all departed in different directions at once.

Second Arkansas Calvary Battalion, CSA
Company D – Bradley County Troop

J.N. Allen

Jefferson E. Andrews

J. Baggett

W. Baggett

J.W. Baker

Stephen Baker

Stephen Barker

W. Barker

John C. Barnes

Nicholas V. Barnett

G.M. Bell

F.M. Bevell

J.B.T. Boone

G.W. Bradley

William Breathheart

J.C. Bryant

S. Brown

J.C. Calhoun

David Cameron

Joseph J. Carson

William H.G. Carson

John S. Cash

John H. Chapell

William A. Clark

G.W. Daniels

N.J. Daniels

Washington G. Daniels

Emanuel Davis

P.C. Davis

P.W. Deadwilder

Joel T. Donham

M.V. Donham

J.M.V. Donham

J.J. Donham

M.G. Duce

E.M. Eads

J.J. Edwards

G.W. England

James M. Ferguson

Benjamin F. Finley

Joseph W. Fitzpatrick

John C. Ford

J.D. Fraser

H.J. Glover

Augustus Goldsby

G.W. Golsby

L.A. Gossett

E.M. Gossien

J.W. Graves

John R. Greenleas

Nathaniel S. Gunn

W.J. Harvey

O. Haire

Thomas W. Hall

Edwin Hallman	W. S. Meachem
Thomas Harlow	W. J. Meachem
James H. Harris	W. W. Merrill
James Harrison	Thomas T. Miles
James T. Hartley	A. B. Mirnel
Edwin A. Hatchett	W. J. Mitcham
Daniel J. Hawks	G. W. Mitchell
M. E. Hayne	J. J. Mitchell
William J. Haynie	Thomas Moore
Robert L. Hobson	Solomon T. Morgan
B. G. Hollyfield	J. A. Musick
James L. Jones	George W. Pickett
James Monroe Kesterman	James M. Powell
Marion M. Kesterman	James D. Powers
Robert Lafaver	John A. Price
John R. Leadbetter	Charles W. Rachley
William E. Leadbetter	George W. Rachley
E. M. Lindle	John H. Reed
A. J. Lindsy	Thomas J. Renfrow
Evan P. Marks	John M. Richardson
Frances Marion Marks	George W. Rodgers
James M. Marks	Hays Rogers
John J. Mathews	Joseph S. Rogers
Gabriel A. J. May	Sampson W. Rogers
William G. May	Baxter L. Seymore
James S. McClellan	John A. Seymore
W. A. McCormack	L. E. Seymore
Elisha L. McMurtrey	Thomas R. Seymore
James Benson McMurtrey	William B. Seymore

William C. McMurtrey
Henry A. Snell
Charles H. Spears
D. T. Spivey
L. T. Sterbart
J. T. Stewart
William M. Stewart
Alfred Stone
William C. Taylor
Wade H. Treadgill
J. R. Todd
D. R. Tolson
George L. Tolson
George L. Tolson
James W. Tucker
William H. J. Tucker
W. K. Varnell
John F. Waldrop
Charles G. Word
David W. Wardlaw
David O. Waters
James S. Williams
J. Williams
William C. Williams
William Woolam
D. W. Wordlaw
J. H. Wright

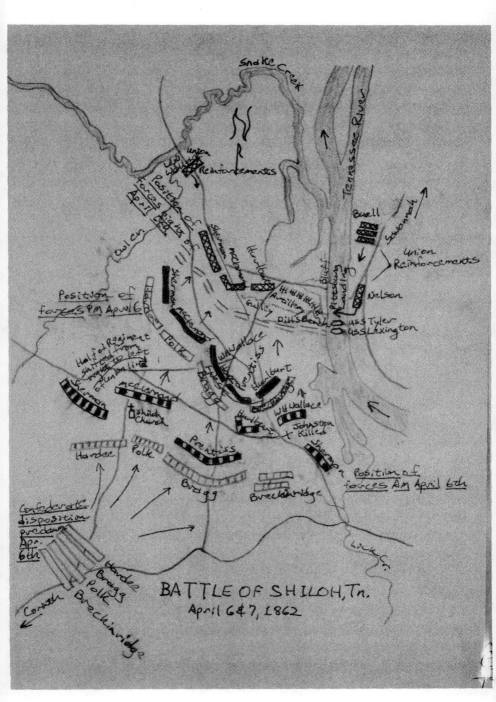

BATTLE OF SHILOH, Tn.
April 6 & 7, 1862

2. Cav. | **Ark.**

D R Leadbetter

Pvt. , Co. D , 2 Reg't Arkansas Cavalry.*

Appears on

Company Muster Roll

of the organization named above,

for _July & Aug_ , 189 2

Enlisted:

When _Feb 22_ , 186 2

Where _Mt Elba, Ark_

By whom _Maj J D Reid_

Period _12 mos_

Last paid:

By whom _Capt Leiper_

To what time _June 30_ , 186 2

Present or absent _Present_

Remarks: _____

Pay due for Horse 40 cts pr day aug $24 80

*This Regiment (also known as 4th Regiment Arkansas Cavalry) was formed by the consolidation of the 2d (Barnett's) Battalion Arkansas Cavalry and the 6th Battalion Arkansas Cavalry, by S. O. No. 69, Corinth, Miss., dated May 15, 1862.
The 6th Battalion Arkansas Cavalry was also known as 1st Battalion Arkansas Cavalry, Phifer's Battalion Arkansas Cavalry, White's Battalion Arkansas Cavalry, and McNeill's Battalion Arkansas Cavalry.
About December, 1864, the 2d Regiment Arkansas Cavalry was reduced to a Battalion and designated 18th (McMurtrey's) Battalion Arkansas Cavalry.

Book mark: _____

(442)

W Sheriews Copyist

---

2. Cav. | **Ark.**

J R Leadbetter

Private , Co. D , 2 Reg't Arkansas Cavalry.*

age 22 years.

Appears on

Company Muster Roll

of the organization named above,

for _June 30, 1862 to Oct 31_ , 186 2

Enlisted:

When _Feb 22_ , 186 ___

Where _Mt Silba Ark_

By whom _Maj J G Reid_

Period _____

Last paid:

By whom _W D Leiper_

To what time _____ , 186 ___

Present or absent _Present_

Remarks: _Detailed as Blacksmith Oct. 14._

*This Regiment (also known as 4th Regiment Arkansas Cavalry) was formed by the consolidation of the 2d (Barnett's) Battalion Arkansas Cavalry and the 6th Battalion Arkansas Cavalry, by S. O. No. 69, Corinth, Miss., dated May 15, 1862.
The 6th Battalion Arkansas Cavalry was also known as 1st Battalion Arkansas Cavalry, Phifer's Battalion Arkansas Cavalry, White's Battalion Arkansas Cavalry, and McNeill's Battalion Arkansas Cavalry.
About December, 1864, the 2d Regiment Arkansas Cavalry was reduced to a Battalion and designated 18th (McMurtrey's) Battalion Arkansas Cavalry.

Book mark: _____

J W Smock

Early Morning Muster

Bridge of Time

On Saturdays in the summertime, when work was all done, there was often time enough left for a trip swimmin' at the not too distant river, taken in lieu of our regular weekly tub bath. Many of the neighborhood boys would ride old mules or horses the three-mile and a half to the pool at China's Ferry. There we'd meet fellows from around other neighborhoods and from across the river to the east, who also came to enjoy an afternoon swim. There's no longer a ferry there now, but for many score years, an old hand-drawn raft carried freight and passengers across the deep channel at the point where the old Princeton Pike met the winding Saline. An old gentleman named Chowning had originated it and his family had operated the ferry for two generations. Pappy told me that when he was a boy, the river crossing was called Chowning's Ferry. He had even shown me an old map that bore the former name. The waterman's name was long forgotten by most, his life's occupation and long residence in the area recalled only by mistaken nationality.

There was and still is a deep, not too swift channel there, that was ideal for towing a heavy laden log raft back and forth on a stretched rope. The same quality that made it a good ferry crossing also made it a good swimmin' hole, even in Pappy's time. Plus, back then it had the added feature of being a spot of much activity, with many comings and goings of horse and wagon alike. Pappy said in the old days, one might see anything from Gypsy wagons, to six-horse stagecoaches and a dozen children swimming in the water. By the time Brother Johnny and I came along, it was more of a cattle watering hole, the ferry having been put out of business by the Union Pacific railroad crossing a mile or so further downstream. Stagecoaches and Gypsies too, had mostly gone the way of the old ferryman, rapidly receding with the dawn of a new century, into a forgotten past.

Though the once busy intersection was no wise as well used as it had been, it still served as a fine swimmin' hole on those hot summer days of our youth. We had many hours recreation, swinging on the old rope that hung from an overhanging willow limb. On occasion, when some unlucky heifer or young steer would wander down to the stream for a cool drink in the summer's heat, we boys would slip up and surround it, herding it into the water. Once in the river, the bottom was too deep for the poor critter to touch the gravelly bed, so he could only paddle about in desperate circles, striving to reach a spot where he might again touch solid ground.

It made for great sport, a group of sprouts corralling the poor beasts from all sides, forever driving them back to the deep channel, where we took turns holding to their tails, letting them tow us to and fro in the normally clear water made muddy by their struggle. We'd keep it up sometimes 'til we were afraid the poor cow would drown from exhaustion. Then someone would break the circle and the "yearling ferry" would bolt for the near shore, clawing an escape up the steep sandy bank, staggering off to hide in the shady woods. Someone was always sagacious enough to call an end to it before we ever let one drown. Had that ever happened, we knew it would mean the end to our fun for sure and likely a good tanning to boot.

We'd just wait awhile though and before long, another thirsty victim would wander ignorantly up, oblivious to the watery fate that awaited it. Rarely did the same animal ever make the mistake twice. But, with abundant free-range cattle as there still then were roving the river bottoms, there were always new, unsuspecting bovines for our crude water sport.

We'd return to the farm after giving our mounts a good drink for the homeward leg, boys near as worn out as the cows we taught to swim. The road from the river wound past Crossroads Methodist Church and cemetery. A mile further on it passed our own community church and cemetery, Camp Springs. Camp Springs is where lie our Great-grand pappy on our father's side, John Sr. and his second wife, Lydia Harris Ledbetter. His first wife, our blood related Great-grandmother Elizabeth Yarber Ledbetter, is also buried there on his right. The church house and cemetery lie little over a stone's throw away through the narrow scope of woods northwest of our homes.

Sometimes when we weren't too wore out from swimming, we might pick wildflowers and take the long way home, stopping to place them atop the petrified-wood headstones of buried ancestors found there, whom we never met, but only ever heard of through accounts from surviving family. We'd also bring home a few new blossoms to Mammy, who always seemed to appreciate our thoughtfulness. She was our step-grandmother, Pappy's second wife. We figured it never hurt to have staunch allies, both of this world and the next, when we were up to typical boyhood mischief.

With all the day's work done before ever we were allowed the leisure of a summer dip, Brother Johnny and I had little to do upon our return, 'cept give Mammy the flowers we'd picked and grab a slice of cold, left-over cornbread from under the checkered tablecloth. We'd then join Pappy out in the shade of the tool shed, to again hear his tales of bygone days, at least until Mammy eventually called us in to supper.

Pappy adeptly struck down any bothersome fly that lit within striking distance of his swatter. Almost quicker than the eye could see, the old man slapped down one after another, keeping a running tally that he occasionally shared out loud at significant numbers, usually at increments of fifty. "That's a hunert,'" he'd say, after knocking yet another from the backrest of an empty steel lawn chair with a resounding ring made by the swatter striking the hollow sheet metal. The ground at his feet lay littered with their tiny mangled carcasses.

"I hate a danged outhouse fly," he'd sometimes remark, "cause ye' know when one lights on you, it's leaving tiny little shit footprints with every step. That's why I keep a dedicated flyswatter out there all the time," he said motioning toward the outhouse with the swatter in his right hand. Johnny and I would laugh every time we heard that, as much from the mental image of a fly leaving invisible little footprints, as from Pappy's rare use of profanity, which he never did within Mammy's hearing.

Mammy's name was Phoebe and though she wasn't actually our blood grandmother, she was the only one we children could remember. Our father's mother, like his father's mother, had died before ever the grandkids of our line met them. Pappy had wed his first wife, Mary Adams Atkinson on January eighth, 1866, soon after war's end, when he was thirty and she was twenty-eight. She was our real grandmother, whereas Phoebe was our step-grandma.

Mary Atkinson was a widow who married Pappy after her first husband died from infection two weeks after Chickamuaga, where he had received a minor leg wound that turned quickly septic. When she, too, later died prematurely, she was buried, unlike the other Ledbetters in this country before her, in her own family's cemetery at Gum Grove a few short miles north of our home place, instead of the older, nearer Camp Springs. Gum Grove was where Pappy and Phoebe also wished to, and would, lie in their own time.

Pappy's father, John Ledbetter, Sr., had wed his second wife in 1865, a year prior to Pappy's first marriage to the widow Atkinson. Pappy's mother Elizabeth had died from abuses suffered at the hands of Union sympathizers, late in '64, during the cruelest stage of the war in south Arkansas. Pappy's father John Sr., at age fifty-six, took for his second wife, Lydia Harris, age forty, on July second, 1865. It was the same deceased great-grandfather, great-grandmother and step-great-grandmother, whose graves we had only just stopped to place wildflowers upon. We'd also paused to place a few blossoms on the graves of Great-great-grandfather James and his lifelong spouse Nancy Moore Ledbetter. They were Pappy's grandparents, often cited as the first of our line to come to America from Ireland late in the eighteenth century.

Having ridden home bareback and cooled 'em down with a slow walk from the cemetery, we'd only to unbridle the horse and mule, then turn them out, before we went to find Pappy alone with his thoughts and the carnage of his fly killing. As we walked up to the tool shed, Johnny and I heard Pappy singing this song in the key of G:

"It was the sixth of April, just at the break of day, the drums and fifes were playing for us to march away.

The feeling of that hour I do remember still, for the wounded and the dying that lay on Shiloh Hill.

About the hour of sunrise, the battle it began, before the day had vanished, we fought them hand to hand.

The horrors of the field did my heart with anguish fill, for the wounded and the dying, there on Shiloh Hill.

The wounded men were crying for help from everywhere, whilst others who were dying, were offering God a prayer.

'Protect my wife and children, if it is Thy will,' such were the prayers I heard that night upon old Shiloh Hill."

We didn't interrupt and our presence didn't deter him in the least from his song.

"And early the next morning, we were called to arms again, unmindful of the wounded and unmindful of the slain.

The struggle was renewed and ten thousand men were kilt, this was the second conflict of famous Shiloh Hill.

"The battle it raged on, though dead and dying men, lay thick all o'er the ground, on the hill and on the glen.

And from their deadly wounds, the blood ran like a reel, such were the mournful sights I saw on old Shiloh Hill.

And now my song is ended, about those bloody plains, I hope the sight by mortal men may ne'er be seen again.

But I pray to God, the Savior, 'If consistent with Thy will, to save the souls of all that fell on bloody Shiloh Hill'."

Seeing he had ended, from the prolonged pause that followed, we applauded. He was still a fair baritone, even with his far advanced years, his voice not yet being all used up. And he was none too shy about it either. He took his accolades with grace, accepting his laurels with a smile and nodding appreciation, while never letting a single fly escape the deadly reach of his swatter.

We laughed at his steadiness and dedication to his task, unfaltering even in fleeting glory. We seated ourselves in the fine store-bought chairs he'd purchased for such occasions, on either side of the blue eyed, white haired, bearded seventy-two year old country gentleman, still bearing his full head of hair.

"Did you boys have a good swim?"

"Yes sir!" we said in unison.

"Didn't see any Chinamen did ye'?" he asked.

"No sir," we said, "nary a one."

"Play any good games?" he asked.

"Just the usual," we replied, casting nervous looks at one another and back at him. "Yep, just the usual."

"It's a right fine day for a dip. If it weren't so far to the river, I'd be tempted to take one myself. Reckon I'll just have to take my swim in the stock-pond with the cows," he remarked, chuckling at the thought.

In an effort to change the subject Johnny quickly asked, "What's that song Pappy?"

"Oh," said Pappy, "that's just a sad old war song that come out of the camps at Corinth."

"Well, you sure sing it right fine," big Brother John added.

"Yep, sure do," I agreed.

"Why thank ye'," he answered. "My Grand-pappy James, who was ya'll's great-great-grand pappy, used to sing right often. He was a fine Irish baritone and he knew many songs from the old country. I wish I could remember more of them now."

Before I could ask him to sing one he did still remember, Johnny asked him to tell us about the song he was singing when we came up.

"Oh, that's just cold potatoes now, water long since run under the bridge of time. Besides, it's too sad a story for a fine sunny day such as this."

I looked from Pappy, over at Johnny, to see just a hint of disappointment in my brother's face. Remembering where we'd last left off Pappy's tales from the War of the Rebellion and knowing the topic was one less dark than the subject of the song, I asked, "Then tells us about your trip to Memphis with General Forrest for his birthday."

A broad, tight-lipped grin spread across his face when he recalled those rare moments of pleasure that he had found in that brief respite from a terrible time. "Well let's see, Polk you're the youngest, you're nine now, right?" he began.

"Ten!" I announced with great satisfaction, proud of my maturity.

"And Johnny, you're what, fourteen?" Pappy asked him.

"Yes sir, but I'll be fifteen come August fourteenth."

"Well then, I reckon you fellers are about old enough to here about my first taste of city life. But not a word of it to Mammy, or your ma."

"Yes sir!" we said in unison, nearly popping out of our seats with excitement.

He could tell by the smiles on our faces that we were enticed. He sat, just grinning for a spell, letting our anticipation build and recalling those far off days to himself, while still swatting down any fly that came in range. A pair of crows cawed from their perch somewhere up in the tree branches. On the humid air, a hawk soared high above, riding the heat currents up to a cooler altitude. His lone screech answered the noisy call of the two crows.

At last, when the racket of the crows had subsided, he began, "As I previously told you Polk, after our return to Corinth from the Battle of Shiloh, General Forrest, who hadn't been officially promoted yet, invited me to jine his entourage on a recruiting trip to Memphis. This was in mid-May, when most of the sixty-odd thousand Confederates under arms in that little Mississippi town were preparing for its evacuation in the face of the slowly advancing Federal force under the command of Yankee General Buell, creeping relentlessly south from Pittsburg Landing. I was very reluctant to abandon my brother after coming so near to loosing him, but he was nearly completely recovered and again insisted I not miss such a rare and fine opportunity as that of accompanying our regimental commander to Memphis. He said I'd be of far more use to him, once't I parlayed the occasion into a promotion of rank. Our new friend Herman Culpepper assured me that he'd watch after my brother and keep close by him whilst I was away. Also, our old friend Manuel Davis promised to take care of Fury, even in the event that the Yanks forced the evacuation of Corinth before our return. They also rather vigorously pointed out to me how it just wouldn't be politic to refuse the Colonel's invitation. Thus encouraged and assured, I gladly accepted the invite.

"I found mostly staff officers gathered in front of the Tishhamingo Hotel, milling around on the street across from the train depot, early that late spring morning. But a peppering of we enlisted were also present with our saddled mounts, all awaiting the soon expected arrival of Ole' Forrest himself. One couldn't help but notice the quality of the breeding in our several animals, my own chestnut gelding being no exception. The Colonel shortly descended the steps of the hotel with some little assistance from an aide, due to his recent surgery for the removal of the Yankee mini-ball received at Fallen Timbers."

'Mornin' boys,' he greeted us cheerfully.

'Good morning Colonel,' we answered, in almost perfect unison.

'Are ya'll ready for a little fun in the city?' he asked us.

'Yes sir!' we responded to a man.

'Well then, let's get those animals in their cars and climb aboard that train afore it leaves without us,' he said in reference to the smoking engine and cars setting steaming on the track. 'They can't wait on us all day, there's a war on you know and they've a railroad to run!'

"We'd become practiced at walking horses onto a railcar by that time and our animals were more accustomed to being loaded, so our boarding went quickly without incident. Once't they was all comfortably situated in their cattle cars with feed sacks strapped on, we had the pleasure of riding for the first time up front in a real passenger car. Up to that point, all we enlisted men on the trip, except for two Memphis boys, had only previously ridden in freight, or cattle cars along with our animals. All this 'Royal' treatment could only be explained, best I could figure at the time, by our commander's appreciation of the good showing we made in the fight at Fallen Timber Holler, when several of us rode to Forrest's assistance. I noticed however, only a few of the enlisted men present in the railcar were fellow Arkansans from my own company D who'd participated with us in the charge when Forrest got his wound. There were far more Tennessee boys along that hadn't been amongst us in that particular ruckus. As it would turn out, the Tennesseans present were mostly all from in or around Memphis. After a little thought on the subject, it also occurred to me that all Arkies present had moved at one time to Arkansas from west-central Tennessee and so, too, were we also born as Shelby and Tipton County Tennesseans. We private soldiers huddled all together around the tables at the rear of the passenger car, whilst the Colonel and his staff officers were seated in cushioned chairs nearer the front. They busily worked over maps and documents, whilst we quietly chatted amongst ourselves, enjoying the pleasantness of the passing scenery. We rolled comfortably along mile after mile, napping at times in the bright sunlight that flooded, with the breeze, through the open windows, lulled by the steady clickety-clack of the rocking rails. The morning soon drifted into afternoon as the distances fell away. Even though our clothes weren't exactly fresh, the breeze, unlike previous rail adventures riding amongst our animals, wasn't filled with the familiar smell of soured horse sweat and horse droppings. Instead, the scents of bougainvillea and daffodils floated in on the sultry air, as we crossed the state line from Mississippi into Tennessee. I heard the Colonel ask at one point, when the breeze blew toward him from our direction, 'What's that odor?' I saw one of his aides motion toward us. I then overheard the Colonel say, 'It's a good thing these boys is soon gettin' new uniforms, else't I might be forced to introduce 'em as the 'critter' cavalry.'

"Just past noon, we were invited to jine in table with the Colonel and his staff. We feasted on fried chicken, fried potatoes and the best fluffy biscuits I'd tasted since leaving home nearly three months prior. The biscuits and chicken reminded me of Ma and Pa and our sisters back at home. It seemed much longer than eighty-three days since we rode out of our yard that cold Redlands February morning. I'd already witnessed much more than I could've ever back then imagined and God only knew what yet lay in store. It made me a little sad and homesick for a spell, even amongst such fine company as I found myself. The Colonel must have noticed the change in my expression, for he was generally as aware of his surroundings and company at any given time, as anyone I ever met. He addressed me from around a mouthful of meat and potatoes, 'Private,' he said between chews, 'I noticed you're not riding that fine looking black stallion I so admire. I'd a mind to try to trade ye' out of him over the course of this trip.'

'No sir I'm not. You may recall how he was wounded at the Holler, shot in the side whilst on our way back from Shiloh,' I answered.

'Yes son, I do now recall that when you mention it. How is he?'

'He's doing well sir, still resting back in stable at Corinth. His wound is pert near all heal't over,' I replied.

"The Colonel said, 'That's fine, I'm glad to hear of it. It'd be a damn shame for a fighter like that one to be so soon lost to our Cause. Who's looking after him during your absence in case they have to evacuate Corinth before our return?'

'A messmate from home sir, Manuel Davis,' I answered.

'You know son, a wounded mount's not nearly as valuable, but I'd still give you top dollar for him right now, condition unseen.'

'You better watch him soldier,' the Lieutenant with the thick Mississippi brogue chimed in, 'the General is quite the horse trader.' He was the same one who'd brought the invitation to me.

'Don't tell everything you know Lieutenant,' Colonel Forrest replied, 'and I ain't made General just yet you know. It still remains for those dandies in Richmond to vote on my promotion and there are those amongst 'em who don't yet believe a man of my social background should rise above colonel.'

'Don't doubt for a moment General, that Beuregard's recommendation will go unapproved by the Congress,' the Lieutenant answered crisply.

'Well sir,' Forrest added, 'in matters of politics I must bow to your expertise.'

'Trust me on this one sir,' said the Lieutenant, to which Ole' Nathan Bedford replied, 'I do sir, indeed I do, because you'll become a Captain soon as I make Lieutenant General.'

'Brigadier General sir!' the Mississippi Lieutenant corrected.

'As you say Lieutenant,' Forrest replied, 'Now, about that stallion son,' he said, returning his attention to me.

'Couldn't part with him sir, not at any price. First of all, he ain't mine to sell, he's my brother's horse and was only on loan to me since mine was lame at the time and my brother was on sick leave with the pneumonia and thusly unavailed of his own animal when I needed a replacement to ride out for Shiloh. Second, he was a gift from our father and it just wouldn't be right even for him to sell you a gift from our Pa.'

'That's fair enough son.' He agreed. 'How's your brother getting along with his illness now, what's his name?' the Colonel asked.

'William sir, Private William Edwin Ledbetter, he's much better now Colonel, thank you for asking,' I replied.

'Good to hear, I, too, have a brother named Will'm. Yours is with your company right?'

'Yes sir that's right, Company D, one of your boys!' I pointed out enthusiastically.

'Fine,' he said, 'we're gonna' need him and every other good man and horse we can manage to muster in the coming months. And by the way, I admire your principles. It wouldn't be too proper for you to sell me your brother's horse that was a gift from ya'll's pa. Even so, I still just may have to pursue this matter a bit further with him when we all do get back to our unit,' he said laughing, at which point all present, including myself, jined in the enjoyment of his jest. He added, 'Do ye' reckon that messmate of yourn', Davis did you say?'

'Yes sir, Manual Davis,' I answered.

'Yes, Manual Davis, well do you reckon he's of any kinship with the President and might perchance put in a good word with his cousin regarding my pending promotion?'

"Again our laughter spread around the table as the Colonel did his best to make us feel more comfortable in his presence. I answered only, deadpan, 'They don't converse much of late sir,' which brought another round of laughter from all."

"You really knew General Forrest that well Pappy?" Johnny asked him with surprise, for the fame of the great cavalryman was well known throughout the whole South, even still after practically half a century, a full two generations removed from those turbulent times.

"And much better before it was done. I'd only just met him at that point," Pappy replied. "We both come to know each other far better with time and experience, the good and the bad. But don't be interruptin' me John." He stated not too sternly.

"Now, it was about that time, not long before we finally pulled into Collierville," he continued, "that the Colonel got down to business, after passing around bottled beers to all. He said, 'Most of you fellers are probably wonderin' how you managed to be ridin' in style, in a train car full of officers, headin' for the bright city lights. That's a mighty good question and one I'm a' fixin' to answer for ye'. I'm in need of ya'll's help, as too is the Confederacy. It turns out that all you boys is Tennesseans by birth and some even Memphians. I'm gonna' spend a little time at my home getting my strength back, convalescing with my family afore we start our next campaign against the Federals occupying Tennessee. Whilst ya'll and me staff find yourselves resting and recuperating in Memphis, you'll also be talkin' up recruitment in the bars and parlors all about town as a means to help belay some of the expense of our trip. We're fixin' to put an ad in the 'Appeal' right away and set up a recruitment station in the lobby of the Gayoso House Hotel, to sign up at least two companies of the best, able bodied men and horses we can muster. That'll bring our little brigade up to near operational strength and with that number, properly employed, we can soon play hell with the Union lines of supply and communication. We'll ride hard and hit 'em fast and make Billy Yank sorry he ever set foot on our sacred Tennessee sod. When we've finished whoopin' 'em, they'll think twice afore carryin' the fight to any other states like Arkansas. You Arky fellers, as I've come to understand, moved to south Arkansas from a little Irish farm colony not fur from here up near Covington. You've been in company of good horses and riders since ye' were mere lads. A lot of boys from up around Covington have been pushed south by the Federals of late into Shelby County and be now residin' here abouts. You Memphians too have plenty kin all about the district. I wish the lot of ye' to ride out to your cousins and uncles, talking up the fine time to be had giving the blasted Yanks what for from the back of a horse. And they can rest assured, that if'n they ride with us, they'll not miss out on the action, for we'll be regularly in the very thick of it, I guarantee!' The Colonel paused to survey our faces and reactions. I reckon he liked what he saw, for the fire flashed in his eyes as a broad smile radiated across his brightening red face. 'You men are not only gamy, but game too, every one,' he said with a chuckle. 'I've seen it in each of ye' with me own eyes on one occasion or another'n. Ya'll are the type of fellers we're lookin' fur and as the old sayin' goes, 'It takes one to know one.' I s'pect none of ye'll have any trouble spottin' the grit in others of your own caliber, same as I had none seein' the fight in the each of ye.'

"The Colonel laughed softly, thinkin' of what he was about to say next. 'And while as we're here on business, we're gonna' mix in a little pleasure too from time to time. Some of you fellers, though seasoned veterans, may yet be a little green when it comes to the gals. As my honored guests, visiting my hometown, I promise that won't be the case much longer.' He paused to let this soak in a bit before continuing. 'We're gonna' throw a little soiree for my forty-first birthday this comin' weekend and I promise it's gonna' be the finest shindig most of you fellers ever before seen.

So enjoy the rest of the ride. We'll be pullin' into Collierville any minute now and you'll have time to step down to stretch your legs and water your horses before we proceed the rest of the way on into Memphis. The Lieutenant has taken the liberty of booking you all rooms downtown in the Tennessee Hotel, not too far from the train station. When we arrive, you'll go with him to fetch your mounts and ride them on over to your accommodations. Your animals will be liveried across the street. Then the Lieutenant will get you reprovisioned with the Quartermaster of the Post.

'Men, we've got some hard campaignin' yet ahead of us before this here fracas is finished. In my opinion, you're probably some of the best soldiers that the South now has to offer. We've got a hard road ahead and some hard recruitin' to do in the meantime, in and around Ole' Memphis. But hear this, I want you to kick up your heels and have ye' a time whilst we're all here together. It may be your last opportunity for a spell. You've earned it and ye' deserve it. And not to disturb you too much, but with the fall of Island Ten and the outcome of our recent engagement at Shiloh, the fates of Fort Pillow, Memphis and Corinth, for now at least, are all likely sealed. What I'm sayin' boys is it's just a matter of but a short while before the Yanks come sailing down the river with them damn gunboats that have knocked out everything we've thrown in their way before now. When they do, our little Memphis flotilla won't be able to do much to stop 'em for long. As a former city Alderman, I know the city fathers have already voted to surrender the town rather than see it bombarded in the likely event that our flotilla doesn't succeed at their bold objective. So look around close whilst we're here, make yourselves familiar with the environs, cause the day'll likely come when we'll ride back in here as attackers, rather than guests, to take it back from the Yanks and punish their arrogance. I'll see you all at my home Saturday evening, if'n, that is, ye' ain't in the jailhouse,' he concluded with a hardy laugh.

"One of the fellers asked, 'Is this Saturday your birthday Colonel?' To which he replied, 'No son, it's not 'til July thirteenth, but we're gonna' celebrate it at home about a month early, 'cause I s'pect we'll be far from here by then, plyin' our trade and dealin' in Yankee misery.'

"We all hoorayed our commander, to a man, thinkin' how fortunate that Providence had provided our Cause with such a fine, unpretentious fellow and how we rough backwoodsmen were blessed to be led by one of our own and not some aristocrat reared in gentility. We were his to command, he had but to direct us and we would go. We knew he'd never ask any man to do something he himself would not do, or hadn't already done.

"We pulled into the station amidst the smoke and clamor of cars, engines and other rolling stock coupling and uncoupling and numerous civilians and soldiers hurrying to and fro. Colonel Forrest shouted to us as he was helped into a fancy gilded carriage driven by a smiling nigra in tails and drawn by a matched pair of speckled gray mares. 'See you boys at the cotillion! Good recruitin!' With that, he and his youngest brother Jeffrey rode off north, cutting a fine figure, to enjoy the privileges of both wealth and rank.

"We soon had our mounts unloaded and saddled for the ride through the cobbled streets of Memphis. The initial excitement felt by most of us was barely controllable and the emotion must have been contagious, for our horses too were nervous and themselves barely contained, voicing their complaints with snorts and farts. After some time clopping along through the busy thoroughfares, the animals finally settled as we approached the taller buildings of downtown. The country boys in our entourage gawked in wide-eyed amazement, mouths agape as we craned our necks to look up at the brick structures, some as tall as eight stories, rising on both sides above the stone covered thoroughfare. Windows were open on all floors and we could see activity inside them in every direction. There was even horse drawn public transportation in the form of trolleys rolling smoothly along narrow gauge rails laid amongst the paving stones in the middle of the streets. Dressed in their finery and regalia, people were walking up and down the paved sidewalks either side of the turnpike. Ladies with parasols, brightly colored bonnets and wide hoop skirts made from yards of whispering fabric, strolled by at regular intervals and gazed longingly in our direction as we rode with backs straight and jaws set. As per the Lieutenant's strict instructions, we bridled in our enthusiasm enough to refrain from the whistles and catcalls that long depravity and isolation inspired in our thumping breasts. 'Wouldn't befit gentlemen,' he stated.

"He managed to keep us corralled past the bars and pool halls, long enough to get us to the hotel and registered as guest of our host the Colonel. A more motley looking bunch you never saw, in our mismatched, threadbare, homespun garb, half washed and rough as a cob. As cavalry recruiters, we'd need to display the dash and flare expected of an equestrian soldier. To accomplish that end, after we'd stored all our gear 'cept our weapons in a corner of the lobby, the good Lieutenant led us again by horseback to the Quartermaster of the Post. Our first order of duty was to fit ourselves with new regulation gray uniforms from the piles of pants and coats lying about the cavernous warehouse so full of precious military material. We dug through stacks of britches with their regulation yellow cavalry stripe running down the out seam, trying on two, or three pair each in an effort to achieve our best fit. Whilst some were busy doing this, others were trying on black leather belts with brass C.S. buckles, or donning high collared frock coats, clasping the bright buttons all the way up the neck to assure their proper trim. Our old frontier garb, up 'til then so precious to us, hit the floor like discarded rags, as we quickly began to shape into a rather fine looking lot. The last items and the most important were jackboots and cap. These were knee-high, slip on, black leather cavalry boots and the gray, unadorned, wool kepis, with their flat crowns, narrow black leather brims and buckled chinstraps. Once't we got all fitted to our personal satisfaction and turned out in our new regalia, we gathered up our smelly, old clothes, which we knew we would soon enough need again and signed for our new provisions, which were charged against our back pay. Already telegraphed to expect our arrival, the Quartermaster had our remunerations awaiting us. We took turns stating to him our name, rank, point of enlistment, enlisting officer and type of weapon brought with us into the service. At that point, we who could, signed and those who couldn't, made their mark with an 'X' and all were paid in full, less the cost of our new regulation uniforms, for the service of our mount, our guns and ourselves for the past three months. Though this was an even greater sum than our original mustering in pay, the money had already devaluated to only fifty cents on the dollar by then. Still, we were mighty glad to have it and right certain that now we could indeed 'kick up our heels' as the Colonel had admonished us.

"Dressed to the hilt as we were, we were anxious to get back to where our waiting mounts stood drinking from the trough with our cutlasses lashed in metal scabbards to their saddles. We proudly completed our outfits by placing their leather shoulder straps over our heads and upon one shoulder, letting the long weapons dangle noisily at our sides. Oh how I wish I had a daguerreotype of those fine boys at that one moment. Our chests were barely contained within the confines of our new coats. Only a couple of Memphis boys in our group grumbled at all about the high cost of our new outfits and the poor value of the crisp Confederate foldin' money.

"At the Lieutenant's order, we interrupted our swaggering and remounted to leave the depot headed back in the direction of the hotel. Our initial enthusiasm was only slightly dampened along the way by the trickling sweat that soon ran in our eyes and down our backs from beneath the wool forage caps and coats, as the little cavalcade pranced through the hot, humid streets on our lively, gaited mounts.

"Once't we got all settled in our double occupancy rooms, we were treated to hot baths, bottled whiskey and fancy cigars, before settin' down to a larupin' three course meal. Even the two city-born malcontents in our midst had to admit this was the life. We all agreed it was too bad that all of war weren't more like this. Someone asked, as we sat smoking cigars and sipping whiskey in the steaming tubs, 'I wonder what the po' folks is doin' tonight?' His comment brought a sprinkling of laughter for a moment, before a cool silence settled in the washroom. We remembered all too well the depressing environment of sickness and suffering that we'd only just left our messmates with back at Corinth.

"But as veterans, we'd learned to shrug off such sad thoughts, lest they deter us from our duty. So we washed the images from our minds with a couple more shots of Lynchburg whiskey." Then Pappy told us something I've always remembered. "Boys, you can't afford to dwell too long on losses, it only hampers and distracts you from all the livin' still to be done." Those were words I've had many occasion to recall. Then he went on after striking down yet another errant fly.

"Our objective, under our commander's direct order, was to 'kick up our heels and have us a time' and that's exactly what we was intendin' to do!

"We were in rare form by supper that evening. We sported clean laundered white shirts and high spirits under our starched collars and new gray uniform coats."

His telling was briefly interrupted by the sound of our neighbor to the north, Ben Kilpatrick, calling his cows to supper. Pappy turned his attention, cocking his head to listen. Sound carried well across the open hills and hollows and we soon heard Ben call again. It was feeding time, come with the cooling of the day. When next Ben's voice cried out the high pitched summons, it bore a different tone, less urgent, telling us the cows had come into his view, wandering up from the shade of the trees at the lower edge of his fields. Now Ben was answered by the bawling of the herd and the lead cow's bell ringing constantly as it rattled on her collar when she hurried toward the barn and her evening meal. We gathered all that from just the sounds and knew before long, Mammy, too, would summon us from the screen door of the kitchen to our own evening's meal.

After the noise of Kilpatrck and his cows had again subsided, Pappy said, "We celebrated that evening, first in the dining room of the Memphis Inn, then out into the gas-lit streets of Memphis amongst its bars and bordellos. Over the course of the long night, I pert near forgot what I'd missed most in the army and had promised myself first when I got to Memphis, a warm, soft bed.

Most of that night I can but barely recall now, other than the recollection that I thought it the high point of my life up to that moment and never before enjoyed a good night's sleep more.

"During the following weeks, we traveled all about Memphis and the surrounding countryside on our well-groomed horses, stopping at any likely gathering spot for locals, to post notices of our intention to enlist volunteers and asking likely looking candidates with good horses 'might we have a bit of a word with ye?' Optimism was then running high in the Southern hearts of the region, due mainly to the recent small successes of the Confederate Defense Fleet against the main U.S. river flotilla up the Mississippi above Fort Pillow at a place called Plum Bend. The battle there had only just been waged between the two unequal forces, out on the water between Osceola, Arkansas and Gold Dust, Tennessee. To the astonishment of most, the tiny Confederate fleet had, for the moment at least, luckily forestalled the further advance downstream of the mighty Union iron-clads.

"We answered inquiries made of us as to the nature of cavalry life and the character of our Regimental Colonel, often recounting for them the stories of Shiloh and Fallen Timbers. We discouraged some and encouraged others, but found none not interested in what we had to share.

"I soon figured out I was along, too, as blacksmith for the twenty-odd mounts in our entourage. The Lieutenant had been good enough to bring along a box of tools and an iron tripod. I made use of an anvil and forge at the livery across the street from our residence in the hotel. When the Tennesseans were done with grooming and feeding out their horses and already gone to quarters, I'd stay on with a helper and tend to their animal's feet whenever there was a need. The helper would pump the bellows and hold the horse's reins. Most of them were steady animals, no trouble to handle, which is always a pleasure by comparison.

"But, when the long days were finally done, I'd spend every spare minute I had down on Front Street, near the boats and wharves. There was always an energy there like none I'd anywhere before known." I saw a fire come into Pappy's eyes when he spoke

117

of this, that wasn't often evident in the pale blue of their color. I glanced at Johnny to see if he had caught it too. He grinned and nodded as if to say he had, before refocusing his full attention back on the old man sitting between us.

"With the many and constant comings and goings of vessels on the waterfront, both military and commercial, there were always tremendous bouts of activity across the cobbled stones of the apron lying beneath the lowered stages, extending at all angles from their respective packet steamers. Boats were moored with gangplanks tied fast from one's larboard gunnels to the next one's starboard, bearing crossings and recrossings of both crew and cargo.

"I'd ride Prince, clopping with the steady upbeat rhythm of his hooves striking the stone paved streets of ole' Memphis, past the shops, offices, schools and houses, headin' west through that shaded, spacious jewel of a Southern city. We'd watch with interest how the complexion of the neighborhoods changed as we grew nearer the great riverside. Massive storage facilities, warehouses and open lots intermingled with occasional bars and bordellos, soon replacing the stores and homes of midtown, until we finally ascended up to the last height that so dominates the surrounding landscape. From our elevated vantage atop the steep bluff lying just south of the boat landing, all the collected splendor and opulence of the river and the city below were revealed to my eyes. It was a thing of fascination that I gazed on many hours," he told us, almost with a sigh.

"The South Bluff where we stood overlooking the tethered steamboats below, was then used as a military gun emplacement, helping guard the watery approaches to the busy docks below. From that point, immediately overlooking a sweeping right-hand bend in the river, artillerists could sight on vessels riding up or down stream. I'd tie off Prince in the shade of the huge, old oaks growing there and visit with the crews at their guns as the summer sun slid slowly down in the western sky.

"When the wind laid, the black smoke from the belching stacks collected in a dark pall that hung low over the boats, resting up against the rising bluffs, shading the labors of all below and depositing oily soot on everythin' from the white cotton bales, to the tops of every wooden cask. The entire bounty of the rich Southern farm country, from both banks, along with military provisions of all description, stood accumulated, stacked and loaded in every conceivable manner and location, crowding both the waterside and steamer decks, layer upon layer.

"At long last, as the heat of the day subsided and the sun turned to a giant orange ball hovering low over the horizon of the far shore, I'd remount Prince and we'd casually descend from the bluff down to Front Street. The clop of our hooves was slower now, as we eyed the entire environment on either shoulder of the granite paved street that paralleled the river and the staging area next to water's edge. Down by the boats, sheltered from the current of the main channel by the lee of Mud Island, Prince and I surveyed the good work of the stevedores and roustabouts ferrying their cargo rapidly along its route. They hustled on deck and ashore alike to complete their daily labors.

"We also saw much activity of other kinds as well, things of a nature prone to be severely criticized and feared by most parsons, although, I've known a few with an eye not unlike my own, toward seein' the spirit of life and a keen relish of it, as a fairly good thing in all its forms and expressions. I attributed most excesses I witnessed there at dockside, to the heady influence of that massive, mysterious living giant, wreathing along its ancient path below the overhanging bluffs of the Front. I say this only after much observation of the many varied forms of human activity, both communal and solitary. Some of the things that Prince and I witnessed there, seemed at times only explicable by way of some unnamed force, relative in strength by proximity to the main channel of the ancient, rolling waters, ever winding along their coarse, but a few yards to the west out beyond any given point along Front Street.

"All those sights, sounds and scents I carry yet clear within me minds eye. But, oh, little wonder, seeing how I so often then did bathe these old orbs with that spectacle in ere'y kind of light and weather, whenever duty would allow. Sunlight and moonlight reflectin' off her ever changing surface always stirred a whole 'nother sense within this breast," he said touching his chest. "Wakes from keels slicing at quarter-speed through the sugar-brown water, mingling with the shadowy reflections of overhanging willows and the sun and lamp light dancing on the ripplin' current of swirlin', boiling eddies, all helped to fill that vast flowing canvas of middle-America. All of the many sights, sounds and scents only seemed intensified by the average person's instinctive reaction to the threat of danger, a thing the beautiful, mystifying river holds so much of. All these things blended perfectly into a satisfying delight, even to rival the art of a master collinear.

"As the sun set in the west, out beyond the channel and Arkansas, the mood began to alter along the earthen bluffs sitting so snugly between the two sweeping bends of Old Man River. Thoughts were then less of work and duty and more a mind of sport and rest from toil. I further developed my hand at billiards during this period, squandering much of my remaining youth by spending many an hour at the tables of Barney's Billiard Room down on Fifth Street.

"But perhaps my favorite variety of entertainment back then was watching a big paddle-wheeler, just past sundown, her lanterns lit, accentuated against the evening twilight, calliope organ tooting out a merry melody above the gay voices and happy laughter blossoming from her decks in the cool of the evening. Then the stillness that followed after the waves of her wake stopped lapping and her sound and silhouette disappeared ever so slowly into the inky, unknown darkness of the night, vanished like a ghost, perhaps never really there to begin with, borne away on the unceasing currents.

"Alone I was then for a brief, few moments with the river, hearing her voice murmuring at the edges of both land and mind, tryin' to somehow share with me a thing not so readily seen. The rivers bear all things in this life. They're like'n to bridges 'cross time, bein' many places at once't, stretchin' the whole length of the land, ever on the move, whilst yet remainin' in the same place!

They are both thoroughfares of and obstacles to movement and commerce. They're boundaries, yet they reach easily beyond all man-made boundaries, constant through the ages, ever plyin' their winding coarse to the sea. They are simply masterpieces of God's own handiwork." He said before pausing, allowing his memory to begin its return from that distant past. Then, much as a hawk returning to rest for a time to its limb, his mind came again back down from the lofty realms of those former times.

"Pickaninnies now play up on the South Bluff overlooking the harbor, where Prince and I eventually made our last stand late in August of '64," he continued with a far less distant look in his eyes. "That same South Bluff where cannon were garrisoned to guard the river approaches of the port city is now, I understand, a small city park. I've been told that many of the giant old oaks and sycamores even yet remain, forty-two years after we sought shelter behind them from Yankee gunfire. Bullets intended for us may still lie imbedded in their thick bark. But, that's a story for another time," he concluded, seeing his wife standing at the backdoor.

We heard the creak of the screen on its hinges, as Mammy stuck her head out of the kitchen to call us to diner.

"You boys go wash up and I'll be in directly," Pappy told us. We obeyed, trying in our imaginations to compare the vastness of the Mississippi to the only rivers we'd ever known first hand, the Saline and the Ouachita, far smaller by comparison.

Johnny poured the drawn water from the pitcher on the washstand into the basin and scrubbed up while I waited my turn. I stood at the end of the dogtrot watching my grandpa in the tool-shed, as he stared idly into space, swatter hanging loosely by his side. I could only imagine his thoughts and the memories that must have visited him there, perhaps recalling some lost love from those weeks spent in Memphis prior to its fall.

Remembrances

The young private, like the other men of his detachment, sought relief from boredom and loneliness in the common recreation of women. The gratification and indulgence found in their arms assuaged temporarily the deep inner longings, but made it difficult at times for him to distinguish desire from romance. He was a full-grown man, in his prime, yet un-crippled by the ravages of war.

She was a black-haired daughter of the Cherokee nation, with dark, roving eyes, sitting at the bar of Rosie's bordello on Gayoso Street, her long, strong legs crossed and showing through a slit from above the knee. He introduced himself and asked if she minded if he sat down with her. She smiled and replied that he was welcome to join her and her friend. She was conversing with a second lady, a blonde, who was also soon joined by another of the Colonel's entourage. The two soldiers introduced themselves and purchased beers, delighting in the two ladies' company. Her name was Karen Doubletree. She would occasionally touch his arm familiarly as they conversed, helping relax his inhibitions, unaccustomed as he was to being much around women. Her laughter was easy and delightful, touching a chord within him. Her brown eyes gleamed over burnished cheeks, set above a radiant display of white teeth encircled within her full and painted lips. When she stood, her frame was tall and slender, with wide shoulders, stout as the average man's. Her voice was like red wine, like Memphis itself, intoxicating to his senses. Sweet oleander wafted through the open terrace doors. In due time, over the course of the warm evening, she took his hand, leading him away up the stairs to her room.

Therein, he found her touch was like lightning on a seascape, illuminating the darkness within the storm, revealing in brief glimpses to the sea tossed mariner so far from shore, the perils of waterspout and wave. He sank into her bosoms as easily as breathing, drawn there by the longing in his soul. Rising gently above her ribs, they were crowned by long nipples, dark islands set in a sea of olive flesh. Following the line of the valley between the peaks, he came to the plane of her belly, surrounding the oasis of her naval. Further south, at the confluence of many waters, he entered the hinterland guarding the decent into the cave of life. Within the darkness of the damp cavern, he was lost in the images and scents beneath the curtain of her course, dark mane, draped luxuriously over his head. He felt the rise of her blood while her slender fingers teased the very cells of his flesh, dancing lithely over his muscles. Their sweat ran and mingled together, as flesh pressed hard against flesh, trying, it seemed, to merge spirits as well as bodies. Her breaths caught, each with a higher pitch, in cadence to their rhythm. Her body tensed and strained for the fruit of their mutual desire. He felt her blossom, opening petals dripping dew. He caught her face in his hands and held her lips pressed hard to his own. Their tongues darted like two sparrows playing on the wind. For a time they were joined as one, mutual energy flowing like the very current of creation. They lay then for a long while in each other's embrace, listening to the sounds of the house and the other's breathing.

When finally they spoke, he asked of her life, how she had come to such a place. She told him she was from Cannon County in middle Tennessee, raised a Christian, the daughter of a tribal elder who had fled into the unknown after killing a man. He'd ridden into the polls one day to vote in an election, when a white man told him Indians couldn't vote. Outraged at the idea, he pulled out his knife and stabbed the impolite fellow, before remounting his horse to ride away, never being heard from again. She had come to Memphis by way of circumstance, where, in the course of her profession, she'd become with child. Her outstanding beauty had allowed her to find employment at the most exclusive bordello in the city, visited by only the finest clientele. By this means, with the help of her sisters and the Madame, she provided for her young, half-white daughter, preparing for her future education, that she might avoid the same sort of life someday. As a blooded soldier, he was acutely aware of the inherent tragedies associated with each of their professions.

He stayed there with her the remainder of the night, snug between the clean, white sheets, happy, the war for a little while forgotten. He shared with her details about his family and how they had migrated from near Memphis to lower Arkansas when he was still quite young. He told her how he yet had some not so distant kinsmen residing in the local vicinity of Memphis and of his mother's people, the Yarbers, who resided in the mountainous regions near her former home in Cannon County. She recognized and responded to a gentleness and gratitude in him not evident in most men she encountered. He retuned after that night, at her welcoming, as often as he could for the remainder of his sojourn in Memphis.

After nearly a month operating in and around the busy city, the dawn of June sixth, 1862, broke clear and warm on the riverside. The previous day, telegraphs had brought the news, while the "*Comeercial Appeal*" bore broad headlines proclaiming, "FEDERAL FORCES, UNDER UNION GENERAL HENRY HALLECK, OCCUPY CORINTH."

On June fifth, without ever firing even a single shot, the Confederates stealthily evacuated the railroad town in the face of the far superior besieging Federals. The army escaped intact, strategically falling back a day's ride to the south, to the more defensible positions around Tupelo, Mississippi, leaving behind the black spirit of a place some said was a mass grave, wherein lay entombed the brave and chivalrous spirit of both the Confederacy and the Southern Cause. It was also said many an abandoned "Arkansas toothpick," forsaken of backpacks for the newer, lighter bayonet, were left behind in Corinth. The Rebs could only pray the Yanks might "enjoy" the environs of their newly won prize as much as had they.

This was bitter news, following hard on the heels of the Confederate evacuation June fourth, after two days of heavy shelling, of Fort Pillow, the only remaining element in the river defenses left between Memphis and the now approaching iron-clads. Beauregard had ordered the evacuation of Memphis on the same day as Pillow's surrender, so by the sixth, practically all, save a small contingent of Confederates camped southwest of town to guard the railway while awaiting the outcome of the soon expected river battle, were already started on the road south to join with the rest of their army at Tupelo. The whole population of Memphis expected the answer to the question of occupation would come any day now, when the Federal Fleet showed itself from around the river bend north of town.

The entourage, now referring to themselves as "the Colonel's escort," hand picked as they were like disciples, was packing up to follow the one hundred ninety-two new recruits that they'd enlisted during their trip, who were already forwarded on to Tupelo. They'd spent nearly a whole month at their enlistment task and as much as they'd like to remain in the lovely city by the river, they also wanted to rejoin their unit and friends and reap some well-deserved havoc on the enemy. Their time in residence at the Memphis Inn had helped rejuvenate their bodies, their spirits and their horses. Now there were old accounts remaining to be settled.

They made ready their mounts, packed up the clothes and other items they'd purchased in the city shops and closed out their accounts at the hotel desk. Most of them had spent their last night before leaving town again at Rosie's and perhaps for the last time, in the loving arms of the ladies.

They were for all purposes, about the only military unit left in the city since Beauregard's evacuation order. Forrest's troopers had been delayed there because the Colonel had gotten out of his sickbed perhaps too soon back in early May and while dancing with Mrs. Forrest at his birthday celebration, "kicked up his heels" a bit much, reopening his Fallen Timbers wound. With the Colonel having to be helped by his brothers from the room during the middle of a dance with his wife, the party in Nathan Bedford's home was cut short that evening. The Colonel's recuperation from the following surgery was being extended as long as possible before impending Yankee occupation of the city required his inevitable evacuation. There was still much hope, however misplaced, amongst most of the civilian populace, that the meager resources of the Confederate Defense Fleet would make short work of the massive Federal Flotilla, much in the same way they had done back on May tenth, up river at the Battle of Plum Bend. But, having seen the destruction wrought by the squat, black vessels during the previous winter at the fight for possession of Fort Donaldson, Colonel Forrest warned his men they needs must pray, for only God Almighty could save the tiny Defense Fleet from sure and swift destruction.

Intelligence reported the Union Flotilla anchored only a short distance upstream from Memphis, off the leeward point of Island Forty-nine. From all indications they were preparing for their downriver run into Memphis. At six o'clock, the morning of the sixth, during the sixth month of 1862, the twenty odd Tennessee Cavalrymen, saddles fitted out for travel with all their gear, mounted up and proceeded en echelon through downtown Memphis, from Third Street, heading west down Union Street and onward to South Bluff, where three remaining six pound James rifles stood with their crews, caissons loaded and teams standing in their traces, prepared as if on the battlefield, to evacuate at a moment's notice. The enemy had just shown themselves steaming around the bend commonly called 'Patty's hens and chickens,' puffing thick, black smoke and coming on hard. Crowds were starting to huddle on the bluffs above and along Front Street, gazing northwest up river. Activity below at the water front was minimal, but frantic, with the casting off of lines and weighing of anchors to get under way the eight little ships that made up the better part of the Confederate fighting Navy. All private and government vessels, normally found engaged in such abundance along the waterfront with the business of commerce, were already long gone downstream to avoid damage or capture by the Yankees. Even the little ferry that spent its days plying the muddy waters back and forth to Arkansas, was now too gone into hiding up some offshoot of the river channel.

The brave little flotilla smoking, steam up, backed away from the staging area in the mists of the early light, wheels splashing frantically, beating the swirling, brown water into a froth, rushing out to meet impending fate. Though unheard by crews over the strain of their belching engines, the sailors received loud cheers and heartfelt accolades from the grateful and patriotic citizens lining the bluffs above, as the sun rose slowly at their backs, soon illuminating the whole scene beneath a brilliant bluebird sky. But, as the Romans said, "sic transit gloria!" Probably but very few present to witness the departure of the unimposing "tin-clads" as they sallied out to meet the fast-approaching, iron-clad invaders, realized just how short lived the praise would be, for the issue at hand was to shortly be settled before breakfast. The Southern Fleet was no more than converted packet boats, mostly side-wheelers, in many cases haphazardly plated with sections of boiler iron that would provide protection from nothing generally greater than a six-pound or less cannonball. Between them they shared a complement of twenty-eight light guns. What they saw facing them as they cleared the point of Mud Island, were dark, menacing, low-riding vessels, belching heavy clouds of smoke, fire and cinders from their short stacks while making rapid headway downstream at full steam, riding four abreast. There was a second and even a third line of vessels visible behind their front ranks. From the distance and angle of South Bluff, it was difficult to make out the number of Union Men-of-War, even with use of field glasses. Their stacks seemed thick as a forest as they mingled and crossed, racing on the current. As the two forces approached within range of each other, the flash and smoke of the first shot issued from the muzzle of the bow gun on the leading Confederate vessel, "Colonel Lowell," followed shortly by the report echoing across the water. The thickening crowd cheered a hooray that even the Yanks could have heard from amidst the racket inside their yet distant floating forts. The Federals then received a full fusillade from the other attacking Confederate vessels. Before the ensuing powder smoke rolled over and obscured the entire scene, the solid shot of the Defense Fleet's guns could be seen bouncing harmlessly off of the angled, iron decks of the Union ships, accompanied by their echoing clangs like unto the tolling of many bells. Then the sixty-eight heavy guns of the Union boats began to unleash their fury, ripple firing on the closing Secessionists. Pieces of the Southern Fleet were soon seen flying pall mall through the foggy air until the thickening smoke settled over the water's surface in the still of the morning, concealing all but the flags, the masts and the stacks of the closing combatants. The flash of muzzles shown like lightning in a thunderhead from inside the dark, acrid cloud, while the guns rumbled continually like peels of thunder. A hush began to settle over the subdued crowd as the masts and stacks bearing Confederate flags rapidly disappeared one by one, sinking out of sight into the thick haze of powder fog.

Knowing their three, six-pound, bronze James cannon could do even less at long range than had the combined twenty-eight guns of the entire Confederate flotilla at close range, yet were sure to draw a deadly response from the heavy guns of the enemy if fired upon, the crews of the bluff-emplaced cannon quickly limbered up and sped their artillery pieces away to the waiting train that sat smoking restlessly on the tracks next to the station. From that point, along with Colonel Forrest and his accompanying escort, they would load aboard the last Rebel conveyance headed south from the fallen port city, to complete the final military evacuation of Memphis, after making one last brief stop south of town to load aboard a small detachment of infantry still guarding the rail lines there. They would all travel together by train to a not too distant point down line at a station short of Union occupied Corinth. After disembarking in Walnut Depot, Mississippi, they'd travel overland by road to rejoin the balance of the Army of Mississippi where they were, for now, safely bivouacked out of Halleck's reach in Tupelo.

The cavalrymen, in their new gray uniforms, upon seeing the victorious enemy warships come steaming, seemingly unscathed, out of the drifting smoke, mounted their horses and proceeded with all due haste to meet their Colonel at the depot. The young private wished dearly to break ranks, as did many of the others, if only briefly, to detour by Rosie's to say a final farewell to their favorite gals. After some strong coaxing and even downright pleading, the Lieutenant, who was a married man, was persuaded to take the column the few short blocks off their route, to ride past the establishment, with the strictest orders not to dismount, or in any way further delay the escorts arrival at their commander's side. Trains couldn't wait and especially not one with the whole U.S. Flotilla and accompanying Marines bearing down on it.

Karen, the lovely Cherokee beauty, black hair and black eyes shining, along with several other of the girls, came out to bid all the boys goodbye. The heartsick private gave the pretty girl a wad of Confederate bills, asking that she use them for her daughter's benefit.

"May I write to you?" the private asked her, "would you write me back?"

"Of course I will John!" she answered with some emphasis. "I only hope I get your letters with the Yankees in occupation." He bent from the saddle for one last kiss, as the Lieutenant ordered, "Troop, forward march!"

As the troopers rode away toward the station, there were numerous comments among them about "Friendly Henrys" taking their place? Some cursed the thought of the Memphis "hoors" left behind with all those "damn Yanks" with their Federal greenbacks. One young private rode quietly on, recalling to himself with a smile, the splendor he had found in Karen's bed and the scent of her on his pillow. He knew you simply don't meet women that gorgeous every day, if ever. A part of him felt somehow left there behind that day. But his face always bore a pleasant grin when he might chance to remember Memphis in June and the heady fragrance of sweet-oleander.

****

The Crossroads

Johnny and I came into the kitchen when we'd finished washing our hands and face. Mammy was still busy setting steaming platters before us as we scooted our chairs up to the table. There was fried chicken, pan-fried taters, hot skillet cornbread, brown gravy, black-eyed peas and Bessie's cold, fresh milk. Mammy smiled at us as she finished setting the table, untied and removed her apron and asked, "Where's your grandpa?"

"He said he'd be in directly," Johnny told her. She went over to the back door to look out at the shed. Without opening it, she peered through the screen at the old fellow still sitting motionless, smiling, in the chair where we'd left him.

"Must be lost in his thoughts," she said, "he's not even swatting flies." The whistle of a six o'clock, westbound, Cotton Belt, express-train drifted out of the south through the timber. The distant sound of rapid-clacking wheels on steel rails was that of a fast flying highball.

"We'll let him be;" she said turning from the door, "he's not much of an appetite of late anyway. What were he and you boys talking about?" she asked, pulling up her chair.

Once more, Johnny being the oldest of us two, answered her. "He was telling us about goin' to Memphis with General Forrest for his birthday celebration, back when the General was still a Colonel."

"Oh he was?" she said and then paused. "He must still be thinking about those old times," she continued on in her proper manner, looking at us with a smile like only grandma's have. "Well, let's have our Blessing then. He'll be along when he's a mind to. Polk," she said addressing me, "could you ask it please?"

"Yes ma'am," I answered, looking from under the brow of my bowed head at Johnny. He smiled smugly to himself, satisfied with not having been asked.

"Dear Lord," I began as the sound of the express faded away to the southwest, "May we be grateful for all of Thy bounty and we ask that You watch over and keep us all in Your care. Please bless this food which we are about to partake and forgive us our sins," I said thinking of the poor cows lying wet and exhausted by the river

132

after our afternoon's sport. "We ask it in Thy Holy name, Amen. Pass the chicken please," I added without pause, hoping to get the pulley bone with the first word. Mammy handed the chicken platter over to me and I took it, beaming a bright smile at Johnny who sat with a black look on his features at seeing how reciting a good prayer reaped immediate rewards. I took my pick from the mound of fryer pieces stacked on the plate, forking a drumstick and a breast to go with my first choice, the pulley bone, before passing the dish to my brother. Mammy never said a word, except to echo the 'Amen,' content to let hungry children work out such matters among ourselves. Regardless of what was left on the plate after it had gone around the table, she would state her views on greed by example, always taking the neckbone, the least favorite piece, leaving all the choice portions for her family. The lesson wasn't lost on me, but there was certain satisfaction in erasing the smug look off Johnny's face.

"How're your little sister Mystic and baby brother Leali doing?" she asked. "I haven't seen them all week," she added, her eyes a kindle with the special love she held for all her adopted grandchildren. She always bore a prayer in her heart that life would use us kindly.

"They're fine Mammy," I said, beating Johnny to it with his mouth full of taters.

"You boys tell your mother to bring those little ones to see me soon," she added. Mammy was a handsome woman. She wasn't overly large, almost petite, with deep-dark eyes that rarely missed anything that went on around her, often glistening with a light of love and life that she shared with her husband and his family. Her nose, short, straight and a little broad, bore her tin-rimmed spectacles that sat above a full mouth and firm chin.

I finished stripping the meat off the wishbone and held it up to Johnny, grasping one side. He took hold of the other, pausing to consider his wish before pulling it in two. When it snapped apart, I came up with the larger portion. Again I radiated a smile at my big brother, who just shook his head in disgust. My wish was to hear more of Pappy's stories and it would soon be answered.

After supper we asked Mammy to be excused and without putting our dishes in the washbasin, bolted out the back door, past the old man still resting in his chair amongst the hung-up tools in the shed. We ran barefoot through the clover of the meadow, disturbing the labor of the bees still at work there, as the sun lingered low in the evening sky.

Johnny took position on the tree-covered hill that dominated the view of the pastures, while I gathered ammunition from the ground and prepared to charge him, dirt clods in hand. We found crawdad mounds made the best grenades for our war game, not too painful if they struck you, and giving a fine impression of an explosion as they burst apart on contact with the earth.

When he was in place behind our makeshift fortifications near the top of the hill, I began my assault, charging up the slope, echoing the Rebel yell from bygone days. Once in good chunking range I let loose a fusillade of clods that burst against the parapets brother ducked behind. When my ammunition was exhausted, Johnny rose up to return fire. I dodged and danced out of the way of the incoming missiles, ducking to retrieve new clods from the hillside, as the dirt showered up around me. With a fresh batch of ballistics in hand, I taunted John, calling him chicken, teasing him with the squawking sounds of a yard fowl. The trick worked, for when he rose up from behind his refuge to throw down the hillside at me, I landed a well-aimed crawdad mound right in his face. The expression beneath the dirt in his eyes and mouth was priceless. He spat, blinked and wiped the grime away from his shocked face that shortly began to show red in anger, inflamed as he soon was by my laughter coming from where I rolled helplessly in its throws on the ground. In the next instant, my pleasure was extinguished by the sound of rocks striking and bouncing off the ground and cutting through the air around my prone position. I realized the fun was now gone out of our game, as Johnny came out from behind the breastworks, counter charging, retrieving gravel from the ground and hurling it as hard and fast as he could. I gathered myself up and ran headlong in retreat down the hill, hollering for help from Mammy, or Pappy or God Almighty Himself as the deadly projectiles flew and ricocheted all around me, fully expecting to be cut down in my tracks at any instant by a solid shot to the back of my head. I leapt panting over the yard fence in one smooth motion, as I heard rocks strike the boards beside and beneath me. I knew from experience that when Johnny was all het-up, he didn't readily regain his calm and that my best plan for the moment was to seek the safety of the house.

I sped past Pappy's now empty chair, thinking the timing of his going in to supper couldn't be worse. But I was soon through the backdoor and into the protection of Mammy's kitchen before my pursuer cleared the fence rails, rocks in hand.

"Good Lord, what's the matter?" she asked, startled by my abrupt entry. "Did a bear get your brother?"

"I wish! No ma'am," I stammered out between gasps, "Johnny's after me with rocks again!"

"That boy," she said, shaking her head. Pappy only grinned quietly to himself, thinking how some things never change, remembering similar situations that took place on the same hillside with his older brother William and younger brother Andrew in their long lost youth.

By that time Johnny was at the door, sweat streaking the remaining dirt down his cheeks. He didn't open the door to come in, but instead, holding his face close to the screen, asked me to step outside in an eerily calm voice.

"Mammy!" I said, spooked by his tone.

"Come in here and wash off your face Little John," she told him in a voice both sympathetic and firm. He hesitated outside the door, still seeing red, not wishing to let go of his desire for revenge. "Stop gawking and come on," she repeated, coaxing him from his anger with her calm. The door squeaked on its hinges as if in protest, as the spring stretched taught, then, as she was about to say, "Don't let the screen door..." it banged to in emphasis of his emotions before she could finish her statement, "...slam behind you," she concluded.

"Sit down there Polk," she told me in a tone that said she knew I wasn't completely blameless in the affair. "Go out in the dogtrot and wash your face like I told you," she repeated to Johnny, "then come back in and sit down with us. Here's a bucket of fresh wash water," she said handing him the pail she'd just drawn from the well to wash the dinner dishes with, knowing the cold groundwater would cool his temper and that he'd feel better with the dirt removed from his eyes, nose and mouth.

"Yeller chicken!" he said sibilantly as he exited the room. "Go on now!" Mammy chided. "And you put your tongue back in your mouth," she warned me.

Pappy silently chewed his food and sopped up pot liquor from the peas on his plate with a slice of cornbread. His wife cleared away the glasses and dishes that we'd left in place where we'd sat for supper, when we'd sped off in our haste to be again outdoors, enjoying the last of the daylight, in the cool of the summer evening. We knew before long the school term would begin again and with studies, combined with our daily chores, such play would be mostly forgotten until next year.

When Johnny came back to the kitchen, the dirty streaks and the red color were gone from his face, but not the menace of his persona. He sat down across from me peering from beneath his tilted brow with a look that said the issue had not yet been fully settled. Noting this, Mammy sent me out to fetch another fresh pail for her dishes. On my return, toting the heavy bucket with both hands, I found Pappy and Johnny laughing together.

To defuse the situation, Pappy began to talk, knowing how we were distracted from care by his tales. "My brothers and I used to play war in that self-same pasture when we were about your age. There was a definite pecking order between us, with Will at the top, me in the middle and poor little brother James Andrew at the bottom. The truth be known, he was probably glad to see his older brothers go when we rode off to war without him that February morning back in '62.

"We were having a dirt-clod fight out there one day," he said, motioning toward the fields out back, "when we was all still just lads like yourselves. Big brother Will, for one reason or another I no longer recall, escalated the engagement much like you did," he said looking straight at Johnny, "by chunking stones instead of dirt clods. He struck our little brother right between the eyes with a good size one and knocked him out cold. He went down like a dead man. We both thought Will had kilt him. It's a wonder he didn't. I took off for the house much like you did Polk," he said addressing me, "to get some help for my baby brother. By the time I brought our ma back up the hill, James was awake, setting up in Will's arms, blood running down between his eyes, around his nose. He looked like some Injun in war paint. Before she even helped little brother up and to the house, she'd sent Will for a switch whilst she wiped the blood from James' face with her apron. When he brought it, she tore his hind-end up right there in the pasture. It was a good spell before Will ever again chunked another rock at anyone. I suspect your ma may give the both of ye' similar treatment if'n she was to be knowin' of ya'll's little spat. Vengeance, you should remember, is a dangerous thing," he added looking directly at Johnny, " believe me, I know. So, I suggest you shake hands and this be the end of it."

"That's okay by me," I piped up, perhaps a little too quickly, betraying my eagerness for protection from Johnny's wrath. My brother, on the other hand, wasn't so quick to leap at the opportunity to bury the hatchet someplace other than my head. But, after a few moments silence under the steady gaze of our grandpa and the gentle nudging from behind his chair of our granny, who peered expectantly at him over the rim of her glasses, he got up and met me half way around the table, where I was already standing with my right hand extended. He grasped it and a smile began to gradually replace the threat that had until then crowded his features.

"That's my good boys," Mammy said, pushing her specs up on the bridge of her nose with a forefinger and smiling at the newly restored peace of the household. "That's what the world needs more of, forgiveness. Now, you two men run along," she added, referring to Pappy and Johnny, "and Polk, before you join them, fetch me one more pail of rinse water so I can finish clearing and washing these dishes," she concluded as she emptied the first one into the wash basin and handed the empty bucket back to me.

"Yes ma'am!" I replied, happy to see my big brother's darker side subdued.

"Jine us on the porch when ya'll are done and we'll watch the sun go down." Pappy said as he got up from the table and started out the door with Johnny.

"Okay sir," I said, remembering my wish with the pulley bone earlier.

"You boys start without me, I've some sewing to be done," Mammy said by way of excuse, knowing Pappy's stories came more easily when it was just the men folk present.

After drawing a second bucket from the deep, dark, three-foot wide well and taking the wash water back to Mammy, I asked if there was anything else I could do for her. She told me, "No thank you son, why don't you go join your grandpa and brother on the porch. And don't do anything to rekindle his anger, you know well how he can be," she reminded me.

"Yes'm," I agreed, hoping the tense moments were indeed passed, glad that I hadn't been struck down in my tender youth by one of those rocks he'd sent hurtling so dangerously near my head, nor wishing to yet take one of Johnny's poundings.

When I rounded the corner from the dogtrot onto the porch, Pappy was performing the ritual of an after dinner chew. He produced his pin knife from out his trouser pocket and shaved off a mouthful of the dark-brown material from the fresh plug he'd just opened. With a gesture, he offered us each some of the tobacco out of jest, knowing full well we wouldn't accept lest our granny appear upon the scene and we all be in trouble. He deposited the dried tobacco with stinging delight in his jaw and worked it around like a cow its cud. After a spell, he managed his first mouthful of juice and casually spat from his chair on the porch out into the already dark-stained dirt and cedar shavings of the ground lying just below his elevated seat.

He reached under the wicker bottom of the rocker and brought out a cedar stick that bore numerous knife marks, yet was big enough that it still held in it some remaining whittling life. He began to slowly and deliberately make long strokes with his sharpened-blade, producing whole shavings that curled into complete circles as they doubled back on themselves from one end of the stick to the other, before falling free onto the gray wooden planks of the porch floor below. The aroma of the fresh cedar was released into the evening air, mixing with the pungent odor of Bull of the Woods chewing tobacco.

Johnny sat to Pappy's immediate right, in the middle, while I sat just to my brother's right. Both we younguns rocked lazily out of sync, one on the forward swing, with the other on the backstroke. Across the fields, the sun crawled slowly behind the horizon, until, with a flash, it disappeared from view. The night sounds began to blossom in the cool of the summer eve. A whippoorwill called to his mate from the hedgerow, while a turtledove up in the branches answered. Down by the pond bank a big bullfrog croaked his romantic sentiments, while the crickets and locusts sang chorus. It was a fitting evening to cap a fine day. The mare whinnied from the barn, glad, too, at the outcome of the evening's events. We could hear Mammy shuffling about inside the house, singing softly to herself as she worked busily at one thing, or another. A slight breeze stirred the curtains in the open windows, making sitting together quietly, doing nothing, a genuine pleasure disturbed only by an occasional mosquito buzzing in our ears.

As dark settled on the moonless night, I lit the porch lantern. It was soon swarming with insects drawn to the flame. We could hear from our seats on the porch, another train rolling through Kingsland some two miles south. I pictured in my mind its headlight cutting through the bug filled darkness. The whistle moaned out a lonesome tune, as the clickety-clack of its wheels kept the tempo of the melody.

The Union Pacific ran from east to west through the little railroad town, past the weathered gray wooden depot that sat on the north side of the tracks, opposite William Marks' sawmill on the south side. The mill was the main industry of the community, providing the majority of employment either directly, or indirectly and most of the building materials for miles around. A couple of miles south of town were the second and third largest businesses in our area, William Marks' gristmill and cotton gin. Kingsland was a crossroads where several community roads converged on the railway and farmers from miles around brought their crops to market there.

The trains rolled through low, wooded hills before crossing massive trestle bridges upon entering the river bottoms east of town, then made the gradual climb to the top of the red-clay ridge where our ancestors chose to settle, through present day Kingsland, before again descending into Moro Creek bottoms out west of town. The coal fired engines, belching steam and cinder, held endless fascination for young boys like Will and me.

Not so many years past, in 1899, Pappy had taken the train east all the way to Memphis, where he revisited scenes from his youth as a soldier for the Confederacy. Will and I both hoped to board a steam train someday to set out on our own far-off adventures. We'd heard so much about them; we couldn't wait to see our first city. But, for now, we contented ourselves by fueling the imagination with tales from our granddaddy's glory days.

It was a test of patience. I knew if I waited long enough, Johnny was bound to ask Pappy to tell us more about the late war, drifting us into a nostalgia for which our generation was born. After a spell, when the sound of the train in the night had subsided, my patience and the wishbone paid off.

"Pappy," Johnny started, breaking the spell of the moment, while ushering in another, "what'd you mean when you said you and your horse Prince made your last stand on South Bluff in Memphis? Is that where you got your belly wound?"

I couldn't help but grin quietly to myself, watching as the old man deliberately drug out the moment of his reply, first slowly turning his head to gaze upon Johnny, then putting his stick and knife down to reposition himself more comfortably, before again taking up the whittling tools and returning his attention to them, much as I'd often before seen him do when I'd laid the bait.

"Well son," he began, "that's a mighty deep subject for such a shallow mind," he teased Johnny.

Mammy overheard as she walked past the nearest window about her tasks and interjected a reprimand for Pappy, "That's not a polite way to speak to your grandson J.R."

"Yes'm," was his sole reply, still playing the storyteller's trick of building anticipation, much as a good cook will fan the pot lid, stimulating more active appetites in the hungry with the escaping aroma, increasing the enjoyment of final delivery at long last.

I practiced at becoming a good storyteller myself, by sitting silent and being a good listener, paying close attention to every detail of both teller and listener.

"To answer your question," he said before another extended pause that lengthened the time since the query was first made to several minutes, "no, I was shot several blocks east of there, but ended up on South Bluff just above where the railroad bridge crosses the river now, whilst trying to escape from our Yankee pursuers. But that was close to two years after where I left the story earlier when we were out back in the shed. I was stabbed by a sword and once cut before that," he said, holding up his right hand to reveal another old scar he bore across his knuckles. "I wasn't seriously shot until August twenty-first, 1864. When Mammy earlier called us to supper, we were talking about June '62."

"Uh huh?" Johnny said quizzically, as if puzzling out the significance of this point in his mind. Then, patience exhausted, almost impertinently, he added, "Then tell us what happened next after you were in Memphis with Forrest in '62!"

Taking mercy on Johnny's evident anxiety, he told us about how on the Saturday night of the big birthday dinner and dance, Colonel Forrest nearly collapsed when the bullet against his spine suddenly shifted, but that his wife caught his fall while he danced with her. He told us that they had boarded the last train out of Memphis as the Yankees dropped anchor in the harbor and sent parties of armed Marines ashore to accept the surrender of the city, after having completely annihilated the Southern Defense Fleet before the watching eyes of a large portion of the city's population.

Once arriving in Tupelo, the troopers were reunited with their comrades and he his brother, William Edwin, when they rejoined the larger body of the Army of Mississippi.

"An army," he told us, "to be sure, is a strange animal, certain to react to cause, though you could never tell just how, where or when. No sooner had we returned to the regiment that we'd all worked so hard to augment with our recent, recruiting efforts in Memphis, than its command was taken from our Colonel by Commanding General Bragg and transferred, along with his staff and escort, including myself, to Chattanooga. I suspect President Davis and ole' Bragg thought more of Bedford's recruitin' abilities, than of his war wagin', simply because Forrest wasn't a West Point graduate like themselves. He was as roughhewn as his men, which made him most popular amongst us, but scorned by many of his fellow officers due to his lack of education and professional military background. One of his detractors was the very unpopular Supreme Commander of the Army and Western District, Braxton Bragg.

"Within the structure of the military, there is order, purpose and action. There can exist a unity of mind and an equality of dress. Good boots and warm jackets affect a man's bearing and increase his opinion of self-worth. Armies feed even at the expense of the countryside. One can rest assured in tasks not mentally overly taxing and a simple devotion to duty, learning a trade amongst brothers. At its best, it can be a good life for simple men. But, at its worst; it can seem an interminable existence.

"Bragg's army, at that point, was the latter. Foraging was strictly forbidden under harsh penalty. Everyday we heard the crackle of musketry, ushering another poor wretch into eternity for some infringement or other, mainly desertion. Most boys had faithfully discharged their duty for the full term of their initial one-year enlistment, but were now held in service by the recently passed 'conscript law.' This made for great contempt amongst the majority of line soldiers, for all officers above the rank of lieutenant and their 'yaller dog' staff officers. Ruthless discipline made us more a'feared of them, than of our enemy. At this stage of the war, morale was poor as ever was. Many had but one burning desire, that being to get out of the army and return to their homes one way or another. This was accomplished, by some, through 'accidentally' chopping off a toe whilst splittin' firewood, or shootin' themselves in the foot in the course of firing practice, or whilst 'cleanin' their weapon.'

"We cavalry were fully aware how we sat in better stead than the poor infantryman. In spite of the popular opinion amongst them, that we got the best rations and provisions and did but little real fighting, anyone of them would have gladly swapped places with any of us.

"The vast majority of infantrymen complained of hardship and depravity. The enlistees had voluntarily given themselves over to a gov'ment with faith in a cause that had now forsaken them with poor, or no rations and gear best foraged from a relentless foe. They said the Confederacy was no more than a dried up teat. The conscripts had an even lower opinion of army life

"But we of the mounted service bore a different opinion. We could see in each other's eyes that we were soldiers, destined to survive off the bounty, or the scarcity of the land we occupied. This was war! We sought to survive at the expense of all else, so as to fight and kill again. As highly mobile cavalry, we were twice bound to cut loose from lines of supply, to move and operate unfettered and unprotected by the main body of the army, striking, then melting back into the landscape. We didn't complain overly, for we knew we would again soon loose the leash and be free from Bragg's tyranny. We made out best we could and oft as not, found our way to greener pastures, which we sore did appreciate in comparison to the days of shortage we also experienced. It was a long contest though and wore more each passing day on the nerves of even the most valiant cavaliers.

"Besides drill, our principle occupations were poker, chuck-a-luck, or louse racing, which we had in abundance at Tupelo. One question I never found the answer to, was whether the gov'ment furnished bedbugs, or if some generous soul brought seed from home.

"Not wishing to be further separated from brother William, and desiring to help him escape the tyrannical atmosphere of the summer camps, I visited the Colonel at his headquarters tent one day with the request that he have Will transferred into his command as part of his personal escort. He was setting in a canvas field chair in front of his open tent flap, adjacent to a folding table that carried his pistol and saber where he'd removed and placed them. I snapped crisply to attention and stood quietly while the Colonel finished studying a map that I noticed was of middle Tennessee. After a spell, his attention seemed to return to his surroundings and he noticed me their, still at attention. 'Oh,' he said, 'young Ledbetter, at ease son. What brings you to see me?'

'Well sir,' I began, 'I'll be brief. It's about my brother William,' I said before pausing to survey the Colonel's reaction.

'Go ahead son,' he said in a tone designed to put me more at ease.

'As you know, Colonel, he and I jined up together back in February of this year, near our home in Arkansas. I was separated from him first at Shiloh, then for several weeks when on detached duty with you in Memphis. We were both mighty pleased to get back together here in Tupelo. Now we get word we're goin' to be transferred out again, all the way to Chattanooga. Sir, you know how it is. You've got both your brothers and your son in your command because ye' can't stand the separation from kin. We promised our ma and pa that we'd look after each other through the course of this conflict and that can't be done if'n we're a couple hunert miles apart.'

"I paused to let my point soak in and the Colonel asked, ever direct, 'What's your point soldier?'

"Wishing to leave no card un-played before the Colonel heard the point of my plea," Pappy said, "I added, 'You remember that fine stockinged black charger I was astride when we first met on the field at Shiloh?'

"After some moments of searching back over the many tumultuous events transpired since those early spring days, he answered, 'I believe I do, a fine animal as I recall, that I'd desired

144

to trade you out of when we made that trip to Memphis. That horse was wounded at Fallen Timbers the same time I was shot, wasn't he?'

'Yes sir, but it was only a flesh wound and he's fine now. You may also recall too, that I tolt' ye' he was my brother's horse, a parting gift from our pa on the day we rode off to enlist. We're both volunteers sir, not conscripts. He and his stallion Fury would make fine additions to your escort. He's more fight in him than me. Only cause of fallin' ill in transit from Arkansas to Corinth, was he not with us at Shiloh. He's fully recovered now sir and itchin' to get in on some action. He knows from your reputation that where ye' go, there's plenty of that.'

"Sensing in Colonel Forrest a growing uneasiness that translated as impatience, I cut to the chase. 'Sir, I've come to request one of two things, though I'd prefer the former, in lieu of your failing to honor that, I ask the second. Could you see fit to arrange for Private William E. Ledbetter of the Fourth Tennessee Cav., to be transferred into your command as an addition to your personal escort that we might serve in the same company and not become further separated? If'n that isn't suitable to your intentions, then I regretfully request that I might be removed from detached service as a member of the Colonel's escort and placed back under the command of the Fourth Tennessee, that I might remain here in Tupelo near him when the remainder of your escort accompanies you to your new duties in Chattanooga.'

"Practicing his best poker face, giving no indication what so ever of his feelings, or intentions, he thanked and dismissed me, returning his attention to his maps, saying only that he'd take the matter under consideration. I had no idea which, if either of my requests he might honor. But, within two days, Will received his orders to, as they said, 'report forthwith to Colonel Forrest's headquarters for detached service from present unit and duty to augment the Colonel's personal escort company and further make immediate preparations to proceed with said officer's command to headquarters Chattanooga.' It was signed, 'Most sincerely, John P. Strange, Adjutant.'

Pappy told Johnny and me how William and he weren't aware of it at the time, but that their names still appeared as 'present for duty' on the rolls of their former Second Arkansas Cavalry Regiment, the remaining balance of which yet operated under the newly acquired designation of Slemon's Cavalry Battalion. It would be November before their names were finally removed. He said by way of explanation, "Military paperwork was approximate at best.

"A telling incident took place about that time revealing something of the nature of our commander and that of the whole Forrest family," Pappy went on. "News arrived in camp of the fate of N.B.'s older brother John Forrest. He was a veteran of the Mexican/American War, left a paralytic by a bullet shot through his lower spine at the Battle of Monterrey. Shortly after the occupation of the environs in and around Memphis by the Federals, Mrs. Forrest, their mother, complained to Brother John of her ill treatment by the Union officer in charge of a detail occupying her farm some six miles north of the city. John, incensed by the outrage, waited outside the Gayoso House residence of the offending Yank Colonel. Upon the officer's arrival, John Forrest, sitting with his crutches, plainly stated to the Yank his intention to break one of his crutches over the head of the fellow if ever he again insulted his mother. Taking offense at the brash words of a mere cripple, the Yankee officer began to rail at John. With the aid of one crutch, John began to stand, fully intending to carry out his threat with the other. The Yankee kicked the one crutch from beneath his arm, sending the elder Forrest crashing to the paving stones. Not to be outdone, John quickly withdrew a Derringer from his coat pocket whilst lying on the pavement and severely wounded said Yank Colonel. He was seized and confined below decks aboard a Federal man-of-war setting at anchor on the edge of the river channel.

"The news sent Bedford into an insane rage, leaving him fit to be tied. After a spell, he calmed enough to dictate a letter to the Union officer in charge of the Memphis garrison. He demanded his brother's release until such time as a civil trial. This message was sent by special courier under a flag of truce and remarkably, immediately complied with by the head Federal of the post. The wounded Colonel eventually recovered after lingering long near death. John was eventually acquitted and the Yank learned, as did we all, not to trifle with a Forrest.

"On June eleventh, we reluctantly left behind, under the command of Lieutenant Colonel Kelly, the new outfit we had whipped together, promising to keep in touch with both old and new friends by written correspondence. We happily departed Tupelo under the direction of Bedford's brother William, en route for Forrest's new command, to consist of Terry's Texas Rangers and the Second Georgia Cavalry. The noose around the Confederate neck, though having thus far somewhat successfully interdicted our rail and river transportation, had not yet been drawn completely taught by the enemy, still allowing on our part some freedom of movement over the turnpikes of Alabama, Mississippi and Tennessee. Our hardy troop of sixty men and accompanying horses," he explained, "carefully traversed the red clay hills of northern Mississippi and neighboring Alabama, moving steadily in a northeasterly direction, employing the best scouts and avoiding all potential enemy contact. At the earliest opportunity in our travels, I told the Colonel how Will and I was much obliged at his generosity on having the both of us directly under his command. He replied, 'Let's see what we think of this new command afore you decide the final verdict on that'n.' In no way masking his utter contempt for our Supreme Commander, he added, 'But the way I see it, the more distance between us and that windbag Bragg, the better!'

"Once't all settled in camp at Chattanooga, we begun to make preparations for our upcoming campaign to follow early in the month of July. Engaged as we found ourselves with near a thousand men, in preparation for the willful killin' of others, I couldn't help but be affected by the shear uncertainty of it all. Like so many others, I wondered would I ever again return home, or have further opportunities to learn more of the pleasures found in a woman's arms? Would I perhaps someday wed and raise a family of my own when the issues of war were again finally settled?

"Having tasted my first blood at Shiloh, this next foray would be my sophomore effort. The questions about my future and how I'd behave through the certain myriad trials and challenges that lay within the scope of action that were sure to shortly follow, were quieted only by staying as busy as possible with the readying of the company mounts."

Pappy explained to us how horseshoes weren't then available as ready-made blanks, but each one had to be cut to length of red-hot, drop forged iron. Then again heated to that glowing sanguine color in the forge and warped into shape by hammering it around the protruding end of an anvil. It was reheated a third time and withdrawn from the flames with tongs for the purpose of bending over the cleats on either side of the heel. Finally it was removed red-hot from the forge a fourth time and the nail holes punched out. Once't reaching this last stage, it had to be cooled for fitting to the individual horse's hoof and shaped on the beveled end of the anvil to its final form, before being applied to the bottom of the trimmed foot by securely nailing it in place. This process was repeated a total of four times each for the sixty odd cavalry mounts in his immediate care, plus the additional accompanying pack and wagon animals of the troop.

He noted that when even the fierce labors of his detail failed to gentle his spirit, he'd find and visit the Quartermaster's herd, to watch the lazy beeves graze. Being reared as a stockman, he found comfort in studying their listless inactivity. "Like any other society," he observed, "they have a hierarchy that they follow by instinct and necessity, as do we humans. They seem blissful in the shadow of their doomed fate, much as are soldiers. Their peace somehow infected my own spirit and at times helped make the moment more bearable."

He continued, "Our cavalry officers knew how homesickness and anxieties of self doubt could cripple the effectiveness of an army, so besides the numerous material and logistical arrangements to be made, the sweltering summer days of late June were taken up with drill, firing practice, feeding, grooming and training of horses, surgeons call and dress parade. Forrest told the troopers in all truth, 'The more you sweat now, the less you'll bleed later.' All those labors made not only for confidence in fine-honed martial skills, but also for a sound night's sleep, relatively undisturbed by dreams of home, or nightmares of the battlefield.

"Slowly, I came to develop a modicum of appreciation for camp life, in spite of waiting in long lines for sometimes inedible chow, the smelly latrines and a complete lack of privacy. But, as water is restless, ever seeking its own level, so too the human heart until amongst like kind. Through daily association, I made new acquaintances and renewed old ones, becoming increasingly at home amongst me fellows. At this stage of our training, horse racing and all other forms of horse play, vinous malts and spirituous liquors were strictly forbidden in camp."

Pappy told us how, "Colonel Forrest participated but little at first in the training routine, not being himself overly familiar with the cavalry manual of arms, but watched the drills intently, learning himself for the first time of maneuvers and bugle commands, as well as their uses and meanings. When a Georgia officer once't asked him why he didn't personally participate more in drilling the men, he replied, 'I'm working too, ye' just can't see it right now.' When he did become involved in drill, it usually resulted in vigorous exertions of both body and language when, for example, green troopers were tossed headlong from the backs of their startled horses upon practice firing their weapons. The General charged out on the parade ground shouting, 'That will never do in combat!' As he became gradually more involved in the training, the horses slowly became accustomed to the Colonel's bellerin' and the discharge of firearms from their backs, making it easier for their riders to remain seated.

"Forrest's proficient use of curse words in the discharge of duty prompted one Georgia recruit to comment within my hearing, 'that damn Colonel, he'll do to tie to!'

"The furnace of summer was fully stoked," Pappy continued, "when, early the following month, we rode out of camp, headed north for a crossing of the Tennessee River, which began on the sixth and we fully effected by July ninth. We had celebrated Independence Day on the fourth, with the sure knowledge that we would soon be engaged in waging no holds barred warfare.

"Our crossing was guarded by two hunert additional reinforcements that awaited us on the east bank of the river. We were now moving with seven-hunert troopers, beyond our lines, into a field of operation which we would often return to in the next couple years, interdicting Federal supply and transportation at irregular intervals, harassing and capturing isolated garrisons and re-provisioning our commissary larder with liberated Union war materials. Our mission objective in this instance was to disrupt Yankee General Buell's supplies coming to him out of Lewisville. Our main target was Murfreesboro, Tennessee, a primary depot on the Nashville and Chattanooga Railroad.

"The Earth is sculpted by God's own hand and if you look close you can see it. The foothills of the Cumberland are a perfect example of the endless variety of His handy-work. If you could iron out the wrinkles in the country above Chattanooga, you'd add twice again the territory of Tennessee. We laced our way through the many vales, past clear brooks and streams that tumbled over rocks and shoals, winding their course through woodlands and fields stacked thick with hayricks. Forage for the animals was no problem. Dominating the entire landscape were the mountains, rising in places near straight up, hemming in the many green glens through which we traveled. We kept videttes ahead and beyond our progress, vigilantly scouting for enemy contact."

"What's a vidette Pappy?" Johnny asked him.

Looking only slightly annoyed by the brief interruption to his train of thought, Pappy answered, "It's like an outrider, riding ahead to scout for any possible trouble. That's what you call a cavalry picket." Then returning to the story, he began, "Now where was I? Oh yes," he said after a brief instant. "We reached the pass through the summit of the mountains at Altamont by the tenth, from which elevation one could take in the splendor of the country for miles in all directions. This was both Will's and my first taste of real alpine country and we liked it, even felt at home in the cool, rarified air. I felt a secret pleasure inside, like that of returning to my native land, but when I pondered the difficulty and hazard these formidable obstacles might exact on our enterprise, the elation was counterbalanced by overriding concern. If we weathered the march, we would have to re-cross this same barrier to escape any would be pursuers.

"Scouting reports indicated that there were few, if any, enemy cavalry as yet on patrol outside the Union pickets, so all we expected to meet on the outward leg, if anything, were infantry patrols, which we knew we could evade, given ample warning. Being largely outnumbered, as we knew we would, surprise was the key to our plan of attack.

"Descending from the great height, we followed the rail line to within ten miles of Sparta, where we jined up with the battalion of Colonel Morrison, bringing our total strength up to a thousand men and horses. This completed our complement. Our new regiment was largely untried in combat, but no way lacking in the desire to inflict harm on the invader. A powerful calm seemed settled on the troops as we rode on through country quite foreign to the majority of us. We were steeling our spirits for the hard purpose ahead.

"Surveying the weaponry of my fellow troopers, on their backs, in saddle scabbards, or carried stuffed in waist belts, or holsters, I noted a numerous assortment of firearms. It appeared to me to be a Quartermaster's nightmare to have to supply ammunition for. The Colonel always preferred to leave that problem to the soon to be captured commissaries of our enemy. A complete Manual of Arms for the outfit would have included carbines manufactured by Smith and Henry, Sharps, Burnside, Maynard, Remington and Merrill. In addition there were muzzle-loading rifles including 1855 model Austrian, 1816 Starr, 1853 British and 1861 Springfield. There were also Jager, Harper's Ferry, Enfield, Spencer and Ballard breech and muzzle load varieties in evidence. For handguns, besides antique flint locks brought from home, our soldiers had scrounged Smith and Wesson,

Allen, Remington, Colt, Joslyn, Lefoucheux and even a few Le Mar revolvers.

"At the time, I personally preferred the Enfield muzzle load rifle that I'd liberated from a dead Yank in the battle at Shiloh Church, for its range, accuracy and ease of obtaining ammo for. I don't mean to butter my own corn but I'd become known as a crack shot in target practice and expected to soon employ my skill as a sharpshooter in the upcoming engagement. I carried it slung barrel down, across't my shoulder, ever at the ready. When the time came, we'd be blowing holes of every caliber in the targets of our wrath.

"Our uniforms included both gray and black jackets and blue, black and gray trousers, besides the requisite denim and butternut homespun haberdashery. For covers we had a seemingly endless variety and color of wide brim and slouch hats, as well as a few gov'ment-issue, gray, wool forage caps.

"You're not much apt to think on the simple blessings of socks until you're slap without 'em. At this stage, many found themselves in just that predicament, but not Will nor I, for I'd purchased several extra pair whilst yet in Memphis, that I distributed most generously amongst the more familiar unfortunates.

"Our trek took us through towns with names like Mount Olive, Readyville and Woodbury, where I feared prying eyes might report our movement to nearby Yankee garrisons. We'd find ourselves returning to these environs many more times over the course of the war when they again became the targets of future raids.

"In two separate instances, upon having to leave the roads to remain undetected by Union outposts, we had to remove the horseshoes of the entire command in order for the animals to negotiate the steep, rocky terrain. While the majority of the men reclined and relaxed, the blacksmiths and our assistants worked furiously to remove, then replace the steel footwear.

"After four days of slogging down muddy roads, climbing, then descending tall obstacles, splashing across treacherous moss covered rock fords and dodging enemy outposts, we approached McMinnville late on July twelfth with but very few injuries received in transit. The next day, the thirtieth, was the actual forty-first birthday of Colonel Forrest that we'd earlier celebrated prematurely in May, whilst still residing back in Memphis. It would also be the day of our attack on Murfreesboro, then still lying some eighteen miles distant. The awaiting populace greeted us as would-be saviors in our mud-splattered uniforms, displaying an uncommon enthusiasm upon our arrival. We were informed that on the evening prior, the Union garrison from Murfreesboro had marched into McMinnville and unceremoniously arrested and carried away nearly every male of the community. There was great distress for their well being in the hands of the cruel oppressors. Colonel Forrest addressed the women from atop his horse in the town square, boldly assuring them that by the following eve their loved ones would be returned. I prayed in my heart that such could be accomplished with good speed. His promise was met with an abundant outpouring of victuals for the men and an overflowing of fodder for our animals.

"After a short rest, at about one in the morning, we were back on the hunt, with strict orders to keep our command well closed up that we might not become separated on the dark night. We made the final approach to Murfreesboro before the chickens were up, undetected by our adversary. Our scouts snuck in behind their outlying pickets, taking them captive without betraying our presence or firing a shot.

"The Colonel, with torch in hand, feeling pert, looking and sounding like a giant, or some king astride his handsome charger in the flickering light, made a final inspection of the troop before we engaged the enemy and whilst we were yet outside their hearing. 'Men,' he addressed us riding cavalierly down the line, 'some of you know this is my forty-first birthday. There is only one thing I would ask of you as my present, the capture of the entire Yankee garrison in occupation of this fine southern town. Reports have it that the enemy is holding some of the brave and loyal Secessionist citizenry in the jailhouse awaiting the gallows. Now we ain't gonna let that happen to our own people, are we?' he asked, to which we replied with a resounding 'No!'

'Your unit commanders have explained the plan. We'll split into three equal columns riding four abreast,' the Colonel said. 'The Yanks have played right into our waiting hands, with their force divided between two encampments on either side of town. Colonel Wharton's command will attack the garrison of the Seventh Pennsylvania Cavalry and the Ninth Michigan Infantry. I'll lead the attack on the headquarters and the jail, to capture the commander and effect the release of the prisoners, whilst the remainder with Colonel Lawton, take the other garrison made of the Third Minnesota Infantry and the Loyalist Kentucky Light Artillery where they're stationed by the river on the far end of town`. I want those artillery pieces. They don't yet know we're anywhere here abouts, so hit 'em hard and quick before they can regroup. Don't hesitate to slice 'em thin with your butter knives and shoot ole' Dutchy down like the lackey dog he is. If'n ye' git hit, stay on your horse if at all possible, he'll naturally take ye' out of harm's way. If your animal should go down, grab another'n. The ox is harnessed, so now we must plow! Prepare to advance the column!' With that, he wheeled his mount and put the spurs to his side, shouting, 'For the honor of your wives and mothers and for the Confederacy, forward men and mix with 'em!'

"Behavior is always more telling than speech," Pappy continued. "You could judge the nature of a commander's ferocity and intelligence by how he employed his troops in battle. I've heard it said you never really know a person 'til you've either worked, or slept with 'em. I'd amend that simply by saying we only fully came to know ourselves, our leader and our messmates when our nature was unfailingly tested of common suffering and danger, like good steel refined through fire.

"As a part of Colonel Forrest's escort, Will and I were in the vanguard that assaulted the town. With the Eighth Texas in the forefront, we moved at a trot up the Liberty Pike, 'til comin' in view of the Federal campfires, where we broke into a gallop. In a charge against a fortified position, there are always some who are reluctant, holding back. You could but drive around them, careening through the formation, closing with the enemy.

"As we sped past the first camp, Colonel Wharton's Texans turned their horses off the road and spurred 'em amongst the tents of our surprised foe, firin' into the faces of the half dressed persons emergin' through the canvas flaps. We rode on toward town. The Rebel yell and firing from the attack on the camp encountered first east of town, along with the thundering of our steel clad hooves on the macadamized turnpike, like the fury of an approaching storm, alerted the garrison inside Murfreesboro to our approach. Our formation split just within the outskirts of town, with Lieutenant Colonel James T. Morrison, leading half off in the direction of the courthouse and headquarters, whilst we dashed for the jailhouse. Colonel Forrest took a small detachment, riding straight through the hotel doors, searching for the Yankee command.

"There was a makeshift breastwork of cotton bales and various sized wooden casks thrown up in front of the brick jailhouse, from behind which Union troops steadily fired at our rapidly approaching lines. It didn't then look none to good for our side. As we poured through the streets with Lieutenant Colonel Arthur Hood bravely at our head, we met a galling musket fire that emptied several saddles around me. The bloodletting increased as Federal snipers, perched in upper story windows, expertly picked even more men from the saddle. But, the fortunes of war are ever changing.

"Prince was swift and never liked to follow behind another horse, so he raced ahead of the pack. If I had any talent, it was that I could see an opening in a defensive line almost before it appeared and Prince was a horse who'd respond with celerity to my command, speeding through a gap like one billiard ball squeezing by another'n, hugging the rail, heading for the pocket with but a hair's breadth to spare. We shot through a looming gap we spotted in the makeshift breastworks, finding ourselves behind the Federal line with others following hot on our heels. I fanned the hammer of my Navy sixer, perfectly riddling one tallow-faced Federal who dropped, drenched in his own blood, instantly finding war's peace.

A trooper riding next to me was hit but remained in the saddle, leaving his head bobbing on his shoulders like a marionette loose on its strings."

Reliving the experience in his memory, the texture of Pappy's voice changed, as a lump seemed to rise in his throat, causing me to involuntarily clear my own throat in an effort to help him regain his usual, familiar tone. He slowly did.

"At this point a number of Michigan soldiers barricaded themselves inside both the brick courthouse and jail, opening up on us with a telling crossfire. I sadly watched one gut-shot fellow, Fred Koerper, who was from Germantown and had accompanied our Memphis recruiting trip, as he lay in the kindred dust of the street, wrestling himself to death from the pain. We were kept pinned tightly down behind cover by a blistering barrage, unable to render him any aid. During the ensuing firefight however I drew a steady bead and dropped more'n one Yank as they fired at us out of elevated windows.

"We could hear shooting and screams coming from inside the jail, as the guards tried to gun down their captives still locked in their cells. Then the bastards set fire to the building with the prisoners yet trapped behind bars, before themselves vacating the premises out the back door, under covering fire from adjacent structures, taking all the keys with 'em. By the time we busted down the front door with a railroad tie, the fire was under good headway, threatening to burn the poor captives alive and choke us all with its thick, black smoke. I surprised a lone Federal who'd taken refuge in an interior closet when I jerked open the door he was hid behind whilst searching for something to fight the fire with. I had my saber in hand and such a scream as issued forth from his lungs when I ran him clean through the breast, as much out of fright as anything, shocked me to temporary inaction as he fell gasping, dead at my feet. But the urgency of the fire wouldn't allow me to long consider his sad fate. Using a length of steel someone brought in as a pry-bar, half a dozen of us stout fellers managed to force the heavy door just enough for the frightened, but grateful captives to slip through. We rushed out of the choking inferno, coughing and spitting, just as Colonel Forrest rode up. As we emerged from the smoking building, I noticed that the streets had filled with the families of the freed prisoners, who rushed tearfully to the sides of their beloved men-folk, ignoring the inherent danger of bullets still filling the smoky air. This caused our boys to raise the cry, 'Long live the Southern woman!' Deeply touched by the scene, wiping tears and soot from my stinging eyes, I'll never forget how the Colonel appeared astride his steed. He was flushed and much excited, eyes afire, hair sticking out from beneath his hat at all angles."

I couldn't help but smile to myself as Pappy's descriptions reminded me of Johnny's earlier red, tear streaked and grimy cheeks.

"You men mount up and come with me,' he shouted, spurring his horse off ahead of us, leaving us to scramble aboard our own animals and follow in the wake of he and his handful of personal body guard. We galloped through the streets heading west out of town, where we overtook him en route to where Colonel Lawton and his detachment had stalled in their attack against the encampment on the east bank of the Stone River. As we rode upon the scene, Union cannon were firing into the adjacent timberline at the hidden Confederates. I watched as Forrest's analytical mind quickly sized up the situation after but brief conference with his subordinates. He immediately ordered the First Georgia and a company each of Tennessee and Secessionist Kentuckians to ride around the camp and attack from the opposite side. At eleven o'clock we heard the noise and saw the growing flames as they set fire to the Federal tents. We could here the holler, rapid fire of rounds cooking off in the blaze.

"Just past noon, as some of us were taking our repast, officers rode in from the direction of town telling the Colonel that a telegraph was surely sent before we cut the lines and we had but precious little time before Federal reinforcements arrived down the rail line. They urged him to cut his losses and get out whilst the getting was yet good. At that point, Forrest's ire was aroused, as if he'd lost his reason and he asked distinctly and succinctly, 'Has

God given you second sight that you can predict the future? I did not come here to make half a job of it. I will have them all!' Then, firing his pistol in the air to punctuate his statement, he ordered our men to hold their fire until his return and with that, raced back through Murfreesboro with his remaining troops and us in tow, headed for the camps of the Pennsylvanians and Michiganers.

"He ordered a ceasefire as we rode up and sent a hastily scribbled note to their commander, one Colonel Parkhurst, saying the troops on the opposite end of town had already succumb to our superior number and that unless he received their immediate unconditional surrender, he'd have every man put to the sword. He added, that, with his vastly larger force, there was no hope of sustained resistance. He concluded that he simply wished to avoid further effusion of blood. This was, of course, all bluster, but keen poker. The silencing of attritions from the direction of town and beyond, left the Union commander with the strong impression that it was true and in his confused and isolated position, not being himself a poker player, he had no way of knowing our strength, or what a bluffer he was up against. Parkhurst received the message and reluctantly surrendered. With that, our commander again wheeled his horse and with all the additional troops freed from further engagement east of town, we sped back through Murfreesboro, to the assistance of our Colonel Lawton and his troopers besieging the western camp.

"Once arrived, Colonel Forrest set about to achieve his final bluff and complete the victory. He sent another message to Union Colonel Henry C. Lester, similar to the one he had delivered to Parkhurst, adding the flourish of signing it 'Brigadier General N.B. Forrest,' even before his promotion, though in the works, was yet to be finalized, perhaps thinking that if there was any doubt in his abilities left amongst the Congress, this victory might just cinch it.

"Lester, himself a poker player, wasn't quite so easily bluffed. He sought assurance that his counterpart opposite town had indeed forfeited and also wished to reconnoiter our strength. Playing straight into Bedford's plan, he requested to be allowed to inspect the condition of the balance of the Union command and to visit with his captured superior, Colonel Duffield, who lay wounded in the home of a local citizen. Our Colonel agreed and had us escort Lester through Murfreesboro, making no attempt to blindfold him or his accompanying staff, or in any way prevent his seeing the number of our command. On the contrary, he sent riders ahead with orders to move troops through the streets in a manner that exaggerated our strength before the eyes of Forrest's Federal counterpart, as he passed by the same Confederate soldiers several times. His own staff, his commander's staffs, as well as Duffield himself, recommended that Lester surrender in the face of such long strategic odds.

"Will, having as I, witnessed all this first hand, reminded me never, ever get in a poker game with our commander!"

"For true!" I agreed.

"Will further stated, after watching me through the heat of the earlier action, 'I hate to put the cabosh on your spirits John, but we need to talk,' he said, fixing me with his clear blue eyes that stood out brightly in the background of his weather bronzed and powder stained face. I could tell by the profound look and tone, he had something important to say. 'There are fellows who run around thinking they're near invincible, kinda' like that Colonel,' he began, referring to Forrest, 'until, one day the sword finds 'em, or they catch a bullet. Then they all wear that same dumb look, like they think some terrible mistake's been made. I don't want to end up seein' that look on you, little brother. It's a sick little universe. We're all just fragile mortals who die. This here ain't no game. Life is short, but once't you're dead, you're a long time dead.' He concluded, 'Start out like ye' can hold out lad, lest we soon loose ye.'

"I agreed with his assessment, promising to take it to heart. I remember looking up at the sky and seeing the smoke hovering low like a thin white sheet, whilst Will bound up my slashed left hand that I had no idea how I'd injured, thinking all the while what had rendered Cain accursed. My right hand shook slightly with a tremor from the post-action afterglow as we shared a canteen. I felt washed out and wasn't sure if the taste of tin came from the water in the canteen, or my mouth as result of the adrenaline that had so recently been coursing through my veins.

"What was said to've happened next, I cannot say for sure, cause in the aftermath of battle, we were far too busy loading captured supplies and tending to the wounded and prisoners. A rumor was soon circulating in that night's camp concerning some of the Colonel's actions that day, about which their were two schools of thought, amongst the minority of whom Will and I sided. He was said to've kilt two nigras. One out of self defense, cause the fellow, a camp follower, emptied a revolver at the Colonel as he rode through the Michigan bivouac after receiving their surrender, one of the pistol balls in fact cutting the Colonel's hat band. The other incident, said to be to his credit, though I'd say to his discredit, is the more disturbing. Word around the campfires was that a light-skinned colored was brought on horseback before him. In typical style, Forrest asked the feller in a flourish of profanity what and who he thought he was, to be riding such a fine horse. The unlucky lad explained he was a servant in the company of a certain Pennsylvania officer, whom he named. At that point, the story goes, in a fit of rage, the Colonel said, 'I spit in your eye sir!' afore whipping out his hog-leg to relieve the poor youngster of most his brains, toppling him limply to the ground in a heap. The story goes, he then added the dead nigra's fine looking Morgan to his own personal herd of spare mounts.

"Whatever truly happened, the Colonel did in fact hang several nigras found under arms in Murfreesboro and again later in nearby Gallatin. He had no trouble finding volunteers for the detail from the less enlightened, easily influenced amongst the rank and file, who bore an unquenchable hatred for coloreds.

"Forrest had become awash with income through the trade in nigras and he considered them no more than chattel. He dictated policy after the raid on Murfreesboro concerning non-combatant coloreds found in employment of the Union Army. They were to be considered runaways and his orders sought to return them to their 'rightful' owners.

"Altogether it seemed rather harsh to my brother's and my way of thinkin', but the result was, nigras seemed much less friendly with Yankees throughout middle Tennessee for a good spell thereafter. And, if we'd have treated 'em like prisoners of war, the abolitionists could have held our poor captured boys hostage in exchange for slaves.

"The story of the murder I don't doubt to be true. He looked mighty worked up when I seen him and perhaps it was as simple as his being caught in the throws of a fierce bloodlust. Whatever happened made for an issue that long plagued Forrest and caused him to grapple with the implications of nigra involvement in the ongoing Federal efforts to subdue the South, compelling him to set an example that would impart a lesson to coloreds across both the upper and lower states. In his defense, I never witnessed first hand such bloody acts by him, though I later had occasion to stir up hatred toward myself amongst some of our own boys, who were, 'til then, my sworn brothers, when I intervened to spare unarmed captured coloreds at Fort Pillow after the Colonel, by then a Major General, was credited with giving the order, 'No quarter, kill the damn niggers, cut 'em down, shoot 'em all!'--- But, that's a whole 'nother story.

"Despite mine and Will's own reservations toward such wholesale killing of unarmed captives, it meant something to ride with Forrest. We were proud to go and do what other units would not, or could not do. Our hectic day in Murfreesboro garnered us six much needed artillery pieces that remained under Forrest's command for the duration of the war, plus many additional small arms with accompanying ammunition, six-hunert mules and horses and various sundry military equipage.

"The war was brought home that day to many more families, as we lost some twenty-five men killed and another approximately fifty wounded, compared to twenty-nine dead Federals, four or five of which I personally dispatched to the next world by my own hands, plus a hunert-twenty more wounded and between twelve to fifteen-hunert disarmed prisoners. We ravaged the rail lines, burned the depot, left the jail gutted and destroyed such supplies as we could not carry off. The Colonel made a deal with the captive Yanks to help us transport our booty to McMinnville, in exchange for parole there, which they happily and heartily agreed to, cheering loudly, 'Hooray for General Forrest!' All in all, it was a fitting birthday present for our commander. Haversacks stuffed to overflowing, any pursuers could have easily followed the track of our egress from the spillage left along the trail," Poppy concluded, spitting into the yard, before falling again quiet.

"Wow!" Johnny exclaimed with a sigh, his mouth hanging agape.

Night birds called out in the darkness beyond the porch light that now began to fade as the coal oil burned low. We sat quietly, considering the implications of all that had transpired that hot July day nearly half a century before. The lamp was still glowing from the window of Mammy's bedroom and her rocker softly creaked on the old floorboards.

Pappy put away his knife and tossed away the used up cedar toothpick that he had fashioned with his whittling. He tugged on the braided leather strap at his waist, drawing out the gold-plated timepiece from his watch pocket, snapping open its cover to reveal the ivory colored face with its twelve Roman numerals. "Quarter of eight," he stated flatly, "church in the mornin'."

With that we sat then silent for a long spell, listening to and relishing the whole of the evening.

Much to our surprise, after some little time, he said, "I reckon we've got a little spell afore bedtime."

Johnny glanced over at me with a grin that told it all. We expected that he'd further share his reminiscence if the porch lamp didn't burn out first. It dimmed and brightened, flickering in its struggle to tap the last drops of fuel.

"Johnny, fetch us some more oil for that lantern and I'll tell ya'll about the vigorous cat and mouse game that ensued after Murfreesboro, with the rolls reversing at regular intervals."

"Yes sir!" he responded with great enthusiasm, hurrying to the fuel reservoir with the barely glowing light, leaving us mostly in the dark but for the dim glow from within Mammy's porch-side window. Pappy and I left our seats and felt our way down the steps out into the yard by the gentle luminance filtering through her curtains, to relieve ourselves under the multitude of glistening stars high overhead. We lingered by the fence at yard's edge, staring at the constellation of blinking fireflies that filled the lower sky of the moonless night. By the time we started back up the steps, Johnny was returned with the light, again illuminating for us the path back to our seats on the porch. We all regained our stations, while Pappy cut another plug and slowly worked up a mouth full of dark saliva that he sent streaming over the rail beyond the lantern's reach. The renewed glow of the restored wick, which rested in a suspended lamp holder screwed high on the wall several feet away from where we sat, drew the attention of the swarming night bugs, while casting a fresh atmosphere to his forum. Then, in his own good time, that neither of us rushed, he rejoined the unfinished episode of his story.

"We rested ourselves and our horses until the eighteenth at McMinnville, after paroling well over a thousand Yanks, all but the officers. The parolees were honor bound by the conventional code of warfare, to return home to their kin, across the Ohio River and remain as noncombatants until such time as a prisoner exchange could be effected between the two apposing gov'ments, when, 'by the rules' they could return to the hardship of army life. Their officers were forwarded to General Bragg's Headquarters in Chattanooga.

"In a short address to the troops before our departure, he stated, 'Most of you men and your fine animals performed admirably, holding nothing back. Those of you who didn't had best take heed of your associates. Oat up your horses boys and take ye' rest, for this is but a short respite. We'll be back in the saddle within four days. We're going after a detachment of five-hunert Federal cavalrymen and their horses, reported in camp not too far distant from here,' Forrest promised with certain glee. By the end of three days, most all detachments had rejined with us and we outnumbered our next intended quarry by two to one, at which time we started underway down the Lebanon Turnpike on a fifty-mile march. One thing you learn from hunting that's similar to warfare is you can't always go about your leisure, expecting an opportunity to exist beyond the moment that you first recognize it, so must act decisively, accordingly, without hesitation, for oh the regret and cost of some lost possibilities.

"Arriving at Lebanon on the heels of the departing Federal cavalry, they had too much of a head start to facilitate our overtaking them. Frustrated at his quarry's escape, our commander conducted an interview with a loyalist minded blacksmith of the town who had shod many of their horses and been handsomely rewarded by the Yanks with a pocket full of Federal dollars. Here, the Colonel proved once again he could be hard and mean. When asked by Forrest where the escaped brigade was headed, in hopes of intercepting them along their route, the burly fellow told him in a somewhat disrespectful manner, 'Colonel, I'd rather go to hell than tell you that,' at which point Forrest drew his revolver and without further warning, saying only, 'I'll be glad to oblige you sir,' granted the brave man's wish, shooting him directly between the eyes. To those present that witnessed the event, he said only by way of explanation, 'You can't wage war using half measures.' Much as life itself, you might say, he was hard, but he was fair, in that he was equally hard on everyone, black, white, Federalist and Sesech' alike.

"The General,' as we'd took to callin' him by then, led us en route the next day to the Hermitage, for a brief visit to the home of former President Andrew Jackson, where we were allowed the better part of the early afternoon to wander as tourists through the grounds and groves. It was perhaps similar to what one might expect heaven to look like, replete with angelic maidens. Properly accompanied by an undermanned contingent of gentlemen companions, twelve young ladies had miraculously picked that same day, the first anniversary of Manassas, to spend picnicking amongst the aged cedars. Imagine our surprise, whilst a half dozen of us, including Will, Herman Culpepper and meself, wandered luckily upon the scene of their festivities and, upon seeing our well-worn cavalry attire, were excitedly invited to jine them. Their grace, gentility and generosity made us think for a moment perhaps we'd been slain on the field of combat and were now come to the pastures of the warrior's paradise. But too soon the bugle called assembly and amongst, in a few cases, tearful supplication, we reluctantly returned to the duty that made us such heros in the unfathomable depths of their approving eyes. On our rejinin' the unit, N. B. said only, 'I believe you boys was eyein' them gals like a hungry man looks at a steak!'

"Climbing back in the saddle, we departed the Hermitage, headed in the direction of Nashville. Scouts soon overtook us, informing our General that Federal General Nelson had arrived in Murfreesboro from Nashville in pursuit of us, shortly after our departure from those precincts. It was determined that in light of the reduced garrison at Nashville, we should move there forthwith to test the strength and determination of the remaining defenders. We rejined the course of the Stone River, following it to within seven miles of Nashville where we encountered Union pickets. General Forrest ordered a charge that captured a portion and drove back into the city the balance of our blue clad opponents. Unbeknownst to us at the time, a marauding band of Tennessee guerillas had simultaneously attacked from the opposite end of town, giving the Federal garrison the impression they were under general assault. As result, we could hear in the distance our enemy's drums play the long roll, calling all to arms and their posts.

"Concentrating our strength, we then moved against a Federal outpost guarding the bridges over Mill Creek, capturing some twenty prisoners and pursuing the remainder up the creek bed where an additional forty men were outflanked and captured. Burning both road bridges in our wake, we moved a further distance up the channel to the rail lines at Antioch Station, where the Federals had determined to make a stand and protect this vital crossing. Colonel Walker and his Eighth Texas quickly routed the demoralized Yanks, capturing another thirty-five prisoners and their accompanying arms and munitions. We again torched the trestle, some rolling stock on a sidetrack and the depot full of stored supplies.

"A platoon was dispatched southeast a short distance down the rail line in the direction of Murfreesboro where they destroyed another trestle, toppled a water tower and burned a quantity of split wood stacked by the tracks for train fuel. They returned after only a couple hours with fifteen more Yanks, each escorting a captive apiece.

"We then moved cross country, prisoners in tow, through the lush pastures, dismantling fences along the way to accommodate our passage to the Murfreesboro/Nashville Turnpike, where we again rejined with our scouts. Cattle raised their lazy heads, ruminating thoughtfully as they watched us pass, then again bent to their grazing.

"The scouts informed Forrest that Nelson and his thirty-five hunert troops were proceeding with all haste back up the turnpike from Murfreesboro in an attempt to cut off our retreat. By that time the sun was settling behind the western mountains and the entire command, both men and animals, were fagged out from a full day that had included everything from socializing with the fairest daughters of the Confederacy to whipping the Yankees multiple times without loss of a single man and coming as close as four miles from the capital building. We repaired a short distance down the turnpike in the direction of the approaching adversary before following our scouts down a dim neighborhood road that off-shot the main thoroughfare. Some safe distance down this by-way called 'the Chicken Road,' we dismounted for a well-earned rest. After grooming and feeding our weary mounts, we took a brief repast of cold hardtack before lying down, not to sleep, but only doze, ready at an instant to remount should the enemy, whom we could hear moving noisily by for hours out on the turnpike toward Nashville, discover our place of hiding. General Forrest worked deep into the night paroling our captives.

"With our pursuers passed in the darkness, we continued the next morning in the direction of Murfreesboro. Shortly after regaining the highway, we were informed by our hard riding scouts that Nelson had been apprised of our movements and was countermarching again in the direction of Murfreesboro. We shared hardy laughs picturing the poor foot-sore Federal infantrymen, tongues lolling out, trying haplessly to catch us, mounted as we were on racehorses. We turned off the pike six miles before Murfreesboro, again allowing our frustrated pursuers to pass on into the sight of our previous raid, whilst we moved, in due time, on to McMinnville where we again rested until August tenth.

"Finding orders awaiting him in McMinnville to proceed forthwith to Chattanooga, he and his escort, including Will and I, were soon back in the saddle in accompaniment of our commander on the long arduous journey through the steep country. It was seventy-five miles as the crow flies, but our horses were not of the winged variety, so the round trip seemed nearer two hunert. We arrived at Braggs new headquarters in Chattanooga to find the Army of Mississippi, soon to be renamed the Army of Tennessee, arriving daily by rickety railcars via the circuitous route required by the surrender of Corinth, going first from Tupelo down to Mobile, Alabama, then across't to Montgomery and up to Atlanta, Georgia before turning northeast back up to Chattanooga. The Supreme Commander was gathering his forces in preparation for an offensive in conjunction with General Kirby Smith, striking deep into the heart of the Kentucky bluegrass country.

"The first order of business on our whirlwind journey was the official promotion of the Colonel to the rank of Brigadier General, the commission postdated July twenty-first, 1862. Secondly, Bragg informed Forrest that he would require the services of his cavalry to scout the advance of his army, as well as, screen his movement and interdict any attempts by Buell to pursue. With that, we were put immediately back in the saddle hurrying to rejine our regiment in middle Tennessee. By the time we caught up with the boys, my hindquarters had calluses atop of calluses from the interminable hours in the saddle. Whilst under temporary command of Lieutenant Colonel Hood of the Second Georgia, the regiment had been obliged to fall back to Sparta, then Smithville and finally

Woodbury under pressure from three thousand pursuing infantry and eight-hunert blue cavalry.

"Stepping down upon our arrival to let our horses blow but for a very few hours, the General again had the entire command underway back in the direction of Murfreesboro. Skillfully weaving around the forces arrayed against us, being nearly trapped on two separate instances when, except for brief advance warning from our videttes, we made a last moment dash, we thoroughly interdicted the railroad between Manchester and Tullahoma, burning all the bridges and capturing a twenty-man picket at Morrison Station. We thence proceeded down the branch line in the direction of McMinnville, destroying all bridgeworks to within ten miles of said place. Feeling tired, but satisfied with our destructive enterprise, we retired from the vicinity and awaited the arrival of Bragg's advance forces to come through the pass at Altamont.

"We pitched camp by a creek in a cove at the foot of the Cumberlands and sent forth scouts to reconnoiter the pass. I took a well-earned sleep that night that only partially renewed my vigor or relieved my aching joints and muscles. But, as I've learnt', there's just one thing that doesn't vary, everything is temporary.

"Returning at first light, our scouts reported to the General and his staff with the alarming news that the Feds, under General McCook, were planted firmly astride the path of Bragg's Confederate Army at the approaches to and the height of the summit, separating us from our planned juncture. Other scouts came in soon after daybreak with more alarming news. Federal infantry columns were advancing toward our trapped position on all three roads converging at our camp from Manchester, McMinnville and Winchester.

"With our line of retreat through the mountain passes cut off and largely outnumbered, the situation looked despairing. With no time for delay, the General had us formed up in line four abreast. We advanced a short distance down the McMinnville Road toward one of the approaching columns. There we turned aside to a deep, dry creek bed that paralleled the road. Using the covering overhang of the rocky watercourse, we bypassed the unsuspecting Federals, who marched by our sheltered position less than six-hunert yards distant. At their passing, we emerged from the wood and galloped some seven, or eight miles, to within approximately another eight miles of the town, where we took a shortcut on a neighborhood road over to the McMinnville/Murfreesboro Pike. Here we encountered a troop of Federals drawn up in line of battle across our path. Raising a loud cheer, we bypassed their opposition by leaving the road and taking to the fields in a sweeping move that left them wondering where we'd disappeared to.

"Finally free from the jaws of the near-sprung trap in which we'd found ourselves, we took a more leisurely pace the remaining distance to Sparta, where, early on September third, we rode into the camps with the forward units of Bragg's army.

"Finding their path blocked by McCook's firmly entrenched position atop the pass at Altamont, the Army of Mississippi, by then officially known as the Army of Tennessee, had backed up and gone round, coming across through passes further east.

"It's said there is no rest for the weary and never was it more true than at that time. With the shoes of our entire command in disrepair, I, along with my fellow smithies, spent the balance of the afternoon trimming and shoeing many of the horses in our company. The long days in the saddle, compounded by the strenuous work stooping and lifting horses feet, caused me to severely strain my lower back. At that point I swore I'd somehow get relief from farrier duty, which opportunity soon provided by way of a befriended Yank prisoner.

"As our infantry resumed its advance, we kept scouts constantly in the field ahead of the army, gathering information of enemy dispositions and reporting all back to headquarters. Under the temporary command of your namesake," Pappy said, directing his attention to me, "General Leonidas Polk, we crossed the state line into Kentucky and our cavalry assisted in the capture of a Federal infantry brigade at Munfordville. We destroyed the tracks of the Louisville and Nashville Road and burned the bridges for several miles.

"We had been actively engaged for better than sixty days, marching on average thirty miles a day and both men and horses were greatly jaded. Whilst sallying forth on this particular foray, Forrest's horse stumbled and fell in the dark of night, rolling over and severely dislocating the General's right shoulder. This caused us great concern, but in typical style he soundly cursed the offending jug-head for being a 'stumble-footed oaf' and remounted to continue the march.

"We reached Bardstown late in September, where again orders awaited General Forrest to report forthwith to General Bragg in Chattanooga. Delaying only a few days, long enough to thoroughly rest the men and horses, Will and I again departed in the General's vanguard to re-cross the lawless regions of a disputed territory.

"As a matter of formality, because of, first, the confusion associated with personnel records after all the preceding outfit reorganizations; second, the further concentration of the whole, vast Army of Tennessee in the vicinity of Bardstown and thirdly, the nearing end of our original enlistment term, Will and me was encouraged to formally reenlist. We added our names, on the twenty-seventh, to the rolls of Company E, formerly of Colonel, by then General Wharton's Eighth Tennessee Regiment. Even so, we continued to have problems getting our mail until well after October, when our names were at long last removed from where they erroneously still appeared as 'absent' on the muster rolls of the original Second Arkansas, who had by then been reorganized, becoming newly designated as Slemon's Fourth Arkansas. The paymaster presented us with our back pay, plus a fifty-dollar bounty for reenlistment.

"Desiring a change from the back killing labors of a blacksmith, the soreness from which my brain was constantly reminded that it was attached to a hard working body, I gave to the company's officer filling out the documents, my occupation as musician, which I proudly demonstrated for the skeptics within hearing. Being always industrious and having scrounged a bugle off a Yank captive who taught me how to blow on it some tentative notes and commands, I'd continued to improve my hand until I could proficiently play nearly all the simple tunes of the duty. Another officer from a distant company came rushing up on his mount in a cloud of dust, wanting to know, 'who was the damn fool blowing false commands?' to which General Wharton replied, 'Our new bugler.' I got the job.

"Having seen the cruelty with which the families of even suspected Confederate sympathizers were treated, as well as the immense number of paper-chasin' clerks accompanying a United States Army Corp, we were obliged to not give the true, present identity of our homes, for fear our families would be visited by official Federal wrath should occupation reach their environs. When Will and I were captured during future operations in '63, we would state, to protect the true identity and location of our folks, that we hailed from the location of that day's muster, Cannon County, Tennessee. We also earnestly professed to our captors to be conscripts, not volunteers.

"We did in fact still have family residing in the district, but of another name than Ledbetter. Our mother's older sister, Mary Louisa Yarber Johnson and her elderly husband Mr. Sam Johnson, were prominent citizens of Woodbury. We enjoyed their immense hospitality whilst briefly garrisoned there. They made it abundantly clear to Will and me that we did indeed have a second home with them should we ever need one.

"After three days hard march, as much up as down, we reported to Headquarters Chattanooga, where much to our dismay and disbelief, General Forrest was again relieved by the aptly named Bragg, from command of the regiment that he had raised and used to such advantage in disrupting the activity of a largely numerical superior enemy force. His and our recruiting skills were again to be employed, this time in middle Tennessee, to raise yet another new regiment of cavalry.

"It's often said that Forrest and Bragg didn't see eye to eye. I can personally vouch for this in that General Forrest stood six-foot two, whilst Bragg was nearly a full head shorter than his subordinate and always had to look up to our commander whether seated, or standing.

"Because of Buell's retreat in the direction of Nashville with his occupying forces, we returned to the vicinity of Murfreesboro, arriving in the nick of time to extinguish fires set to the courthouse and several residences by his recently withdrawn rearguard. General Forrest, not wishing to draw further Federal wrath against any of the citizenry, established headquarters in the fire damaged public building rather than a private residence and we earnestly set about the task of gathering to the General a new force with which to carry war to the enemy."

With the coming of the nine o'clock hour, so too the approach of a long, westbound express train, whose engine passed through Kingsland and on, the whistle of which could be heard in the cool night air blowing clear out on the trestle over Moro, while the clickety-clack of the trailing cars still rattled back in town.

"We came to love the generous spirits and open armed hospitality of the Tennessee people," he said above the distant din of the railway. "They were called 'volunteers' not only for their willingness to be thrown into a contest, but also for the forthcoming indulgence by so many of them to our wants and needs, giving freely even before asked." Spitting his spent chaw into the darkness beyond the lamp glow, Pappy rose, unfolding his tall frame and stretching his old bones that popped in protest of the exertion.

"You boys have been a mighty good audience for an old man's tales and don't think I don't appreciate it," he stated frankly.

"Thank you, sir," we answered, in unison.

Noticing Mammy's lamp extinguished, he added, "But now it's time for bed. Run along home afore your pa comes down the road worried and lookin' for ye'. Say your prayers like good boys and tell your folks, Good Lord a'willin', we'll see ya'll before church in the mornin'."

We reluctantly vacated our chairs and in turn hugged the old gentleman's neck, expressing our love for him and bidding a good night. He said to our departure, "I'll keep the lamp on and watch for ya'll 'til ye' round the curve."

We strolled slowly out the gate onto the dirt road, whose dim borders we could just make out as our eyes adjusted to the twinkling starlight. An owl called hauntingly from above our heads. Before we rounded the road bend in the direction of home, where we would soon be able to view our own lit porch lamp, I looked back to see him still leaning against a post at the top of the steps, with what appeared as a shining hallow around his form, backlit as he still was by his own glowing porch lantern.

Leadbetter John

Co. D , 8 (Smith's)
Tennessee Cavalry.
(Confederate.)

Musician | Private

REFERENCE SLIP.

is filed with

Leadbetter John

Leadbetter W.

Co. D , 8 (Smith's)
Tennessee Cavalry.
(Confederate.)

Private | Private

REFERENCE SLIP.

is filed with

Leadbetter William

175

Again to Storm the Heights

With the coming of September and the fall, so, too, came the new school term. In 1910, the government was yet to declare Labor Day as a national holiday. So, on the morrow, after finishing all the chores of a typical Monday morning, we children of age would report to the schoolhouse less than two miles distant in nearby Kingsland. This knowledge weighed heavy like impending doom on my mind that first Sabbath in September.

As the elder brother, Johnny was responsible for most chores around our home-place, while I was detailed to attend to the daily tasks on Pappy and Mammy's neighboring spread. This meant I spent most nights at their home, except Saturday, when on the following Sabbath, all but the chores essential to the care of the livestock were left for another day. On Sunday mornings we were allowed the luxury of lying in bed until the sun shone brightly in the window. Most nights through the week, while staying at the home of my grandparents, I had my own private bedroom, but back at my parent's house on Saturday nights, I shared a bed with my big brother. On each new Lord's Day, I always hoped to snatch a few more minutes sleep from the clutches of another dawn, but the happy mockingbird could not wait, singing noisily at our window all the various melodies he borrowed from the several other species common of our region.

The house was a flurry of activity with our mother, who we always called Mommy, preparing our younger siblings for church meeting, followed by Sunday school. While she continued her struggles with the uncooperative toddlers, the men of the house, of whom I became officially a part upon turning eleven, leisurely sipped saucers of hot, black coffee after finishing our breakfast, resting easy in the sure knowledge that our own final preparations for worship would be much less time consuming, requiring only the donning of clean pants and shirt, running a comb through our oily hair and giving our dusty boots a thorough final wipe down with a well-used, oil-saturated rag.

Eventually, John and I would fetch Sparky from his stall in the barn, to set him in his harness and traces, then hitch him to the wagon, with plenty of time left for the young ones to clamber noisily aboard from all sides, a familiar racket that no longer startled the Sumpter mule. Then, with all crowded in close together, we proceeded down the road in the direction of the tall, white, frame church house built in 1890 to replace of the original old log one, circa the 1850's. En route we rode past Pappy and Mammy's home, where we paused long enough for them to join us up in the buckboard for the short balance of the trip.

I leapt out to tie off the mule when we pulled into the crowded churchyard already filled with sundry other teams and wagons. There were a handful of neighborhood girls huddled together by the steps in their rustling, white dresses. I noticed how they immediately caught Johnny's eye and his full, undivided attention. Being not yet much interested in such matters, I rolled my eyes in self-righteous disgust at the newly acquired silliness on his part. We slowly unloaded our wagon full of family members, both old and young, then all entered into the Lord's house together in a single file. When we came to our familiar pew on the left side near the front, Johnny filed in first, with me trailing close behind, Pappy next, then Mammy followed by our mother, Mommy, who kept the little ones corralled between she and our father, Poppy, who always came in last and sat next to the center aisle.

Our pastor was a Methodist circuit rider who, with his tall, disheveled frame and drooping hound-dog eyes, always reminded me of pictures I'd seen of former President Lincoln. Even despite that strong point many might have counted against him, his gentle nature and genuine, abiding concern for his fold, ever endeared him to the hearts of our rural congregation.

For a spell then, sitting quiet and still in the pew between my big brother and my grandpa, watching and listening to the parson's grim warnings, the sad thought of again reentering school was temporarily assuaged by the presence, grace and mighty power of our Lord. After the parson's sermon was finally finished, we joined off-key voices in hymns played on the out-of-tune piano. At my regular weekly request, we almost always sang, among many others, my favorite selection, number one twenty-one in the Cokesbury Book, "Church in the Wildwoods."

But the services, though normally plenty long enough for vigorous boys, weren't in fact that long and I soon found myself again back outside in the bright midday sun, reminded once more of the impending doom awaiting us on the morrow. I looked on school as something akin to a prison term and said as much when asked by Pappy what was eating at me? Knowing perhaps, how the promise of a story would distract me from my cares, he said, "Prison, huh? You don't know nothin' 'bout no prison boy! After our lunch I'll tell ye' what them Yankee 'hotels' was a really like."

Having been both reprimanded and tantalized at the same time, I sat quietly imagining the black and smelly dungeons of Yankee captivity.

We turned our rig back toward home and soon had the entire family unloaded in Pappy and Mammy's front yard, where we proceeded indoors to eat the meal Mammy had mostly prepared the evening prior and had but to rewarm, except to bake a fresh skillet of cornbread to go along with it. While busy visiting with her younger grandchildren and our mother, Mammy accidentally let the cornbread overcook a tad. Our hungry eyes watched as she flipped the steaming, black-bottomed bread from out the round, iron skillet onto a plate in the center of the table and quickly said before Pappy might comment, "It's not burnt, not really, just nice and brown... nice and brown."

I glanced around the table to see silent, tight-lipped smiles spreading on the faces of the three, seated adults. Johnny and I grinned too, as Mammy finally took a seat amongst the gathered clan, before asking her husband to return thanks.

After our dinner was done, the young ones played gypsy circus in the front yard, building a makeshift big top with a few of Mammy's old quilts propped up with beanpoles and broom handles. They paraded the unhappy tomcat about in their toy wagon where he was held captive like a caged lion beneath an upturned potato crate. Baby brother Leali noisily banged on the bottom of a metal pail with a wooden spoon, using it for a drum until Pappy asked him to, "Hush up that confounded racket!" He stared for a moment in stunned silence before tuning up for a cry, having been frightened by the mild, unexpected scolding he received from the normally quiet, white haired, old gentleman. Mammy scowled sternly at her husband before gathering up our little brother into her comforting lap.

After a time, the children were again loaded into the old wagon and taken home by our folks, where as was customary, they all retired for a Sunday afternoon nap. Johnny saddled up the mule soon thereafter and rode off down the rode for a visit to one of the young ladies I'd caught him making eyes at in church when our heads were supposed to've been bowed in prayer. Mammy, too, took the rare opportunity to rest herself from the endless tasks of running a household. This left only Pappy and me sitting together in the porch rockers as the sound of squealing children, still at play in the rear of the receding wagon, faded down the road.

Pappy, saying only that he'd be back directly, ambled inside where I could hear through the open window as he rummaged in his bedroom desk drawer before again returning to the porch with a folded letter that he carried pinched between the fingers of his left hand. He retook his seat and then after unfolding, reviewing and refolding the paper, began his discourse.

"We recrossed the wild country from Kentucky back to middle Tennessee, some hunert-sixty miles in five days time and spent most of October scourin' Murfreesboro and the surroundin' countryside for new recruits. We even tried findin' would-be equestrians amongst some of the infantry units garrisoned in the region. We mounted 'em up on the most long-legged, orneriest, captured Yank horses we had and run 'em quickly through their paces. We derived many a heartfelt belly laugh watchin' the poor flatfoots bouncing gracelessly in the tall saddles, 'til shortly being toppled head over teakettle, where they generally wound up all sprawled out on the ground in a cloud of dust, not too injured to limp away sheepishly whilst our Sergeant bellered out, 'Next up!' in between our gasps of laughter.

"But, within a mere four weeks, with the addition of the Thirty-second Alabama and several companies of young Tennessee Militiamen, along with another thousand fresh levies, we'd again managed to scrape together yet another mounted command for the General's use, our success due as much from the growing fame and reputation of our leader as from our tireless efforts in every hamlet and burg within the surrounding four counties. However, men and horsepower were, as always, only a portion of the equation. Just as with our first regiment put together back around Memphis and Corinth, this command too needed effective weaponry. But as Forrest was most want to do, he intended to glean from our enemies all we lacked. Plunder was a way of life for the Southern cavalryman, much like the Comanche's of the Southwest, living off the prey of our adversaries.

"Before breakin' camp and strikin' out behind enemy lines, the General assembled the troop for an address. 'Men,' he began, 'I wish to welcome ye' all to my command. I say to you in all earnestness, neither I, nor your Captains, are men ye' should trifle with. Let there be no coy dogs amongst ye', nor for that matter, any puffed-up roosters either. I don't cotton to such and have no truck with that sort. Your officers expect ye' to do your duty without hesitation or argument and won't suffer no whining cowards. Those who don't can expect transfer forthwith to the most unpleasant duty possible. You've only to put your trust in God, your officers and me, though not necessarily in that order. Accept your destiny as ordained by the One and the order and discipline imparted to you by the others and you'll find the cavalry to be a happy home for ye'. It surely do beat bein' a blasted flatfoot by a fur piece!'

'And fear not, for he who answers the last muster in the service of his nation's need is of the noblest sort. A life given for one's country is never spent in vain. It blossoms anew in the hearts and freedom won for his people.'

'Right now, I'll be dad blamed if'n ye' ain't the raggedest, most wore out lookin' bunch I believe I ever did see, but the Yankee railroads we're soon to be a'goin' after are strewn with jewels ripe for the pluckin'. A few days from now we'll take some depot, warehouse, or train cars and you'll have ample occasion for re-provisioning. And one more thing afore we strike out. I've found what eventually festers up most relationships is someone gets to thinkin' they're irreplaceable. I promise not to do that and I s'pect the same of ya'll. I welcome ye now to Forrest's Cavalry Regiment. Make me half as proud as I've been of my last two commands and we'll be happier than a whole litter a pups when everybody's got a teat! Good day to ye' then and good huntin'!'

"His rousing speech was met with a grand hooray and 'three cheers for Forrest!' Shortly afterwards, the larger portion of our new command moved out in lockstep, headed in the direction of Nashville, drill weary heads now held high by both men and animals. The new recruits moved to a forward position at the little village of La Verge, only some fifteen miles distant from Nashville.

"Receiving information to that effect, the Union commander in the Tennessee capital, one General Palmer, sent out a large force in an attempt to surprise and capture the unsuspecting greenhorns. Following a well-laid plan of attack, he succeeded in routing the new levies, who fled back down the road in our direction of Murfreesboro. Receiving word of the impending catastrophe, two-hunert veterans quickly accompanied the General in a flying column, racing to stem the tide of reversal that seemed rapidly attempting to overturn all our most recent efforts. We found the turnpike swarming with our unarmed refugees, many in nothing but their nightshirts, who reported the Federals were hot on their heels, mopping up all they encountered. Deploying our force in a strong position on a ridge across't the road, we watched the enemy appear, then suddenly cease their pursuit and turn 'bout-face back in the direction from whence they'd just come. We followed them close into LaVerge, where the fleeing blue coats abandoned their fresh won prize, marching quickly back toward the safety of Nashville. Once't more the General had just managed to avert impending disaster, barely retrieving from capture the larger portion of his men, animals and irreplaceable equipage.

"Gathering the remnant of his scattered flock back to the forward outpost in LaVerge, we soon again managed a field ready force totaling near thirty-five hunert strong. Wishing to quickly remove the hanged-dog looks from the faces of his freshly spanked volunteers, we immediately struck out from there, rapidly interdicting the railroads into Nashville at every juncture. As the General had promised, we began shaping our troop into one of greater military bearing as homespun and squirrel rifles were effectively replaced with Federal gear from stores and armories captured as we swept right up to the very outskirts of the Tennessee capital. The new men had ample opportunity to gain much valuable combat training through the experience, as they were engaged with the Federals in several running skirmishes. The fresh troops began showing great promise during that period.

"It was soon after, early in November, that Bragg's new orders attached our regiment to the command of Fightin' Joe Wheeler, another West Point professional, ten years the junior and a head shorter than our own forty-one year old general. We rested for a spell in camps near Murfreesboro with a large contingent of infantry that was concentratin,' at the time, around middle Tennessee in preparation for approaching operations. Our tether was then soon again loosed as we began striking independently at the scattered units of invasionary forces surrounding and occupyin' the sacred halls of state gov'ment, ever probing for their strengths and weaknesses. This Yankee occupation of the Tennessee capital, perhaps above all else, rankled Forrest most, causin' him to repeatedly beseech his superiors to move with him against the garrison there, to remove the offending abominations as soon as possible. At one point, on November sixth, General Breckinridge at last concurred with Forrest's assessment of the weakened state of Federal affairs within the vicinity of the capital, agreein' to coordinate with Hanson's Infantry in an effort to assault and dislodge the U.S. troops from the very Capital steps. An esprit de corps and enthusiasm unlike any I'd previously witnessed was displayed amongst our ranks as the battle plan was laid and preparations made for its execution.

"At the appointed hour, our cavalry moved out of LaVerge by way of four different approaches to Nashville and affected a juncture near the outskirts of the city soon after dark. Will and I were amongst a troop one thousand strong in company of General Forrest, when on the following sunrise the order 'prepare to charge' was passed down the line. As the nervous tension mounted and all said their final silent prayers before the battle was jined, word came again down the line that by direct order of General Bragg, far removed from our theatre of action, we were to cease the attack and counter march immediately to LaVerge.

"Unsatisfied with the effect to morale such action would incite within his troop, the General, without the hoped for aid of Hanson's supporting infantry, ignored Bragg's ill-advised 'suggestion' and led our cavalry contingent alone against the main Federal force anyway, who, though strongly entrenched, were routed and fled the field before our furious mounted charge.

"Such was the artillery dual as then ensued between our battery and the well-placed Federals, as I rarely witnessed during the whole of my stead in the service. For a time it seemed our battery would be destroyed, as round after round plowed through their ranks, or burst in air above their position. But the courage of our boys kept them at their pieces, operating their guns with coolness and great skill, giving back to the Yanks better even than what they got. Henceforth, all who witnessed their daring display treated these men, the survivors, with an extra accord.

"Back in camps at LaVerge, we rejined the running debate with Hanson's infantry about who had the best duty, infantry or cavalry. The flatfoots claimed they had it the worst 'cause when the apposing armies sally forth, they were the ones officers sent to their deaths charging on foot across open fields into the face of a well-armed and entrenched foe. They were weeks marching over hill and dale, footsore, ragged and ever weary, arriving on the heels of the cav., which had already confiscated any provisions in an area before their coming. In rain, they complained how pulling mud ached both hips and knees 'til ye' felt you're legs were bein' pulled apart at every joint, whilst totin' a heavy musket for a spell soon began to feel like an anvil on your back. And to top it all, they nearly started a riot when one from their ranks said, 'I ain't never seen a dead man wearin' no spurs.'

"We, on the other hand, argued it was clearly the cavalry who had the harder lot. Colonel of Cavalry and fellow Arky, John C. Wright probably said it best when he stated plainly, 'The infantry marches at a leisurely pace, followed by a baggage train bearing for them all the niceties of life, to then camp for weeks, or even months in one location, needs readily met by requisition, with their only duties being stated hours of drill, or to act as occasional picket guard, with plenty time left for relaxin' and socializin' amongst themselves and the local community. Though they most often bear the brunt of fighting when two armies are arrayed on the field of battle, it may be months before they are again called on to face such trial, where they find themselves part of a great mass of men moving in unison, participants in the brilliant pageant of martial grandeur, nerves steeled by the sound of fife and drum played grandly amidst many bright flags and regalia, all designed to greatly ease their trepidations.'

'Whilst at the same time,' he continued, 'the cav. are never long in one spot, constantly on the move, scouting right up to, or even behind enemy pickets, intentionally drawing fire on a regular basis to determine the adversaries strength and position, loosing men habitually in these less known, unsung engagements, gone forever from home and family, often unburied, their fates and final resting places forever unknown. Constantly vigilant to protect the infantry from surprise attack, this daily attrition amounts to fully match the appalling losses suffered by the infantry when pitted in pitched battles. When the infantry's day is done, they lie down to a good night's rest, secure in the knowledge that the cavalry is guarding their bivouac. Whereas, after long hours in the saddle, the cavalryman must first tend to the needs of his mount before his own, leaving him often too weary to even eat before he naps, one eye open, ever vigilant against surprise, ready at a moment's notice to spring again into the saddle to screen the balance of the army from attack. In retreat,' he concluded, 'it is usually the cavalry who stand and fight, greatly outnumbered, whilst the larger portion of the corps make good their safe escape from the pursuing foe.'

"This unending argument went on between the two branches of service throughout the war and even afterwards, but I admit I greatly preferred the independence and self-reliance of the cavalry corps, where a man could readily act of his own initiative in the smaller sized detachments, away from the tyrannical boot-heel common of so many infantry commanders. Infantry moved as one, under orders from the mind of one, a tiny part of a much greater whole, much liken to mindless ants, their every move under the eye and will of their superiors. And they made easy prey for enemy cavalry unless constantly screened and protected by their own cavalry. Though never admitted by me to them, I would not have cared to trade places."

Holding up the folded, dog-eared, yellow parchment that had been in his hand all the while, he said, "This here letter came from a member of the Third Arkansas Cavalry, whilst they was servin' dismounted as foot soldiers. It was written to my first wife, your blood granny, from her first husband, another Dallas County boy, who, in October of '62, just one month prior to the composition of this correspondence, charged afoot in the terrible, final assault against Union held Battery Powell at Corinth. He, too, much preferred the mounted service over the life of a flatfoot. I'd like ye' to read it when ye' git' the chance," he stated, referring to the letter in his hand, written by her long-deceased husband to the woman who, over the course of the war, married two different local cavalrymen.

"For me, there was no match to the spirit of abandon and the excitement of a thunderin' charge, routing and ridin' over a demoralized foe as they fled before the tramp of iron-clad feet.

"That, I reckon, was what I most missed when held captive, the thrill of the chase, ridin' amongst men and animals of fortitude and courage. Truth be known, we mostly didn't fight for the Confederate Gov'ment, or even the Cause, as much as we fought for each other and the thrill of the hunt. After seein' so many blunders and losses and the frequent mishandlin' of the few military successes achieved by the South, we, like our General Forrest, were inclined to question if those sittin' on the seats of gov'ment or their chosen commanders even knew remotely what they was doing? Yet we always found our glad companionship in the field that enabled us to keep ever at the unnerving and unending tasks laid before us.

"Under orders from General Bragg to take post in the vicinage of Columbia and prepare for an expedition into west Tennessee, we moved thus on December fourth, with eighteen-hunert men. We took position on the banks of the Duck River and began the task of assembling our force for a treacherous winter campaign into a region fairly swarming with Federal forces. Having sent a contingent ahead of the column to scrounge ferriage for the crossing of the swollen Tennessee, we arrived in the company of our general at the shores of the ice-cold, winter-swollen obstruction near Clifton on the thirteenth. We had no baggage train and thus no tents to protect either enlisted, or officers from the freezing drizzle that came steadily down. Using flat-bottom boats arranged for by our advance party, the men and artillery were ferried across to the far shore, whilst horses and mules swam the treacherous tide. Instructed by our officers to look to our powder upon reaching the far shore, we discovered most of our ammo and percussion caps were ruined by the inclimate weather and the hazards associated with the crossing.

"On the sixteenth we bivouacked to allow the troop to dry out clothes, rest and regroup after the trials of our treacherous crossing. To the great relief of all, a private citizen arrived in camps that evening with some fifty thousand percussion caps for both rifles and shotguns to replace those lost in our amphibious crossing.

"On the seventeenth, we pushed on toward Lexington, Tennessee. Here we encountered our old regiment under command of General Frank Gurley and with the aid of our former comrades, attacked and captured an occupying garrison of Loyalist Tennessee Cavalry along with the Eleventh Illinois Volunteers. That day I found ample opportunities to exercise my new duties as bugler, sounding one charge after another.

"It was there that the legend of Private Kelly was born, of Kelly's Troopers, Russell's Alabama Regiment. In a charge against a Federal battery that was causing our entire command great discomfort, Private Kelly rushed to the fore, being the first Confederate to reach the Yankee guns. As he dismounted in front of the guns and dashed to assault their gunners with his pistol in hand, the enemy touched off the loaded weapon directly in his path. The result was horrendous, severing the poor lad in two. His middle exploded like an over ripe tomato, leaving him a terribly dismembered fragment of his former self. He was said to've lived just long enough to send his love to his mother back in Alabama."

Pappy, now an old man become more kind and wise with age, paused here briefly, considering the sadness that still accompanied the memory of this bygone tale of personal sacrifice and valor. Then he continued.

"Meeting no further resistance after Lexington, we reached the vicinity of Jackson on the afternoon of the eighteenth. The pickets were rapidly driven within their epaulements, whilst troop trains were heard arriving in rapid succession to reinforce the occupying garrison. Union General Sullivan surrendered all the precincts outside Jackson-proper and awaited developments within the relatively safe confines of his earthen fortifications. Confederate cavalry were dispatched in the directions of Bolivar and Humboldt to destroy all tracks leading into the beleaguered city to prevent the arrival of any further enemy reinforcements. Upon return of these raiding parties, the inferior weaponry still remaining in possession of our men, was replaced with the abundant, captured stores of our enemy, brought in confiscated wagons from various supply depots that had fallen undefended into our hands.

"Seeing little else he could accomplish under the circumstances and commenting with a rakish air, 'Pigs get fat, hogs get slaughtered,' Forrest had us fall back to the vicinity of Spring Creek and using recently captured Federal drums, the General kept up a ruse of superior numbers of Confederate infantry by beating the instruments in the manner of a large force in our quarter, whilst furthering the illusion by maintaining numerous, scattered camp fires throughout the night. The balance of our scattered command rejined with us at Spring Creek on the following morn. We had now in our possession twenty-five fine new Federal wagons, an entire section of captured artillery and adequate small arms for the whole of the command. We then proceeded to destroy all bridges on the Mobile and Ohio Railway within striking distance, capturing further men and materials. Another hunert-twenty hardy new mounted volunteers, from Hickman and Perry Counties, jined up with our regiment at that point. Leaving behind the Fourth Alabama at Spring Creek to bring up the captured Federal infantrymen, we proceeded on toward Trenton.

"Here a notable incident occurred that tells something of the character of our General. Using only the small number of his escort and a pair of cannon, we assaulted and captured a much larger force ensconced safely within strongly fortified walls. At first the Federals made a show to put up a great fight. They were inside a massive blockade, bristling with gun-barrels extending in every direction through the numerous rifle ports. Not wishing to waist the lives of his men needlessly, Forrest had the artillery brought up and unlimbered. He helped aim the guns and within discharging but three rounds, white flags began to replace the muskets sticking out the gun slots. Upon unconditional surrender of the garrison at Trenton, Forrest received the sword of the Union commander, one elderly Colonel Fry, who sadly explained the saber had been in his family's possession for three generations. After brief examination of said sword, General Forrest returned it to its owner, saying, 'Take back your heirloom, but the next time you employ it, may it be in service of a nobler cause than the subjugation of your fellow countrymen.'

"After emptying the wooden fortress of its occupants and its fortune in valuables, we warmed ourselves with the huge blaze of its destruction. A wide-brim hat has several practical applications, not the least of which can be a shield for your face from the heat of a roaring blaze.

"Our success at Trenton garnered for us no less than three-hunert captured nigras, a thousand head of fresh mules and horses, fourteen additional wagons, four-hunert thousand rounds of small arms ammunition, twenty thousand artillery rounds and a hunert-thousand daily food rations, as well as a large supply of cavalry stores, from which I personally liberated new, knee-high, black leather boots to replace my well-worn ones and a fine new McClellan saddle, with all the accoutrements. Prince was notably happier with the lightened load of the well-designed saddle, as was my backside with the easier sitting seat. From the captured Federal animals, the whole command was well mounted.

"Shouts of glee could be heard as the troopers burst open crates of warm winter socks. Also, I saw many boys leaving the storerooms with as many as three and four U.S. Army issue Colt revolvers stuffed in their waist belts. Counting the Navy-style Colt brought with me from home, I myself then had three different six-shooters, plus several extra cylinders that could be pre-charged for quick replacement of an empty one during the heat of battle.

"On the morning of the twenty-first, we resumed our advance toward Union City. En route we captured another stockade and its garrison of thirty Feds before burning it and another railroad trestle down. We pushed on to the Obion River and after crossing over, encamped for the evening, feeding and resting our animals and ourselves. Scouts arrived in the night with the news that some ten thousand Federals were in pursuit of our force, approaching from the south, in an effort to cut off any retreat by us back toward our own lines. Nonetheless, not one to be easily deterred, the General proceeded toward Union City and there again assaulted a Federal garrison. As fate would have it, after driving the Federals inside their stockade, Confederate Lieutenant Colonel Collins and the Fourth Alabama were seen from half a mile away, across large open fields, moving with the vanguard of paroled Yanks left earlier in their care, at the same time as a parley was in session for terms of the garrison's surrender. This distant force appeared to the surrounded Federals to be a large number of reinforcements coming to the aid of the Confederates. Our pokerfaced emissaries encouraged this misconception and the Yankees quickly capitulated, seeing no way to withstand such a numerically superior force.

"On Christmas Eve and Christmas Day we spent our efforts singing carols whilst dismantling railroad trestles high above the frigid, swirling Obion. We rested that night amidst mixed feelings of satisfaction with our work and deep longings for home and hearth intensified greatly by sentiments of the season. The weather was so severe that the skin of my hands, as well as many of the others, was painfully cracked open from the prolonged exposure.

"On the following morn, we were set in motion toward Dresden, where en route weary men slept in the saddle, whilst wet and footsore horses stumbled on. We encamped to rest our command and receive scouting reports of enemy activity. We then continued toward Huntington where we camped at McKenzie Station on the Memphis and Louisville Line. The Federals had seized all passable bridges over the Obion to prevent our safe return to the banks of the Tennessee River where, once crossed, we would be back within our own lines. Scouts reported to the General that there was one rickety, un-held bridge that our enemy had neglected, thinking it totally impassable. We galloped as quickly as the winter roads would allow in its direction, arriving to find, much to the mortification of officers and men alike, a treacherously precarious span over the turbulent, ice-choked stream. Apparently undaunted, our General immediately set us about the chore of shoring up the crossing to facilitate the movement of artillery and wagons. Over the long hours required for completion of this task, the steel-gray sky hid the sun by day and the stars by night, constantly pelting us with sleet and rain. From time to time it came down so hard, I heard some fellers say, 'Now it's a comin' down cross-legged!'

"We kept a huge bonfire blazing on the near bank for warmth and light, fueled from the several wagons of captured railroad wood that couldn't now be carried across the unreliable structure. Even so, my ravaged hands ran with blood that froze almost instantly in place, whilst my toes went completely numb over the course of the crossing. Yet I was one of the more fortunate that didn't suffer from severe frostbite as did so many.

"The rickety bridge was far too dangerous to support the heavy laden wagons, so, much to our chagrin, we emptied them, filling the pot holes of the approach with the much-prized sacks of captured flour, meal and coffee. To instill confidence in our completed handiwork, General Forrest himself drove the first team and wagon over the swaying span. Continuing in this way to work through the pitch black, freezing night, we threw our complete regiment across the swollen watercourse by three the following morning.

"Without pause, we trudged four more slippery miles into McLemoresville, expending the remaining hours of the predawn and the balance of our precious, little-remaining energy, slogging through waist deep mire with the artillery and other equipage. Here the troop was gratefully halted for the remainder of the morning, being badly in need of warmth, food and rest, which were provided by the generous souls of that little burg. This short respite was made shorter by news of a Federal force pressing hard in our direction. Before noon the whole of the command was back underway in the direction of Lexington, through steep, muddy hills, over roads not designed for the heavy movement of a mounted army in winter.

"On the twenty-ninth and thirtieth, we rested a few miles beyond Lexington, next to Flake's Store at Parker's Crossroads. We learned from the store-keep that the area was known as Red Mound because the soil was full of rusty colored clay and iron, similar to that of our home-soil in Redlands. We treated our poor, sore hands and chapped lips with captured lard and dried out, or replaced our tattered clothing with Yankee stores from the wagons we worked so hard to carry over the Obion.

"The General kept patrols afield to advise him as to Yankee whereabouts and early on the afternoon of the thirtieth, one under command of his brother William, returned with the news that a large force of enemy infantry were approaching our camp at the double-quick. We fell back a short distance from the intersection of the two roads, threw out strong pickets in their direction and prepared to make a stand. The Feds, upon arrival, drove in our pickets and deployed in line of battle across the road junction. Here took place another brief, but hot artillery dual, that caused the Feds to withdraw from the crossroads and fall back a short piece within the cover of the woods, whilst still blocking our escape route to the south. We were dismounted and told to advance slowly through the trees whilst the vast part of the work was done for us by our cannoneers, who poured a steady fire into the opposing ranks. Out flanking 'em on both sides, we gradually came to surround their position and slowly tightened the noose they now found themselves in. With no reports of enemy reinforcements in the area, we leisurely drove them back on themselves until, with nowhere left to retreat, our enemy took cover in the zigzagging corners of a waist high split-rail fence. Here we kept them pinned down with small-arms fire, being careful not to overshoot our targets lest we fire into our own men on every side of the cornered Yanks. The artillery was brought up to a closer proximity from which to fire into their midst and began a galling fusillade that splintered the shelter of the fence, sending deadly wooden shards cutting through their ranks. Finding themselves in desperate straights, they twice came out from behind their wooden barricade to form a charge in an effort to fight their way from the deadly trap. Twice they were driven back to the rail fence. Then, acting independently of Forrest's orders, one Colonel Napier led a bold, but foolhardy mounted charge against the Federal position, in which he and his horse were both felled dead at the fence line, leaving his badly mauled command to fall back to the cover of the trees.

"At this point, shaking his head over the pointless waste of good men's lives, the General repositioned his artillery to fire into the Federal left, enfilading their entire position. At the same time he sent strong reinforcements around both the left and right to prevent any chance of retreat to their rear where our position was weakest."

Not understanding his terminology, I briefly interrupted. "What's enfilading?"

Turning to look at me, he explained, "That would be to shoot down the length of a line of men from one side, or the other, instead of firing into their front, or rear. Enfilading fire usually negates the benefit of whatever cover the targets are crouched behind and allows artillery to continue pouring it on even when friendly troops are advancing."

Nodding my understanding with a smile, he continued uninterrupted.

"Again for a third time the Yanks charged out from behind the cedar rails, in growing desperation mounting their strongest effort yet to escape. Barrels level with the terrain, loaded with grape and firing directly into their massed formation, our field guns cut bloody swaths through the advancing lines, leaving open lanes in their melting ranks. Afoot, we then pressed home our advantage, driving in on their line at the fence as it scattered in great confusion. The dismounted cavalry quickly leapt back in the saddles of our waiting mounts and drove them headlong through the woods, where killed and wounded Yanks were trampled under hoof, like the strewn leaves littering the forest floor. White flags began appearing from all quarters and the firing slowly subsided. The slaughter was mercifully ceased whilst our officers conferred with theirs to arrange for surrender. If you listened, one could hear the pitiable moans of their wounded, coming as it were, from all points of the compass.

"Then, as we were just settling our backs against trees to swig from our canteens and take a breather from the hectic activity of combat, firing again broke out to our rear. We were at first astonished, as was the General, when stampeded horses and their holders swarmed around us, fleeing the surprise attack from behind. Unsure what was happening, the General called to his escort to mount up and follow closely. Closing to within a distance of the firing where an occasional bullet clipped twigs from the trees thick around us, the General ordered us to dismount and wait behind the cover of their great trunks, whilst he slowly eased forward in attempt to make out the situation. Riding slowly from tree to tree, he disappeared from our view in that manner. The minutes crept by as the firing grew ever more intense and increasing numbers of mini-balls could be heard slamming into the bark above and around us. Then, in great haste the General reappeared, galloping and weaving a path through the woods, whilst ducking his head to avoid low hanging limbs. Speeding past where we were already scrambling to the saddle, he shouted only, 'Follow me lads!' We did as he'd suggested, glancing over our shoulders to see what had put the 'giddy up' in his step. After only a short retreat, he pulled up and explained briefly, with great excitement, that he had nearly been captured when several blue bellies stepped from behind trees, demanding he dismount and surrender. Telling them he had already forfeited and suggesting he return a short distance through the woods to bring up the small remnant of his decimated command, he turned and slowly rode out of their sight before spurring his mount in a hasty egress, at which point he rejined us. He gathered up his scattered command to implement a charge against this new threat, hoping to quickly counter it. He ordered men who were out of ammo to fall in anyway, so's to aid in the show of force he hoped would extricate us from our now trapped position between the remnant of the force we had up 'til then so badly whooped and the newly arrived Federals that had somehow managed to slip around the rearguard he had posted for the express purpose of preventing just such a situation. Sending word by courier to the commands of both Russell and Starnes to keep the demoralized Thirty-ninth Iowa out of the action, he shouted, 'They got us right between the rocks and shoals boys, so there's nothin' to be done but charge at 'em both ways!' With no more than his escort of seventy-five men and a small portion of Dibrell's command not exceeding another fifty, we spurred our mounts back in the direction of the fierce firefight, in hopes of driving off the Federals before their whole contingent could be brought to bear. When we emerged from the cover of the timber, we were facing a line of cannon trained on our advance. They immediately discharged a volley that unseated several in our

195

midst, whilst we advanced as rapidly as our weary mounts could manage. Glancing around during the charge, I noticed that Will and Fury were nowhere to be seen. Given, he had a wife and daughters to consider.

"Prince and I sped through the accompanying cloud of dust and smoke until we could see the flaming tongues of the belching cannon, that fortunately had yet to find the range, sending the majority of their whistling missiles sailing harmlessly overhead. Guns blazing, we dashed in amongst the smoking cannon, driving off most of their infantry support and cutting down the rest. Seeing this, the gunners scattered like a covey of quail. I rode down on one poor feller I remember in particular, whose head I leveled my rifle barrel at, only to have his brains and blood splatter over Prince and me as we sped past his exploding skull.

"Thusly, we managed our escape from the enemy's grip in mid-afternoon, as Russell and Starnes, along with the balance of Dibbrell's command, rejined us as we rode the length of the forming Federal line, before disappearing from their sight, receiving in the process but little disorganized, long-range fire from their small-arms. Once't safely beyond the immediate threat of the much slower pursuing infantry, we rested and watered our mounts, topping off our canteens in Beech Creek.

"Whilst Prince and I rested bank-side beneath the shade of the great old beech trees from which the little stream took its name, my nostrils were assailed by the odor of Yankee blood that stained my cloths, my saddle and my horse. The sweat associated with the arduous activity of combat sat chill against me skin beneath the heavy wool of my uniform as I picked small pink pieces of the Yank gunner's brain from my hair and clothes.

"We proceeded toward the friendly environs of Lexington, which were gained around six that evenin', where we again took brief respite from flight to properly tend to our much suffering wounded, before resuming our march southeast in the direction of Clifton across the wide Tennessee.

"Upon arrival at the shores of the great river, we were met by a force of a thousand Union Cavalry, attempting to block our escape to the other side. It was here that we taught our blue-clad counterparts a valuable lesson in mounted warfare. I sounded the charge on my bugle, that was echoed down the lines and as the two opposing regiments rushed in clouds of dust across the open plain of the river valley, they came on, sabers drawn, prepared to do battle in the Napoleonic fashion of cavalry engagements, whilst we brandished our Navy sixers. A thick cloud of mallard ducks was flushed by the charge from a backwater where they had sat feeding, rising across the path of the sun, for a time darkening the sky with great quacking and commotion until their passing.

"Many in our ranks carrying scatterguns would rather have employed 'em to bring down some fresh fowl for supper, but under the circumstances, instead opened on the closing Federal Cavalry at the proper range, getting in their deadly work and permanently dismounting many a Yank. Their gleaming swords, though menacing in appearance, were little match for revolvers at close range. Before they come near enough to effectively employ the long blades, we had shot most of their front ranks from the saddle. We then continued to advance into their midst as the two sides collided and mixed in a hurly-burly encounter that left fallen men and animals of both sides entwined one atop the other. I ducked and dodged flashing steel, at times poking my hand guns right into the sides of our enemy at close quarters. In one instance, I was shocked to see a hole the size of your fist appear through a feller's chest upon pointblank discharge of my weapon. Pistol cylinders empty, I felt obliged to draw my own saber from its sheath tied securely to my saddle, to lung and parry with more than one Federal in the thick of the contest. We mixed and mingled until there was no semblance of unit order, or integrity left. Still the struggle continued, slashing and firing in hand-to-hand, horse-to-horse gridlock. The ground became so tangled with heaped bodies until animals stumbled, tossing their riders onto the muddy ground underfoot, adding to the bloody mayhem. Finally, over the sounds of shouts, grunts and screams, the Yankee retreat could be made out as it issued from their buglers. As they tried to extricate themselves from amongst us, we further decimated their number, severing limbs held up in defense and decapitating hapless refugees.

"The scene was replete with blood and guts in spades. The stains on my clothes from the Yank gunner slain at Parker's Crossroads were overlaid with the blood of several more in the close proximity of struggle that occurred there on the sandy ground next to the Tennessee. Many wounded and dying of both sides, man and beast, crawled to, or fell at water's edge, their blood mixing with the current as it ebbed from their slashed and shot bodies, flowing away downstream.

"After the fury of the collision between the equally matched forces, I searched amongst the living and the dead for William and Fury. To my great relief I found 'em unharmed near the sunken flatboats we'd left in expectation of our return crossing. The two of them appeared unhurt and unstained, quite the contrary to Prince and me. Prince had received a serious gash across his right flank where I'd dodged a saber only to have it strike him. I'd been stabbed through the flesh of my side by a lunge from a Yank who I in turn unseated with a blow to the side of his head with the barrel of my heavy pistol. Seeing our bloody disheveled appearance, Will bore a horrified look, not knowing where our blood ended and Yank blood took-up. Nearly collapsing from the McClellan atop of Prince, Will caught me and eased me to the sandbar on which he stood. He dampened and dabbed a kerchief from around his neck at the splattered blood on my cheeks. It was only weariness and the subsiding of the rush of adrenaline in my veins that had caused my near swooning. As I returned to my senses, I found my head cradled in my brother's arms, whilst he examined me to determine my wounds. The sensation of pain now proceeded from my side, which we quickly decided was the worst of my injuries.

"By now activity swarmed all around our position as men waded into the shallow water and brush that hid our ferriage and began hitching lines to the sunken vessels to extricate them from the their anchorage. We moved off a short distance to be out of the way, where Will stopped the flow of blood from my flesh wound by stuffing a rag in the hole. Together we then began to tend to

Prince's wound, with me holding tight his reins whilst Will sewed closed the gap in his hip with curved needle and a strand from his tail. Will said nothin' 'bout my part in the melee, only occasionally glancing up at me, shaking his head. After several of these looks I finally countered with, 'New Years Eve is as good a day as any if you gotta' die. I ain't cryin', why should ye?' Despite my savoir'-faire, I knew why brother was both concerned and disgusted. He didn't relish having to someday tell our folks how I'd met my demise. He still only shook his head and drew the suture through Prince's flesh.

"I was of little use during the river crossing and rested with my animal in the shade of a cottonwood tree. The majority of the uninjured command, not searching through the tangle of stricken at the sight of our cavalry battle, extricating wounded, or shooting crippled horses, labored to put us across the winding Tennessee to safety from further Federal assault. It was a scene of tremendous activity. From my seat against the tree, it looked at one time, as if fully a thousand animals, including Prince and Fury, were swimming desperately to gain the distant shore, six-hunert yards away through the swollen, swirling and icy current. This would prove good practice for future trials.

"A crowd of bundled-up Tennesseans, who'd witnessed our rout of the Federal horsemen, stood in the blustering wind and cold, cheering our crossing as we came over in boatloads from the far bank. After half a day, roughly twelve hours, with the aid of the civilian spectators and their skiffs, at eight in the evening on the last day of the year 1862, we were all back across the Tennessee to the relative safety of our own lines. We had lost in this winter campaign, deep in enemy territory, roughly a hunert mule and horses and something less than three-hunert men all told in kilt, captured and wounded. Though individual losses of fine men can't readily be measured, the liberated animals and new recruits that now augmented our returning ranks negated the numerical loss. We had destroyed or carried away a tremendous amount of Union military stores, fully equipping our new command with all the necessities of an army in the field in winter, including a baggage train sixty-wagons strong, with canvas shelters, bedding, hordes of rations, ammunition, a large number of captured colors, sound remounts and six cannon. We had captured and paroled a number of Federals so large as to which I would not care to guess. This was achieved with a Confederate force no more than twelve-hunert strong. We often had advantage in that we fought mere inexperienced milk-fed, mid-western lads, who shrank from our tumultuous approach.

"All told, it had been a highly successful venture, fraught with difficulty and close-calls, yet one that left the enemy in awe of our cavalry, frightened dast they dare move against us, due to our seeming invincibility even in the face of long odds. It instilled in our own ranks a pride and daring second to none. The green horsemen were now seasoned veterans, raw frontier skills sharpened on the crucible of combat. Anyone who'd seen our ragged lot before we crossed the Tennessee on the fifteenth past wouldn't have recognized us as the self-same army. What a difference a fortnight can make. Those fresh, green troops had gone where no one else dared and had acquitted themselves with dash and valor, rendering folly all efforts at our apprehension by the stricken foe. We were 'bad' and we knew it. There was a new swagger in our walk that had not been before seen. We thought ourselves rakes and ramblers, peddlin' and tradin' in Yankee grief.

"Still, we were wore to a frazzle and had lost dear friends along the trail, each new loss bringing back the painful memories of all previous ones. Each time we lost a friend, it was like they became part of us, taking up a small corner of our souls.

"We couldn't remember when last we'd awoke rested between clean linens. But, for a while, the end of the trail was proverbially in sight. We would go into temporary winter quarters on the fifth upon reaching Columbia, Tennessee, to mend our wounds and re-shoe our mounts, while protecting the left flank of the army. As we entered the outskirts of Columbia, word was passed that the heroic Forrest's Regiment was returned from a great victory. The ladies turned out in droves bearing gifts of all variety sustenance.

"Two incidents occurred here worthy of mention, both concerning General Forrest. As escort to our commander, our unit camped near his tents. Late one evening, after the General had entertained his staff with poker and hard liquor, a great hubbub ensued from the direction of his rather-large command shelter. Fearing some sort of assault on the General's life, Will and I rushed with our weapons in that direction. We found a number of soldiers holding General Forrest's larger, younger brother William, who had a mad look in his eye, to restrain him from assaulting Bedford. After some minutes the provost guard disarmed and escorted him from the scene to cool down and sober up. After their forms receded into the darkness beyond the lanterns and campfires, General Forrest addressed the gathering of troopers, like myself, who'd been drawn to the racket. It was the only time I ever witnessed in the General's eyes anything remotely resembling fear. He said only, 'God only knows what will get Will'm riled up, or when it might happen, but for certain he's bound to shoot his guns and even drunk,' the General added, 'he rarely misses!' The next day we saw the two brothers again in each other's company, seemingly as if nothing had ever happened.

"The other instance was when the General, watching my brother Will and me feed our horses, came over, as he strolled through the campground wearing his brocaded hat, saber rattling at his side and asked us 'How you boys doin'?' Will replied, 'Right tolerable, if'n ye' don't look too close sir.'

"The General chuckled at the jest, then in a more serious tone, commented that he'd noticed how Fury never seemed to appear at the forefront of any of our charges during the recent enemy engagements. Will explained how he couldn't seem to drive him to the front no matter how diligently he tried. 'He's a handful even to get to follow near the rear of the pack,' my brother said to our commander.

"Forrest said, 'You'd think he'd get tired of eatin' our dust.'

"In Will and Furies' defense, I offered that, 'Ever since being shot at Fallen Timbers, Fury's trust has been betrayed and being a smarter than average jug-head, with balls and a mind of his own, he simply ain't yet got over it.'

"The General then leaned over and whispered in the black stallion's twitching ear. When he turned and walked a short distance away, I followed and inquired what he'd said to the animal. He replied that he had threatened to geld him if he didn't learn to charge and that if he was indeed so smart, that should change his timidity.

"The General was joshing us, but at the same time there was always a serious side to his nature that never relaxed. Horses under his command, like soldiers, expected to be put in for transfer if'n they didn't meet muster in the eyes of either their General or his staff. Leaning close to me, as if to share a confidence, he said in a hushed voice, 'We've still a lot of ground to plow, Trumpeter Ledbetter. I asked that your brother be transferred to my command at your request. Continue to make me proud. In my experience hedgers generally always get the worst of it anyway.' Noticing me favor my wound, he added, 'Now, take care of that side of yours. Have my surgeon Dr. Cowan examine it. You know his tent,' he said, nodding in that direction, before again strolling leisurely off to further inspect the troop and spread his jewels of wisdom. When I returned to Will's side, always the optimist, he said, 'The good thing about Fury bringing up the rear is, at least from that direction, I can always watch your back.'

"Having suffered under the plague of a terrible soreness and at big brother's urging, I made my way directly to the quarters of Dr. J.B. Cowan, where, tapping gently on the tent pole at the front flap, I was happy to find the good surgeon in. 'Yes son?' he asked, drawing the flap but a few inches aside to prevent the loss of precious heat from inside. 'General Forrest suggested I ask you to examine my saber wound, sir,' I reported. 'Come in then,' he said opening the flap fully whilst lightly grasping my arm above the elbow to encourage a more rapid entry, before quickly drawing it to behind me. I could appreciate his miserly attitude toward the luxurious heat we experienced within. His iron camp stove crackled with the happy sound of a roaring fire on a cold morning.

'Take a seat there,' he said, motioning to a stool beside a table where sat his medical bag. He took hold the stove-handle with a makeshift potholder as he stooped and stuffed another stick of wood through the already full opening, before closing the metal door with a clang. Turning to face me he said, 'Now, how can I help you?'

'It's my side, sir, right here,' I said, indicating my left waist, in the fleshy area below my ribs. 'Let's have a look,' he said, helping me tenderly remove my shirt over my head. The stab wound was wrapped in the remnant of the blouse that I'd worn when first receiving it, rinsed out since and torn into long strips for use as bandages, its usefulness as a shirt mostly spent. The dried blood stains in the fabric, that washing would not remove, caused the doctor to betray a look of great concern, though experience had taught him to withhold judgement until closer examination. Once't unswathed, he relaxed visibly, his practiced eye noting the profusion of blood evident on bandage was not freshly leaked from the wound. He probed the cut with his tools, creating an uncomfortable sensation that I tried not to squirm away from. 'I see you've got a little red here around the edges. That's not uncommon with a stab wound. What happened here?', he asked. 'Yankee saber at the battle on the banks of the Tennessee before our crossing,' I told him.

'What you've got is a little secondary irritation, not uncommon with these type injuries. I'm going to dab it with some alcohol to clean it up. This is gonna' sting a bit,' he said applying a cotton-ball on long forceps to the inflamed saber cut. The burning was severe, proving to me the doctor was a master of understatement. I'd often heard sawbones were as slippery as lawyers and parsons and weren't necessarily to be trusted at their word. I withdrew a preordained bullet from my pocket to bite as he swabbed the edges thoroughly with what felt like a hot brand. After he withdrew the forceps, I exhaled, relaxing the tension in my muscles as tears came in my eyes. More gently, he sewed the gap closed, plunging and drawing the needle through the soft flesh beyond the raw edges like an adept. As he'd planned it, the burning of the alcohol overrode the prick of the needle. I could feel the edges as they drew together under his practiced hand.

"It took only six stitches,' he told me, as if pleased with his handy work. Then he withdrew from his case a length of wound cotton bandage, courtesy of the U.S. Army, that he gently applied to my still burning underbelly, wrapping the balance of the cloth around my waist beneath my upheld arms and tucking the end into the wrap. 'Come back and see me in a couple days and I'll change that for you. Try not to use anymore of this bloodstained, homemade bandage,' he said holding the offending item at arms length by his forceps as he deposited it in the waist-bin. 'When I see you again I'll provide you with an extra change of dressing. By then it should be in good shape if you'll keep it dry and that infection doesn't worsen.' He turned to drop his forceps in a basin of alcohol with a holler clatter, then scrubbed his hands in an adjacent basin, all atop his table next to his medical bag. As he dried his hands on a white towel he added, 'Stay clear of that unkind steel in the future son,' to which I replied, 'That would be my intent sir. Thank you for your attention doctor.'

'Anytime lad,' he added, 'Now remember, I wish to see you back here two days hence,' again ushering me as quickly as possible through the portal of the tent, without appearing overly rude, leading me gently out the opening by my arm. I thought to myself, 'don't let the tent flap hit ye' in the arse!'

"When I emerged into the frigid air, it was a momentary shock after the comfortable warmth of the surgeon's tent. Standing in the now falling snow, still next to the flap I'd only just exited, I could hear the good doctor inside again open his stove to wrestle another stick into the roaring blaze.

"As I rejined William at our tent, he looked up into the rapidly falling flakes and said with a broad grin, 'The old woman upstairs must be a'pluckin' her geese.'

"The trauma of the surgeon's call left me feeling wrung-out, so I went to lie down for a spell. Inside our shelter, relaxing on my cot beneath a pile of warm blankets, I could hear the sounds of camp life going on around me. Busy hands rattled pots accompanied by the sound of water poured from one container into another. From a short distance I heard a sergeant inspecting a muleskinner's rigging, rattling the trace-chains. He called to the attention of the driver a twisted harness strap, blistering the snow-filled air with his adjectives. Then I drifted off, lost in dreams of the snow-covered fields of youthful play.

"I awoke sometime later to a hush. It was so quiet I thought at first I must have napped 'til taps. But then, wiping the sleep from my eyes, I noticed there was still pale daylight showing through the tent-canvas. Gingerly rising on the cot, I slipped on my new Yankee jackboots and held the tent pole as I stood and poked my head out-of-doors. A gray sky hung low over the brilliant white and hushed landscape. All was still beneath the falling snow, now collected several inches deep this early January eve. Reaching my head further through the opening to crane my neck, I could see a large body of men gathered, singing around a roaring bonfire. Turning back inside for my stolen Yankee overcoat, I wrapped it around my shoulders and headed out through the near knee-deep accumulation toward the aroma of cooking food.

"As a child, I always enjoyed the snow, considering it a friend and a playmate. I wore a smile as I trudged down the way, past men and animals shivering in the bitter cold air of a frigid evening. It would be an even colder night. Thank God for the captured Yankee stores and the eighteen-hunert heavy wool blankets we'd carried away in their stolen wagons. As I approached the gathering about the fire, I began to make out the strains of the old cavalry song, 'Boots and Saddles.' There in the midst of his men was General Forrest, singing the loudest of all. We passed the evening feeding on hot stew, passing bottles and trading tunes. The flurries kept up all night. We were lucky to have a wagon full of firewood, care of the locals. The only fighting we saw for near a week after that, was with snowballs.

"We recuperated our animals and ourselves through January and the first week of February, awaiting the roads to dry out enough to facilitate renewed military activities. Our cav. units patrolled the territory between the Yanks and us, constantly skirmishing with their cavalry patrols. The two main bodies of the opposing armies stood like two men, sabers drawn, glaring at one another, parrying with their weapons for some weakness, or advantage. In this case, the drawn weapons were the opposing cavalry corps. This following period was fraught with daily acts of courage and hardihood by the lone cavaliers.

"One cold day, after I's pert near heal't, whilst on patrol, William, and I come across some shivering nigras hiding in a barn. The look in their eyes when we discovered them was one of fright beyond any of my own experience, even with all we'd been through. It was a fear of one with no power of his own, no rights and no friends. Even in our worst conditions, we had our brothers-in-arms and the respect of our foe for the skill and unity we exhibited. The nigras couldn't even count on one another in many cases. They weren't allowed even their self-respect, not by most Sesech, or for that matter many Yanks I ever saw. When we were held captive, or imprisoned on various occasions, we saw nigras generally treated worse by Federals than would most Southerners. We were inside fences whilst the darkies were on the outside, but the walls around them were much higher and stronger, if invisible, than ours.

"At Will's urging, knowing we should be back in the comfort of our own tent by nightfall, barring any unexpected encounter with trouble, we tossed 'em the rolled up blanket we each carried tied to our saddle for emergencies and some hardtack, leavin' 'em where we found 'em, figurin we all had trouble enough without our interferin'. By dark we were indeed back to and grateful for the comfort and safety of our camp. We never spoke of the incident and no one ever mentioned the missing blankets."

From time to time Pappy would pause to swat a pesky fly who was foolish enough to bother him in his tale, then continue.

"But alas, the cavalry life is a gypsy life and we were soon again bound for the road.

"On the tenth of January an expedition was undertaken at the bequest of General Wheeler, to move against the Federal gunboats and fortifications near Harpeth Shoals on the Cumberland. Due to my infirmity and Will's charge as my orderly, we did not sally out with the large portion of the command that participated in that undertaking. We felt for our absent companions, for freezing rain, pelting sleet and heavy snow fell incessantly throughout their mission, causing great loss and suffering amongst the poor souls, including loss of digits to frostbite and even deaths from exposure. However, the force did manage to burn, or capture three transports and a gunboat and destroy a considerable stockpile of quartermaster stores.

"On the twenty-sixth of the new year, the General was again summoned to appear before the Commanding General at Headquarters Shelbyville, who informed him of a new assignment in the offing to attack Federal held Fort Donaldson. Against Forrest's better judgement, we hurriedly broke camp and in company of only his escort, raced over treacherous, ice-covered roads to catch up with the balance of the regiment that had moved forward in our absence under command of Major General Wheeler. After two of the most miserable days I ever spent, being constantly exposed to cutting winds and freezing precipitation, we rejined our comrades fifteen miles short of Dover. We went into camp in a draw, somewhat sheltered from the 'blue northern' that blew without ceasing. Still, the cold soaked in our bones nights and stayed there the whole of the day.

"A complete inspection of the troop, including Forrest's and Wharton's Brigades, was conducted, revealing the command had been poorly equipped in the General's absence, for such an expedition in winter. The men had less than twenty rounds each of small-arms ammo, clothing poorly suited for the climate, little sustenance and no means for cooking.

"The General was in a state at seeing how his fine troopers, who'd brought more equipage into the hands of the Confederate Gov'ment than any other single unit in the entire service, were so badly mishandled. He had been sneakily called to headquarters by Bragg so that Wheeler might steal away with his command on some ill-fated assignment to attempt capture of a fort that could not be long held under fire from the numerous gunboats that plied the waters of the Cumberland with immunity. Giving himself sufficient time to cool, Forrest reported to General Wheeler his views on the poor likelihood of success for such a plan, with a great chance for disaster in return for so little gain. He argued that we would soon be out of food and ammo and unless initially victorious, would have to forage from the bleak winter landscape a hunert miles from support and pursued by an obstinate enemy bent on our destruction, who would only become more emboldened at our likely failure. His views of the operation being one fraught with peril and pitfalls and greatly inclined toward calamity, passed unheeded by his immediate superior.

"I've watched animosity and discontent build between men until nothing short of coming to blows, or drawing weapons will again restore reason to their minds. This, in my estimation, is what began the civil conflict we know as the War of the Rebellion and this too is what proceeded from that day forward between Forrest and Wheeler.

"We were put on the River Road for Dover at the first streaks of dawn with the temperature well below freezing, in company of a force eight-hunert strong, consisting of portions of the Fourth Alabama, the Fourth Tennessee, Cox's, Napier's and Holman's Battalions, and Woodward's Kentuckians. We were accompanied by a complement of four six-pound James rifles. General Wharton with a command some two thousand strong, with two artillery pieces, advanced by way of a left-hand road, where they encountered and engaged a strong force of Union Cavalry, capturing all but a handful who escaped to sound the alarm amongst their compatriots in Dover.

"On our final approach, under direction of Major General Wheeler, only recently arrived upon the scene, we occupied the Confederate right, atop a crescent shaped ridge surrounding Dover by the east and southeast. What lay before us was a similarly shaped, fully occupied rifle pit some eight-hunert yards to our front, that surrounded the whole of the town. Beyond it we saw a redoubt atop a knoll on the same elevation as our own. In our immediate path lay a narrow valley, cut through with numerous gullies and ditches, that would present great hazard and challenge to a mounted attack.

"About this time we noticed General Wharton's troop arrive and deploy perhaps half a mile distant, at the opposite end of the line of battle from us, on a prominence to the far Confederate right.

"At the appointed hour I was instructed to sound the charge, the note of which was repeated by other buglers throughout our ranks. We immediately threw ourselves and horses forward, down the gradual slope of the ridge we occupied. The sun was making its first brief appearance for several days, whilst the wind had gratefully laid. The rock of the saddle, riding pall-mall, clearing ditch and rail, to the sound of pounding hooves, was for a moment glorious. But then, the abandon of flight was quickly replaced by the crude realities of war. We carried the rifle pit in the face of warmly delivered musket fire. The enemy's various six-pounders and a much larger gun firing from behind the earthen redoubt, atop the opposing knoll, swept numerous men from the saddle with grape and cannister. My perceptions of war were greatly affected that day as result of events that transpired thereafter.

"Front line soldiers come to accept death as a constant companion, ever at our shoulders. One too many near misses begins to wear on ye', giving the feeling that calamity is stalking, waiting for the inevitable one wrong move. If you let it worry you, such fatalistic conjecture can take the heart right out of an army, one man at a time. Anyone who's ever seen it knows, momentum can get you through many a dangerous situation, but once't lost, it can be sore difficult to again retrieve.

"I myself cut or shot down close to a hunert foe on the field of conflict during my stead as a soldier, many to their deaths. As a Confederate cavalryman from '62 to '64, I was expected to do no less. Duty is a seductive maiden that we followed after lustily. Those she did not swallow, followed her until it was beyond hope, for that is the nature of duty!

"I watched in disbelief as a trooper just ahead of me was dislodged from his saddle in a leap across one of the ditches in our path. He tumbled rearward, landing on his head and breaking his neck. With no room to maneuver in our tight formation, my horse couldn't avoid trampling his motionless body. I turned in the saddle as Prince cleared the same obstacle, to find the fallen man lost to my sight amongst the trailing dust and horses. I learned later he was indeed killed just that quickly.

"The main body of the Federals manning the outworks made good their retreat into the redoubt, taking with them their two fieldpieces, whilst we followed close on their heels with shouts of 'follow them into the works boys,' believing they would shield us from frontal fire. However, the firing from the elevated fortification and surrounding two-story buildings was merciless, coming from every angle as it was, being largely unobstructed by the presence of our fleeing foe. General Forrest went down right at the foot of the wall, his horse shot from beneath him, disappearing from sight whilst a blistering fire poured down on us. We fell back, firing as we went, our attack broken at the disappearance from view of our brave leader. The spirit of our soldiers was dashed, fearing the loss of one so respected by us all. But as we found relative shelter beyond the trench, what sight should we behold, but our dauntless General beating an ungraceful retreat on foot. We cheered his return, a small group riding out to cover his retrograde.

"Though our ranks were thinned, his appearance renewed our vigor and we quickly regrouped, again starting down the slope en-echelon, this time dismounted. We pressed hard on the Feds, driving them from the freshly reoccupied trench and surrounding outbuildings, felling many as they fled back over the bloody ground. We pressed them to the earthen walls of the redoubt where several of our best men and officers were gunned down by the unrelenting rifle and canister fire.

"In the front lines, every man, from the highest to the lowest rank, takes responsibility. Each one serves his comrades to protect their lives, even at the cost of his own. There can be no shrinking from the ultimate responsibility that falls to the fighting soldier. Unlike our various walks in civilian life, as military men, the boundaries of wealth and class dim in the heat of conflict, where all must face the ultimate test of courage.

"At the order, I sounded the bugle command and we marched shoulder to shoulder out of the Federal rifle pit that we'd momentarily occupied whilst reloading and regrouping. We started the long march across the hotly contested, remaining open ground. We could see their blue caps and jackets as they knelt and stood in rows behind the embrasure some two-hunert yards to our front. At the greater distance where we then found ourselves, the enemy couldn't yet use their elevation to fire on us, for fear of shooting their own fleeing comrades again running before us. We stayed close by them, to gain as much of the deadly no-man's land as possible before the enemy found shelter behind the emplaced battery that would then open its deadly work. Like the Yank riflemen, their cannons, too, were quiet, yet their gunners stood at the ready to once't more shower us with steel-toothed death at the earliest possible instant. We marched at the double-quick in long rows abreast. I looked left and right, seeing the line squirm forward at a brisk pace. The center would first curve a bit ahead of the balance of the line, then slow to realign, allowing the flanks to fall in. Our officers encouraged our pace and wills, steadying us for the hail of lead that was about to race horizontally over the field, shearing our corps like crops at harvest. Within moments the ground would turn to mud, wet with the blood of our bold fellers. I glanced over my shoulder to see the second, third and fourth ranks, mere yards between us, pennants flapping gently in the soft breeze. Then we raised the rebel yell from a chorus of voices that stood my hackles on end.

"I felt super-sensitized at that moment, looking ahead up the remaining gentle slope that was only occasionally interrupted by earthen terraces. I could feel the bugle bouncing loosely against my back and the dry-grass stubble poking at the bottoms of my feet even through my thick socks and heavy soles of my boots. It was a good feeling that I recognized as somehow special. The breeze caressed my cheeks as it picked up in our faces. That too was good, for it would carry the smoke from their first volley to help obscure our advance. But that was of little consequence, for the line of fire they would bring to bear could effectively hurl blindly through the covering smoke into our consecutive advancing ranks. We crossed another terrace, firing a last volley into the backs of the Federals retreating into the works. I held my empty weapon waist high, muzzle and bayonet pointed forward.

"My mind turned to home as the pulse pounded in my ears and my breath came in short gasps. I thought of our dear sisters and our old parents, their familiar faces passing afore me' mind's eye. The sunlight seemed sharper, like cut crystal, making the whole of the world stand out in bold relief. I glanced left and my eyes met Will's next to me for but a brief instant, we each managing a brief and feeble smile. The pores of his skin shown like the shell craters that marked our path. Fear and courage shined forth from my brother. Perhaps, I thought, our blood might soon mingle in the soil beneath our feet, knowing we could fall side by side at any instant after taking our last step together in cadence.

"As the fleeing Yankees cleared out of the enemy cannon's path, their guns suddenly blossomed smoke from their barrels, one after another down the line. The sound shortly followed. They were aimed at a high trajectory, sending screaming loads arching over our heads. In the next instant the canisters erupted in white puffs with a hollow report. Men dropped, or were flung at horrible angles. Screams of pain rang out above the cries of battle, accompanied by the unmistakable thud of jagged steel ripping into human flesh. Great gaps then appeared in our advancing lines, as we yet moved ever forward at a brisk, and steady pace. The company officers called for a shift in ranks to fill the new holes appearing in our lines. Men hustled to restore order to the growing chaos that suddenly held sway. A hot shard whistled past my right ear and Leo Sumler, a fine Tennessee lad, was gone from next to me. I looked to my rear then down, to see him horribly sprawled on his back, twitching, his face but a bloody pulp. I looked left to Will to see his jaw set, eyes burning like red hot coals. I noticed our files hugely reduced within the oily smoke that blinded us, burning in my nostrils, obscuring our view of the ramparts now but a few yards ahead.

"The crack of the exploding canisters sang out above the roar of the unseen cannon. We raced more quickly to try and reach that infernal wall whilst we still had strength enough in numbers to overrun the stubborn defenders. The cannon fell finally silent as we outran their field of fire. The wall had to be just before us, but was yet unseen through the descending cloud of smoke. With the cannonade halted, we'd soon outpace the thick, acrid smoke rolling down the hill, to see the gleaming bayonets of a hunert rifles trained on our advance. Then they'd let loose a point blank, deadly accurate volley that would strip our ranks further still! Only with luck, would we yet have men enough to sustain the attack and rout their position. Then we would turn the steel hail on them as they again fled before us. But the smoke hid our strength from my eyes as well as theirs and I could not say with any certainty if we were yet strong enough to carry the works. Men were spread apart two and three yards where we had before stood shoulder to shoulder. Will was still to my left, in no way holding back, rushing headlong to meet his fate, a few steps ahead of me.

"Then, out of the gloom, we began to make out the earthworks, capped with dark blue forms, less than forty yards to our front. As a man, our voices rose again in unison with a frightful battle shout, its power causing shudders in the ranks of Yanks. But they stood their ground as we closed the gap. Thirty, then twenty, then their raised muskets rang out as their corps commander's sword dropped. Again the wall vanished from sight in a rushing pall of white powder smoke. Will's rifle was knocked from his grip, landing at my feet. One of the last things I remember was looking down to judge my step so as not to trip over the pieces that were wrent in two at the stock, realizing in that brief instant that a mini-ball had snatched it from his hands, shattering the wooden stock where it met the forearm. I looked back at Will to see him gaze up from his empty hands toward the wall only some fifteen yards away. Before we could close that short gap, another volley erupted in our faces, deafening me with the percussion afore my world went black. The echo of the muzzle blast and the ringing in my head went on, though all other sounds of battle were, like our troop, nearly wiped out."

Pappy then paused and pulled out his pipe and tobacco, leisurely filling the wooden bowl as he'd done so oft before. My anticipation mounted, anxious to learn what came next. He completed the operation at last and struck a match to light the smoke. Then, examining me to check the effect of this interruption, he smiled at my strained patience and took a few puffs on his pipe before resuming the account, blowing first a few smoke rings into the air.

"I caught a ball right here," he said, pointing to the part in his hair, "that scalped me clean to here," he demonstrated with his forefinger, indicating a line halfway across the top of his skull. "As time goes by, we tend to forget some of the hardship we endured and remember only fonder times, but this wretched memory will not recede. I remember looking up from where I lay on the ground, on my back, into the depths of a clear blue sky, watching men scramble over me. I don't remember their faces that seemed so unimportant in relation to the vastness of that deep blue sky. My face must have been twisted in fear and pain until I began to pass. I slowly relaxed, until suddenly, beyond the sky, I could see rows of angels, trumpets blaring, drowning out the din of battle coming from all sides. The battle receded then completely from my consciousness.

"The glancing blow of the bullet knocked me unconscious for quite a spell. When I finally began to come to, I could hear the moans of other wounded and the murmur of Yankee voices moving amongst the fallen in the fading light of day. An odd sound kept preceding the silencing of excited voices. I gradually regained my senses and began to recognize the familiar sound, but it was somehow different. It was that of a bayonet stabbing into an abdomen. The oddness of its sound must have come from the fact that the bodies being stabbed were prone against the earth, instead of upright, as I'd only previously heard. As the voices of the Yanks brought their deadly work nearer, I drew in my breath and tried to still the now trembling extremities of my trapped body. Being, as I was, a good deal covered by inanimate, fallen comrades, I could only hope their lifeless forms would shield me from the lethal stabs. I peeked out of one, swollen, blood-incrusted eye to see if I could catch a glimpse of my immediate company, checking for some sign of life like a rising and falling breast. I saw none. With each beat of my heart, my head then began to throb terribly where I'd been shot.

"They came nearer, speaking in low, determined tones, rummaging through the effects of the dead, whilst the sickening sound of their cruel blades systematically silenced the murmurs of the dying. I tried to remember the call of angel trumpets and to be elsewhere, gone from there and the dreaded bayonet probing the innards of Sesech all around me. I lay stiller then than the dead atop me, who instead caught the stabs I dreaded. For the longest moment of my life, I played possum whilst the two hoodlums tugged on and removed the tall leather boots from my legs where they stuck out from beneath the pile. The fact they didn't also take my socks spoke volumes about the differences in provisioning for the two opposing armies.

"When the murderous, thieving Yanks moved along down the line, I again lost consciousness, receding into the netherworld, now filled with demons in place of the former angels. Such sights as I beheld in that fever dream, only Christ Himself returned from Hades, could tell of. Those vague memories are thankfully only brief glimpses of a hellish realm I fervently pray never to return to.

"When next I woke, it was to the deep bass sounds of gunboats firing as they stood out on the river lobbing shells upon the battlefield. The exploding bombs ripped apart many bodies. The bayonetists were gone, along with the sun and the moans of the wounded, leaving only our silent dead and the carrion critters rummaging amongst their carcasses. A pale moon cast an eerie luminance over the whole scene. At first I wasn't sure if I were alive, or dead, surrounded as I was in a cloud of ground fog. I was shortly overcome by a sensation like what drowning must be like. I was under and couldn't get up, pinned down by the lifeless, gray-clad bodies. I thought I might suffocate beneath the surface before

I finally, instinctively pushed free of the corpses pressing on my chest and stomach. Once freed, I fully opened my blood-encrusted eyes, only to see the stark reality of my situation come tumbling in with startling clarity.

"I became fearful for my safety, moving as I was, in the open amongst the knots of bodies. At a distance, I saw a nigra grave detail laboring at their gruesome task, under supervision of two blue clad, white men holding rifles and lanterns. I crawled slowly through the gore, from one twisted tangle to another. The fog covering the valley dampened the stench of blood and helped conceal my movement. Of all the myriad smells of the battlefield, there was one more familiar, if no less repugnant, that reminded me to always attend to my constitution before going into a fight.

"I struggled through the clutter of limbs and trunks, verging on panic, having to purposefully, calmly talk myself through. Eventually I gained one of the ditches that cut through the swag and crawled as rapidly as I could toward the shelter of the tree line. Looking back from the lip of the ditch to survey from whence I'd just come, it appeared some two hunert of my fine comrades-in-arms littered the valley floor. Many dear friends and fine men lay amongst them. Still partially dazed, I stood to my stockinged feet, teeth chattering in the numbing cold, and whilst stooping to stay below the cover of the gully, started to flee. I had progressed but a short distance before I had the presence of mind to stop and retrieve a fairly good fit in bootery from a fallen comrade near the ditch. Then I again fled as swiftly as I could manage in search of my company and hopefully my yet surviving brother." He paused an instant, long enough for me to turn my head to look at him, then finished.

"The body I robbed the boots from, was that of the soldier who'd fallen from his horse and broken his neck in the first charge. In the light of the rising moon, his body covered with frost, I could see the shocked look in his lifeless, almost accusing eyes, peering over one shoulder from a twisted neck. Prince's hoof-prints, amongst others, were clearly visible, even in the dim light, on his misshapen back."

Again he paused in the gruesome narrative to relight his pipe grown cold. I knew not what to say to all of this, overwhelming as it was. It seemed unimaginable to experience something that horrible. There was much more to this old world than my brief twelve years of sheltered experience had yet revealed to me. A chill ran through me, causing me to shiver on the warm August afternoon.

"Fetch me a cold drink, would ye' boy?" he asked me.

"Yes sir, straight away," I said, glad for the distraction from the gruesome sights crowding on my mind. "This water ain't so cold Pappy, I'll draw us a fresh bucket from the well," I said, tossing the pail full into the yard and hurried off for another. When I shortly returned, after cooling the heat of my brain with the first bucket drawn, he sat puffing his pipe and speaking to a young couple who rode slowly past in their surrey. I handed him the dipper full that he drank right down, with a deep satisfied sigh before wiping his lips on the back of his hand and asking with a smile, "How 'bout another'n?"

"You betcha' Pappy," I said, glad to be of service to this man who was lucky even to be here. That thought then reminded me, so, too, was I lucky to even be, for he hadn't started his family until after returning home from war. As I pondered the implications of that, he returned to that sad, long-ago day of February third, 1863.

"I was picked up around nine o'clock in the evening by a scouting party from my own regiment and returned to the retreating command, camped some three miles away from Dover. I was happy beyond words to find my brother with little more than a mild flesh wound received from a Yankee bullet. Also to my relief and satisfaction, there, too, was my trusted Prince. A horse can be as close a companion as a dog and that noble animal was as good a friend as perhaps I've ever had. Will, too, was overjoyed to have his lost brother, given up for dead, restored to him yet again. He told me, 'Kid brother, you must keep your guardian angel ever at her task.'

"I related my escape to a campfire gathering, grimly recounting the atrocities and how the Yankee corpse robbers stabbed and snuffed out the wounded, to which a black oath was sworn by all, to avenge the blood of our comrades upon the culprits of the Eighty-third Volunteer Illinois Infantry.

"After my having been knocked unconscious, our charge, they said, was repulsed with great loss, the gallant boys, ammunition completely exhausted, having no other choice than to fall back. Forrest had yet another mount shot from beneath him. A number of the finest officers in the Confederate service were killed, including Colonel Frank McNairy and Lieutenants Summers and Chapman. In addition, several more were severely wounded and/or captured. All told, some two-hunert sixty men and officers were lost in that folly ordered by Fighting Joe. After surveying his wrecked brigade back at camp, Nathan Bedford, in a towering rage by then, told Major General Wheeler, 'Sir, I'll be in my coffin afore I ever again fight under any command of your'n!' He was, I think, as disappointed in himself for having been talked into going against his own better judgement, as he was with his commander's folly.

"Fighting for life to survive the battle was one thing, but living with the memory of what had happened was entirely another. It was a long time before I stopped frighting wake nights with that feeling of drowning. Some dreams you don't dream, they instead dream you. And you know," he added, scratching his head, "my scalp still itches right here some days," he said in reference to the grazing wound atop his skull.

"Two days later, on the fifth of February," he continued, "our seriously diminished ranks were augmented by the addition of the Second Kentucky Regiment, First Tennessee Battalion, the Texas Brigade and an Arkansas regiment of the Third Cavalry. We were then officially designated as a full cavalry corps made up of roughly forty-five hunert men. Company A of the Third Arkansas consisted of Dallas County lads and there was much rejoicing in our camps that evening as old friends were reunited for the first time in well over a year. They shared an abundance of news from home and told us of their winding path down the trail of war that had brought them thus to service beside us. Not having received mail from home since leaving Tupelo, Will and I learned for the first time of brother James Andrews's conscription into infantry service with the Nineteenth Arkansas. This left us with many new concerns for both him, our parents and our sisters back home, with none of us now there to look after 'em in the face of the growing Yankee threat in south Arkansas. We were mortified to learn of 'Jayhawkers' now operating within the environs of Dallas and Bradley Counties. They would ride out of Federal occupied Pine Bluff, we were told, crossing the river at night under cover of darkness, raiding homesteads to the west, stealing every horse and mule their thieving hands could snatch, to take them back across't the river to the Union garrison in order to be exchanged in return for Federal gold. Redlands and Saline Townships lay in easy striking distance, with plenty of swamps and bottoms to hold up in during daylight hours. These dislegalists operated against our very homes, with carte blanche from the U.S. gov'ment, robbing and vandalizing the unprotected citizenry of the region.

"We were told of all this by a boy from our community named T.A. Atkinson, who we knew from the swimmin' hole and who was at that time, your deceased Granny's first husband. He later died in the war at Chickamauga. T.A. was a steady, likable sort, elected First Sergeant of Company A by his fellows. Also amongst the newcomers to our ranks were Douglas Kennedy and his older brother Corporal Allen Kennedy, who we knew well all our lives and had gone to school and church with. This reunion went a long ways toward renewing our spirits after the fiasco at Dover. We discussed how we had been, in our opinion, foolishly dashed against the works there, only to have our story pale by comparison to their own. Seems the Third had only recently had their horses restored to them, having before that been employed as infantry since their initial enlistment. They had been present back in October when Van Dorn attempted to take back Corinth, probably then the most heavily defended piece of property in the entire country, wasting as result, thousands of the South's finest. This letter," he said, again referring to the paper in his hand, "was written to your Grandma Mary Adams Atkinson Ledbetter, by her husband at the time, First Sergeant T.A. Atkinson, describing some of the carnage that he witnessed. I'd like you to read this son and whilst you're readin', remember that it's only because of your schoolin', that resumes on the morrow, that you can cipher the meaning of that hand." He looked at me sternly to add emphasis to his point, while awaiting my response.

After a few moments, realizing he expected a reply, I said simply, 'Yes sir,' in a meek voice, perhaps a little ashamed of my earlier complaining in light of these latest revelations.

"I think that's enough for today. I'll tell you 'bout bein' in Yankeedom's prison camps next chance we have to visit. But trust me when I say, school and prison have very little in common."

Holding out the letter for me to take, he said, "Carry this home with ye' and read it a little later." Still grasping it between his forefinger and thumb, even as I took hold of it, he added, "Take care of it now, this paper may have once't saved a young life."

"How's that," I asked?

Letting loose the document that I then held gingerly in my own hand with reverence, like some old Bible, he began to explain briefly.

"I'd returned home during the latter half of '64 and by '65 was fairly well heal't from my stomach wound. From time to time, wayfaring young-bloods would come through here some evenings on the neighborhood road, in need of a meal and to sit a spell.

"Your grandma, my deceased wife Mary, had spent hours in my parents' home nursing first my ill mother before my arrival, then on my unexpected return, me. She was widowed; her first husband and my friend T.A. having died from wounds received at Chickamuaga. He authored that letter to her in the winter of '62 after his experiences at Corinth with the dismounted Third Arkansas. I'd forwarded the letter to her after T.A. passed. She gave the letter to me on my homecoming and I reread it several times as I convalesced. I kept it then thereafter in a coat pocket hung by the door. When I'd occasionally ponder the possibility of returning to my outfit, I'd take out the letter and it would remind me of all the futility of war. Between it, the bad dreams and Mary's sweet eyes, I was able to free myself from the grip and call of duty.

"Of the several regiments originally mustered back in '61 and early '62, few were still actively designated for service because attrition had so greatly depleted their ranks. They'd been consolidated and reconsolidated with the remnants of other units. The Arkansas Infantry Regiments of the Nineteenth, Sixth, Seventh, Second, Twelfth, First, Ninth and Fifth were eventually all consolidated under the much-debated designations of the Seventh and the Nineteenth Infantries. Their officers were given furlough to return home and recruit young men just coming of age to bring under-strength regiments near as possible up to strength. I was laying low, lest they find me and send me back, or hang me for a desertin' scoundrel.

"I got wind of those officer's touting their tall tales of honor and glory for the Confederacy. The war was already lost by then, it only remaining to be fully proven out to some. The final results were written in the hand of scoundrels the world is too oft visited by, with the lives of young-bloods who should never have been sacrificed upon that altar to a gov'ment already withered on the vine.

"Sitting here on the porch, I'd watch and listen to visiting younguns in their eagerness to get into the fray. I was reminded of my own naïve notions back in the spring of '62. I'd like to've known how to stop 'em from goin' down the war road, but one's gotta butt with one's own head. I could only share my accounts 'bout the true realities of war with the occasional lad come wandering down our path, in hopes it might sway their thinkin' and perhaps head em back in the direction of home.

"By this time, my mother had passed, my father hadn't remarried and I was yet to ask the widow Atkinson to be me' wife, so's it was just us two old bachelors alone with our ghosts in this empty log-house. We welcomed some occasional company, especially young folks, to restore a little life and vigor to the old haunts. Having learned well how to batch whilst in the service, I did most the cookin', except for meals prepared and brought right regular by the many war-widows with eyes set towards Pa and me.

"After an evenin' meal and some small talk with the war-bound sojourners, we'd retire toward the barn to check the livestock and share in a nip from a jug I kept by for socializin'. The conversation would generally work its way 'round to the question of enlistment in the Cause of southern freedom. Once asked of my sentiments on the war, I reckon I felt bound to make some sort of effort to, pray, save a life in repayment for all those I'd taken. Thusly had I opportunity on a few rare occasions to read aloud the soldier's letter home to a handful of would-be Johnny Rebs.

"With the advent of war, schooling was a secondary concern, what with the farm tasks falling to the few younguns still remaining back home. Education was neglected and far too many lads couldn't write even their own names, much less read a communique. So, I'd pull the pre-placed letter from the pocket of my black frock coat where it hung next to the back door and without further introduction, but to make a show of unsheathing and unfolding the manuscript, I'd recount those sad feelings so accurately captured in time.

"On at least one occasion I know of, the un-whiskered naiveté returned back up the road toward home in the direction from whence he'd come, after hearing an account of the wastefulness of war."

With those final words, our visit for the day drew to a close. My ma, Mommy, could be heard calling from down the road for me to head that way. The morrow was the first day of school and there were things that needed tending. Reluctantly I shuffled down the steps, hands in pockets, dragging my feet in the dust. As I turned to latch the yard gate behind me, I looked up to see Pappy grinning broadly. He said simply, "Study hard son, someday you'll be glad ye' did. Learn ye' letters well and be careful your hand."

"Yes, sir," I replied, feeling of the paper stuffed deep in my trouser pocket, anxious to soon have a read at it. It would be near bedtime, later that evening, before I could settle in with a flickering lantern to decipher the faded scrawl that crowded onto every inch of the pages, paper having become so rare and valuable by the stage of the war when it was written.

BATTLE OF CORINTH

224

The Letter

Oct. 19th, 1862

My Dearest Mary,

How I do miss you and our three little ones. Do they speak of me much? Oh how I do you, telling the boys of ya'll often. I would appreciate a kiss from you now more than any I ever got. I cannot exaggerate the pleasure your letter last gave to know you and the children were all well. I pray this letter finds you likewise. The boys are always joshing me about you. They delight in telling every gal we meet in our travels that I am the married fellow amongst them. I do not mind though, for I know you are as fine a wife as can be found in all the Confederacy. I fear the next few months apart from you and our babies will be the longest of my life. I so long for peace to return that I may come home to you all.

We have seen some hard campaigning of late, with some loss to our number. We buried Billy Scarbourgh just two days past after he fell in our most recent battle. Rest assured I am yet well to this point. There is much talk of our soon being given back our horses. Our good Colonel Sam Earle sent a letter directly to General Sterling Price requesting the immediate return of our mounts from where they are still billeted there near home as yet awaiting recall to our service. All company's officers signed the petition and Colonel Earle personally delivered it to our commanding general. Should our request be honored, of which we have great hopes, a detail will be dispatched across the Mississippi to retrieve our animals. I am hopeful to be included among those forwarded on such duty. My dear, please pray that such will be the case, for I so long to soon hold you each within my embrace once more. Hug the little darlings for me and tell them each how very much their absent father loves and misses them.

I carry a great burden as First Sergeant, standing as I do between the enlisted men and the officers. I have not before told you fully about my life over here, for we live daily with death and tyrants. I know not if this will be the last letter I'll ever write you. This war has been filled with a long string of frustrations, one arriving quickly on the heels of another, with so many opportunities for defeating the invaders lost at such cost. So we take bittersweet pleasure from the rare instances when we are allowed to actually be victorious. Too many of the officers consider the enlisted as less than gentlemen, though I wouldn't give a plugged nickel for the scruples of most of them "gentlemen" when compared to the common soldiers who do the real fighting. As the highest-ranking, non-commissioned soldier in the ranks, most officers consider me "almost" a gentleman. I beg you forgive my sour attitude, but there are none here for me to share these thoughts with, for the officers would consider it treason and the men would likely be incited to mutiny should they hear their First Sergeant express opinions so like their own. But, I must needs give vent to my feelings lest I soon loose in part my sanity. I thank you for your forbearance.

As an example of the terrible mishandling of troops in both armies, I will in a hurried manner try to recount some of the sad transactions of our most recent campaign, in which it was my lot to take part, as did ten-and-one-half thousands of my fellow companions under General Price's command, first on the attack, seizure and eventual defense of Iuka, followed by our ill-fated attack on Corinth. It is said that honest confession is good for the soul. All experience teaches us that communion in an honest and confiding spirit with our fellows refines and improves our minds and hearts. As

226

iron strengthens iron, so, too, do men draw strength from their own.

On September 14th last, we marched against the Yanky garrison at Iuka, some twenty miles southeast of Corinth down the Memphis and Charleston Railroad. The Federal garrison fell back at our advance, evacuating the town before our superior force. We re-provisioned from the badly needed supplies left behind by the retreating Unionists and took up their abandoned quarters. The Mississippians of the place happily welcomed our arrival. Shortly thereafter, an order came to General Price from General Van Dorn to join our two armies in concert to assault the heavily defended railhead at Corinth. That same day however, the 17th, the Federals attempted to trap and encircle our 15,000 Graybacks within the confines of tiny Iuka. Approaching from the north under a flag of truce, Union General Ord sent a message to General Price telling of a recent Confederate defeat at Antietam, saying that he thought the outcome of the war was thus decided on that far-away field in Maryland and that our surrender would avoid useless bloodshed. General Price replied that such a case, were it true, would only move us to redouble our efforts and that no laying down of arms would occur 'til such time as the Union recognized the independence of the Confederacy. Sensing a trap, our commander then prepared to march us south, away from Ord's blue columns. But in so doing, we shortly encountered the other jaw of the trap laid for us by Rosecran's Federals approaching quickly from the south.

We formed for battle in the recently abandoned Federal rifle pits. I had no more compunction that day about killing Yankys than I did about eating my breakfast. We were all anxious for our unit names to be redeemed from the many defeats we'd suffered at their hands. But what happened next nobody wanted. Those Iowa farm boys displayed themselves honorably, yet it was one of the most horrible sights I've witnessed in my

227

stead as a soldier. My flesh trembles, creeps and crawls even now at the very thought of it. We were safely behind works, ready and waiting when they marched out into the open ground and began their long trek to assault us. They knew their drill well enough and stepped along smartly like a fine-honed blade cutting our way. Our fingers tightened on stocks and triggers. A few anxious looks were exchanged within our ranks, whilst most stared steadily down their sights at the approaching blue hordes. I attempted to steady the men, speaking calmly as I moved down the line, encouraging them with a pat on the back and a "steady on" spoken as I passed each position. I heard over the clank and clamor, another sergeant down the line shouting, "Here's them Yanks we promised you, boys. Aim careful now!" I looked either way up and down our trench and then to our front at the awesome sight of half a thousand men under arms, bayonets gleaming in the low angle of the sunlight, closing steadily with our company of Dallas County boys hunkering down in a hole in the ground.

The lads under my command came from all corners of our county. We'd been whooped pert near every time we'd been committed to action. We'd seen our colors fall before and felt we'd been so far cheated, with no fair chance to prove our worth as soldiers. We only wanted now to have at 'em. To a man, we were determined to regain our honor and have those now approaching colors. The time was finally at hand. All the wheels of creation had turned, since perhaps the very dawn of time, aligning to grant us the tenfold-retribution that was about to be wrought from these invaders. As they drew ever nearer, the knots in our stomachs were not as much from fright at seeing the deadly tusks of the charging elephant, as from the desire to take the gleaming tusks for a prize all our own. Didn't they know, I wondered, what was fixin' to happen? As I watched their good order, dressing their line as they quick stepped across the remaining ground, I became more certain they did indeed know, but were good soldiers, proud to go as ordered into the breach. I encouraged the boys to hold their fire, being of the mind that long distance fire, taking out but one of ten was easier to mentally absorb and men would continue to advance in the face of it. Whereas if we were patient, being careful not to hesitate too long, delaying our fire until the last possible moment, we could easily take out six, or seven of ten with every volley. In those circumstances the enemy will more readily break under the shock of such smashing heat.

When I finally gave the order to fire, the Yanks were as near as fifty steps. We disgorged a belching breath of destruction, dropping them all along their front. They quickly and expertly closed up, faltering but little in their advance. But our second volley was on them before they'd even closed ten more paces and their ranks further thinned to reveal many open spaces back through their slowing advance. We quickly poked down another round, stabbing our ramrods in the soft soil of the trench-front and fired again. True to my theory, the greater shock value of the solid wall of accurate fire began to tell. The third volley decimated the ranks of desperate men yet standing. Still they retrieved their fallen banner each time a bearer was cut down. It was a frightful, appalling sight, the very thought of which yet staves the blood from my heart. I began to wish they'd stop coming afore we'd kilt them all. The few remaining were close enough by then for us to easily read the 17th Iowa on their pennant snapping atop its staff, shrouded even as it was within the darkening powder gloom. Only a few coarse throats still carried their defiant battle cry. The groans of their fallen began to replace it. We reloaded and fired until but a handful of them remained to achieve the rifle pit they'd so valiantly assaulted. Some fell on bayonets, while a few were spared, simply knocked unconscious by a rifle butt in an effort to spare their brave and foolish lives. The Iowa flag went down under a hail of fists and was snatched from the grasp of the last bearer. We surveyed the daunting scene and the wrecked brigade lying before us, squirming in their agony beneath the low hanging cloud of dust and smoke. I spoke aloud to no one in particular, "Welcome to the wrecking ball boys!" The taste of our retribution turned sour in our mouths and sat like bitter fruit on our stomachs. Their colors had fallen right into our waiting arms as the final bearer showed us how a condemned soldier meets his fate. I was happy to learn a little later that the brave Yank had suffered only some bruises and cracked ribs within the storm of blows that met him as he reached our trench. The fingers on his right hand had been broke as they pried the flagstaff from his iron grip. Somehow, I knew right at that moment our time in the mouth of the tiger would soon enough again come.

We rose from the hunkered down position we'd held against the assault, watching the pitiful remnant of those 17th Iowa boys beating a hasty, disorganized retreat back through their fallen brothers. Sporadic cheers began to go up at intervals along our line, but were short lived for lack of support after the drifting smoke cleared to reveal such awful and total destruction as lay before us. The sounds that replaced our few victory shouts came then from the dry throats of the many dying and wounded Yanks. I prayed God forgive us what we'd done. One soldier said, "That was quick, weren't it?" to which I replied, "Killing don't take that long, it's living that's supposed to last awhile. But now it's all but done for these boys." We poured out of our trenches and drove the fleeing Feds before us, making good our escape from the would-be trap intended for us. We won the day, but our time would soon come at Corinth, for what goes around surely comes around.

We made a forced march around by the south and joined up with Van Dorn's troops west of Corinth near Ripley on the 28. By Friday morning, October 3, we were ready for a joint offensive of our two armies. T'was one of those bright and beautiful mornings that makes the heart leap for joy, helping remove most of our remaining trepidations about the slaughter at Iuka. The day found us wending our way under marching orders from Generals Price and Van Dorn, having previously prepared three days rations and told to be ready to march at a moments warning.

Our march was uninterrupted until near the middle of the afternoon, when suddenly the sound of artillery burst upon our ears; the couriers flew madly by us, the orders were received for the 3rd Arkansas to double quick into line, an order often given and obeyed before.

In a few minutes the brigade was formed in front of the first line of defensive works around Corinth. Shot and shell plowed the ground around it and through it, but oft before had it unflinchingly faced the enemy and now confidently it awaited the order to engage. Nor waited long, the bugle note called at once the onset, a short, sharp assault placed the works in our possession and the march was resumed.

On every road leading to Corinth from the south were heard brisk skirmishing and then all would be silence for a while. Then again the skirmishing would begin a little nearer the main works and a little more stubbornly contested. Late in the evening, as the sun nearly hid below the western horizon, looking red and angry through the clouds of battle smoke, the hottest engagement of the day was in progress. Green's Brigade fiercely assaulted the last outwork, which was being stubbornly defended. A courier dashes up to our brigade officer and again the bugle sounded the assault. With one immense shout that fairly shakes the Earth, of which ears unaccustomed to the sounds of warfare can have no idea, our brigade carries the works and furiously drives the enemy up to the very front of the main works, establishing itself far in advance of the fast-converging lines, all now leading to the same point at Battery Powell.

The sun set in a fiery blaze, beginning a long and moonless night. Now dark, very dark and the flanks of our brigade are exposed to the enemy sharpshooters. Orders come to the center, for my own company to deploy on the right as skirmishers. Imagine yourself there, ordered to deploy in pitch darkness against an enemy already posted, firing at everything they hear, with only the flash of their muzzles to guide you, then you have one of the more trying duties of a soldier.

That contest kept up until midnight when our friends were formed so as to protect our flanks and we returned to our place in line. We lay down, not to sleep, but to ponder over the events of the day and to think of tomorrow. All who started with us in the morning are not with us now, some lie in hospital with limbs torn and bleeding, lives fading slowly away; some are maimed for life, while others will recover and soon stand again with us in battle line. Some are already filling a soldier's grave, uncoffined, unshrouded, wrapped only in their soldier's blanket, taking their last long sleep, their Earthly warfare ended.

Thoughts of home and kindred and friend come crowding thick upon our minds. Oh, dear wife of my lost youth, how I did sore miss thee then. Our precious children presented themselves each one to my very heart and how I longed to bounce them once more upon my knee. All thoughts of kindred, love and friendship seem doubly dear when we know on the morrow we may forever be separated. Too well we know death will very soon reign supreme and who will be its victim?

Everyone knows our work. In front of us are more than forty guns, loaded, ready at an instant to open on our advance. To our right and left stand strong forts mounting many heavy guns and we are sheltered from them now by only the steep railroad embankment that we hide behind, which for the time at least, completely

232

shelters us. But too well we know that as soon as we assault those works, lines of bayonets will gleam fiercely out from behind them.

Here I confess that no circumstance has ever so tried me before, or since and I pray shall nary again. For ten, long hours we were left thus to our contemplations and reflections. There is no language to express the emotions that rise in the breast under such surroundings. Oh, dear wife and all who may read this, so far removed from such trial by time and distance, greatly contemplate these things. Let an earnest prayer ascend to Him who rules over all things, that neither you, nor our children, or their children, may ever be similarly so tried.

The first gleam of light in the east was the signal for the artillery to begin its deadly work. Fiercely the enemy assaulted our own artillery, but what could our light field guns do against emplaced heavy guns? The contest was unequal and our guns were quickly silenced. The sharpshooter's next began their long, fierce contest. The sun is high, but still no bugle call to assault. All are tired of this delay and desire to end the intolerable suspense. The sun rises yet higher and still the uninterrupted rattle of skirmishing continues. Ten o'clock is here, will the assault never be sounded? Yes, at last, clear and loud by the same high note that has so often before called to action. Sounding the assault, most determinedly is it obeyed. Concealed batteries and rifle pits before unknown are stormed and like the incoming sea, our column drives everything before it, assaults the works, carries every gun, sweeps away the first line of supports, assaults and scatters the second like chaff before the wind. A third line of reserves more stubbornly contests. Our own fire is weakened, but our momentum is too great! Their third line waivers, breaks, it rallies a little Oh, for a few more minutes and it too will be driven; but no, on our right and left our friends have failed and fallen back. Now both our flanks are assaulted causing them to begin doubling slowly back on our center. Fierce commotions are repeated, with everyone knowing that only complete victory, or utter rout shortly now awaits us. Pale-faced are our reserves. Twenty minutes placed the works in our possession while for forty more we contended as men seldom ever continue, but still not one friendly bayonet in sight. Our flanks are pressed further back upon our center. We are broken, routed, but so fierce we find was the assault, the enemy now so shattered, that we are not pressed as we withdraw. Still their artillery plows mercilessly through our broken ranks, coming at us from three directions. It is over; with not one half of those brave men who obeyed the summons to assault given this morning, returning to meet us at our evening camp located only a few miles from the fatal spot.

Our regiment gathers about our, alas, only remaining field officer. The officer names on the letter of request for remounting, reads like a roll of the dead. Our campfire lighted, no word is spoken and no thought even whispered. Those hardy men clustered together, without uttering one word, much like frightened children.

That morning they were determined and not unworthy participants in one of the most bloody scenes ever enacted, with cheeks unblanched and nerves of steel, but now the tears flow down every cheek, as in perfect silence they contemplate the wreck of our once proud brigade, who only wished to boast that it rarely assaulted a foe in vain.

Thus began and thus ended a sad day, a Sabbath, one which came from the hand of the Great Creator, bright and clear, a most beautiful and lively day as it came from the hand of the Great Giver. But oh how marred, how desecrated by the hand of man, to whom it was given in mercy for rest!

I realize now how little control we have over our own destinies. The generals gamble their reputations and we are the stakes of their wager, won, or lost at the *roll of the dice, or the drop of a card. So if it is ours to die, not to go like sheep to the slaughter, but rather to fight and die with honor! It is now late and we have reveille before the dawn. I will finish this on the morrow.*

My dear Mary, in reading back over these words I fear they may disturb you too greatly, but some peace now returns to my heavy-laden breast from sharing of this burden with you my love. Kiss the children for me and pray we may soon be remounted. Perhaps I may be detailed to fetch our horses and can soon see you all. Write as often as you can and give my love to all. God bless and watch over you in my absence. I will write again at my next opportunity.

Your loving and ever faithful husband unto death,
Sgt. Thomas A. Atkinson

(After studying the frank tone of his correspondence, the Sergeant decided against sending it to his wife at the time for fear it would too greatly distress her. The mere act of writing it had granted some relief to him from the ponderous burden he bore. He would carry it on his person over the next year until just prior to his death, occasionally rereading the solemn lines, grateful he hadn't forwarded it at the time of its composition.)

Mars' Spawn

The tellings never took place outside of the picket fence that surrounded the old house built in 1855 by his father. Starting over after the war practically from scratch, Pappy added the fence, erecting it with his own hands, fixing its borders around the sanctity of their home. He took great pleasure from its neatly spaced palings and orderly design. He'd set the boundaries of the yard with those rough-sawn cypress boards and then within that perimeter, aided by his new, first wife Mary, they elaborated on the little homestead, planting flower beds thick with daylilies, building a new hen house and laying out a generous vegetable garden.

On January eighteenth, 1866 he'd wed his nurse, the Widow Atkinson and helped her rear his new stepchildren, Sergeant Atkinson's orphans, Jewel, Betty and Byron. Then, late in 1866, she bore him a son, my father, Charles Edwin. Again in 1870, she would bear him a second boy, who lived but a month, just long enough to assure their broken hearts. They both loved and lost more than once. The little one, named William for Pappy's older brother, lies with other past generations at Camp Springs, their graves marked by fallen leaves, collected in the sunken depressions of the Earth, enriching its red clay for future generations. Grandma Mary never recovered from the loss and died soon after, joining the others and leaving Pappy to raise Sergeant Atkinson's three young children and a toddler of his own, my infant father.

We sat together, Pappy and I, on that day in steel, lawn chairs beneath the broad shade tree adjacent to the vegetable garden. The nip of fall was in the air and here, too, the leaves drifted down around us and collected in the furrows between the fallow rows. The harvest was in, so now the tilled soil, within its neat borders, was only a garden of memories from Pappy's cultivated mind.

"My life as a soldier was keenly divided between pre-Dover and post-Dover," he began. "For the first time in years my uniform no longer seemed a proper fit. It felt too tight. And I'd lost on the

237

battlefield, the wide-brim, slouch felt-hat that had served me so well up 'til then. I thereafter took to regularly wearin' the gray wool and black leather gov'ment issued kepi I'd had since Memphis.

"Some say my head wound changed me. I knew it was not the physical effects of the blow to my skull, but rather my descent into death's dark cavern, whilst I lay lifeless amid the pile of dead and wasted Southern boys. Death was cold and silent as it sat heavy on my heart like a great stone, its weight altering forever the composition of my soul. Upon that field of carnage I awoke to a strange, vertiginous feeling and the sound of someone screaming. Frost was settled on my ears, eyebrows and beard and the screams, it turned out, were mine own. Often after that I'd awake myself nights with similar cries of fear. Those chilling memories I hold yet in my heart, fully and intact." With that he fell silent for a spell, before again continuing.

"After my experience at Dover, I soon tired, then altogether sickened of war. But the circumstances of bein' enlisted for three more years and my sense of duty to my mates, wouldn't allow me to yet leave the army. Nor was there any assurance that war wouldn't soon come home to Dallas and Bradley Counties, a fact that only worried Will and me the more about our women folk. With James Andrew by then away in service, that left only our Pa to protect 'em. We found what solace we could in the fact that they was all resourceful, stalwart, pioneers. Faced with orders and committed to combat, we couldn't yet go home, so, but else was to fight or die. And so we did, to the point that with me the rage and habits of soldiering in the heat of action became as much a part of my character as almost any other aspect of my basic nature, equaled in stature only by my natural tendencies toward compassion, sensitivity and spiritualism. As such, my soul has been ever restless, stirred as it is by such confounding opposites, like two armies upon the field within striking distance, only minutes away from confrontation with one another, ever shifting, probing for some weak point or advantage, that one may overwhelm the other and thus vanquish it.

"Every night in the army was a campout, wet, or dry, summer, or winter, whether in quarters, or on the move. We rested at Columbia for some days after our fearful exposure to the harsh winter conditions and the severe battle losses we suffered at Dover. Not long after being reinforced by the Third Arkansas and others, about March sixth, we were thrown across the Duck River to take up post with headquarters at Spring Hill.

"Whilst preparing to ferry the Duck, one of the boys found a rabbit den in a mass of logs drifted on the riverbank. He called together the several companies near the spot and surrounded the pile of logs with clubs, as he set it ablaze. The wood was high up on the sandbar, full of small tender and very dry, so the whole affair was soon engulfed in swirling, crackling flames. The rabbits altogether commenced to abandon their refuge, darting in every which direction, where they were struck, or turned by flailing missiles, or stomping feet. They screamed with a high, terrified voice in their helpless panic. It was a similar scream as I've since heard coming from field hospitals and prisons.

"Hardly a cottontail escaped and the troops feasted that night on every conceivable form of rabbit meat, though I could eat none, put off by the whole spectacle and their hunerts of tiny screams, mixed with the whoops and thudding blows from our boys. I gnawed on hardtack instead.

"Once in position at Spring Hill, we established outposts and picket lines. A series of sharp, spirited skirmishes took place for the next fortnight, fraught daily with the ring and flash of steel and splendid acts of courage and hardihood. We made the enemy pay dearly encounter after encounter, but its customary attendants upon the field of conflict saddened the joy of our victory. For every fiery, glowing description of military glory, there is a dark counterpart consisting of every form of mutilation and disfigurement imaginable. The romance is dampened by the realities of war. I recall faces distorted in pain so as to scarcely appear human after encountering the swift messengers of death, their bandage and clothes clotted with blood, with no good couch on which to repose, save some straw scattered sparsely upon the ground. The uncomplaining fortitude I witnessed of so many wounded and dying, on both sides of the conflict, helped raise my opinion of our race.

"Our initial bloodlust quenched in the main, after having met the elephant so often, many began to weary of killin' and bein' kilt.

"It was at this time a group of us met some Yanks about dark at a spring near our evening's camp. I was standin' guard whilst other troopers quietly replenished hands full of canteens. Some Yanks wandered up figurin' to do the same. I saw 'em first and had 'em dead to rights, looking at 'em, along with others of our detail, right down the barrel of our carbines. When first they saw us, they knew it was too late, we had 'em cold. They froze in mid-stride. It was yet light enough to make out the eyes and rank of a Yank sergeant lookin' right back into my one squinted eye and the bore of my piece. I could see they were cav. from their noisy, dangling sabers and the yellow stripes on their trouser legs. Gradually I lowered my gun and smiled at the blue belly, then nodded to the gurgling spring. He took my meaning and began to relax, then speak to his detachment, telling them to go ahead with their task as he glanced back over his shoulder to insure he'd read me right. There we all were, weapons pointed at the ground, or into the air, within feet of the selfsame enemy the generals had flung at us and us them, so many bloody times. I suppose the unspoken, temporary truce that fate had ordained was evidence that we'd already seen enough ambulances filled with mangled, bleeding freight and unless duty strictly required it, maybe we could drink quietly for a spell from the same spring without tainting it with our spilt blood. With no generals, or colonels around to tell us any different, no one got trigger-happy.

"When our lads finished fillin' canteens on our side of the little pool, we gathered them up and headed out in the direction of our camp. Our armed guards continued to stand easy, but ready for any aggression 'those people' might make against our backs as we withdrew. Under the vigilance of their spared sergeant, the Yanks kept their nervous fingers away from their ready triggers and pointed no weapons at us. We filed out of their line of sight, covering each the other's flank whilst we egressed from the spring. I looked the Yank sarge once't more in the eye, in the fast fading light of day, without the distraction of my saddle rifle staring him down. He straightened to attention and snapped a crisp salute to his cap bill and held it until I returned it with an easy, almost cavalier one of my own, touching the brim of my cocked hat with just two fingers of my right hand. We both sensed something unusual had just transpired that would long be recalled by all present years after our stead as soldiers was past, as a thing less horrible than most encounters, to help balance out some of the harder experiences.

"I admonished the boys not to speak of the incident lest we be brought up for cowardice in the face of the enemy by some overzealous officer with an axe to grind. With the dawn, the truce was long since past and the trumpets called us again to arms as we prepared afresh for battle with the enemy.

"The young Yank sergeant's face was still clear in my memory and as the Lord admonishes us to pray for our enemies, my morning prayers included a mention of him and his men, that they might not come under our guns and yet have to suffer at our hands. Our thirsts were for a time quenched by the drink from the cool spring, though nothing so quickly makes one's mouth go again dry as armed conflict. We were about to face the enemy in the coming days with redoubled fury, to again kill at our superior's behest. God help us all, I prayed.

"On March fourth, scouts sped into headquarters with news that a large force of Federal infantry were headed toward Spring Hill on the Franklin-Columbia Turnpike. Dispositions were immediately made to meet the enemy some four miles north at a place called Thompson's Station on the Tennessee/Alabama Railroad. On the following dawn we secured the heights above a narrow valley cut through by both the train tracks and the dirt turnpike. We occupied the far Confederate right with approximately two thousand mounted troops and a section of Freeman's Artillery. At about half-past nine, with the sun just up good above the surrounding hills, the Federals appeared marching down Columbia Pike with five regiments of foot soldiers, another six-hunert odd mounted troopers and a full battery of artillery. They immediately began deploying in line of battle across the valley floor and occupied the opposing hill with their artillery. The cannon opened, whilst the Yanks moved admirably up in the face of heavy fire, closing to within less than two hunert yards of our own lines. Whitfield's Infantry, under direction of General Van Dorn, sprang forward to meet their advance. From our position on the hillside, we watched as the two forces traded musket volleys in the open ground for over half an hour, until the Federals finally fell back in good order, surrendering only the ground they'd earlier crossed.

"The Federal artillery presented a nuisance to all Confederates afield, firing as they were from their elevated position with a view of the entire theatre. Seeing no threat to our own position by any advancing blue bellies, General Forrest sent Colonel Starnes, with his Fourth Tennessee, around under cover of the surrounding hills, whilst the remainder of his command, including his escort in which Will and I rode, rushed to cut off the Yank route of retreat toward Franklin. He intended to crush the enemy betwixt the upper and nether millstones of his cavalry and Van Dorn's infantry.

"Colonel Starnes, with the guidance of Major McClemore of the Fourth Tennessee, who was born and raised only a few miles from the very place, surprised and routed the Federal artillery from their fine vantage point, to beat a hasty retreat to the rear. They also drove the infantry west across the railroad and up on the far ridge, where they made their next stand with stubborn determination.

"Apparently having seen our rearward movement, a large Federal detachment occupied a stone wall to protect their army's flank. These men made an admirable effort to maintain this position in the face of two very determined and hard fought charges by our troopers. However, on our second attempt, we overran them and after exacting a heavy toll from amongst their ranks, they were forced to surrender. Throwing down their arms, they were marched from the field in the direction of Spring Hill. We then continued our march north to cut off any potential retreat that our commander's keen military eye had seen as inevitable. But as we broke from cover, we could see the Federals were by no means yet about to quit the fight.

"We were formed for another charge, which we shortly made up the steep slope of the hill yet occupied by the stubborn Yanks. The blue clad infantrymen poured a telling fire into our approaching columns, causing heavy losses to our mounted troops. But for nerve and pluck, the charge would have been broken then and there. No man distinguished himself above another. All faced their duty admirably and the glory of one was the glory of all. I watched as our escort commander, Captain Montgomery Little, topple dead from his saddle whilst riding next to Forest at the head of our charge. Major Edward Trezevant of Memphis was also slain in the final assault. The very elements of Heaven and Earth seemed in one mighty uproar. My mount staggered as the ground jarred and shook beneath his hooves. But our advance moved steadily forward and within a few more moments we were upon the enemy. In the fury and confusion of the melee, I clearly remember looking up to see General Forrest personally draw his sidearm and level it within a few feet of the Federal commander's head, one Colonel Coburn, demanding his immediate surrender. Further resistance appeared to have been in vain to the Yankee commander from his precarious vantage looking down the barrel of Forrest's .36. The Federal opposition soon subsided at his command.

"It was at this time that King's Battery of Van Dorn's command opened on the Federal position, narrowly missing killing all within a few feet of Federal commander Coburn, including General Forrest and myself. I admit I saw only the dirt in front of my face for the next little bit because of hugging the Earth until a courier could ride to tell Van Dorn's artillery of the success of our attack and to cease firing. Until a man has experienced shelling, he can't imagine the numbing terror of it. I don't think a flapjack could have lain any flatter than did I those long tense moments with the dirt erupting and showering down around us. My heart beat a hole in the ground beneath me. A few of both sides fell wounded from the 'not so friendly' shrapnel.

243

"Before taking Colonel Coburn to meet General Van Dorn, General Forrest rode back down the slope to the side of his fallen young officer, Captain Little, kneeling by his body, he openly wept, saying simply, 'Brave man, none braver.' Looking on the now lifeless body of the once handsome Little, shot between the eyes and trampled repeatedly by passing horses, I was reminded that a body without a spirit is just a body.

"Coburn's surrendered command consisted of the Thirty-third and Eighty-fifth Indiana, the Twenty-second Wisconsin Volunteers and the Ninth Michigan. We displayed to these brave men whatever courtesy we could muster and a sort of genuine camaraderie developed between those who just minutes before fought so fiercely. We had a new found respect for each other's skills, courage and in this case, fairness. There existed a bond between fighting men that transcended sectional differences, or color of uniform.

"Our closing charge had exacted the heaviest toll of the day. Back in camp that evening at Spring Hill, Will and I visited our friends of the Third Arkansas to determine how they'd fared in the events of the day. We found their spirits somewhat subdued as well and learnt' that their revered Colonel Samuel G. Earle had been amongst the hunert twenty-five Confederates killed in the day's action. We also learned that a fine man of the cloth, Regimental Chaplin Crouch had succumbed to wounds received. He was a fine Methodist parson, whose services Will and I had attended more'n once't. In route back to our own cantonment, we dropped in on the bivouac of the Fourth Tennessee, to learn they'd also lost their Captain Alfred Dysart in the assault against the Union artillery. None went without loss. But the war provided little time for mourning such.

"Picket skirmishes resumed with heated fervor as we probed the Union lines around Franklin. The weather turned bitter, almost constantly raining, or drizzling and cold as charity. Running battles took place throughout the next week. We withdrew to the vicinity of Columbia in the face of an approaching, extremely superior force on the twelfth of March, after a dicey crossing of the flood swollen Duck and its tributaries.

"With the passing of the Union threat and upon effecting repair to the pontoon bridge that had washed out in the rising currents of the Duck subsequent to our crossing, we again accompanied our commander in re-crossing the river and relocating his headquarters back to the Spring Hill vicinity by the fifteenth. At this time General Forrest was assigned to command a division, made up of his present command and Armstrong's brigade, including the Eighth Tennessee.

"The General's escort, on the twenty-fourth of March, in company of Biffle's Regiment, the Tenth Tennessee, the First Tennessee, the Third Arkansas and the Second Mississippi, deftly wound our way through the lines of our enemy, eluding detection right up to the very outskirts of Brentwood, where at dawn, we brushed aside the pickets and captured with the loss of but one poor Confederate, the entire Union garrison previously in possession of the place. From there we made a sweeping movement, leaving behind rising pillars of black smoke, whilst capturing spoils and prisoners from there to Triune and back. Within a few miles of our return to Brentwood, we broke for repast, only to be interrupted by an alarm that our retreat was being cut off by a large force of Union cavalry. Quickly remounting, we dashed to the point of contact, where we found the Federals in a threatening position surrounding some captured wagons that were being forwarded to the safety of our own lines. We immediately formed and charged, sending the Federals scurrying for cover with loss of some fifty of their men and animals. With no further hindrance, we camped near Hillsboro that evening, before continuing back toward quarters at Spring Hill next morning.

"Frequent petty outpost affairs now occurred, amounting to many injuries, but little consequence strategically, except that I relearned a very valuable lesson shortly after the turn of April. These violent encounters between small bands of mounted adversaries became so frequent as to be considered almost routine. The area we were assigned and had patrolled for days had been totally void of all sign of Unionists. Reporting directly to the General each evening the fruitless results of our scouting, he said, 'It's just as important to know where they ain't, as where they is.'

"Will was back in camp on April third, whilst I was out with some others taking yet another turn at mounted patrol. We'd been in the saddle the larger part of the day when sometime about mid-afternoon we stepped down to let the horses blow a spell. On patrol, with but half dozen men in a detachment, I never brought along my bugle. Thinking we were nowhere near the enemy, I stood my carbine against a tree and hung my waist belt with knife and pistol from the upraised barrel before stepping off a few paces behind the cover of a suitably wide tree for a constitutional. No sooner had I shucked my britches, than a detachment of Federal cavalrymen swooped in on us, firing their side-arms point blank into the faces of my surprised companions, where they stood holding our horses. One comrade raised an arm to shield himself from a saber blow, only to have the limb struck from his body. They were left on the ground, bleeding out their eyes, ears, mouths and other holes in their heads, whilst our horses scattered. I could do no more than raise my hands in surrender with my britches still around my ankles, as the rascals laughed at my embarrassing predicament. Their laughter meant nothing though, in light of the scene of my dead companions on the ground before us. The only good part of the whole incident was that all our horses had fled back in the direction of Spring Hill. My hope was that Prince would return with the others to our cantonment and thus, to Will's care, not becoming part of the Yankee's regiment. Yanks were known to be notoriously cruel to their mounts, abusing and neglecting them, going so far as to shoot jaded animals in favor of fresh ones when in hostile territory, to deny their being left behind for potential rehabilitation and return to Confederate service.

"The lesson I relearnt' at that time was never, ever be more than arms length from your weapon when in potentially hostile country. I was allowed to very slowly raise my trousers. They bound my wrists tightly in front of me and led me rapidly away at a trot from the place where lay my fallen comrades. I took one last look over my shoulder at the sanguinary pools spreading in the road dust beneath their lifeless forms.

"I was quite fortunate in that, upon being trotted on foot behind my captor's horse into the Yankee camp, I luckily encountered the cavalry sergeant whom I'd spared at the freshwater spring. In his business with his duties, he did little more than glance up at the prisoner being paraded through their midst. But making a double take in thinking I recognized him, I chanced a call in the form of, 'Hey Sarge!' When he looked back up briefly, even though my hands were bound together with a rope drawn by my captor, I attempted to repeat my cavalier two-finger salute and tried to grin the same grin that had accompanied it. Noting all this, he called to my captor, 'Hold up there, soldier!' Drawing in the reins of his mount, the Yankee private turned to see why the sergeant had halted him.

"He came over to my position behind the Federal mount, saying to my captor, 'I need to inspect your prisoner' and looked me closely in the eyes. After a moment he asked, 'Don't I know you?' to which I replied, 'We met briefly at a local waterin' hole not too long ago.' He said surprised, 'Well I'll be damned Reb, that is you ain't it! Appears you've had a bit of bad luck,' to which my captors responded, 'Not as bad as the fellers that was with him, they're all dead. This one was in the middle of his business when we come upon 'em. You might say we sorta' caught him with his pants down. Where'd you know this feller from Sarge?' Grinning in a friendly manner, the Yankee sergeant said, 'This here is one of the Rebs that let us go when we were filling canteens that evening a few weeks back at the spring Willie discovered.' Apparently the story of forbearance on the part of their enemy had circulated somewhat within their camps. 'Well I'll be damned,' said the private, 'now I'm glad we didn't kill him too.' 'Me too,' said my new friend in blue uniform. Looking me in the eyes he stated, 'Well ain't you in a fix.' I could only agree, 'Seems so.' Then turning back to his men he concluded, 'You boys leave him be, I'll see to him now.' It appeared my luck was, for the moment, somewhat improved.

"The sergeant took charge of me from that point, escorting me to his tent where it was pitched under a large oak tree just beginning to show its first buds of spring. He sported a Remington 'New' Army revolver in ready reach on his hip. The canvas of the tent was covered with a heavy layer of yellow pollen from the overhanging shade tree. I found his temporary quarters nicely apportioned with only one cot, indicating he didn't have to share his canvas shelter with anyone and could occasionally find some privacy. There was also a camp table and a second stool for company. We pulled the low-backed stools away from the table and took our places facing one another, as my host brought over a kettle from the near by fire and poured us each a tin cup full of real coffee, the piping scent of which it had been some time since I'd smelt. I first savored the rich aroma, cradling the warm tin in both hands as I held it steaming beneath my noise. The sergeant smiled at my evident enjoyment of the fresh, hot beverage. After I'd gingerly sipped at the piping liquid he'd only just removed from the fire, he offered his hand to me and introduced himself as Sergeant Huie Smith of Pittsburgh, Pennsylvania, presently serving with the Eighth Pennsylvania Volunteer Cavalry, with whom we'd mixed and matched arms on several previous occasions.

"I found my eyes quite watery from all the pollen in the air and was sneezing regularly. Sergeant Smith offered me a kerchief from his own satchel where it hung on the back of his camp chair. I thanked him for all his kindness, generosity and hospitality, noting to myself how sometimes just the smallest service can come back to you many fold. He said to me, 'Til that evening at the spring, we'd thought of you Rebs as mostly wild animals, best shot like a rabid dog.' We'd since taught them the lesson of mercy that he'd not forgotten. I've always tried to remember and live by that when I could, including most the remainder of the war. My earnest prayer was then this, spoken to the Lord nearly everyday from that time forward until the war's final end, 'Heavenly Father, cure thy children's warring madness. Bend our pride to thy control. Remove our hearts of stone and replace them with hearts of flesh.' In His own good time, my prayer was answered and I thanked Him that both Will and I had lived to see the day.

"As we stepped back out-of-doors, I admired his shiny new black McClellan saddle, blanket and gov'ment issue bridle where they hung on a lariat strung taught from tree to tree. His mount was away in pasture, foraging. The contrast between our equipage and our adversaries was dramatic. Whereas they seemed to have the best of everything, wanting for nothing, we had our comforts little attended to by the Southern gov'ment, being poorly fed, poorly clad, poorly armed and poorly paid, 'cept for what we could despoil from the Lincolnites through our efforts raiding against their supply depots, owing our frequent successes mainly to the fine leadership, planning and considerations provided for us by our cunning regimental general. But we still continued to get damned little mail, despite all his best efforts.

"Soldiers are often said to be rude, crude, coarse men, hard-set for the most part, if not to begin with, then made so by the rigors of their occupation. And this is all quite true. But through our pleasant conversations, never have I found a warmer heart, more full of gratitude manifested for the former sparing of his and his men's lives. I caught myself soon being turned in my sentiments about Yanks by the sergeant's friendly persuasion. I was again reminded of the importance of accepting a man for the caliber of feller he is, regardless, be he Johnny Reb, or Billy Yank. Working on the home place after the war with hired-hand freemen who come wanderin' through our country, wondering what to do with their newfound freedom, I came to better understand this was equally true of coloreds, as much as with whites.

"Upon refilling my coffee tin, he made the second cup an Irish by tipping in a snort of rye he had held by. After another refill, we could have settled the war in half an hour, if'n it'd been left up to us. Lubricated by the oil of gladness, we spent as pleasant an evening as perhaps I ever passed in the company of men. Huie introduced me to some of his closer acquaintances and we ate, drank and smoked in good company around a lovely outdoor blaze, with fiddle music and song in evidence. The Yank musicians, not surprisingly, played many of the same tunes as us."

The wind was slowly rising as we sat next to the fallow garden and the sun settled nearer the horizon. "Looks like it might rain," Pappy noted, studying the great cumulus clouds gathering dark blue above the trees, far to the south.

"Yep," I answered.

"Son," Pappy said, "I need you to fetch up on that roof and replace those missing shingles. That last little blow picked a few off," he said, pointing toward the top of the potato shed. Rising from his seat, he led me toward the tool room, where he picked up the hammer and some nails while pointing out the homemade ladder and hand-drawn cypress shakes stacked in the corner. I obediently placed the ladder carefully against the gray wooden outbuilding and slowly climbed up to a point where I could slide the replacement roof covering into position beneath an overlapping one. There were only a few missing, so the chore didn't take long. Pappy stood below and steadied the ladder while he handed me up the various tools and materials to complete the handicraft. "There!" he said, expressing great satisfaction with my completed task. "Now I won't have to worry 'bout that little problem no more. That's been weighing on my mind right heavy of late. Thank ye' son, I'm much obliged!"

After returning the tools to their respective places, we shuffled through the crackling, dry leaves to retake our seats next to the old garden. "Now the taters won't spoil from their gettin' damp," he said, looking pleased with the benefits derived from our simple task. The sound of a peckerwood knocking at an old tree rang out in the evening air. Pappy pulled out his chaw and cut a plug, buttoning his coat to the collar, to settle in and watch the sun set. I, too, turned up my own collar and awaited him to tell me more about his captivity among the Yanks. It was but a short wait until he spat and again took up the tale.

"Next morning, after the pleasantries of the previous evening, Sergeant Huie asked me what I was a'fightin' for and why the South had been so rash as to attempt secession.' I explained what I understood of the matter as this, that the North had elected a president bent on depriving the South of her property as guaranteed by the U.S. Constitution. The North had further refused all the South's attempts at reconciliation and then sent troops in an act of aggression to try and force our capitulation to their will. As such, we were left with no other course than that of war in defense of our rights, our freedom and our sacred honor. The sergeant jumped up, grabbing his sword and swore loudly, 'If I was to think for one instant that I been fightin' to free the Nigra, or to deprive the South of even a single sawbuck, I'd toss away this saber on the spot right here and now, never to again take up arms!' But, it wasn't long left to the sergeant and me to settle all the differences of our two nations, for my host just then had to follow protocol and turn me over to far less friendly hands, who owed no debt to any Southerner, save one of vendetta.

"As mean a lookin' a white man as I ever seen in the uniform of captain, walked up to Sergeant Smith's camp right at that instant, asking, 'What's this Rebel doing here?' Before the good sergeant could even begin to explain, he was told to turn me over to the Provost Guard forthwith, lest he be brought up on charges for consortin' with the enemy. Having no other choice than to obey, Sergeant Smith escorted me to the Colonel in charge of the Provost, whispering a good word on my behalf to the Marshal, before shaking my hand warmly and retreating reluctantly to his camp. Along with other captives, we were being forwarded to Nashville and a temporary prison there.

"The very damage we'd so recently done to the rail lines through the country between Spring Hill and Nashville required that we take a wide detour, completely avoiding the wrecked tracks of that contested ground. The Yankees therefore, shipped us like cattle east to Murfreesboro, where our ranks were consolidated with and held amongst a large number of other captured Confederates who'd been taken near Woodbury.

"We received our paroles at Murfreesboro before being sent on to the Tennessee capital. Just after our noon meal of slop, we were paraded in long lines before a rickety wooden table, where sat

Union officers. They smelled of coffee, bacon, onions and cigar smoke, all the things I missed most, besides a soft warm bed. Most of the Confederates claimed to be unfamiliar with the art of writing, so the Provost Marshal wrote our names for us, requiring only that we mark an 'X' next to it, that he notated as 'His mark.' Then it was 'Thank ye very much,' and 'move along.' Not wishing to invite trouble by letting on I could indeed read, I made no effort to correct the misinformation I noticed written on my prisoner parole. It stated that I was captured in the vicinity of Woodbury, like most others being held there, even though my capture had come at far distant Spring Hill. It was an insignificant detail, that didn't amount to a hill of beans and I was no wise inclined to do anything to help my captors. Not that they'd've appreciated it anyway.

"We were again crammed aboard railcars to start north to Nashville. En route, there was a poor young lad, fevered and unconscious, whom no one seemed to know to what unit he belonged. I tried to feed the poor lad some water, that only ran down the side of his open mouth. Upon arrival at the train station in Nashville, a kindly, older surgeon, one Captain Jerome Ross, was there to meet the train and pick up our sick and wounded Confederates for transportation to the temporary hospital on the grounds of the Female Seminary. In sight of the U.S. Stars and Bars flying over the capital rotunda, I helped Captain Ross load the languishing lad into an ambulance for removal to the ward.

"For the next week, before my being forwarded on to Louisville, Kentucky, I assisted the surgeon in ministering to our many ailing soldiers. The situation was most pitiable, the doctors being denied nearly everything the condition of their patients required. It was a scene of melancholia, with few careful, or cheerful nurses to assist the poor lads so far from home and family. The boy from the train made a brief rally, before again failing and finally passing. I visited him almost daily when my orderly duties allowed. Even as the mists of death stole slowly over him, he would always brighten at either mine, or Dr. Ross's appearance. It is a pleasant reflection to think that we made his long, painful hours seem shorter and perhaps smoothed his path to the grave. God knows our charges needed a hunert fold greater care than we could afford them, but we withheld nothing that was in our power to impart. The boys I witnessed in those hospital cots thought not of themselves as martyrs, or heroes and wished only to be again united with family and home. Far too many were never granted such a humble request, being instead carried from their sick beds and laid in unmarked, shallow graves, with no loved ones near to lament their passing. The prisoner's plight was regrettable, but doubly so for the infirm.

"I don't say I know everything, but in my short stint as a hospital orderly, I came to recognize the smell of death on the breath and in the bowels of the ailing. Ever after I could tell you three days before a man was gonna' pass.

"Dr. Ross said that he could not attest that his patients had received the care, or sympathy to be expected from the local southern citizenry of Nashville that should have been afforded to the boys who'd come there from across the whole of the South and fought valiantly for the freedom of Tennessee, braving both the disease of the camps and the hazards of combat with little complaining.

"After one week of this sad and solemn hospital duty, the hunerts of parolees, including myself, were loaded tightly aboard packet boats en route down the Cumberland River for Louisville. The elderly Dr. Ross could have been paroled, too, but chose to stay at his labors in the Nashville prison barracks with those too ill to be moved.

"We arrived in Louisville about the middle of April, where we spent one day and a night, before reboarding the packets en route to the joint prisoner exchange depot at City Point, Virginia. This was one of the last exchanges of the war, for the system soon broke down with charges of bad faith made by both sides toward the other.

"The most notable thing to me whilst held in Yankee hands, was the concentrated effort of our enemy to break down espirit de corps. The humiliations suffered at our captors' hands, were disheartening. Our march into captivity at Woodbury was in a line some twenty yards wide, as far as the eye could see forward and behind. The demeanor of my fellow captives in that march, was much like that of cattle, resigned to their collective fate. I found myself wondering, 'If all these are conquered, might not we all soon be?' I found myself often asking, 'What then was there left to fight for if the fight was already lost?'

"They near starved us, causing full growed men to weep from hunger. What little food we did get, was contaminated with all manner of vermin, worms and beetles. Trying to make the best of a bad situation, my comrades joked that, 'The soup may be too weak to drown worms, but they soon die anyways from starvation.'

"Outfits were broken up as quickly as possible in captivity, separating boys in many cases for the first time from fellas they'd been with since leaving home. Upon capture, officers were immediately cut out from enlisted in an effort to deprive us of coherent leadership. That wasn't always so bad though for enlisted men, considering so many officers were promoted to rank not as result of any talent, or skills, but for political favor. This promotion of the undeserving over the more capable was the bane of the southern army, if not in fact, its ruination.

"After being turned over to the Confederate authorities at City Point, we were shuffled along en route straight away back to our former units. There was no talk of furlough and no time to waste in getting us to our respective commands. It seemed to me the situation was becoming more and more desperate for the Cause. I found myself rapidly reloaded along with the hunerts of other freed Rebs, from boats to trains and back to boats, treated little better, if in fact as well, by our own southern government as we'd been by the Federals. None the less, many a former plowhand, turned soldier, kissed the gumbo riverbank soil when finally set ashore back in Dixie.

"It was certainly more evident than ever, after my stint in Yankeedom, that the enemy had far more resources and capabilities for war waging than did our Southern States and a will to use them. It would yet be a long struggle, with what appeared to be one inevitable conclusion.

"Shortly after the turn of May, a month and a week to the day from my capture, I was reunited with my brothers-in-arms, to find both William, Fury and Prince not much worse for wear. The regiment was just returned to the cantonments outside Spring Hill, only a short distance from where, on the third of April, I'd been captured and all the other members of my patrol had lay down for the last time. Will explained that when the horses had come wandering back into camp one at a time without their riders, another patrol, including him and Fury, was quickly dispatched to find us. After extensive searching, that took until daylight the following morning, they came across the sad sight that I still clearly recall so well. They sought me amongst the dead that looked as if buckets of red paint had been cast on the earth about their heads. Will happily noted that I was not amongst them, leaving him to figure I was most likely captured and carried away. How right he was. I told how Sergeant Huie Smith, of the Eighth Pennsylvania Cavalry, had taken me under his wing that day and eased my first night in captivity, before being put into the prisoner exchange pipeline. Will told me that they had continued to clash regularly with that same outfit, before breaking camp and heading south. We drank a toast to my Yankee friend's health and I hoped he was well.

"I was never again thereafter without my sixer close by, stuffed in my belt, or tucked under my blanket at all times, the ready feel of its grip ever imparting a sense of security. For many years after war's end, I still toted a hog-leg as if it was just another part of my wardrobe.

"Prince looked stronger than I'd seen him in awhile. After a full year in the hard riding service, he'd been left behind at Spring Hill to recuperate when the balance of cavalry made a long drive into north Alabama and back. With the late snows of that year, there was plenty of early grass for him to fatten on whilst resting. I on the other hand, had grown gaunted from my hungry time amongst the Yanks. I couldn't get enough to eat for the first week

255

back, feeling like I had both a hollow leg and a hole where my belly ought to be.

"The regiment was only just returned from the sweep through northern Alabama, chasing Colonel Able Streight's Yankee Cavalry. They'd ridden clear across the state and into Georgia, where our boys captured the whole Yankee outfit. Will told me of a night attack they'd made during the campaign, where they snuck up on the Federal camp through the underbrush, surprising many of the unsuspecting Yanks in their last breath. They were so successful, he said, as to intercept practically all sounds of alarm, exclamation, or fear before they could even issue forth from their lungs. It had been a deft exercise in deadly precision and stealth, catching the Yankee troopers unsuspecting and off guard. I couldn't say I was sorry to have missed it and I wasn't looking forward to cutting any throats.

"The next month spent in camp at Spring Hill, was as peaceful a time as I'd spent for awhile. Except for the inevitable picket skirmishes, we were not overly in contact with the Federals. The one notable enemy encounter that occurred at this time involved the capture of our videttes near Carter Creek before the end of May. The Federals, under cover of darkness snuck in behind our pickets, surprising and carrying them away. So, in retaliation, on the night of May twenty-first, a detachment of the unit on which muster roll Will and I appeared, the Eighth Tennessee, laid a trap for the unsuspecting Union cavalry. Showing themselves to the enemy as advanced pickets not long before nightfall, they then, under cover of darkness, removed the plank flooring of the bridge they'd been seen observing and withdrew to the shelter of a cedar break. Here they waited for their plan to unfold. The ruse worked, with the apparently exposed position of our men as seen at sundown being too good for the Union commander to resist. With the guidance of a local nigra, the Federals came up behind the supposed position of our pickets as last observed before dark. The boys of the Eighth sprang from their hiding places in the cedar grove, driving the surprised blue bellies headlong in retreat for the floorless bridge. As they galloped into thin air, numerous horses and riders fell into the dark chasm between the timbers, leaving telltale traces of blood, skin and hair plainly visible in the light of the following morning. Riding out to survey the sight of the clever deceit, Will and I were impressed with the amount of damage that must have been inflicted on man and beast from evidence of so much of their hide and hair left behind. The Federals, henceforth, kept their distance for a good spell afterwards.

"With the exception of daily fisticuffs between one feller or another within our own camps, the proceeding weeks passed in relative peace. Our animals and men had fair rations and so healt' and fattened, as fat as you could get on army grub. The biggest threat to our ease at that juncture, was the General himself. He chafed at being up under his superior and in lieu of active combat to distract him, he was like a caged lion, not to be trifled with. He was drinkin' again a good deal of the time and his humor was almost always intractable. He was as much feared and despised by most of the men during those sultry days, as he'd before been loved and appreciated.

"Despite that important consideration, Will and I agreed he should put in for a furlough whilst we were relatively inactive, to visit his wife and daughters and check on Ma, Pa and our sisters. Having had none since his enlistment and under the circumstances of our women folk being left unattended in James Andrew's absence, it seemed only fair and reasonable. And as a show of good faith, I'd stay with the regiment, to prove we weren't just wanting to goldbrick together.

"Herein is a perfect example of how the army worked, or should I say, didn't work. The application was first looked at and signed by the sergeant, who forwarded it to the Corporal, then on to the Lieutenant and the Captain, then the Major, the Colonel and finally the General. The first time the General looked at it, he denied it, citing, 'It ain't right, the Adjutant ain't approved it and now the date's expired.' The General's objection required an entirely new document be prepared, correctly dated and once't more carried from hand to hand and signed off on by every preceding officer again. This time through the chain of command, each officer seemed to find some minor detail for which to reroute it back through the entire pipeline. He carried the little ragged shred of paper from hand to hand, doing all in his power to see that each officer correctly signed the document, to get the dang thang approved.

"When Will had finally jumped through all the proper hoops and brought it again before Forrest, the General was in his command tent sharing a game of five card stud with his staff officers. It's said, 'Lucky at love, unlucky at cards.' That bein' so, the General must'a been getting' some, cause he was sure losin' big. He was too preoccupied to be bothered with such trivialities as a private's furlough. But, jaws taut and showing the 'Ledbetter' in him, Will had just about had enough of the run around and this meanish behavior on the part of our formerly trusted leader. He insisted on pressing the General for an answer. The General locked him in his mad gaze, eyes, Will said, flashing like lightning. Without getting up, the commander snatched the furlough from my brother's fingers. Taking a pencil from another of the card players, N.B. wrote, 'I tole you once't already goddamit, NO!' Taking back the dirty little snub of paper from the General, Will read it, not knowing what to expect. When he saw the answer, he looked up from the 'furlough' to the General's glaring eyes that seemed trying to burn a hole through him. Will could see our commander was spoiling for a fight, saying nothing, but hoping Will would make a move. They stared at each other a long moment, before Will did the only thing he could do, wad and toss the furlough at the General's feet. He saluted and turned on his heels, saying only, 'Keep it, sir!' Then further adding as he walked out the open tent flap, 'I wouldn't have a thing so unwillingly given.' The General kept his seat as my brother stomped off into the night, taking a long, solitary walk to cool down.

"Dr. Cowan was present at the card game and noting the effect of hard feelings resultant of the incident with one of the General's own escort, tolt' Will that Bedford was inconsolable at the time, himself having put in for a ten day furlough to visit his wife that he hadn't seen since the previous May in Memphis. It, too, was denied by Bragg himself. This seemed only fitting and we took some solace in the justice of it, thinking it was good enough for him.

"Dr. Cowan further encouraged Will by quoting a scripture from Proverbs 16:32. 'Remember what the Bible says son, 'He who is slow to anger is better than the mighty and he who rules his own spirit than he who takes a city.'

"It's said an army reflects the personality of its leaders. It's also said an army should never stay inactive in one place too long, for tedium and monotony will soon take their toll. Never were these two precepts more true than through the hot dry month of June, '63. Our Pa used to say, 'Weather can have strong effect on men's personalities and a hot, dry spell is the worst.' This too seemed true enough at the time.

"As water seeks its own level, so, too, firewater follows after firewater. So many bawdy houses popped up around Spring Hill that month, it was like a perfect Sodom. Horizontal refreshment was a regular past time for many. There were a lot of boys from Irish stock, like ourselves, real blow-tops and they'd everyone fight at the drop of a hat, while carrying three hats with 'em everywhere they went. Those were some of the orneriest men I ever saw, with more swearin', card playin', dice shootin', and brawlin' than I've ever seen anywhere, save maybe Main Street Kingsland on a Saturday night. Without firmness, you'd soon come to be as bad as the worst. Our Pa always told us 'Good dogs never teach the bad dogs good tricks. It's always the bad dog,' he said, 'that teaches the good dog, bad tricks.' We strove not to fall victim to like behavior as the more barbarian in our midst and at times wondered aloud, 'How could God ever favor an army made of soldiers so wicked?'

"It was during the same week following Will and the General's clash, when, on June thirteenth, Forrest fatally stabbed a fellow officer on the steps of the Masonic Hall of nearby Columbia. Caught in one of the General's fiery gazes, Lieutenant Andrew Wills Gould was provoked into drawing a pistol from his coat pocket and firing wildly after their discussion turned heated, subsequently wounding Forrest in the hip. Thinking himself mortally injured, Forrest put the blade of his jackknife through his young victim's chest, then stalked, shot at and missed the scared, dying young man as he fled bleeding, accidentally wounding instead a bystander in the leg. The whole affair originated after Forrest besmudged the artillerist's honor with public accusations of cowardice during a particular engagement on the pursuit of Streight's Cavalry through Alabama. No charges were brought after the event, civil, or martial, against either party, with the younger soon buried in the ground, expired from lung fever resultant of Forrest driving his knife blade home into the young feller's lung.

"But, the General was nothing, if not acutely astute in his observations and it wasn't long before he realized, undoubtedly with his surgeon's gentle nudging, the effect his drinking was having on morale, both his own and his soldiers'. It was about this time when Ole' Forrest swore an oath of abstinence and within days we were again breaking camp, heading south with the whole of the army, retreating before the threat of a reported Federal offensive said to be designed in mind of pushing Bragg's army out of Tennessee. Nathan Bedford's compass began to swing again true and you could soon see a marked difference in the entire command. I often after heard N.B. say when offered a drink, 'No thank ye', my staff does all my drinkin' for me now!'

"Once't more sober-minded, I think the General had a new-found respect for my brother William, admiring his pluck to say what was on his mind and play the bigger man, by lettin' it lay, even at the point, some would say, of provocation. He never apologized in words, but he made a concerted effort at showing my brother and me his lack of ill will. With renewed action lurking on the horizon, the furlough was never again mentioned."

Here Pappy paused, removed his spent chaw and studied the angle of the sun sitting low on the western horizon and the dark clouds building to a tempest as they approached from the south.

"I believe it was the twenty-fourth of June that summer, when we started toward Shelbyville and a rendezvous with General Leonidas Polk's infantry. Upon approach of the river crossing outside Shelbyville, the sounds of a furious tangle were heard. Forrest sent an aggregate force dashing ahead of the main body of cavalry, to survey the situation and inform General Wheeler's cavalry of our impending arrival on the scene. I was amongst the contingent that burst through the Federal rear and sliced our way onto the bridge across't the Duck, to find Wheeler's hard-pressed troopers about to torch the route of our escape. It so happened to be the Alabama boys of Russell's Brigade, with whom we had served under Forrest within the preceding months before their transfer to command of Wheeler. No sooner were we arrived, than the Federals made a concerted effort to push us off the bridge and take its possession. Here was as fierce a hand to hand battle as ever was fought, with our men trying desperately to hold on until the balance of our command came up to attack the Union rear and save us and the bridge. But, our cavalry did not ride to our rescue in time and at Wheeler's command, we abandoned the bridge and fought our way out of the desperate mix, with blades and balls filling the air around us, to plunge into the river in a bid for the relative safety of the far shore. Now jined with Wheeler's outfit and separated from our own, we quickly patched up our wounds, of which there were many, as best we could and rode southeast up the riverbank, in hopes of making a juncture with our stranded command at a ford or bridge somewhere further upstream. This rejining with our own force was accomplished within four miles further up the river's course, from whence we proceeded in the direction of Tullahoma, the vicinity of which we achieved the following morn.

"During the action at the Shelbyville Bridge, we lost our brave leader Colonel James W. Starnes. His capable, evenhanded guidance through thick and thin was sorely missed thereafter. We acted, in conjunction with Wheeler's troopers, as rearguard to the main body of the moving army, engaging and falling back from the pursuing bluecoats time and again. As we sped through one small hamlet in the foothills outside Chattanooga, the escort in close proximity to our general, an old woman, brandishing a broom like a club, appeared in the doorway of her little cottage shouting at our commander as he galloped past. In his haste, I wasn't sure if Forrest made out the words of the old crone, but following closely on his heels, Will and I clearly heard her taunts. In a shrill voice, she called him a, 'great big cowardly rascal,' saying, 'Why don't you turn and fight like a man, instead of running away like some whooped pup? I wish Forrest was here,' she added for emphasis, 'he'd make you fight!' We tipped our faded hats and rode on in pursuit of our leader, trying not to fall out of our saddles as we bent double with laughter.

"We next ensconced at Kingston, Tennessee, snug within the towering foothills of the Appalachians, some fifty miles southwest of Knoxville. William and I, along with several companies of the Eighth Tennessee, were from there detached, under the command of Colonel George G. Dibrell, to Sparta, to employ our proven skills as recruiters. As we operated in those environs, there was a strong force of Federals in possession of McMinnville. On the ninth of August, this Federal cavalry, under Minty, attacked our camp, driving our pickets in an attempt to stampede our animals and capture the dismounted troopers. Thanks mainly to fast thinking on the part of the men and the swiftness and rested state of our horses, the Federals were spoiled in their later efforts, but caused us to fall back in the direction of Wild Cat Creek, taking up strong position there. We were able to pour on a crossfire from well hidden positions in the rocky high ground above the approach to the creek ford. As the superior numbers of Minty's cavalry bravely, but fool-heartedly charged again and again, we unseated an unprecedented number from their ranks and dropped many of their animals in their tracks, leaving the lawn across which they came, strewn with the victims of our intense rifle fire. After enduring more of this abuse than seemed reasonable, the Federal Cavalry finally gave back, leaving us with little more than five wounded amongst our own ranks. Then, under direction of our Colonel Dibrell, himself a local and well acquainted with the vicinity, we were led to another and better position for defense at the summit of the Cumberland Mountains, where Frost's Turnpike made passage through a cut.

"At that place we were jined by a contingent of the local citizenry, men and women, bearing hunting rifles and food respectively. It was at this time that we were introduced to the famous Tennessee partisan and guerilla fighter, Champ Ferguson, who was a resident of that county. We rested from our rigors, enjoying the hospitality and excitement of the gathered mountain folk. We partook of their favors but one evening only though, finding ourselves again the following morning in pursuit of the fleeing enemy. That day we were jined by two-hunert of Colonel McClemore's command, sent to our assistance with ammunition and support, after Forrest received word by courier of our being assailed.

"We stayed in the region for the following fortnight, closely observing the Federal movements. On the seventeenth day, of the eighth month, 1863, the enemy renewed their attempt to force a crossing of the ford on Wild Cat Creek, where we had so seriously repelled them back on the ninth. Their memories served them well and they were not as unwise as before to race into the open approach to the creek. As such, their attempts were easily repulsed until dusk, when our commander deemed it prudent to again fall back to the more defensible position where Frost's Turnpike crossed the mountains, with only mild pursuit by the demoralized Yankees.

"Word come within two days to rejine the main force of Forrest's cavalry at Kingston. It was at this time that a mutiny, long brewing and whispered of amongst the enlisted, came to fruition. As we prepared to recross the mountainous country from Sparta to Kingston, some two-hunert of the Eighth Tennessee Cavalry, most of them residents of the surrounding counties, were averse to leaving their homes and families with the Federal threat so near and prevalent. To further incite discontent, rumor had it that Bragg was evacuating Tennessee, leaving it unprotected in the hands of the invader. The apparent surrender of Tennessee by Bragg, following so closly on the heels of the resounding Confederate defeats at Gettysburg and Vicksburg on the 'black holiday' of July third and fourth respectively, soon reached even the most remote mountain hamlet.

"When a large, dark cloud passes overhead, it's hard not to get caught in its shadow. With the news of such resounding defeat, the morale of the South was at its lowest ebb up to that point. It was becoming ever more obvious that we were engaged in a lost cause. We had to ask why even a politician couldn't understand such simple truth? The furlough incident with Forrest burned in my brother's mind, as did the question of the well being of his wife and children and our elderly parents and young sisters back home. Were they not in like circumstances as the families of these Tennesseans? The fun was gone out of it sure and we wanted, like most, only to return to home and peace. But unlike the other two-hunert local mutineers, we had only a few cousins and our Aunt Louisa and Uncle Sam Johnson living in the vicinity and were yet far away from our true home and family across the wide Mississippi.

"Aware that as a deserter he'd be a wanted man, not only by the Union, but the Confederacy as well, William still decided to take his chances without rejining the balance of our command awaiting our return to H.Q. His plan was to reside with the other men of the Eighth that were refusing to leave middle Tennessee, fight with them as a partisan and try to make his way back to Arkansas at the earliest practical opportunity. He intended to accomplish this, he said, with the aid of a forged furlough from the Lieutenant Colonel who was also disaffected and himself a participant in the revolt against the authority of our General and the Confederate gov'ment.

"No one deciding to return to regular service was in anyway accosted by the 'rebellious' Rebels, nor were the mutineers severely frowned on by the faithful. Tearful farewells were made and Will and I once't more found ourselves separated. I'd never done anything more difficult afore in my life than ride out of sight, as he stood astride Fury atop a high promontory, along with many of the others, waiving long and hard. We neither one knew if we'd ever again meet in this life.

"Within the year, most of these men, including Will, had fallen into the hands of the Federals and were, on October eleventh, 1863, sent to Camp Morton Federal prison in Indianapolis, Indiana. There they sat out the balance of the war until receiving their paroles on May twenty-second, 1865.

"We, of course, didn't know it at the time, but it would be nearly two years before we again laid eyes on one another. Thus separated from him and Fury, I was left with an uneasy feeling that there was then that much less yet standing between death and me. Upon later receiving news of Brother's capture I ever after kept a sharp eye out for Fury whenever we encountered mounted Yanks, or came upon any of their dead horses. I never again saw him though and could only hope he met with not too sorry an end"

The sun dropped behind the trees and a low rumble proceeded from the gathering storm. A strong gust swept up the collected, brown leaves, bearing them once more aloft and sweeping them along on the chilly air. Pappy stood and stretched. I could hear his old sinews pop as he did. "Look at those clouds would you? Your roof repair will soon enough have its test. I believe I smell somethin' good, don't you son?" he said in reference to the aroma of fried foods wafting on the air. "Help me with these chairs," he said, dragging his to the shelter of the tool shed, while I followed suit, doing likewise with mine. The tale was again for now ended. We marched slowly in single file toward the old house where Mammy was just setting our supper on the kitchen table. I followed thoughtfully in his wake, shuffling through the noisy leaves beneath our feet.

appears as signature to an
Oath of Allegiance
United States, subscribed and sworn to at
Morris, Indianapolis, Ind., May 22, 1865.

4 Cav. Tenn.

William Ledbetter
Private Co. D. 4 Tenn Cav

Appears on a

Roll of Prisoners of War

forwarded from Louisville Military Prison to
Camp Morton, Indianapolis, Oct. 10, 1863.

Roll dated Headquarters District of Kentucky,
Louisville, Oct. 10, 1863.

Where captured Cannon Co. Tenn

When captured Sept 17, 1863

Remarks:

Number of roll:
297

W. Woodruff
(829) Copyist.

4 Cav Tenn

Wm Ledbetter
Pvt Co D. 4 Reg Tenn Cav

Appears on a Register of

Prisoners of War

received at Military Prison, Louisville, Ky.

Where captured Cannon Co. Tenn

When captured Sept 17, 1863

Discharged:

Terms C Morton

When 4 Oct 10, 1863

Remarks:

Louisville, Ky., Register No. 2; page 205

W. H. Jenner
(829) Copyist.

268

8 Cav. (Smith's) **Tenn.**

Wm. Ledbetter,

Pvt , Co. D , 4 Reg't Tennessee Cavalry.

Appears on

Company Muster Roll

of the organization named above,

for May & June , 186 3.
Not dated.

Enlisted:

When: Sept. 27 , 186 2.

Where: Bardstown,

By whom Genl. Whorton.

Period: 3 years.

Last paid:

By whom: Capt. Sharp,

to what time April 30 , 186

Present or absent: Not stated.

Remarks: Absent without leave
since August 1st Left at
Rome.

This regiment was organized in January, 1863, with ten companies A to K. Companies B, C, H and I had formerly served as Companies C, H, I and F, respectively, of the 4th (Murray's) Regiment Tennessee Cavalry; Companies D, E, F and G formerly served in a temporary field organization known as Davis' Battalion Tennessee Cavalry, and Companies A and K were formerly independent companies; Company L was added August 1, 1863.
The regiment was mustered in the field as the 4th Regiment Tennessee Cavalry but was officially designated by the A. & I. G. O. as the 8th Regiment Tennessee Cavalry.

Book mark: ....

F. C. Pratz,

(842) Copyist.

L 4 Cav. Tenn.

William Leadbetter

Priv Co. D 4 Regt. Tenn. Cav.

Appears on a

Roll of Prisoners of War

at Camp Morton, Ind., desiring to take the Oath
of allegiance.

Roll not dated.

Where captured Home, Cannon Co. Tenn.

When captured Aug 17 , 1863.

Remarks: Conscripted July 20 1862
Cannon Co. Tenn. Desires to
take the Oath of Allegiance
return to his home in Tenn.
and remain a loyal man.
Recommended

Certificate shows: "Sworn to before me this 9th day of
December, 1863. 1st Lieut. MARK A. HOYT, Invalid Corps."

Number of roll

79; sheet 2

(532b) C. E. McLaughlin
Copyist.

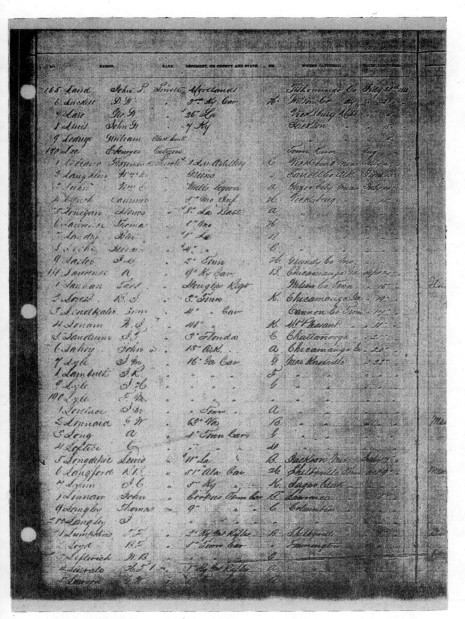

Camp Morton, Indianapolis, IN Prisoner Roll

The Tempest Renewed

After supper, Pappy asked me to start a fire in his bedroom, while he remained chatting in the kitchen with Mammy as she finished clearing the table.

The piney woods of our country are blessed with an abundance of rich, heart pine, left at the core of fallen and rotted yellow pine logs. Those familiar with it know what fine kindling it makes, full of resin and as flammable as kerosene. I took a knot from the wood box and readily chopped it into small slivers with a hand hatchet, before stacking the pieces together under the dog-irons. I sat a nice, big, round backlog against the bricks at the rear of the fireplace, then placed dried, split white oak in front of that. With the whole arrangement properly laid, I had simply to touch a lit match to the glistening, red splinters stacked beneath the well-cured oak. Within moments the entire affair was engulfed in flame from the rapidly ignited kindling below. A roaring blaze soon illuminated the dark corners of the bedroom and fought back the chill that crept with the evening into the house.

I set the fire screen across the face of the open hearth and then pulled my wicker chair up closer, staring into the consuming blaze that hungrily devoured all within its reach. I could hear the muffled voices of my grandparents as they visited together in the adjoining room. I couldn't make out their words, but the gentle, loving tone of their conversation, mingled with Mammy's occasional laughter, told me all was well between them. Outside the storm had arrived, as evidenced by the scratching of the hedge as it swayed in the wind against the side of the old house, accompanied by the first drops of rain beating hard against the windowpanes.

Pappy soon joined me in the pleasant glow of the warming fire, checking his pocket watch against the clock on the mantle. Satisfied of their synchronicity, he took his pipe from where it sat in the wooden stand atop his desk. Filling and tamping the well-used bowl in the familiar manner, he sat the fire screen aside and lit the contents with an ignited broom straw. He then settled back into his chair to enjoy the simple pleasure of an after dinner smoke. The rain beat harder against the glass, as the wind rattled the window in its frame. "Quite a blow out there," he noted. We sat listening to the rising sound of the deluge, taking comfort from the crackle of the reassuring blaze.

Then, he again let his mind wander back across the passage of time, to those former days of wrath and fury. The smoke from his pipe rose up like some specter, hovering above his head in the still of the bedroom air, mingling with the other customary odors of the place.

"When the recruiting party of the Eighth Tennessee Cav. arrived back at Forrest's headquarters in Kingston, the General was none too pleased with the fact that we'd returned with fewer than what we departed with. The mission had been counter productive to its goal of augmenting our ranks and had instead, diminished them by near two hunert much needed men and horses. Uncharacteristically however, the General didn't immediately fly off into a rage. He seemed to at least sense, if not share, the frustration of the average fighting man as to the course and character most recently taken by the war. Noting the change of temperament within his ranks and being fully aware of the adverse effect that a spirit of defeatism can have on the morale and fighting ability of an army, General Forrest immediately called together an assembly of the entire troop to address the problem. Having us all gathered in close around him, so's all could see and easily hear his words, he began. 'Men, most of ye' have by now seen some two years of hard ridin' and hard fightin'. You're some of the toughest and finest horsemen to probably be found in all the world, else't ye' wouldn't yet be here today. The nat'ral familiarity with horseflesh ye' brought with ye' to the mounted service has now been honed by your rigors to a keen edge. There ain't no one, nowhere that can out ride, or out fight the lot of ye', even at four to one odds. You've all seen it time and again and ye' know what I'm speakin' of without me even have'n to voice it.

'What you may not yet know, or maybe just don't now recollect in light of some of the more recent reverses to our shared

Cause, is this... once't ever ye' set abouts to do a thang, don't never then hedge. Be holdin' nothin' back, for when ye' wholly commit, unseen forces'll come into play to ye' favor. 'Be not lukewarm!' God can find no favor with such and withholds his hand from their aid. And remember this, too...you can always do more'n ever ye' suspect ye' can, so don't never give up whilst there even remains the merest glimmer of hope for success. Our Cause is a just one and as such, should find ready help from the Devine, if'n we can only stand the test of our faith, stayin' ever true to our goal of Southern freedom.

'I promise this one thang, to lead ya'll well, same as I've always tried to do in the past. Ye' have me sacred word on that as one fighter to another'n. I won't be found guilty of wastin' your blood or courage in some vain effort to little end. And know this, even in the most desperate situations, I always leave an open out. I've never been one to walk into a room without first knowin' where to find the back door.'

"This last statement brought a chuckle to the ranks, for our leader's reputation was well known amongst us. 'I've been as proud of ye' boys as if'n ye' were me own sons. I think of ya'll in that way and treasure both your devotion and the trust you've placed in me as your general. I'd put not a one of ye' in harm's way 'fore me own sons, or brothers. We all drink of the same cup,' he added. That was nowise untrue, for both his younger brother William and his kid brother Jeffery, as well as the General himself, had ridden at the very head of pert near every charge we'd executed up to that point and no one expected otherwise. Even his elder son, then only seventeen, was exposed to nearly all the same dangers and exertions as any other common soldier in his command. The General was indeed hard, but fair.

'I only wish to add this one final thang 'fore we set off,' he concluded. 'The Union has dispatched General Rosecrans from Nashville to try and drive us from Tennessee. It would appear that we're turning tail, not wishing to give fight. Well, that's just exactly the appearance our commander-in-chief is hopin' to give. Rosecrans'll soon be thinkin' he's pursuin' an army in retreat and when he relaxes and lets down his guard, we'll turn on him quick, on ground of our own choosin', to destroy his forces piecemeal.

'We've still yet some hard fightin' and ridin' ahead of us, but the rewards reaped can be great if'n only we can keep the faith in our good Cause. I know ye' men have got plenty of all that yet in ye', so I'll be s'pectin' to see it when the time comes. We'll be movin' out at first light on the morrow. Our immediate duty is to screen the main body of the army from enemy assault during our southward march. But just ye' remain patient a little longer. Soon enough we'll turn the tables on our pursuers and strike back hard!

'Now, may the road rise to meet ye' and may we all rise together to meet the many challenges it still yet ahead holds. Pray God bless our best efforts!'

"With that, the men gave him a rousing cheer and I felt a new pride swellin' in my chest. I did note a conspicuous absence of any mention of the so-called 'deserters,' or, in light of most of the missing men remaining to defend their property and families, any appeal by the General to defend the honor of our homes and the 'Southern woman.' He was astute enough to know there remained many under him with dear friends and family now amongst the two-hunert or so absent men.

"The path lay long before us, but we knew we followed as brave and equitable a commander as one could s'pect to find amongst the ranks of either army. Whilst I yet remained in his service, I intended to serve as truly as was in my power, as honor dictated. If I fell in duty well rendered, then t'would be to my eternal credit.

"I say on the 'deserters' behalf and to their credit, when they felt they couldn't no longer give of their best efforts to the Cause, they would not stay on just to avoid legalities. I believe the General understood and appreciated as much about the newly absent fellers, who'd followed him unflinchingly on all previous occasions, though the office of his rank would not allow him to openly express such sentiments.

"But of those remaining, we all knew there could be no reservations held. Our utmost efforts would be no doubt required at every approaching turn. Oh, how I then missed big brother Will in whom to confide.

"We were a community brought together by fate. We fought an enemy better equipped and far superior in numbers, with vast untapped resources yet at their disposal. Most of us held little or no hope of ultimate victory, but fought on undaunted against long odds to defend the collective honor we shared with our brethren-in-arms. Through our unflinching tenacity and that of our valorous general, we would yet snatch victory from the jaws of defeat on numerous occasions.

"About the sixth of September, we passed through the main body of the infantry, heading for picket duty along the Ringgold/Lafayette Pike. Soon after arrival in our assigned quadrant, word was received that mounted Union troops were pushing for Dalton and the rail lines there, attempting to cut off that vital supply link bearing the lifeblood of our army. By the eighth, the cavalry of Generals Wheeler, Wharton and Martin had hooked up with that of our own near the pass between Sand and Lookout Mountains, to block the intended advance against our lines of communication. Upon seeing our formidable force arrayed on the heights against them, the Union generals did an about face with the forces in their command, heading back in the direction from whence they'd so recently arrived. As soon as the last bluecoats disappeared from our view around the road bend, we were back in the saddle, under the direction of General Forrest, racing for Ringgold Gap.

"We reached our new destination by good dark on the tenth, to discover Crittendon's Federal Infantry pushing to sever General Bragg's army in two. Two whole blue-coated divisions were crossing at Red House Bridge, where the East-Tennessee Railroad passed over Chickamauga Creek, some ten miles out of Chattanooga. Our couriers rushed to speed the word for Bragg to bring up his much larger infantry corps, then not more than six miles distant, to crush these two isolated divisions. But no Confederate infantry were forthcoming. Bragg, upon notice of so uncommonly favorable and dispersed dispositions of his enemy, inexplicably repaired in the opposite direction, towards Gordan's Mill. What Bragg was so unwilling to do, Forrest desperately attempted, with a force no greater than nine-hunert men and horses. With no expectations of additional support, at first light on the following day, we launched an assault against the front ranks of this advancing enemy force."

Pausing in his recital, he bore an unpleasant look, more in his eyes than the expression on his features. He puffed his pipe, grown cold, finding no relief in it from the phantoms disturbing his thoughts. Then, not bothering to pluck and light a broom straw, he stood and took a match from the box on the mantle. The sulphur, so precious to one who'd had to live without it, flared at the end of the little stick, as he drug it across a chimney brick. After it had burned down passed the sulphurous portion, he touched the flame to the content of the pipe, drawing in the odorous tobacco smoke like breath. After a few puffs, he seemed satisfied with the result and again, with a little time, settled back to his tale.

"We hit 'em hard, then fell back rapidly, stopping to give fight at every rise in the convoluted ground. The far superior numbers of blue infantry grimly bore down on us repeatedly, falling in large numbers before our sharpshooter's eye. We'd often had advantage in the past, in that we fought against mere milk fed lads, still wet behind the ears. But these were tested veterans, bending staunchly to their deadly task. As they closed again and again, we simply evacuated the cover we held, for the next advantageous concealment we came to, utilizing every favorable position to its fullest benefit. At Confederate Hill, where the most pitched battle of the day was waged, we doggedly held our ground, losing our only man killed in this running engagement. He was a close messmate and a fellow member of the General's escort, from Shelby County, Tennessee, named Private Zack Rogers. Both General Forrest and Prince were also slightly wounded that day when hit by nearly spent musket balls." Pappy paused, puffing his pipe and thinking of times shared with Rogers around the many campfires of their campaigns. The rising smoke from his pipe wafted on the still air of the room while the rain beat steadily on the roof, intense, but not violent. Once more he proceeded.

"Rosecrans's Federals had become badly divided into three vastly dispersed forces, separated by winding, narrow mountain roads. Our own forces were in an ideal interior position to strike at each of the divisions and crush them in turn with our superior numbers of seasoned veterans. Forrest repeatedly urged Bragg to seize the day and act on the unprecedented opportunities Providence had provided us, whilst the Yankees were yet so widely divided and thus weakened. Bragg continually delayed and slowly, ploddingly, the Union forces again came together, consolidating into a force by then far superior in strength to our own.

"Oh, for a Ceasar of the South to have then taken the situation readily in hand! Would one such as he not have crushed his enemies piecemeal, in detail, as Forrest had envisioned and so urgently chided his superior to do, driving the invaders headlong out of Tennessee? Perhaps never before in all of history was such a desperately needed, pat-hand for success on the battlefield dealt to and so wastefully folded by a so-called military commander!" he said, words dripping with cynicism.

"One thing you could say for General Forrest, he was equally intolerant and impatient of ignorance and incompetence in his superiors, as he was with his subordinates. He was no great respecter of rank for the mere sake of rank. He had never much cared for Bragg before and in light of the latter squandering such great tactical advantages, the tension between them fast came to a head." Again he puffed his pipe, raising a fresh cloud of smoke upon the air above our heads.

"Being thus able to do no more than slow the advance of the Federal Infantry whilst exacting a heavy toll for their crossing of the bridge on the Chickamauga, we broke off the engagement after one final stand at Tunnel Hill.

"That evening, encamped near the General's own tent, we could hear Forrest singing, in a loud and what sounded like, a drunken manner. Next day, word was, that at his surgeon Dr. Cowan's urging, our commander had broken his vow of abstinence, taking some whiskey to belay the pain associated with the removal of this latest bullet from near his spine. We rested quietly in camp for the next week, recovering from our brisk encounter with the enemy near Ringgold on the tenth. By the seventeenth, all opportunity to destroy the far-flung thirds of the Union Army of the Cumberland had been completely squandered. Thanks to Bragg's inaction, Rosecrans had miraculously slipped the noose that had hung so precariously around the neck of his entire army. The formerly separated Union divisions were by then concentrated, facing the Confederate Army of Tennessee from across the sluggish waters of the stream who's Injun name means 'River of Death.'

"The result of Bragg's indecision would be another ruinous blow to the Southern Cause, leaving seventeen thousand seasoned Confederate veterans lying upon the fields bordering Chickamauga Creek whilst sending its waters running literally red with the blood of both sides.

"A mass assault against the whole Union front was instead decided on by Bragg and set for the morning of September eighteenth. However, some overnight realignments made by Rosecrans, had moved the Federal positions from where they were expected, to be instead some two miles closer to their lines of communication and the city of Chattanooga. As result of these unforeseen developments and the required alignments of our own front associated with the discovery, the actual battle was nearer noon actually getting underway.

"Along with one battalion of Kentucky Cav., the General's escort was to the right of Bushrod Johnson's infantry regiment when it first went in near Reed's Bridge. Whilst supporting the advance that pushed the Federals far back from the creek banks to a nearby tributary called Pea Vine Creek that feeds into the Chickamauga, we encountered a force of Union horsemen under Colonel Minty. This fierce collision kept up until Johnson's infantry came forward to help drive off the blue-coated horsemen in the direction of the bridge.

"Soon after the Federals retreated from our immediate front, General John Bell Hood and his corps arrived straight from the train station, fresh from General Lee's failed eastern offensive in Virginia and a nine-hunert mile ride aboard the rickety train cars. Hood took immediate command of the Confederate right flank as the battle cooled for the night. We camped that evening away south near Alexander's Bridge, in rear of Hood's battle line.

"On that fateful night I left our own tents and called on the bivouac of the Third Arkansas. I visited with your grandmother Mary's first husband, T.A. Atkinson, for next to the last time. With the absence of brother Will, I was the only Dallas County boy left in the General's escort, so I never passed up any opportunity afforded for visiting with homeboys. As a result of our visits together, T.A. and I had cultivated a fine friendship over the previous months. I found in him a feller similarly like-minded as myself, a gentle spirit never previously one for strife, forced only by the circumstances of war to become acrimonious.

"We knew instinctively that on the morrow, there would be many who would no more return to camp. So we took opportunity that starry night, to enjoy the simple pleasures of breaking bread in the company of stout fellers and to share the thoughts of home and kin, perhaps for the last time in this world. We stood or sat round scattered fires all throughout the encampment. The faces of every sort of soldiers reflected the amber glow of the flames. Looking down on the scene from a nearby hill, the army looked to me like a flock of fireflies, flickering across the dark canvas of a cloudy night.

"Around our particular pile of embers sat men with marching drums and a pair of fiddles. The assorted brogues of various states mixed in songs of melancholia, life and death. Irish folk ballads touched a note in each our breasts that spoke of the bittersweet feelings of love, loss and the inevitable fate of mortals, conjuring up memories of home and family and comrades lost. We, too, imagined the soon to be seen sight of 'the elephant' and the threat of death that the morrow would bring.

"Sweet harmonies sprang forth from the welling hearts of those present for loved ones so far removed, sharing a mystic bond as we sat together suspended between this and the next world.

"Slowly our comrades departed the gathered circle one by one, much as we depart from this world. Some found their beds, eased to sleep by the stout liquor coursing through their veins. Others sat alone with their silent prayers, fears and worry. God was then there amongst us, as, too, was the reaper of souls. Their presence could be noted in the solemn words spoken in hushed tones. Life seemed evermore precious on the eve of a battle that would bring both death and glory.

"Left finally alone with only the wind, the flickering lantern and the low burning coals, T.A. and I chuckled softly to ourselves at the jokes that had been made and shared that evening between brothers-in-arms. The liquor in our veins sharpened the senses until we thought we could hear the strains of Yankee voices drifting on the breeze. In the quiet of mid-night, their muffled sound came softly through the woods. Smoke drifted across the tent tops as a chorus of snores echoed through our files. I pulled my collar up a little tighter as the temperature settled further and the wind fanned the embers again to a blaze, brightening the view all around. Stands of arms were stacked like tepee poles and scattered throughout the encampment, ready for the bugle call that I was too soon to sound. Reminded by their sight of my duties, I at last bid my friend goodnight and wandered off to find my own blankets. It is all a bittersweet memory to now recall, even after so much time come between our last pleasant evening shared."

He paused to tap his pipe on the dog-irons and adjust the wood within the hearth. "Fetch us another log from the box, son," he suggested. I did, placing the stick on over the hot coals that he then adjusted to his satisfaction with his iron poker. The flame thus renewed, he resumed, while the rain still beat steady against the glass.

"I rode Prince back late that night to our campsite, to see the General only just returning to his tent from a council of war he'd had with Generals Hood and Bragg. Knowing tomorrow would be an active one, I lay quickly down to take a few hours fitful rest. Long before first light, I was roused to call reveille with my bugle. My trumpeted command was echoed down the line of encampments as the Army of Tennessee came again to life. We quickly saddled and rode out at a brisk pace to reconnoiter the most recent dispositions of our foe.

"What greeted us was the sight of a formidable array of Union infantry to our front near Jay's Sawmill, ready in battle line. Horses were becoming more of a premium all the time, so, not wishing to jeopardize our means of transportation, the troop dismounted and prepared to meet the fresh attack afoot.

"Prince and I were dispatched to the rear as courier, to carry the news of the impending clash to General Polk. Arriving at Polk's headquarters tent, I found a flurry of furious activity that made it difficult to see my message delivered to the commander. After cooling our heels and taking some fodder and breakfast from the General's commissary, a message was brought for delivery back to General Forrest. Again we dashed back across the rolling landscape at breakneck speed, knowing that battles are often won, or lost for want of an expedient communiqué.

"Lathered up and panting, Prince and I sought and found the General in the midst of a desperate defense against overwhelming numbers of Federal infantry. The enemy attacked in wave upon wave, breaking their energies against the bulwarks of the stubborn Confederate artillery and riflemen. I found General Forrest personally directing the fire of a gun battery. Piloted to his side, I reported Polk's reply to Forrest's request for infantry reinforcements. My commander dispensed a string of fiery adjectives as he read the message I handed him. The note expressed the fact that no infantry were available to his disposal at the time, but what cavalry could be spared would soon arrive, if only Forrest could hang on 'til then.

"No sooner was the paper bearing this unpleasant news tossed aside in a wad, than we heard the sound of Dibrell's bugles, as his battalion rode to our relief. Moving to greet and direct the fresh arrived veterans whilst leaving overall command of the action

283

temporarily in the hands of his brother Colonel William, the General sped off with nothing but his bodyguard of half a dozen stout fellows, augmented by the addition of Prince and myself as guides.

"We raced for the rear, where I'd previously seen unengaged infantry troops lounging in the shade of an oak grove. Riding up to find the gray-clad foot soldiers still at their leisure, Forrest demanded to know whose command he was addressing. We were directed to a Colonel Claudius C. Wilson, in command of a brigade of Georgians. Ordering Colonel Wilson to bring up his troops immediately, Forrest directed them to fall in on the faltering left flank of his dismounted cavalry. This strengthened and extended that portion of the Confederate line beyond the Federal position. Thus invigorated, led by one who ever preferred to be on the offensive, our desperate defense turned to a hearty assault. Bolstered by the three-hunert Georgia foot soldiers, our dismounted cavalry moved out in fine infantry formation, driving off the Federal assault so quickly as to overrun and capture a battery of their deserted cannon. Dressed as he was in a long white linen overcoat, the General was readily visible, personally leading the thrust that captured the Union artillery. The trophies of both the Seventy-seventh Indiana and the Sixty-ninth Pennsylvania colors were also gained and carried from the field.

"Remaining close to our staunch general throughout the day's engagements, I had ample opportunity to observe him as he maneuvered men from one critical point to the next, bolstering our line as it sagged first one place, then another, under the telling weight of the greater sum of Federal attackers. Our flanks were increasingly threatened as the widening Federal front overlapped the ends our own line time and again, only to be countered by Forrest interior talent for anticipating his adversaries' next move. Through the artful movement and manipulation of his limited forces, he repeatedly stemmed the blue tide at the last moment. But, eventually our lines were spread too thin and the ever widening Union lines were able to position their cannon to pour an enfilading tempest of furious missiles down our entire length, as we were unrelentingly subjected to the waves of salty, veteran blue bellies crashing against our front.

"We eventually gave ground, driven back whilst leaving a deplorable number of brave soldiers on the contested ground. When I had directed Forrest earlier in the afternoon to where the Georgians waited in reserve, they were a handsome lot, fairly well dressed, looking to have the pride of soldiers instilled in them. They were seasoned and ready for a fight. When they came into action, the tide of momentum was turned on the Federals. Now, as we backed away from the heavy fire of the three deep, blue ranks, overlapping us at either end, we passed by our dead and wounded, many of them proud Georgians, fallen in the advance. Men were shot from the crown of their heads to the soles of their feet. Some lay with blood pouring from multiple holes. Some had their eyes shot out, another his jaw blown away, tongue lolling around where a chin once't was, wrecked and broken. Another poor lad was hobbling away from the firestorm, using his musket for a crutch, when he tripped and fell as his feet became tangled in his own dragging guts.

"At that moment occurred one of those strange coincidences of war. To my amazement, I heard an old familiar voice I knew from back home in the neighborhood, calling out to me in our retreat. Searching around the horrible scene upon the field, there lay a close neighbor from Dallas County, shot clean through his upper thigh. Hillard Harris had up and gone off a month afore war broke out to jine up with the Georgia infantry, back in the state where his folks had come from and he'd been reared. I hadn't seen or heard from him since March of '61. Turns out he'd returned to his childhood home to enlist amongst family and friends with the same Georgia outfit that I'd led the General to earlier in the day. I helped my wounded friend from the bloody ground and to the rear. We retreated with order, falling back only some four hunert yards, carrying off most of our injured, surrendering no more ground than what we'd taken since eleven that morning. We stopped our rearward movement at the position from whence we'd first begun the fight. I quickly turned Hillard over to the care of an aid station in the rear before hurriedly returning to the General's side. After all the excitement of the engagement was passed, I tried to locate Hillard in the hospital, but would not find or hear from him again until March of '65, when he once't more returned to Arkansas, four years and four days after his departure.

"At that point, General Walker arrived on the scene in response to the courier message I'd delivered to General Polk hours before. He personally relieved Forrest from the command of the engagement, quickly bringing his fresh reserves into action. With the addition of rested troops, the Confederates again gained a temporary advantage, surging forward, until the Federals responded in like kind, driving the Rebels back again from the bloody ground to whence we'd started. The contest continued after this fashion throughout the P.M., surging back and forth across the same ground until it was thoroughly awash with the blood and bodies of both sides.

"Resting from his vigorous labors, whilst observing the continued ebb and flow of the battle's tide, General Forrest noted the Union troops about to outflank the left of Maney's Brigade. Sending me hurrying to recall Dibrell's battalion, who, too, were resting at the rear after having been relieved, he led them rapidly to the relief of our hard pressed right. Forrest again took personal command of the artillery, directing their fire so near the Confederate front, that Maney rode up to ask the General to redirect his fire a little less near to his men. He did as requested, but still brought the guns to bear on the blue hosts within a mere fifty yards to the front of the crowded gray backs.

"Late in the afternoon, the engagement reached a stalemate with the belligerents contented at last to settle for simply holding the ground from where they each had started early that morning. We retired from the front to rest the fagged out horsemen, who were unaccustomed to the additional rigors of fighting dismounted. We were glad to be riding to camp, instead of marching, as muscles we didn't even know we had began to ache before much later that evening.

"We could still hear a furious contest underway to the south, on the far left of the Confederate line, as Generals Stewart, Hood and Cleburne pushed hard in that sector against Rosecrans's embattled Federals. The racket continually rose and fell at uneven intervals. Near dusk, it began to finally fade, then intensified yet again, until, long after dark, only occasional skirmishing remained to be heard scattered about the arena of conflict. The front ranks lay down in battle line, to bivouac in position for the following day. They rested their heads that night on nothing but their arms.

"Right after dark, General Armstrong's Brigade of cavalry jined our bivouac. Their heads hung low on their shoulders from fatigue, as the dusty warriors and their weary mounts drug into camp. Amongst their ranks rode the Third Arkansas. I observed closely as Company 'A' filed by, watching intently for all my friends and acquaintances to appear in the parade. A knot tightened in my belly as more and more filed past without any sign of Sergeant Atkinson. Finally I stepped up to a close messmate of his in the Third, sitting wearily astride his mount. He answered my inquiry as to T.A.'s whereabouts, with the news that he'd received a not too serious wound near his knee, that was sure to take him out of action for a spell, but that chances were he should again return before too long. This was a relief, though one never knew what the result of even the most minor wound could be, should it turn septic. All that I could discover as to where he'd been carried was that litter bearers had taken him from the field en route to hospital somewhere in the rear. With preparations underway to renew the contest on the morrow, there was no time for locating him within the hodgepodge medical system of makeshift field hospitals. The report that he was not seriously injured had to do for the time. I could only pray God's mercy on him.

"Back from yet another council of war at Bragg's headquarters, General Forrest reported that the battle would commence on the dawn, beginning with an advance by the right and move successively left down the line, with the intent of sweeping Rosecrans's army south away from their lines of supply, whilst cutting off their route of retreat toward Chattanooga. Being on the far right flank, that meant we would be some of the first to engage and would begin the attempt to herd the Federals south. The twentieth promised to be another long and difficult day.

"Before the first light even began to brighten in the eastern sky, I was sounding reveille. The bone-tired men marched away north to take their position for the coming assault, set to begin at seven. The main body of our horses was again left behind, with our cavalry to act in concert as infantry with Breckinridge's Corps. Only those acting in command and as couriers remained in the saddle. Forrest directed his dragoons beyond the farthest reaches of the Union left, where all awaited the distribution of morning rations. The mistakes of sending weary men into combat on empty stomachs at places like Shiloh and Corinth were not lost on our general. Once't well enough fed, Forrest issued a command to sound the charge and with that fateful bugle note, I sent eight thousand to meet their destiny and helped launch one of the worst encounters of the war. Overlapping the enemy's flank, Bedford turned his force south and the hearty warriors swept all before them. Riding near the General for the purpose of sounding bugle commands as necessary, I was able to observe the brave actions of men unaccustomed to foot soldiering, marching unflinchingly into a wall of flying steel and lead.

"Captain George W. Winburne of Company G, Third Arkansas, with Private J.P. Carrol at his side, were both shot dead moving at the head of their men. Still the stout souls pushed on, teeth bared and gritted, rifle barrels aflame. Men fired and reloaded so rapidly, so often, that their powder flashed from the heat of the gunmetal when poured into the muzzle. The advance moved doggedly up with the Federals steadily giving ground before it. The dismounted troopers behaved so admirably in the face of stiff resistance, that I was witness to a scene often spoken of thereafter.

"Not recognizing the pennant of our cavalry, the renowned and venerable infantry commander General D.H. Hill inquired whose infantry was doing such a fine job of crowding the Federals. Upon being informed they weren't infantry at all, but in fact cavalry unhorsed for the occasion, he rode up to Forrest and delivered his compliments on the ferocity and tenacity of the troopers and Forrest's fine handling of steady, well-trained men. Being himself still quite busy overseeing the affairs of the field, the General simply tipped his hat in gratitude for the kind remarks and rode on about his tasks. Following in Bedford's wake, I turned in the saddle to see Hill grinning, shaking his head, as he spoke with the company of his aides.

"As the day settled on toward evening, the Union were evacuating the field in great disarray, as their center had been broken when Rosecrans pulled a division of blue bellies from that quarter to bolster the faltering Federal left. The efforts of Forrest's Regiment and Breckenridge's Corp smashing against the beleaguered left flank of the Army of the Cumberland, had caused this fatal blunder on the part of their Yankee commander. The keen military eye of General Longstreet had instantly noticed the movement of men away from his immediate front, prompting him to rapidly move his corps to exploit the weakness. The Confederates surged through the hole like water bursting from a dam, sweeping away all resistance in their path, driving the blue lines back on themselves in mass confusion. But for the grim determination of Union General Thomas where he stubbornly sat astraddle Snodgrass Hill, the rout would have been a complete debacle for the enemy. Without Thomas' cool, even-headedness, the retreating throngs of bluecoats would have been slaughtered in numbers unequalled in the history of warfare. His unrelenting determination to quit the field in good order however, bought the precious time needed to place ground between the pursued and their pursuers. As the last of Thomas's divisions finally quit the arena that evening, the whole of the Confederate Army of Tennessee lay down exhausted upon the killing fields of the Chickamauga, to lick their wounds and tend the dead, whilst Rosecrans scuttled on north through the choked mountain passes, hurrying desperately to reach the relative protection of Fortress Chattanooga. Only Forrest and four-hunert mounted troopers gave any chase at all, following after nightfall hot on the heels of the vanquished. Riding through the darkness, our path lit only by starlight, we arrived at dawn upon a detachment of Federal horsemen just out of Rossville. Waking me from sleep in the saddle, the General called for a charge, which I immediately sounded, rousing many others from the reverie of dreams. Without hesitation, in column of four abreast, with Generals Armstrong and Forrest at the lead, we plowed into the center of the line of mounted rearguard where it stretched across the road. Our shouts echoed off the canyon walls, giving the impression of a much larger force. This was another instance where the fighting was fast, but furious, with numerous enemy falling under our guns in a very short period. Riding at the front near the two generals, I probably unsaddled near ten men. The resistance was quickly broken, sending the blue-clad horsemen racing headlong for the covering guns of the retreating infantry, whose flank they'd been until recently guarding. In the chase, the enemy spun in their saddles, firing wildly at our front ranks. Only feet behind and just to the right of General Forrest during this horse race, I was suddenly showered with a stream of thick, red blood, as it spurted like a fountain from a wound to the neck of the General's mount. I watched as the General coolly leaned forward in the saddle, plugging the bullet hole with his finger and plunged on in rapid pursuit of the enemy. We spurred our animals up the steep incline to the summit of the pass, picking men from the saddle without discretion. Once't reached, we encountered a heavy fusillade from the riflemen ensconced amongst the many boulders on either side of the pass. This quickly halted any further action on our part against the fleeing foe. Repairing rapidly back down the mountain only a short distance, just out of range of their sharpshooters, we waited but a short spell until the last of the Army of the Cumberland had vacated the summit. We then returned to the high promontory close upon their retreating heels.

"As we dismounted to rest our weary mounts, Bedford released the hold on the bleeder and the poor beast shortly sagged and collapsed, bled dry by the rapid pounding of her excited heart. She was a fine looking, tall buckskin. I stood by her side, rubbing and soothing her in her last minutes, watching the bright red liquid pulse from her neck, all the while grateful it wasn't Prince.

"The Federals had left in such haste, they'd abandoned a pair of signalmen in a high tower, built in a great tree at the summit of Missionary Ridge. These two Federals were dislodged from their perch and relieved of their fine brass field glasses. The two generals carefully scrambled up onto the high platform as we waited below. After some time they descended from the great height and fired off a dispatch to General Polk, urging the rapid pursuit of a defeated and demoralized foe. Prince and I were spared the rigors of that particular courier duty back across the treacherous landscape, in favor of a less jaded horse and rider. Asking permission to ascend the observation platform, I, along with another private from the General's escort, climbed the rickety ladder far above the tree line, to a splendid perch where only hawks and eagles normally trod. The height and view were literally breathtaking in their breadth and scope. Before us lay a panorama beyond description, the thought of which even now stands the hair upon the back of my neck. Far away to the north, within the confines of Chattanooga, we could plainly make out the tremendous bout of activity being undertaken with the first arrivals there of our panicked adversary, whilst winding for miles below us through the narrow goat trails, on what the local mountaineers call roads, were the unorganized throngs of frightened Yankees whose rear guard we'd just driven from the summit. We watched as wagons were shoved over the sides of steep precipices to make room for the mad flight of frantic men. There was plainly a rout underway, even with as yet no persecution of the pursuit by the balance of the Confederate Army of Tennessee.

"We shortly retired from the windy precincts of the mountain top, falling back but a short piece to the shelter of a refreshing arbor in a little mountain cove. It was our commander's intention to await the vanguard of Bragg's Tennessee Army, protect and hold the pass and continue observing the movement and activity in Chattanooga below. That afternoon and evening, we enjoyed the freshness of the high mountain air and the songs of birds, whilst our comrades back at Chickamauga were treated to the reeking smells of putrid, decaying flesh. The song of all birds was absent from that other place, driven off by the fury that had filled both Earth and sky, replaced with the groans of the maimed and dying. We knew what grim wreckage we'd left behind and former experience made us glad to be away, though our hearts were rent with pity for the living, as well as the dead still upon that horrid field. Nowhere else but the banks of the Chickamauga did I ever see a stream so completely filled and flowing with the blood of men and horses. The sight returned to me again and again as I tried to rest that night, driving me from my bed upon the Earth, to seek comfort in gazing on the spinning constellations, until sleep finally found me on my rocky perch just at dawn. Before drifting off, alone with the wind whistling through the fractured rocks, I reached out my hand to touch the stars that seemed so near in the high, thin mountain air. I lifted up a prayer to the star-filled heavens for the safety of brother Will, our loved ones at home and poor T.A. and Hillard, lying that night somewhere injured in hospital back at the battlefield.

"On the high mountain top we rested between the two mighty armies, each of which still reeled from the blows exchanged in the previous days. I was by then fed up with it all! I asked myself what would I do when next committed to conflict? I wondered could I press the fight as before? But, it seems, it is the questions about ourselves that we least wish to ask, that God so often most likes to pose.

"Seeking guidance, I pulled my compact Bible from my saddlebags. Turning in The Book of Luke to chapter 9, verse 37, I read, 'Now it occurred on the next day, when they came down from the mountaintop, that a great multitude met Him.' And so it would be.

"After two more days guarding the pass, awaiting the main Confederate force to come up, Prince and I rode in the vanguard of Forrest's escort, near the General's side, back down the mountain trail. We retraced our steps back to Bragg's Headquarters, where we found it incredibly still located, as before, on the bloody banks of the Chickamauga. There, yet encamped around the headquarters, sat the entire Army of Tennessee, still licking their wounds.

"Bedford marched out of Bragg's tent after failing to cajole, threaten, or coerce the commander-in-chief to capitalize on his costly victory, by moving whilst opportunity yet remained to rend the desperately needed Southern industrial center of Chattanooga from the grasp of the addled Yanks. Standing close by, I heard him ask Dr. Cowan in disgust, as he swung angrily into the saddle, 'What in God's name does he fight battles for anyway?'

"Before we were sent out again, I asked Dr. Cowan to help me locate Sergeant Atkinson and Private Harris within the far flung facilities of the makeshift hospital system. He made inquiry through the proper channels, only to be told they were probably held in one of three main facilities set up for the wounded. This left me with the unpleasant task of searching bed by bed through these wards filled with the long suffering, until I might at last come across't one of my fallen comrades. The conditions I found our wounded kept in were deplorable beyond description. To say there was a severe want of sanitation is the height of understatement.

"At last I discovered the resting place of my dear friend from home, T.A., amongst the throngs of other groaning men. He lay on a cot within the stifling confines of a captured Yankee tent, stenciled with the large letters 'U.S.' on its roof. A blanket with like insignia covered him from the chest down. The stumpy remnant of his mangled leg protruded from beneath the corner of the covers. My heart sank to my bowels at the sight of the pale, emaciated fellow lying weakly before me, but a shell of his vigorous, former self. The stump remaining above the knee had been hurriedly swathed in a blood-clotted, homemade bandage. My first act was to stir the flies from where they lit upon the ugly dressing of the missing limb. It was instances such as that one, that instilled deeply within me a greater hatred for those disease ridden little pests, than for any other creature under God's firmament. The sound of that swarm rising upon the still, hot air roused T.A. to open his eyes dimly and look up weakly. I put on my best poker face, wanting to appear as cheerful as possible for my fast fading friend. At first, no recognition came to his drawn features, but then, slowly, as his eyes began to come more into focus and the realization of his sad condition and hopeless surroundings returned to him, his pale orbs brightened slightly and a feeble smile came to his trembling lips. 'John,' he said in recognition, mustering all his remaining strength for the effort, 'by God it's good to see you.'

"He quickly noted the pained expression and trembling smile that my brave face could not conceal and sought to somehow soothe my concerns. 'The doctor says its nothing an artificial limb won't cure. I should imagine you fellers are gonna hafta' carry on the fight without me for a spell now. I don't s'pect I'll have much use for a saddle anywise soon.'

"I swallowed hard to put the great lump in my throat back in its proper place before I dared try to speak. At last I managed to get out in a trembling tone, 'I don't know 'bout that, tough as you are, the generals'll probably be a want of your services right soon. Probably figure out a harness to hoist ye' in the saddle so's you can again lead your stout company at its front.'

"To this he only answered, 'Lord-a-mercy, I hope not. I'm right fed up with this whole affair. Won't bother me none for them generals to carry right along without me. They'll rightly figure it out of their own.'

"I gently settled on the edge of the cot, nearer my ailing comrade. With that, he grimaced, as a pain shot up the remaining half of his missing right leg. I leaped back to my feet, embarrassed and apologizing whilst askin', 'What can I do for ye', T.A.?'

"Seeing my guilt at having unsettled him, he said, 'It ain't you J.R., them blamed phantom pains where I got shot come back from time to time. Doc says it's normal to feel the missing limb on occasion, even long after it's been gone. At times I could swear I feel the tiny feet and wings of them blasted flies a'crawlin' on me toes. I try to wiggle 'em, but they ain't there to wiggle no more.'

"I gently settled again on the cot side, this time with no ill effects to my frail friend. As he spoke in weak tones, I smelt the familiar odor of death on his fetid breath. He yet clung to but the thinnest thread of life. I knew then, this would be our final meeting this side of the veil. We sat then quietly for a spell, his hand resting gently on my knee, just enjoying the company of one another's presence, together, we each sensed, for one last time. I thought of his poor wife and children that he'd often spoke so fondly of. How would they manage without their husband and father? Two tears crept into the corners of my weary eyes. I quickly brushed them aside, not wishing to further sadden my suffering messmate with my grief. As we rested there together, the smells of the ward mingled with the scents borne on the slight breeze that had just begun to stir the heavy air. There was the good smell of the Earth in fall. Coffee aroma, too, carried on the breeze into the tent, mixing with the unrelenting odor of fetid flesh associated with flies and late summer heat. I could tell the worst of the odor came from the nasty bandage on T.A.'s nub.

"Rising gently from his side after sitting a long while, I went to find an orderly to change the dressing. With some difficulty, I managed to persuade a young overworked soldier, grown jaded to the suffering of his fellows by so much exposure, to bring a basin and fresh wraps to assist my friend. Rousing him from the delirium that he drifted in and out of, I explained to T.A. our intentions of cleaning his diminished leg and changing his bandage. Bravely, he nodded his understanding, knowing too well the discomfiture that the slightest movement rendered to his irritated nub. I pulled a mini-ball from out my trouser pocket, placing it gently between his clenched teeth, as the orderly began his gruesome task. Upon unwrapping the dried and clotted cloth, the rotten binding cracked open, releasing a stench that instantly turned both our stomachs. I grabbed my mouth and nose, but stood my ground as he peeled back the layers to reveal the most despicable sight of all. Beneath the original dressing, applied the week prior, right after completion of the surgery, were maggots swarming over and in the discolored flesh. 'Good Gawd!' said the attendant. T.A. fell blissfully into unconsciousness, as I ushered the poor lad out of earshot by the scruff of his neck. I was in a fighting rage, ready to whoop somebody for allowing this to happen. But futility rendered me harmless after only a few moments. 'How God, could this happen?' I asked no one in particular, feeling how completely helpless we'd become to control our destiny.

"Together we took whiskey from the surgeon's commissary and after bracing ourselves with a stout belt and gently treating T.A. to a sip, we poured the balance of the bottle over the little white vermin, wiping away their writhing carcasses from the ragged flesh and cleaning the pitiful, pale limb as best we could. T.A. was mercifully unaware of most that went on, allowing us to rewrap the whole affair with clean white strips of cloth and nestle him gently back on his bed. The excitement had been too much for him in his weakened condition and he lay in a fevered sleep, mumbling and tossing fitfully. I sat with him yet awhile before duty required I return to camp and the affairs of soldiering. Knowing this would be our last visit this side of the grave, I leaned over and gave a light kiss to his forehead. As I stood to leave, he feebly grasped my sleeve, tugging me back closer. His eyes opened in slits and the corners of his mouth turned up slightly. In a whisper that I had to lean in close to hear, he said, 'John, when you get home, check in on Mary and the children. They'll need a protector afore all of this is done. God bless ye' ole' soul!' With that his hand dropped back to his side on the cot and his eyes again closed. His breathing was shallow and labored, but he was peaceful, perhaps from knowing his request would not go unheeded by a friend so dear.

"I left him there in sleep and the care of the young, overworked orderly. I pressed the few Confederate dollars from my pocket into the medic's hand, reminding him to take extra care of the dying man, lest I should learn otherwise and return to insure he met a like fate. He solemnly assured me he would, stuffing the near worthless currency into his trouser pocket.

"As I was about to depart, a folded letter dropped to the floor from the pocket of T.A.'s coat where it hung on a chair-back next to his cot. The orderly retrieved it to inspect, noting the name scrawled on it's front. 'Mrs. Mary Atkinson,' he said aloud as he read. After brief examination, he handed it over to me and I stuffed it in my own pocket before leaving the hospital. I told him where we were posted and asked he keep me informed when the inevitable occurred, or if he might learn of any news from Hillard.

"War gives expression to the two furthest extremes of emotion, both love and hate. At that moment, I was filled with the twain, love for a friend and hatred for the foe that had felled such a goodhearted man and for the commander-in-chief that squandered and neglected his brave boys to no avail. All the blood and thunder of Chickamauga had proved fruitless. Rosecrans was back safely inside the strong defenses around Chattanooga and the war would drag on indefinitely. The Cause was now good as lost. It had all become just killing for the sake of killing. I was filled to overflowing with an intense rage toward the methods of the world as men had made it. In those days of infamy, I, too, would for a time, succumb to that same blind rage that infected parties of both sides, making us, oft as not, no more than gangs of miscreants, sworn against all law, order, or peace. Those were the darkest days of America's history, as well as my own darkest hours.

"I wept that night as I read the letter T.A. had composed to his wife the year prior, but never posted. I then wrote an accompanying letter explaining subsequent events to the soon to be Widow Atkinson. We had never met, I only having seen her from afar around the community back home, never being formerly introduced at anytime before the war. Little did I know what lay in store for the both of us upon my homecoming, anymore than I then knew if'n I'd ever again in this life see home. It makes you wonder if sometimes God doesn't call one from this world to make room for another'n.

"I held the letters un-posted until the next day, when the young orderly showed up with the news of T.A.'s painful passing. His day to die had blessedly come, deep in the night. I informed the lads in the Third Cav. of his demise and we all toasted as true a man, save the Christ Himself, ever that walked the Earth. There was still no word of Hillard. He too was lost for the time in the confusing aftermath of battle."

Pappy paused here to listen to the quiet following the rain shower. Occasional drops pelted the window glass, as it dripped from the tree branches. He stirred the fire, drawing in a deep sigh. The painful memories were troubling to his old soul, but like the bullet that had lodged against General Forrest's spine after being wounded on the retreat from Shiloh, it was better to get it out, than to leave it festering, awaiting silently to dislodge and debilitate at some unexpected, inopportune moment within the rigors of mounted warfare.

"Our next orders," he rejoined, "were to ride east to Harrison, to scout the dispositions of Yankee General Burnside. I was glad to be leaving the camp on the banks of the Chickamauga, for it held most painful memories. The distraction of brisk activity was the prescription my soul then most needed. I was actually looking forward to our next encounter with the enemy. Nor would I have long to wait.

"The next months were like a fevered dream, of which I recall but little. A form of madness seized me. The toast we drank to T.A. started a drinking bout that lasted into the following spring. I rode with an almost suicidal abandon and fought with a fury hitherto unseen. With both Will and T.A. gone, I spent more and more time alone with only my dark thoughts.

"In those months of muttering thunder and gathering storm, soldiers of both sides were participants in an unholy rebellion, caught in the middle between the two heartless gov'ments. Gone were the glory days of the Confederacy. To be shed of him, Bragg once't more reassigned our General Forrest to a new command, this time to organize and lead the mounted troops of north Mississippi and west Tennessee. But for the successful affairs of Forrest's command in those areas of operation, more and more defeat and humiliation lay ahead for the South's men-in-arms. I no longer cared much one way, or another. I walked around vacant eyed with an attitude both sour and mean, causing me to become feared by even me own mates. I had both my hand and nose broke during that period from brawling. I learnt from that period in my life how easy it can be to develop a bad reputation, yet how difficult, once't gained, to live it down. I suppose I'd made up me mind that we were all soon gonna' die anyway and so, held nothing back, forgetting restraint in both war and play. An unruly spirit ruled over me. But some force unseen protected me through that long, reckless period. No doubt the prayers of family back home went not unheeded."

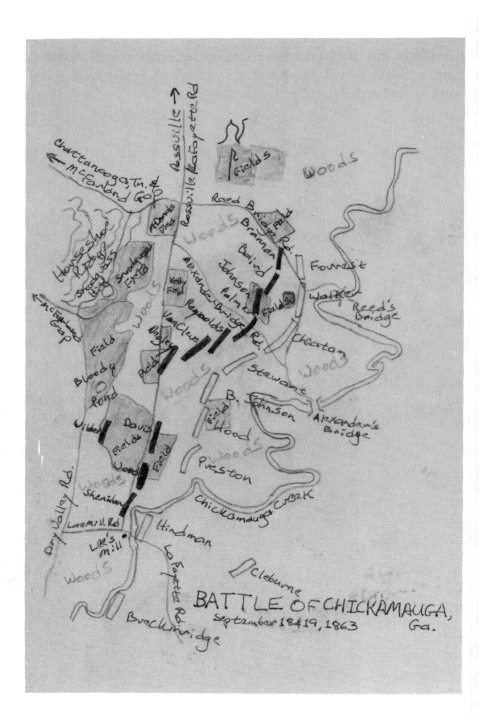

BATTLE OF CHICKAMAUGA, Ga.
September 18 & 19, 1863

Came the Horsemen

"Sometimes I feel like I might could just sit like this from here on out, satisfied simply to survey all the familiar surroundings of home, restin' easy after a long life of toils and labor. I've spent many an hour sittin' here rockin',' watchin' all the birds and clouds that sail 'cross this patch of sky. After dark, I've watched the many years as the stars and moon continue along their ceaseless transit. It seems everything's forever a'changin'. At any given moment the air's a'stirrin,' plants are growin' and our thoughts be restlessly a'rovin', all whilst clouds drift aloft, the Earth spins ever round and the seasons march steady onward," he concluded. Then after a brief pause, added, "But as I sit here at me leisure son, someone's gotta' keep the place in repair and I want ye' to know just how much I do so appreciate all ye' help in that regard," he stated, as sweating from his bidding, I joined the old man where he sat in one of the pair of green-painted, steel armchairs beneath the cool of the broad, shadetree.

It sometimes seemed I couldn't get a new installment of the story about his stint with Forrest's Cavalry but that I first fulfilled some task about the place. He was a fine project supervisor, a talent he no doubt honed while in the army. Ever since the conclusion of the war, when afterwards they first began to have blacks on the farm, he'd been known to occasionally work a farmhand nearly to exhaustion.

With former slaves wandering the roads of the south, wont to do with their newfound freedom, they eventually found their way into areas like our neighborhood where Africans had never before played a part in agriculture. With my grandpap, as with many other founding Irish families of our little community, the homeless coloreds with a simple and abundant knowledge of farming, soon found ready employment as sharecroppers and tenants on the land. The harvests produced of their labors, in conjunction with the broader markets made available by the railroad's arrival to these parts back in '76, helped fulfill a dearly held hope for newfound prosperity on the farms and timber holdings that first took in the new citizens, giving them humble shelter, a renewed purpose in life and gainful employment. There is a long tradition since the war, of coloreds working side by side with our family and treated as such fair and equal. And as you'd expect, like old Forrest, Pappy, too, could be hard, but fair, working a white hand every bit that of a black one.

"Yep," he said, looking out over the various log buildings and pastures, "this view reminds me of Parson's portrayal in his sermons of what heaven's a'like. Onliest difference is, here there's birds singing and roosters crowing 'stead of cherub songs played on angel harps."

After sitting a spell, listening closely to the many sounds of life surrounding us, he said, "I sat right here on this very spot and held both ye,' your big brother and even ye' daddy afore ye,' when you was each yet only babes."

Then he added with a touch of excited anticipation edging his deep voice "Feel that breeze! Somethin's a'stirrin'," he noted in reference to the sudden refreshing gust moving the 'til then heavy air. "We could surely use a good shower 'bout now!" he concluded.

The wind felt pleasant against the beaded perspiration on my skin, helping cool my brow as I rested out of the warm Indian summer sun. I soaked in all the pleasant sights of the place, its orderliness standing as a bastion against the myriad chaos of life, while leaning back comfortably in my seat with both feet up off the ground, listening intently to all the varied country sounds. Some clouds gathered slowly to the south, darkening the sky as yet ever so slightly. The rustle and rush of the breeze around the shadow of the house, softly hummed in my ears. I relished the afterglow of a good task well rendered and patiently looked forward to my reward in the form of a properly thought out tale from one whom I believed to be a master storyteller.

To my surprise he pulled out an oily rag with a pistol wrapped inside. It was his 1860 Army Colt six-shooter, the very one he brought home with him across the wide Missisip back in '64. With apparent fascination, he held it in his hand, cocking and pointing it at various targets within his periphery. He snapped on empty

303

cylinders, one after another. All understanding of gun safety seemed to've been temporarily suspended as he targeted various pecking chickens and every other moving thing in the yard. Then, after his turn clicking off empty rounds, he reversed arms and handed the weapon over to me for examination. The contagion of its feel in my hand was immediately intoxicating. There was a balance and natural grace to the handling of the superbly tooled piece. It led my hand to twirl and point it with threatening accuracy about the premises.

"How many?" I asked, glancing up from the weapon to look directly into his pale, blue eyes. My own eyes narrowed until I was watching for his reaction through only slits.

His face grew grave and ashen in color at the thought, while his voice remained unchanged by emotion. He asked in reference to my inquiry, "Dispatched to eternity?"

"Yes, sir, with this," I said holding up the sixer.

Frowning slightly, almost quizzically, he answered, "Hard to say." After an extended pause he explained, "You see, I carried so many weapons over my two and a half years as a hard-bitten trooper. But that one you're holding was probably my favorite. I had better than a half dozen other Colt revolvers, mostly Navy models, but none were as well built as that Army version I took off a dead Yank lieutenant at the Battle for Fort Pillow. None of the others had the balance, or smooth action of that brass fitted one there. And when it was emptied, it made a fine club for unsaddling an opponent in a close melee."

I hefted it in my hand, checking the weight, then swung it to and fro as if to conk some poor fellow about the head.

"Too many," he concluded in answer to my inquiry, still wearing the grave expression of one facing his past with a sense of remorse for his actions. "It's a dangerous and seductive feeling to point your trustee pistol at a fellow and let fly with awesome accuracy and result. It could almost make you feel like Ole' Mars' himself."

"Sir?" I asked, not taking his meaning.

Some of the gravity of his thoughts was lightened by my puzzlement, as he chuckled softly before explaining. "That was a sort a joke amongst N.B.'s boys. The General had some forty-odd personal slaves in his service on and off throughout the war, acting as body servants, cooks and wagon drivers. They called him 'Mars', which was short for master. 'Yassa' Mars', they'd reply whenever he barked out some direction or other. But we turned it into 'Ole' Mars' in honor of the Roman god of war, said by the ancients to've been red in complexion, cause when in a battle the General would get just as red as a beet from his collar up. Just like ole' red Mars himself."

"Oh, I see," I said, chuckling to myself at the play on words.

Reaching over and again taking the gun from my hand, he eyed it carefully, remembering specifics about its history with him. "There was this one time, near Tishamingo Creek, at the Battle of Brice's Crossroads down in Mississippi, when moving in advance of the main body of our troop, we came up against a numerically superior bunch of bluecoat rearguard under command of General Samuel Sturgis. I believe it was June tenth of '64, not long before the raid on Memphis. We'd been marching for days through occasional torrential downpours and were tired and wet to the bone. We'd routed their initial stand at the crossroads and a small contingent of our force was dismounted, pushing hard on their retreating flanks, far out in advance of our main body. After initial heated contact with a large number of their rearguard protecting the retreat of our fleeing enemy, we quickly took up position in the cover of some standing and dead fallen timber. Sensing the weaker numbers of our yet isolated small force, the Yank infantry turned and made repeated, hard-fought charges against us, causing us to fear we'd be overwhelmed several different times. The Yankee drums beat the attack as if to bust their heads. Mingled with the martial sounds of fife and trumpet, 'twas enough to drive forward even a paralytic. More than once't their frontlines came to within but a few yards of overrunning us, when we lay down our empty rifles and drew our revolvers. The blood beat in my ears like the thunder of four-hunert hooves. I emptied cylinder after cylinder in the short span of time whilst they were in our immediate front. I painfully recall how accurate my bullets flew in the desperation of those short moments. When the blinding smoke began to clear, we'd driven them back in confusion with great slaughter. Their dead and wounded were strewn in heaps that we used to quickly reinforce our breastworks against further attack until reinforcements finally arrived to relieve us. Another coat of Federalist blood was added to my clothes there on the bloody creek bank. That day I realized I'd come to enjoy killin' and it was a sobering thought that jolted me to my core. I reckon my second life began there and then. I was ready to have done with all the maimin' and corpse makin'. I wished only to return to from whence I'd come and again be a simple farmer.

"The Federals eventually made good their escape after suffering terrible losses and we were left with the gory detail of collecting the dead and wounded, along with their provisions, from the battle scarred terrain. The shouts of combat were replaced with a gentle breeze whispering through the trees. The smell of spilt blood and rotting flesh in the summer heat was evident everywhere we went as a constant reminder of the business at hand, that of waging war on our enemies.

After a long pause, he shook his head slightly, then again rejoined. "I wish your late grandma Mary could've tolt' ye' 'bout her life during that dark period when her first husband and I were away with the majority of the other men and boys from these parts. Your grandma Phoebe still remembers, but she don't talk much about it. We came home to learn what it had been like for the women and old men back here with southern Tories ridin' roughshod over the defenseless rural folk. Those black-hearted sons-a-bitches came by torchlight, bandanaed to hide their identity. But folks figured out who they was anyways. When the rest of the hardened veterans came home in '65 and heard from the women and old men that hadn't perished at their hands, what the murderin', stealin', torturin' sons-of-dogs did, there was swift retribution. A posse of former Confederates was formed in those all but lawless days following the fall. Some 40 Jayhawkers were systematically ridden down and summarily hanged from the nearest tree. There are dozens of old oaks still standin', most of 'em near crossroads, where the tormentors of old ladies stepped out into thin air en route to their own special hell.

"Greed can prompt men to do things inexplicable, so one can never be too careful in your estimations about other folks. Occasionally we come in company of persons who we find are more mercenary than faithful, even some we've called friend. 'Tis a painful experience no doubt, but one ordained. As such, they bear watching, for they regard ambition in a perverted sense, deeming to rise above the squalor of their own wretched lives above all else and material gain at all costs a worthy goal, regardless of concern for even the most basic needs of their neighbors. Their motto is, 'Grab all you can, any way you can, as fast as you can!' But I believe to my soul that God's hand is in all things and that honor and morality have both their rewards for observance and penalty for ignorance. All friendliness for them was lost."

There was suppressed emotion, perhaps anger, percolating within the inflection of his voice when he proceeded. "Only one of 'em managed to escape the noose by breaking and running for cover before we cornered him. He turned out to be a fool even in his last action. Instead of ducking and jinking in his flight, he ran headlong straight away, focused only on putting the maximum distance between him and his pursuers, a feeling I, too, have often been familiar with. It's the easiest shot there is, the goin' away shot. You just draw down on the target," he said, extending the pistol out in front of him with both hands at arms length, lowering it until the sights were level with his old eyes. "Get the sights lined up without hurrying, no need even to figure lead, then gently squeeze the trigger," he concluded as the hammer dropped with a snap on the empty chamber. "The hammer slammed home," he said, lowering the barrel "and the low-slung, long-striding figure abruptly folded in a wrenching, rag-doll tumble, landing at last in a motionless heap. That was probably one of the better shots I ever made with this weapon." I was silent in the presence of the pair of stone killers. He handed the revolver back to me handle first, as if

307

glad to be shed of its power. "He was one of the men responsible for my own mother's death," he went on. "She perished from being strung up by the neck on her tiptoes, him tryin' to make me Pa tell 'em where was the gold and silver that greed had 'em believin' my folks possessed. In their ignorance, that gang of miscreants mistakenly assumed since the Ledbetters were such long-time, upstanding members of the community, that must equate to accumulated wealth in the form of minted coin, hidden somewhere about the place. Ma would probably have survived the ordeal little worse for wear but that the fools used a rotten limb to string her up. When they put tension on the rope, the thick branch broke, striking her on the head and shoulders as it fell. For whom so ever else I kilt' or maimed, the Lord knows I am indeed truly sorry, but that one's killin' I've never once't regretted," he concluded.

As I held it quietly, pondering the words he spoke, I felt the latent power of the weapon. I again cocked and dry fired it, drawing back the hammer with my thumb each time, then dropping it with a squeeze of the trigger, round upon imaginary round. Click, snap, click, snap, it said without discharge as I pointed it at the birds flittering about the tree branches unscathed.

"Tell me how you came by it, Pappy, would you?" I asked. Eyeing the gun as it sat in my two hands, he scratched his beard and pondered, recalling the events of that infamous day.

"That's probably one of the most talked about events of that damn war. But what'd they expect when you drive men to the limits of endurance, not only for themselves, but their families as well. It was right similar to what happened back here with the 'Jayhawkers' after the war. Fort Pillow was a hotbed of Tory abuse in that section of Tennessee. From that den of thieves, more old men and women were tortured and robbed of their meager worldly possessions than ever came this way out of Pine Bluff," he said by way of comparison to the Yankee base of operations, that had supported the terrorization of locals in our own country.

"Pillow was garrisoned mostly by the homegrown Southern Yankees of the odious Thirteenth Tennessee Battalion, who much like the cusses back here, saw an opportunity to steal anything their

Confederate sympathizing neighbors owned, with the full blessing and power of the Federal Gov'nment behind 'em. And serving beside them were former slaves, dressed out in full U.S. Army uniforms and firing bayoneted, gov'ment issue weapons at our boys as they came on. Under those circumstances you couldn't rightly have expected things to've turned out much different. If 'n you ask me, the real parties responsible for the atrocities were the Federal generals who put the poor, colored men garrisoned there in the circumstances that led to their capture and demise.

"It was in the spring of '64. We were returning from some months of hard fighting in Mississippi, with intention to establish Forrest's headquarters in a lovely little town in west-central Tennessee called Jackson. The preceding campaign through the Magnolia State was some of the toughest times Prince and I spent in the cavalry. We regularly clashed in running battles back and forth across its northern counties. Our opponents were no longer the 'buttermilk cavalry' we'd been previously accustomed to, but were now experienced warriors like ourselves. There was instances like the Battle of Okalona, where the General, along with many others, both Yank and Reb alike, lost kid brothers on the field like Jeffery Forrest. Tupelo and LaGrange, Guntown, Ellisville, New Albany and Booneville are but some of the places that made me come to dread the very thought of Mississippi and Yankees alike.

"As I've said before, horses were at a premium by that stage of the war for both sides and the Federal troopers we were fighting were the hardest on them. Whilst most Southerners prided ourselves on respecting both women and horses alike, blue bellies would neglect their mounts, ridin' 'em into the ground, then shoot 'em, leaving 'em rotting by the side of the road, rather than chance lettin' 'em fall into Confederate service. The roads we crossed in Mississippi and en route from there to Tennessee were littered with the corpses and skeletons of horses and mules left lying where they fell after pouring their hearts out for the harsh masters. Packs of wild dogs and hogs stripped the corrupt carcasses and scattered their bleaching bones. For years afterwards those bones were gathered, ground and used for fertilizer. I've heard better than three million pack and saddle animals died, or were slain during the whole of the war. The few we did retrieve from the enemy at that stage, were undernourished, suffering from various ailments, the most common being greasy foot."

"What's that Pappy?" I asked him.

"It's a type of hoof rot associated with a lack of victuals and chronic exposure to damp conditions. It's caused mainly from neglect of proper foot care. And without adequate salt in their diet, the swarms of flies were debilitating, driving the animals to constant distraction during the warmer months. As often as not, the few captured animals we did gather up, had to be rehabilitated first before they could be again pressed into service. I often worried about poor ole' Fury, as well as Brother Will, after I got news of their capture. I bore a grief for Fury akin to my sense of loss for my own flesh being in Yankee hands. I prayed Prince would never suffer such a fate. The thought of loosing my faithful four-legged friend made me treat him with extra special care. I shared my rations with him and rarely neglected to groom him out from head to foot at the end of a long day, no matter how bone-weary I might be. In return he never failed me. He was surefooted as a mountain goat and hardy as a mule. He'd carried me all over three states, through rain, hail, snow and blistering heat. We'd been in more battles together than I could count, both wounded on numerous occasions. We'd swum more rivers and forded more creeks in two years than most people see in a whole lifetime and probably crossed ten thousand miles of territory together. On guard duty he was tops. He always warned me of something approaching, even on the darkest nights. I could not bear to think of parting with him after serving together so long through thick and thin. When I was so ill from my wound after the Battle of Memphis, the only thing that brought me safe back here was Prince, himself deeply battle scarred, steady making his way for home, as I lolled half-conscience, barely hanging in the saddle. The good Lord must've heard my prayers to protect us both, cause without Him and Prince, I wouldn't be here with you now. And for that matter you wouldn't be here either, now would ye'?" he asked.

"No, I reckon I wouldn't at that," I offered.

"At the end of March we recrossed the state line just to the east of Union-occupied Memphis, heading on north for Madison County. I was mighty glad to be back in the Volunteer State, even though the country in that corner of the region is more akin to north Mississippi than most of Tennessee. We forded the always-muddy Wolf River at a point where it was little more than a meandering creek lost in a winding riverbed. Further north beyond the Wolf, we encountered a massive, dismal, tupelo swamp, riddled with islands and streams, with the waterlogged terrain giving us far more difficulty than the equally porous Yankee patrols, which we skirted at will. Once't free of the slough country, we passed immense farms, formerly abundant in cotton production, but now fallow. We forded the Loosahatstchie, then the Hatchie, before coming to the Forked Deer. Cottonwoods and sycamores lined the stream banks. Once beyond Forked Deer Creek, the land took on an ever more rolling character, becoming ever steeper the further north we went. The farms here were smaller, nestled amongst the numerous hills. Within a few days, we'd reached Jackson and set up quarters in public buildings there. The General had learnt' to avoid the hospitality of loyal locals for fear of retribution against the good folks once't our duties required our presence elsewhere.

"Reports were soon swarming in from the country to our west, all the way from the banks of the Mississippi, that Tories were raiding the property of every Confederate son away from home. The very things that we common soldiers were fighting for, more important than our leaders and ourselves, were our women, our families and our homes. Now those so precious to us were being laid waste whilst we were away in service.

"On patrol we saw abuses beyond number, or description. Those were terrible days of shortage and long suffering for all the South, especially those contested territories crossed and recrossed by both armies. Commerce and industry were so absent, a still like that of the Sabbath lay over the whole countryside. Congregations were torn apart by differing sentiment and the church houses went empty, helping make a rapid decline into barbarism more and more imminent. Life's comforts were completely absent and the necessaries most difficult to obtain to a degree unimaginable in a country not made victim to war's foul deeds. It was a blighted land, looking much like the Biblical descriptions of a land infested with locusts, as indeed it was, though rather that of the two-legged variety. And the comparison went further, for like locust, normally passive and solitary by nature, when they swarm, they alter in attitude and color, becoming all of the same voracious hue. When these raiders put on the blue uniform, they, too, were altered, acting as one, causing even normally harmless souls to jine-in stripping the South of her former bounty. As such, they could but be destroyed.

"We reported back to headquarters of finding hamlets where some homes were burned in between others left untouched, the difference being the political inclinations of their occupants. Unburied, charred bodies lay in the ruins, too burnt for even the carrion to bother with. The burned-out neighbors were sent packing, if not killed outright, for their son's serving of the Confederate Cause. Near a quarter-million southern women were said to've become refugees during that time. Orphans were everywhere. And the same Tory neighbors, completely unharmed by the roving Yankee patrols consisting of armed, uniformed nigras and Tennessee Federals, watched quietly whilst their longtime 'friends' were drug from their beds in the night and treated worse than dogs by the marauding scum. Captain Freeman had to be restrained by enlisted men from retaliating on the spot against the unmolested Unionist neighbors who had stood by and watched. Though the inhabitants of the infamous fort didn't conduct all the raids, their presence at Pillow, as with other Union garrisons throughout the South, emboldened the pro-Union elements of the populace to abuse those of a different mind. The partisans of both sides were undoubtedly far worse in their actions than regular army," he said, eyes squinted, with a look so serious as to stand your hackles. I sensed the presence of death and killing that settled over his spirit when he thought on it. "But the tarnished-honor of the dead and homeless Tennesseans was not to go unpunished!

"Never one to rest long on laurels won, the General determined the nest of vipers had to be rooted out and we were the very wild hogs to do the deed. We were a capable force, not overly reduced in strength by our recent forays and capable, as always, of taking on a much larger foe.

"On the ninth of April, the balance of Forrest's troopers, under command of Colonel Chalmers, were dispatched before dawn from the environs of Jackson to proceed in the direction of Fort Pillow. Later that same day the General's staff and his escort packed up and broke camp at Headquarters Jackson. We rode due west, out of Madison County, through Haygood County and on into Tipton County, where we camped that night at its seat in Covington, my old childhood home. The reports by locals of the many children made orphans only strengthened our resolve to rid the country of the pestilence then residing in the former Confederate stronghold on the high bluff above the Mississippi River. Chalmers' troopers were already beginning to gather for the attack at a point just east of Pillow when we lay down to sleep that night, still some twelve miles away east at the County seat. We would cover the remaining distance with the General early on the morrow.

"Long before light, on April twelfth, I girded for battle inside the warm, dry comfort of my canvas shelter. I slipped on my good boots, pulling my pant legs down over their tops to keep out the pouring rain. My sleep clouded eyes looked toward the heavens, scanning the ceiling of the tent that was being pounded, as my ears beheld the rumble and crack of violent thunder flashing just outside in the wet and windy night. We prepared to ride, steeling ourselves for the trial and hardship awaiting us in the darkness and storm.

"The first streak of dawn found the storm but little abated and us winding our way through the hillside farms west of Covington. Every rise we crested revealed several more in all directions, each sporting a barn and house, or what was left of 'em. It looked much like the approaches to Shiloh, a broad, open, rolling land, interspersed by pastures surrounded by ruined fences and thick stands of timber where the terrain made farming unmanageable. Approaching nearer the river, we encountered great flocks of seagulls feeding in the weed-choked, overgrown fields.

"The day of the attack was a dark, stormy one, cyclone weather. The wind moaned in the treetops with a foreboding sound, muffling the noise of distant thunder. The horses were wide-eyed and skittish in anticipation of what the haunting wind would bear. Our company of roughly a hunert souls, carried weapons strapped to our backs at the ready, barrels pointed down to protect from rainwater running in their muzzles. Our mounts included sables, palominos, buckskins, blacks, roans, chestnuts, grays, paints, bays and appaloosas. As we rode through the deep gullies near the fort, we were at great peril of being surprised in a crossfire by Yanks hidden in the cover of the labyrinth of ridgebacks, boxing us into an untenable position from which there would be no defense and little escape. To protect against such, we swapped turns as outriders, charging up and down the steep inclines to guard the flanks of the company as it wound the valley floor between rises.

"The land rolls up to great heights there along the banks of Old Man River, offering a distant view of Osceola, Arkansas, only a mile and a half away across't the river and broad bottoms. First Chickasaw Bluff was as perfect a location for a river fort, looming over the channel, as ever there was, until long after war's end the Mississippi changed course on September eighth of 'aught-eight' and moved away to the northwest. Some say the river itself was offended by the 'massacre' that took place there on its banks and abandoned the sight, leaving eighty-acres of former Arkansas hardwood bottomland stranded between the new channel and the old fort. The old channel is now called Cold Creek Chute. But before that, the Confederates had constructed the works so immediate to the navigation channel, that one could not fire a pistol, or even chunk a stone without expecting to come mighty near your mark below. The smoke from steamboat stacks discharged practically at eye level to the fortifications. In that way, it is similar to the ground around Pittsburg Landing. Guns could fire at passin' vessels from several angles, whilst being virtually free of direct retaliation because of the steep angle required by passing ships to return fire. It was however vulnerable to long range mortar rounds being lobbed over the protection of the earthen walls and as result, was abandoned by the Confederacy June fourth, '62, after two days severe shelling by the main U.S. flotilla standing off upriver. But, since Confederates originated the defenses, we had maps of every inch of the trenches and rifle pits in existence there and furthermore, we had good intelligence on the nature and composition of the garrison ensconced within, provided by local guides all too willing to aid in its interdiction.

"We began to hear firing as we made our last approach to the fort at about the hour of nine o'clock. Chalmer's approaching troopers were already trading volleys with the outworks. The General immediately set about to scout the ground, with complete disregard for his own safety, as well as that of his bodyguard and all their mounts. The open timber and not overly steep terrain made good ground for horses, so we were able to gallop through the cover of the big trees to within yards of the outer breastworks. So near the guns of enemy sharpshooters did he ride, that he had two horses shot dead and a third wounded beneath him in his reconnaissance. I dare say the animals of his stable were relieved when he was finally satisfied with his plan of attack and fell back to relative safety. So often did the General go directly into harm's way and live to tell it, that it seemed the same spirit that's said to've protected the Sioux chief Crazy Horse from the bullets of his enemies, visited him also.

"The plan called for us to storm the outer works on horseback, which we shortly accomplished in a quick-mounted dash to the earthen wall, overwhelming the blue-clad nigras with our repeating pistols and the shocking pound of charging hoof beats. We made short work of them, riding 'em down in their flight before the thunder of our hooves. Most of the time, my saber remained safely in its scabbard, lashed beneath a saddle stirrup strap. I even once't employed it as a cane when I had a broke foot received in a tumble from my mount. But on certain occasions I proudly unsheathed it. I recall a young white lieutenant trying to rally his fleeing charges whilst turning to fire that very revolver at me," he said, nodding to the pistol, now lying still in my hands. "I heard the round as it flew near my head. In the next instant I had laid open the side of the poor feller's head with my saber, as perfectly as the drill had taught us. It was as if the sword had taken a'holt'of my hand and led it, rather than the other way 'round. T'was an odd sense of accomplishment, having achieved the grace of a pair of matched athletes, horse and rider working together to perfection. Upon seeing the bright brass fittings of the Army model Colt lying in the mud, I drew up Prince and bounded off his back to retrieve it from where it had fallen from my victim's hand. Upon first holding it in my own hand, I was elated with our performance and the capture of such a fine sidearm. Yet on consideration after catching sight of the vivid red liquid flowing from his scalp, I moderated my elation when realizing the consequences our actions had for the poor lad, barely old enough to wear a mustache, that lay bleeding and dying at my feet. But such thoughts of concern for one's enemies have no place in battle. In the heat of action, with bullets ripping the air all around and men toppling from the saddle, other matters are quickly at hand and you go into a battle mode. I checked the cylinder to see how many unfired rounds remained in the chamber, stuffed the newfound treasure into my belt and rapidly swung back into the saddle to rejine the pursuit of the fleeing nigras, trying to forget the clear vision yet held in my mind of the shiny brass lying next to the bright-red puddle.

"Once't we got in their rear, chaos took command and panic reigned. The wind added to the effect, so high by then that hats were snatched from heads unless a chinstrap held them in place. Once't within the perimeter of the outer works, we dismounted, leaving our precious horses hidden behind the cover of the screening hills with horse-holders standing at the ready in case things went bad for us. We were soon able to position ourselves to snipe at them in their embrasures. Their commander was picked off early in the engagement, which left their fate in much less capable hands and added to the slaughter before the day was done.

"The Union artillery fell back after just two hours, taking cover inside the final redoubt of the fort. We stormed the steep hills, guns at the ready, hearts pounding, lungs burning, with our labored breaths matching the roar of the wind. I skirted a pitched firefight in the last rifle pits outside the fort, where I saw men of both sides, in plain sight of each other loading, aiming and firing as quickly as their hands, in many cases swathed in bandage, could manage. The majority of Confederate injuries came at that point before the last of the Federals were driven from the final outworks.

"As he'd done so often before, Forrest, by this time a Major General, called for a temporary truce and went forward under a white flag demanding the surrender of the battery, or he promised to put every man to the sword if forced to risk further injury to his men by having to take it. Here is where the loss of Yankee Major Booth was so telling, for his subordinate, seeing their desperate straights, still refused to capitulate, stalling for time that our wizened General was not about to allow him. He hesitated beyond the terms of the ultimatum and with that, the final assault was ordered, resulting in the utmost effusion of blood. As we began the attack, their cannon, manned by Company B, Second U.S. Artillery, appeared threatening as they brimmed through the portholes, but were in fact completely ineffective due to the fact they couldn't achieve the angle to fire on us down the steep terrain. But for the deafening concussion and frightful sight of flame and steel discharging from their barrels, the fusillade flew harmlessly over our heads.

"When we broke over the top of the revetments, many blacks quickly fled down the various ravines and steep bluff facing the river to their rear. There was sport made by many of my messmates, accompanied by hoops of laughter, whilst picking them off, one after another'n as they stumbled, slid or rolled hastily down the inclines in their terrified flight. I witnessed a white Union officer rush to the flagpole within the fort to strike the Union Jack, but a bullet cut him down as he struggled to lower the colors. The wind had wrapped the flag around its staff, hiding the stars within their blue field, leaving only the thirteen red and white stripes showing, making it near impossible to bring down the tangled emblem. Under the rules of war, this meant that no surrender had been made and the carnage went unabated, even after most resistance was ceased. I rushed to the flagstaff and cut the lanyard with my sword in an attempt to bring down the Federal colors. Only after what seemed several minutes of struggle did I finally achieve my goal, watching as it drifted down into the churned-up mud. Still the firing raged around me. I could see no officer nearby to order the blowing of recall, so I decided to sound the bugle command without orders. Even as I blew with all my might, the frenzy of killing continued. I don't believe Jesus Christ Himself could have stopped it. I climbed the southwest wall, where I forlornly watched the continuing mayhem inside the walls and the doomed plight of the fleeing, colored Yanks making for the river. I myself even drew a bead with my Spencer on a couple different nigras, but fired at neither one as they desperately negotiated the steep bluff, hastily making for water's edge. I watched with hope for their safe escape as they waded into the river and disappeared, their skin blending with the dark water. Perhaps some Yank atop the bluff in Memphis returned the cosmic favor four months later when I, too, fled for my own life into the same river.

"Slowly, most of the firing finally ceased. I had occasion afterwards to protect some of the few surviving blacks from the continuing wrath my own Confederate comrades, who were more than anxious to finish the job. Several drunken fellers, who'd robbed the Union commissary of its liquor stores, were yet takin' target practice on a group of bound nigra captives. But for their advanced state of inebriation, none of their charges would have survived. General Chalmers, coming upon the scene of wholesale slaughter, drew his sword, ordering in a loud voice that the killing cease at once't. He then ordered me and a number of others to form a double cadre around the helpless, terrified coloreds for their protection from the mayhem. After he'd ridden again away down the line, some of the drunkards resumed in their insistence that we step aside that they might forever 'free' the remaining nigras from their shackles of slavery. I told the rowdy lads that to kill 'em now, unarmed as they were, was nothin' short of murder. My belligerent comrades were oblivious to reason and became even further enraged by my intervention, though to no avail against my vigilance.

"One frightened darkie, seeing Chalmers' handling of the whole affair, asked if he'd just seen General Forrest. I had to laugh out loud after the tension of the previous moments and answered him, 'No that ain't the devil himself, just one of his minions.'

"After the immediate threat to their safety was passed and we were able to gradually relax, I asked the nigras whilst rifling through their pockets, what Uncle Abe paid a Yankee private. I wasn't surprised to learn that where as white soldiers was paid fourteen dollars a week, coloreds received a mere seven. Other inequities we observed were the snug log structures that housed white infantrymen, whilst nigras were quartered in thin canvas tents with only earthen floors.

"When General Forrest finally rode upon our position, inspecting the captives, the colored Tories did indeed think they was beholdin' the devil himself whilst I pointed out to them that here was the real General Forrest. His eyes were afire with the customary glow of battle, whilst his face burned red as always during and immediately following a heated engagement. When he removed his hat to wipe his brow with a coat sleeve, his hair was even sticking up as if horns sprouting out either side of his head at angles where it had been unprotected from the elements by his cover. I heard them comment as the General spun his horse to ride away, 'Lawd, Lawd, it shorely do be's the devil.'

"At the celebrations next night back in Covington, some said the General had stood on the parapets shouting in the heat of the conflict, 'Kill the niggers, no quarter!' However I cannot say, for it was quite loud and smoky and I heard no such orders. As the smoke drifted away and I finally caught sight of him, he was personally directing the sighting of captured guns at the approaching Federal warships on the river below. In his defense, when they didn't surrender the fort at the promise of annihilation, he had no choice but to play out the hand lest he be thought only a bluffer from then on. And, too, he was again making an example to discourage other nigras from jining the ever-burgeoning Federal ranks. I believe one of the maind'est reasons many white Southern soldiers mercilessly slew captured nigra Yankees, was their fear of the pride, determination and overall bearing of freedmen trained-in-arms. They would soon become a formidable foe if emboldened by success. They were frighteningly formidable to those in our ranks who'd spent their whole lives oppressing them and could not, in their estimation, be allowed even a toehold. Still, I found it a sickening event that further soured me against the war and my part in it. I bore no great animosity toward the nigra, for I was given to understand from my earliest memories that none of us can help what we were born.

"Amongst others, I helped direct the surviving captives in the burial of their dead. We acted in great haste, for Federal gunboats, loaded with fresh reinforcements, were menacingly patrolling the river below, attempting to trade volleys with the captured cannon of the fort and threatening to put in and offload their fresh troops. Our captives drug the bodies to the ditch at the Southwest corner of the embrasure for interment. I saw one black hand grasping for the light as the sandy soil was shoveled over it by his own people, just before a round coming from the mortars below landed twenty yards away in a spray of blood, dirt and noise, blowing pieces of dead nigras into the air whilst still clutching shovels. As the falling dirt covered the dead and dying, the gunboats were finally hailed and signaled to put in under a flag of truce to retrieve their wounded. I gladly volunteered to climb down the cliff with the stretcher detail to load the stricken aboard the vessels, attend to the dead at water's edge and escape the ghastly scene within the fort. Some wounded were accidentally toppled from their litters, compounding their injuries, as the bearers slipped negotiating the steep, treacherous paths down to the water.

"I took opportunity to wash my soiled hands in the river and it was then that I was about to conclude there must indeed be a difference between nigra and white blood. I had had both Yank and Sesech' blood on my hands many times before, but never had I had such difficulty washing it from them. I scoured my palms with river sand and rinsed them again and again in the flowing stream. But it was two full days before the sanguine stains finally came off. As I squatted on my haunches there at water's edge, watching the Yankee boats retreat upriver around the bend with their fresh troops still aboard, as well as their retrieved injured, the stiff wind that had blown all day, laid and the storm's track began to follow them up the river channel. The evening sun shone bright on my face from the western skies breaking clear over Arkansas, whilst the rain still poured down on our heads in cloudy Tennessee. It was all enough to make a hardened veteran weep. The shower hid my tears of grief."

After the briefest of interludes, he went on. "I was raised to see import in the signs and, too, like all good farmers, to read omens. That day, the twelfth one in the fourth month of 1864, I saw several. Amongst them was the rain on us in Tennessee, whilst the sun shone bright over here. Another'n was the Federal flag wrapped around the staff, hiding the stars of all the states and showing only the stripes of the original colonies. Another'n was the unrelenting stains on my hands from handling the dead nigra corpses and finally, as we began our egress from the hills around Fort Pillow, one of our troopers accidentally discharged his rifle into the air. As he stood looking embarrassed by the dangerous mistake that caused many in our company to flinch and draw weapons, a branch wrapped in a vine dropped from a large tree high overhead, knocking his hat from atop his head and sending him momentarily to his knees. The tension of the trying day was relieved by the comedy inherent to such a sight. After a good spell, when the laughter of all the fellers was finally somewhat subsided, I bent to retrieve the branch. I found that it was dead, choked of life by the fatal embrace of the strangling vine wrapped tightly around its base. It put me much in mind of our own situation. The South was somewhat like'n to the branch, the agricultural economy of which had built the foundation of our nation, but was now being choked to death by the vine of the North that was itself all dependent on the branch for life and support. Too, it was a symbol of the Southern economy, so dependent on the Africans for labor to support commerce, yet choking off and now killing the very source of its former lifeblood. And it was not unlike the Army, the private soldiers being the strong limb upon and off which the officers live and hold tightly in their grasp, to the point even of strangulation. Also, I was put in mind of the relationship between horse and rider. And finally, it also reminded me of our branch of the family, spreading to the west, whilst other limbs grew in other directions. As we rode toward Covington, I resolved to look up long lost relatives still found in residence of the west Tennessee town towards which we were headed.

"Much of my trepidation about the days events was at least temporarily forgotten upon our triumphant arrival next morn, back at my childhood home of Covington. The storms of the previous day were passed and our equipage blinked and rattled from our saddles in the prevailing sunshine. As we entered the little burg, our boys doffed their hats in an exaggerated courtly fashion to the ladies outlining the puddled streets, whilst our horses snorted, and stepped sideways nervously, tossing their heads, ears and tails twitching.

"I was reunited shortly thereafter with my older, third-cousin Ruel Ledbetter, meeting and dining with his wife and younguns' through the better part of the afternoon. Over the meal, we shared accounts of family history as they had unfolded down the separate branches of its widely dispersed members. After a prolonged family visit, I eventually rejined the regimental revelries.

"The ladies of the vicinage, being much bereft of able-bodied men and having heard of our success, gathered at the courthouse to receive the General's staff and express their profound personal appreciation for deliverance from further outrages, loss of life and property to that band of ruffians, now so completely uprooted by our operations against them. Every expression of their heartfelt gratitude was experienced the late afternoon and evening of the thirteenth and on into the early hours of the fourteenth. I met up with a purty, lil', redheaded gal that had been a childhood sweetheart and my first love back in '55 afore we moved far off to the 'Bar' State. We shortly fanned our ole' flame back into a fresh firebrand. Once't I got her alone, t'weren't too long 'fore we were spoonin'. Then purty soon, we's forkin'," he said with a glance in my direction, accompanied by a grin and a wink. "That was a night of such unrepentant debauchery, that the memory stirs me even yet in me old age," he said, shifting in his chair. "Then it was time to bid again farewell to the love of me youth as we proceeded to reestablish ourselves at Headquarters Jackson by the fifteenth.

"And with that young feller it's time we bid adieu for the day," he concluded, holding out the oilcloth for me to replace the pistol in. "Thank ye' again for all your good help. I don't know what I'd do without it."

"You're welcome Pappy," I replied as I gently laid the shiny piece back into its safe cover. "Thank you for the story."

"You're welcome lad, my pleasure," he said rewrapping it in its protective cocoon.

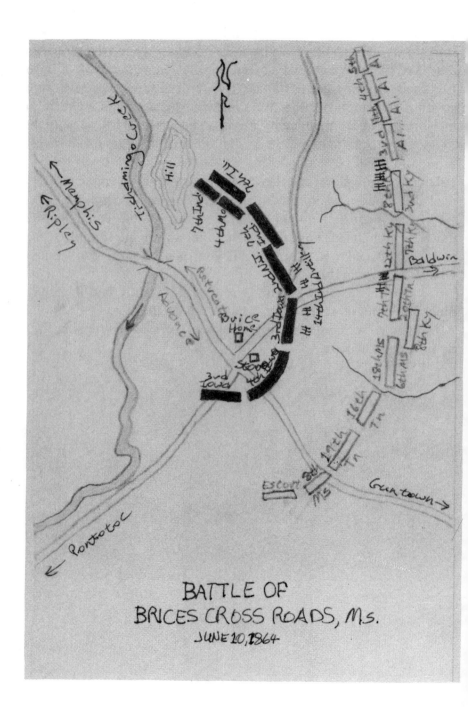

BATTLE OF
BRICES CROSS ROADS, M.S.
JUNE 10, 1864

Brice's Cemetery

Forrest's Cavalry Remnant 1911

Homeward Leg

With the turn of the year 1911, we were visited with terribly cold weather all across our region. It was so severe that winter, the river at the old ferry crossing froze from bank to bank and bend to bend thick enough to carry a four mule team and wagon. This meant it was a good time to go into the bottoms to harvest hogs for scalding and smoking. Our community as a whole still let much of our livestock run wild in the lush plains along the creeks and rivers of the countryside throughout the spring, summer and fall seasons. Then with the onset of harsh winter, the cows came in from the bottoms to feed on the hay that had been stored in barn lofts during the summer. The hogs, however, could stay snugly in the freedom of the wild, living off acorns and tubers they rooted from the rich earth. Bores were lured into wood-frame hog traps with shucked corn for bait, where they were castrated and fattened to lose the wild flavor and toughness associated with their gender, while the many sows made for great sport, to be ridden down from horseback and shot. After being field dressed, they were loaded on mule drawn skids and brought home for final preparation. But the sport was not without hazard. The flashing tusks of a sulled-up, 400-pound boar were deadly blades to be avoided by baying hound and hunter alike.

I was by then twelve and a half, near as tall as my brother John and ready for my first hunt. During those frigid days and nights camped away from home, using our hunting dogs to track the swine, "we splashed through bogs, ate like hogs and slept like logs." This was only done during the coldest days of the year so as to avoid contamination of the fresh kill from buzzing flies. Pappy, recently turned 75 and weakening, didn't make the hunt that year, but gladly greeted our return, being invigorated by the cold and memories of campaigns and hunts in such by-gone conditions.

Once home with the meat, we built a great fire in the barnyard, beneath a large barrel used for a boiling pot. When the water was at just the right temperature, lye was added, then the gutted, whole hog was dipped and turned, loosing the hair from the hide for easy picking. In this way, we soon had a clean, hairless carcass to be quartered and covered with salt in washtubs. After a week, these salt-soaked sections of pork were strung up in the smokehouse, where a hickory fire was kept smoldering beneath them for a month, to preserve enough meat for all the following year. Hereafter, we could go anytime to the smokehouse to slice off a section of delicious smoked ham, or bacon from where it hung from the rafters.

Throughout this process of scalding and sectioning, a good fire was kept roaring in the yard to heat the water and to warm ourselves by. Next to the fire, Pappy sat, ever attending to its needs, keeping it fed and stoked. While he sat watching us at our labors, his trusty poker in hand, he helped pass the time with the story of his return home from the war.

"I's hurt pretty bad when I finally got back here to Ma and Pa. I was shot, skinny, scared and pale. I rode in from the southwest on account of the side roads from that direction runnin' through more sparsely populated bottomlands. I'd thought to abandon all stealth so near home, bein' a wounded veteran back in my own land. But even with my weapons again clean and charged, I decided not to chance the more direct route with 'Jayhawkers,' home guard and the like patrolling the byways. I was, after all, away without leave and not relishin' the thought of a return to battle line, least ways not anytime soon. I'd seen more than my share of wing dings by then and 'the Cause' had become but a withered and dyin' vine, bearin' only its bitter fruit. No matter how much we suffered and sacrificed, all the Southern blood in the world would not, by then, buy us ultimate victory. Try as we might, in all faith, it was pointless, for it was like warrin' with the angels themselves, so vastly superior were they in every respect. I wanted only then to rest long enough to recover from my wounds, be near my dying mother and again find some peace in the simple dignity of labor.

"When Prince brought me to the doorsteps of this old house," he said nodding toward the stacked, hewn logs that had housed our family so long, "there was no sign of our faithful ole' hound

Buster. I learned later the ravagers shot him down when he attacked 'em. The front door showed signs of havin' recently been stove in. Pa peeked out from behind the window curtains, armed and cautious. I'd grown a full beard and Prince and I were both emaciated beyond recognition. I heard my mother ask him weakly from inside the room, 'Who is it John?' to which he answered, 'Don't know Elizabeth, some soldier boy.' Before sliding unconscious from the saddle I said, 'It's me Ma, your boy John. I've come home to ye!'

As we wrestled another sow into the boiling water, my brother Johnny asked Pappy, "Tell us how you came to leave the service, would you, sir?" This request initially met with only silence from the old man, at which point Johnny added, 'Please!' Pappy watched the pig turn slowly round in the steaming caldron and thought about the events that had returned him miraculously home. Then in due time, he began to unfold the tale, like so many from those dark days, seeming at times more incredible than true.

"Afore we descended on Memphis that hot August day in '64, many things had occurred that altered my feelings about the war and my duty, Fort Pillow bein' one of 'em. But another equally as compellin' was an execution we were made to witness when in camps with Bragg's Army of Tennessee. There was this one lad that Murchison's Provost Guard took in hand and tried, without success, to break to the will of command. He reared up against authority every time they'd go to rein him in, or beat him down. 'I ain't subject to no man's leave,' he'd say. They bein' who they was and he speakin' the plain truth 'bout the real state of affairs, he gave 'em little choice but to shoot him. No matter what they did to him, he didn't break, remainin' a true rebel right unto death. 'It's funny ain't it,' he'd say in his slow Mississippi drawl, 'that the very thang this here war is about is a second American Revolution, to finish what the first one started in this land, the birth of liberty. That friend, is freedom from tyrants. The very thang this here Confed-er-ate gov'ment claims to be opposin' is the selfsame thing they themselves is red-handed guilty of! I heared somewhere's once't how all rebels are eventually betrayed by their own cause.

Reckon I can't argue wid' 'dat.' Shaking his head, he'd ask, 'You mean to tell me that Jeff Davis has gotta' press a bunch a fellers into arms again their will to promote liberty? One tyrant to replace another'n, does that seem rat to you?'

"He'd cuss 'em to their faces too, as the whip was cuttin' his hide and call 'em the yaller lackey dogs they was, until he'd pass out. I believe, to a man, the private soldiers hated the Army when we were made to stand at attention through the beatin's he took. He was a true patriot of free men everywhere, North, or South. And many of the enlisted grew to love the bigmouthed bastard for sayin' what we often felt. When I call him a bastard, I mean no disrespect, for he was one by his own admission. He said his daddy had been a northerner, come down south drummin' hardware in lower Mississippi back in '47. Said he had no quarrel with no Yankee, save maybe his long lost Pa and he weren't lookin' to settle that one. Unlike myself, he was a conscript. He didn't want to fight and didn't think he orta' have to. But he couldn't find anyone with any say in the matter to agree with him. So's, he kept talkin' with nothin' they could do to stop him, save limit his audience. 'I ain't ashamed of no man's scorn. Better a livin' dog than a dead lion, I say. Real dignity comes from truth to self, not some unworthy standard strangers may place on ye'.' They shortly executed him by an eight-man firing squad, in front of the entire regiment, to be shed of his mouth and make an example against desertion and treason. I suppose they probably wished they could take the same measures with radical newspaper editors who fired broadsides at the many inexplicable actions of the gov'ment. He spoke the hard facts 'bout the state of the war that the officers didn't want us hearin' and made no bones about our Cause bein' lost, a fact becomin' more and more evident, though few seemed to openly acknowledge it. Their pride and fear of the provost wouldn't allow 'em to.

"I drew detail mucking out stable stalls for a month afterwards for unofficially blowing taps on my bugle when they chunked his body face down in the customary shallow, unmarked hole prescribed for 'traitors.' Had I not had such a fine record in combat, I could've met the same fate as he for my action. But I didn't mind the lousy duty it earned me one bit though. I thought it was the least I could do for one so brave and defiant to the final breath, with more nobility of character than near all the butcherin' bullies who sat over us. The last thing I remember him sayin' was he preferred to be laid to rest posterior up, 'so's the whole damn world can kiss my arse! It ain't never been nothin' but hard on me and I don't s'pect to miss it much,' " Pappy stated, before falling for a time quiet, further recalling to himself the unflagging admiration he still held for that misfortunate, impious comrade from long ago. Then again he spoke in a soft voice, gentle as goose down.

"The following months, after the action at Fort Pillow, were fraught with many spirited clashes against the Federals. It was more of the same we were so familiar with, the details of which vary little from my accounts of other battles. We were almost constantly in the saddle and regularly under fire, covering an area bigger'n hell and half of Georgia. This took a hard toll on men and animals alike. As tough as it was though, we found humor in our situation. Boils were increasingly a problem for our saddle-weary hindquarters. Many of us became proficient at using a heated bottle to draw off the swelling of the painful sores. Poor ole' H.C. McCorkle came to me one day during a short break on the trail, so irritated he didn't think he could bear to remount a saddle for the balance of the trip. Asking me to help out, I agreed. As I heated a knife blade and an empty bottle for the procedure, he said he 'weren't much looking forward to the operation.' To that I replied, 'Well, you know, it ain't exactly the highlight of my day neither.' This brought a round of laughter to all of us working around the boiling pot.

"General Forrest," he went on, "was ordered by supreme command to relocate his headquarters from Jackson, Tennessee to Okalona, Mississippi. Shortly following the first of June, we began a northeasterly march from that village to interdict Sherman's line of supply as he inched ever nearer Atlanta. Our regiment consisted of elements from the Fourth, Fifth and Eleventh Alabama Cav.; the

Third, Seventh and Eighth Kentucky Dragoons; the Seventh and Twelfth Kentucky Cav.; the Sixth, Eighth and Eighteenth Mississippi Cav. and the Seventh, Sixteenth, Eighteenth Nineteenth and Twentieth Tennessee Cav.; as well as with my own unit, the General's escort, made up of hand picked troopers on detached service from various Tennessee Cavalry regiments.

"Before we were half way to our destination in northeast Mississippi, couriers overtook us, bringing word of a large force of fifteen thousand combined Federal infantry, cavalry and artillery under command of General Samuel D. Sturgis, marching southeast out of Memphis into northwest Mississippi. This was the breadbasket of the west and thus vital territory to the Confederacy that had to be protected. Crops were evident in abundance there, due in large to the fact we yet owned the Mississippi hill country. Reversing our march and heading due west to meet this new threat, we intended to exact a heavy toll for Federal encroachment into the rich farming region.

"We galloped with abandon across broad valleys winding through low ridges. As was so often the case on the day of a battle, the clouds were a steely-gray overcast. With no sun in view, we rode through occasional cedar groves so similar in appearance as to make one think we were riding in circles.

"Scouts met us on our advance with word that amongst Sturgis corps were twelve-hunert black, Missouri Federals shaking their fists at the local population as they marched through communities along their route, shouting, 'We'll show Forrest we are his masters,' whilst pledging vengeance for the events at Pillow. The General grinned what I'd have to term as an evil grin when he heard this, saying nothing, just looking around at the men in his company and chuckling softly to himself.

"Around noon, while we closed the last few miles to a nearby crossroads, we heard the opening shots as our scouts encountered Federal scouts just east of Brice's store. As our main body came up, the Federals fell back to a strong position they had established under support of their artillery, across the road intersection on the high ground. Our officers began to dismount our ten thousand strong and direct them into battle-line for an immediate advance along a half-mile front. With escort in tow, the General rode the length of the line from right to left, taking his final position on the far Confederate left. At a point south of the Baldwyn Road, he ordered roughly half his escort to fall out and shore up a gap where the Sixteenth and Nineteenth Tennessee Cav. jined on each other. I was amongst those thrown into the slot. He came to me briefly, in an urgent state saying, 'When you hear Sgt. Gaus blow his bugle on our end of the line, blow hell outta' your'n!' Before riding on south, he addressed the lounging cavalry where they took rest from the hard riding of the preceding days. 'Get up men and prepare,' he shouted, 'I want you to charge. When you hear our guns on your left and the bugle sounds, the whole line must move out quickly. Do this and we'll give them hell and make 'em holler!' With that, he rode on toward the Pontotoc Road as the weary troopers climbed again to their feet as directed.

"I stood ready in line next to a fellow member of the escort, detached of service from the Fifteenth Tennessee Cav. It was the young feller I once't helped rid a boil from his bottom, H.C. 'Corky' McCorkle. We'd nick named him 'Corky' because of how he bobbed up and down when on horseback trying to avoid sittin' on his saddle sores. The ground before us was grayish, gumbo fields, interspersed with scrub forests and occasional areas of dense brush. The washes were littered with ancient seashells from when this had been the floor of some long receded ocean. Distant, sporadic gunshots and bugle calls, mixed with the crowing of roosters from surrounding farms, echoed over the meadows. Across the open expanse, atop the next rise, we could see our enemy spreading out north and south from the frame buildings scattered about the crossroads, readying for the fight. Stalks of tall grass, looking like inverted stands of swords, lined the edges of the cultivated earth.

"Shortly past four in the afternoon it began. Through the roar of cannon and the crackle of musketry, we heard our bugle command over the din of battle. At that, I repeated the same notes on my own horn, blowing for all I was worth. We swept down from our hilltop at the double-quick. During the dismounted advance, under heavy fire whilst traversing a draw between high ground, my lucky kepi that I'd had since my recruiting days in Memphis, was snatched from my head. With no time to think on it then, we moved ever forward. Sure enough, the Federal line broke under the telling weight of our unified advance. We pushed 'em north along the road back toward Tishamingo Creek, where hunerts of their number were slain tryin' to cross over the rain-swollen stream, or negotiate the traffic-choked bridge. By that time our cannon had achieved the height of a long flat Injun mound that dominated the scenery for miles in all directions. From that ideal vantage point adjacent to the creek, where it lay just northeast of the bridge, they fired almost directly down on the only Federal line of retreat, that by then had become a choked bottleneck. It soon became a killing field where the desperate refugees were trapped and for some time, quite terribly slaughtered.

"After the action, I walked from the crossroads back over the ground of our initial assault. There were gray clad bodies strewn at intervals on the sloping fields. I retraced the ground where we had first rushed the Yanks, looking for my lost cap. I found it with a hole shot through the crown, lying next to 'Corky' McCorkle's lifeless body. Inside the kepi were the spent lead ball and a black cricket that had taken refuge in its shade.

"Dressed in red stained butternut, my friend lay on the valley floor, amongst the tall stalks of purple thistle. Mists from the rain-swollen air settled on his face, running down his boyish cheeks as if tears. Gazing on his lifeless features, I began to perceive the sun burning through the overcast, only to realize the brightening glow I witnessed on his face came not from a star, but perhaps his soul as it departed the flesh. At the same time, I looked up to see another sign in the sky. I had long since regarded fish hawks as an omen of death, since having seen one immediately after the passing of both of my paternal grandparents back in 1860. There, flying casually overhead was a flock of osprey that I counted as a hunert twenty-five strong, slowly winging their way southeast. It was a moment unforgettable that brought the mists to me own eyes.

"Later that evenin', we gathered up our fallen comrades, bearin' 'em to a cemetery already in existence behind Brice's store. The boots of both the living and the dead were heavy with collected damp clay stuck to the soles. We buried a hunert and five lads from sixteen different units in the sticky soil. From the collected dead you could tell who'd done the heaviest fighting. The greatest losses had been from the Third Kentucky mounted Infantry, the Twelfth Kentucky Cav., Eighth Mississippi Cav., Seventh Tennessee Cav and the Sixteenth Tennessee Cav. One soldier, a victim of artillery fire, with no head to lie upon his earthen pillow, was buried unidentified in the southwestern most corner of the plot. Another twenty died later in hospital from wounds received and lie buried in nearby Okalona, making the total number of our deceased a hunert twenty-five, same as the flock of osprey. As sad as was the detail of laying to rest old comrades, one had to learn to cope with the losses so common of combat, else't you'd never have found a moment's peace. Perhaps the hardest part was havin' to move on so quickly.

"The surviving Yanks not taken captive were sent scurrying back to their Memphis barracks with far greater losses than our own, leaving north Mississippi, for the time, again in peace. Besides over sixteen-hunert captured, the Federals left behind more than two-hunert dead and nearly four-hunert wounded, along with two-hunert teams and wagons, plus twenty artillery pieces. Lightened of baggage as they were, it was jokingly said the ground they covered in four days to reach Brice's Crossroads, took only four hours to re-cross back to Memphis. Oh but what price victory?

"In his typical offhand style, General Forrest nonchalantly explained in one sentence the hard fought win over Sturgis' forces. 'I got there first with the most men,' even though he'd done neither.

"Shortly thereafter, toward the end of June, General Forrest took some time off from command to recuperate from his several injuries received in the previous months of hard fighting. The escort, too, enjoyed a well-earned rest over the following weeks. He again returned to his command during the early days of August.

The forces of our regiment were badly dissipated at that time by supreme command's desperate shuffling of various battalions about the theatre, like knights on a chessboard, in stopgap efforts to stem the swelling tide of each new Federal offensive. Much of his remaining command was widely dispersed with a view toward recuperation of men, whilst findin' adequate succor for the much-jaded animals.

"The Federals were continuin' to make threatenin' movements on multiple fronts, causing great concern throughout the region of north Mississippi and west Tennessee. The courthouse at Oxford Mississippi was burned to the ground about that time by Federals raiding south out of Memphis, whilst General Forrest was away on leave, adding insult to his injuries. In an effort to slow these increasingly aggressive actions, it was determined to strike a hard blow against the enemy garrison at Memphis. The idea bein', it would force 'em to pull back large numbers of men and materials from their systematic invasion of the South, to guard instead the vital river port base of Union staging and supply. With that goal in mind, we made preparations for a movement north against the city, scheduled for the last week of August. We consolidated our forces, whilst refitting and reshoeing our mounts for the darin' excursion. I didn't relish the thought of more hard riding and fighting, but found some solace in the hope of an opportunity to see the lovely Cherokee girl, Karen Doubletree, whom I'd grown so fond of whilst recruitin' in Memphis back in the spring of '62. Though it had been less than two years since we evacuated the city, it seemed much longer. We intended to ride right up into the middle of the town that many of us were so familiar with.

"Calling into headquarters detachments of both Bell's and Neely's Brigades on August eighteenth, the General personally hand picked the fittest men and animals of the units to carry out his daring plan. He selected roughly two thousand troopers and their mounts for the task. Along with a battery of Morton's Artillery, we set out for Panola in north Mississippi. Up until this time the season had been unusually dry, but the spring rains began just prior to our departure. It came down incessantly in sheets as we labored through the muddy thoroughfares, overtaxing both men and animals. When we halted for rest breaks, we sat beneath the bellies of our horses seeking what little protection they afforded us from the drenching downpour. Every stream was swollen bank full or fuller, causing great difficulty in the crossing. Marching nearly non-stop, we finally made Panola by the gray of early morning on the nineteenth. At that juncture, Forrest determined to return half the artillery battery to headquarters in Oxford because the additional cannon were too greatly slowing our advance. Also, better than a company of horses and riders, on the verge of collapse from the strenuous march, were dispatched to escort the fieldpieces back.

"Moving steadily north after our brief rest at Panola, we crossed the swollen Tallahatchie River and pushed on toward Memphis, timing and surprise being essential to our plan. The sun shone brightly on the nineteenth, but did little to dry out the sodden roads. We camped that night near the tiny burg of Senatobia, to allow the men and animals adequate rest in preparation for the contest scheduled for the following day. The rains returned that night, swelling beyond the point of fording, the first stream we encountered on our march the next morning. With no bridge to be found, we split off into patrols, searching for any materials that could be fashioned into a crossable structure. We disassembled gin houses and barns in every direction, returning to the likeliest sight for a crossing with planks and telegraph poles of all description. Using grapevines for rope and rickety flatboats for pontoons, we tied the conglomeration together with the wild vines to form a crude affair. This was a precarious conveyance at best, so we carefully led our animals across one at a time. Our two remaining cannon were disassembled and toted across by hand. Reassembling the guns and our troop for the final dash into the city, we were greatly disappointed to find just six miles further along our trek, Coldwater Creek presented no less formidable an obstacle. The entire process was again repeated by the weary soldiers, allowing us to all finally cross over late that afternoon.

"We camped that night in Forrest's childhood home of Hernando, still twenty-five miles distant from our objective, to rerest what portion of the regiment had not fallen out of column from fatigue and injury. Before bedding down, the General called together a council of war. I was ordered to attend. General Forrest being familiar with my time spent in Memphis and record as a soldier, wished me to help guide one of the three prongs of the attack on the following day. The goals of our raid were threefold. Following the same pattern of our urban raids since Murfreesboro back in '62, the fifteen-hunert remaining cavalry would split into three roughly equal columns after entering the city limits, each with a specific objective. The General explained how one group, under his brother William, would engage the better parts of the six Union regiments that our spies informed us made up the garrison. The soldiers we would be facing were of the Hunert thirty-seventh and the Thirtieth Illinois, the Thirty-ninth, Fortieth and Forty-first Wisconsin and the Forty-fifth Iowa. As was becoming more common, these units contained both black and white troops. The primary objective of the first prong of our assault was to keep the infantrymen away from our other two columns and capture as many horses and mules as possible. A second column, led by the General, would dash through the streets for Union headquarters at Gayoso House, in an attempt to capture Stephen Hurlburt, the commanding general of the Union forces. The third column, that I was to act as guide for, would continue on toward the river, making the deepest penetration into the city with intent of freeing Confederate prisoners held in Irving Block Prison and capturing any unsuspecting transports moored at the wharf. Thinking on Brother William's being a Federal captive, I was hopeful of freeing some of our boys from the jail, though it was doubtful he would be amongst 'em. With our plans laid and after preparin' our gear, we retired to a restless night in our bedrolls, thinking long on the events of the morrow.

"We rolled out of our blankets at three in the mornin' to feed the animals and soldiers afore saddlin' up for our final advance. The regiment was in motion within the hour. We approached quietly, as riding near the front of the winding column, I watched Captain William Forrest go forward ahead of the vanguard into the early morning fog whilst we waited in silence. He trotted right up to the pickets of the Hunert and thirty-seventh Illinois stationed on our approach down the Hernando Road. We listened as the guard called out, 'Halt, who goes there?' To the hail, Captain William replied, 'Detail of Confederate prisoners.' I learnt' later that disguised in a dark overcoat, he'd ridden right up to the sentry and laid him out with a pistol blow to the side of his head. He came loping back out of the mists to report the capture of the guards. With that we advanced some distance further afore encounterin' a second picket outpost. Being detected by these Yanks, the General gave the command and all hell broke loose. As I sounded the bugle, the Rebel yell split the quiet of the pre-dawn as we thundered through the cobbled streets. We shortly met resistance in the form of a Wisconsin battery, but they were soon driven in flight from their guns, as riders of the first column split off and descended upon them with a terrible fury. The remaining two columns flew through the tree-lined streets, block after block, dodging the beehive of bullets buzzing about our heads. Things went fairly well even so, with but few injuries, as General Forrest's detachment, with him riding at the front, split off south in route to Gayoso House Hotel. I didn't know at the time I'd never lay eyes on the General again.

"We remaining troopers of the third column spurred our horses on until we approached the campus of the Female Academy. When the brick buildings of the school came into view, we were met with the sight of blue-clad infantry lodged firmly behind the makeshift fortifications they'd thrown across the street. They loosed a volley that stopped us in our tracks. As we spread out to form for a charge, we were continually fired on from upper story windows in the masonry structures all about us. The flying lead came at us from all sides like river-bottom mosquitoes. As we ducked for cover, the organization of the column began to come undone. Prince and I sped for the shelter of a nearby alley. No sooner were we within the protection of its walls, than out stepped a pair of Yanks, rifles leveled, one aimed at me, the other at Prince. Seeing the danger of our predicament, I dropped the Army Colt from my hand where it clattered to the stones. 'Step down and disgorge old fellow and let us see what else you've got,' said one of them. Federal infantrymen being normally bereft of side arms, one of the Yankee foot soldiers quickly retrieved my shiny weapon from the paving stones, whilst the other kept his weapon trained on me. Climbing down, I stood arms in the air. The Yank, with my pistol in his hand, leaned his musket out of my reach against the brick wall and climbed up on Prince. 'How do I look as a cavalryman?' he asked his companion. He jerked the bit in Prince' mouth, roughly handling the bridle reins, causing him to rear up with defiance against the stranger on his back. This mistreatment of my trusted, four-legged friend triggered some deep-seated revulsion within me. Before I could think, or even realize what I was doing, I'd leapt up behind him. Grabbing his full beard with my left hand, I twisted his head around at a terrible angle, whilst grasping the pistol in his right hand with my own right hand. Overpowering him, I stuck the gun barrel to the back of his head and depressed the trigger. Brains sprayed out through his erupting forehead from beneath his blue cap, a pink mist suddenly blossoming in the cool of the morning air, as he crumpled in my grip. I held onto my retrieved pistol, but was unable to keep a holt' on his suddenly limp and bleeding body for use as a shield against the fire of his companion. Slipping from my grasp, he crumpled to the stones with a sickening, heavy thud. His friend, though momentarily stunned to inaction, quickly regained his composure and steadied his weapon on me. Trying to shock him into flinching, I reared Prince again on his hind legs, flashing deadly hooves in our opponent's face. Still he held his bead. As Prince stood again on all fours, he discharged his weapon from only yards away. The mini-ball struck the C.S. belt buckle at my waist, deflected up and penetrated my stomach. The thudding hammer of explosion struck me square in the middle. I rose out of the saddle from the force, then landed back in it, before doubling over and clinging desperately with my thighs, trying not to come unseated.

Then, enraged at thinking he'd kilt me, I rose up from my crouch and fired the pistol into his surprised face. He tumbled backward, dropping his rifle and staggering a few paces before collapsing in a heap. At that very moment, having heard the shots, a group of other Federals came charging around a corner into the alleyway. Clutching at my stomach with one hand, I turned Prince about quickly and spurred him back out into the continuing fracas on Madison Avenue, whilst our pursuers fired after us. Prince was in charge by then, as I lolled barely conscious in the saddle. He sped away from the clash between the opposing forces, heading not back toward the Hernando Road, but across the campus lawn, deeper into the city in the direction of the river. All I could do was hold on and try to remain conscious, as waves of pain rolled over me. The wind whistled in my ringing ears, accompanied by that once familiar clop of hooves on Memphis cobblestones. I raised my hand from the wound to see it covered with my own blood and bile. I was gut shot.

"Bein' shot is one of the most unpleasant experiences I've ever known," Pappy said. "I saw it happen to others often enough, including my own mount beneath me, but it doesn't prepare you for the shock of jagged metal slamming into your flesh, ripping a path through bone and muscle. I sit now in the evening light and share with God the beauty of the day and know how good it is yet to be alive.

"Prince knew the streets as well as I did, so I concluded he was making for the safety of the stable where he'd been liveried during our time in occupation two years prior. Residents of the town stared in dumb amazement as we trotted past. They could hear the echoing racket of the early morning engagements that were occurring throughout the city and they weren't sure at all what it meant. As we ventured further into the downtown area, I desperately tried to think what to do. I decided our best hope was to find our way to Rosie's bordello, where I'd once found solace and shelter from the ravages of war. Perhaps I could now again find sanctuary there.

"Though it had been but a couple years since that time, it seemed much longer. In the period proceeding, my youth and innocence had been siphoned away. Where once we'd ridden erect these same streets as proud warriors full of hope, now I was a hardened, grizzled rag-a-muffin bouncing roughly astride a worn-out animal, fleeing desperately for our lives.

"Surprisingly, we went blocks unmolested, finally rounding the corner down the street from Rosie's. There, to my dismay, were Union officers mounting their horses right in front of the bordello. It was too late for they'd already seen us. Before they could react, I spurred Prince and he sped directly passed them, not ten yards away, as they stared in disbelief. I swear I noticed general's stars on one of 'em's uniform. As we galloped toward the river, the group of Federals hotly pursued us, firing their weapons from our rear. We rode on untouched. Prince labored up the final rise that led to the southern most bluff overlooking the great river, where he and I had so often come years before to survey the activity at the wharves below. As we reached its crest, our pursuers were gaining on us. To add to our troubles, there stood a manned battery on the same ground once't occupied by Confederate gunners. They, too, were shocked to see our ragged figures bearing down on their position. Rushing to their rifles stacked in a stand at the center of their enclave, we gave them no time to take aim as we raced on, following the lip of the bluff away to the south. Bullets ripped into the bark of the giant trees we wove our path between.

"Looking out on the Mississippi below, I could see it was quite low and barely a hunert yards wide. The rains we had experienced over the past days had obviously been localized and had not attributed to any rise in the late summer level of the river. As I looked ahead, surveying for a path down the steep cliff, I was met with the sight of a mounted Yank coming right at us. The fellow was rushing to discover what the firing was about and probably as surprised to see us as we him. It was but seconds before our paths collided. Prince' momentum knocked his horse sideways over the edge of the bluff and sent the both of them tumbling in a cloud of dust down the precipice into the thick undergrowth. We continued to make haste along the lip of the bluff looking for a way down the face to water's edge. I thought of dismounting in an attempt to lead Prince down the almost vertical wall, but decided the underbrush, if not the angle of the slope, would prevent our success and lead to our capture or death. Our pursuers were now closing on us and our situation looked ever more hopeless. Then, at a hunert yards distant, I saw where the bluff made a dip, perhaps twenty feet down to a drainage gully that cut a path barely manageable for a horse and rider if they were desperate enough. On reaching the declivity, we turned to face the Yanks we had been racing for our lives. There was not a moment to waste. We began our angled descent of the eighty-foot deep wash with bullets tearing through the foliage and whizzing in the air around us. We gradually worked our way down through the alluvial sand, at times barely upright, whilst the Yanks collected on the bluff above us. Once't at the base of the cliff, I spurred Prince the seventy yards across the bar and splashed headlong into the shallows. Lead thudded into the sand and zipped through the water around us. Prince never let up as his feet were lifted from the river bottom and the current took hold, carrying us away downstream. I fully expected to be struck from behind by a messenger of death at any moment, but the firing from the heights subsided as I was unsaddled by the force of the swirling water. I slid gently backwards, grasped Prince's flowing tail and hung on for dear life as my trusted friend struggled for the far shore. Prince was experienced at river swimming and knew to work with it, not against it. Trying to lighten the load, I abandoned my bugle in midstream, along with my spade and all but one pistol. I held on to the rest of my weapons for fear I'd need them again. Our strength ebbing away, we made the slack water none too soon. We came out the other side with most of our equipage intact, if soaked. My percussion caps and powder were ruined, rendering the carbine and shooting iron, for the moment, useless. We made landfall in Arkansas a couple hunert yards downstream on the inside of a westward sweeping bend, right below where the railroad bridge now crosses.

"I went back to Memphis on the train in '99 and looked out the window of the coach from up on the high trestle to see below us the spot where we'd returned to Arkansas soil the morning of August twenty-first, 1864.

"I lay for awhile in the sand of the riverbank, gathering my strength, as Prince grazed on the nearby grass. Looking back upstream over my shoulder, I was surprised to see the Yanks in Tennessee waving to us, as if they were glad we survived the treacherous crossing and wished us well. They could, after all, have struck us down as we struggled for our lives in the dark waters. As soon as I was able, I drug myself back into the saddle and pressed on, seeking safety in cover. The undergrowth above the sandbar was thick with briers that tore at my clothes and our skin. We fought through the sting of the thorns and came at last into a small clearing in the midst of the thicket. I dismounted, bleeding from my many scratches and crumpled on the ground, exhausted by the effort and our narrow escape. Slipping into unconsciousness, I slept for a long spell whilst Prince stood nearby. When I awoke, I lay still for a time, studying our surroundings. The signs told me this clearing was the lair of a great buck deer. The spot was trampled with his tracks, with low narrow trails leading to the opening from all points of the compass. By the aid of the several trails, he could flee away from the approach of a threat from any direction.

"The fire burned in my stomach. It felt like boiling hot coffee was burning a hole right through me. I lay on my back and pulled open my shirt to inspect the wound. Dried, masticated food from my last meal surrounded the hole. Bile oozed out as the flesh gapped open and closed like the mouth of a fish with my every breath. The bullet had gone into my stomach without injuring a bowel or making an exit wound. Not knowing what else to do, I figured some food was in order. Gazing around, I saw ripe muscadines hanging in abundance from the vines above my head. I struggled to my knees and pulled myself up using the stirrups of Prince's saddle. I could feel the bullet shifting inside my stomach as I moved. With my cap, I gathered all the fruit within my limited reach, sharing the wild grapes with Prince. At first, the acid of the tart fruit intensified the burning in my gut, but then the fire began to subside.

"The day was well-nigh spent as the sun set in the west as a fiery-red globe, whilst fog crept in low off the river. I removed the saddle from Prince's back and lay my head down on it, not knowing if it would be for the last time. At least, I told myself, Prince was back on the soil of our home state and had a better chance of escaping Yankee service should I fail to wake on the morrow.

"I wondered about the buck whose scent and spoor were all around us where we hid within his sanctuary. Judging by the size of his hoof prints and their depth in the soil, he was of relative old age. The tracks were splayed like the forepaws of an old male. Like me, he spent his every waking moment on guard lest some hungry hunter take away his life. His trails into the sanctum were surprisingly small for such a large animal. 'God bless him,' I said softly 'and God help us,' I added. I wished then that I knew more about herb poultices. I tried to wipe the ragged edges of the gaping hole in my belly, but found the touch of anything to the inflamed injury was enough to again reduce me to near unconsciousness. I lay back, staring into the azure sky, so full of stars, weighing my options should I see the other side of midnight, before finally settling into a fitful sleep.

"The dawn found me still in this world. I awoke to the sound of birds singing and a distant steam whistle blowing out on the water, with the terrible burning still in my midsection. The rest had somewhat reinvigorated my body and my spirit. Prince snorted and looked at me as if to ask what was my plan. 'Prince,' I said, 'we're agoin' home. I've made up our mind about doin' without the army for a spell. Ma'll know how to ease this pain in my side.' There was but one path for us now, that leading back to Bradley County. Should we make it, our war would hopefully be done with.

"I had a breakfast of muscadines, that promptly began to leak out the wound. Prince nibbled at Spanish mulberry leaves whilst I carefully placed the saddle on his back.

"I knew from military reports that everything in the section of Arkansas where we were, north of the Arkansas River, was said to be in Union control. The trek would be fraught with perils that we had no way of knowing. Travel was dangerous, with outlaws of both Secessionists and Union sympathies, lying in the woods along the roads to shoot any man in transit suspected of attemptin' to jine in league with the opposition. But naught was to do but to do it. Much of Arkansas was still mainly wilderness and if careful, possible to cross without too great a fear of detection.

"We emerged carefully from the thicket on the side opposite the river, watching for enemy patrols that might be searching for us. We skirted open plantations, slinking through the underbrush of overgrown fields. We avoided the main roads and traveled where the leaves were thickest, sometimes riding long distances through the winding course of shallow streams. I was keenly aware of every sound and movement within range of my heightened senses, alert for any potential danger. All my experience for survival through the previous two and a half years was employed.

"Briefly emerging from the cover of the forest onto a dim, dusty road when a thicket blocked our trail through the woods, we came across't a pool of dried blood in the road where some poor soul had fallen victim to treachery. Parallel boot-heel marks in the dirt led to where his body had been dragged out of sight. I was leaky-eyed and my heart hung heavy when I viewed his robbed and carrion-ravaged body, partially hidden beneath an overhanging bush next to the right-of-way. I would have liked to bury him, but there was no way under the circumstances. I had no spade, not to mention that the effort of digging would have been impossible in my condition. All my strength had to be preserved for the journey ahead.

"We trudged on through sloughs, bayous and thickets, skirting open ground, ever watchful for any sign of humans. We stuck to the isolation of black-water swamps, full of razorbacks, water moccasins, mosquitoes and everything that kills, stings or cripples. I was fearful of Prince being stung by a snake as we moved through high weeds in the thick-forested bottomland so like that of home. Old trails were plain through the bogs where someone had figured out long ago the best route across the many creek branches. This was some of the flattest ground I'd seen since leaving Arkansas in the spring of '62.

"Finally we came to the banks of the Saint Francis River, looking across to Crowley's Ridge rising rapidly above the broad plain as far as could be seen to the north and south. We drank our fill, cooling our heated heels in the shallows. Then we easily waded the Saint Francis and shortly began the climb to the ridge top. God's handiwork was plainly evident there. Some giant hurricane from before the time man ever saw the light of day, had pushed up barrier islands in the shallow sea that once't covered this coastal plain, as demonstrated by seashells littering the gullies and washes.

"The high ground, though more difficult to negotiate, was easier to hide in and a relief from the monotony of the flat country of patchwork farms we had wound our path through for the previous two days. We followed the sandy ridge south for a spell thereafter, careful to avoid trails and using the backside of slopes to mask our presence from occasional homesteads. We stopped at intervals to eat our fill of muscadines, scupanines and persimmons hanging in abundance from their vines and trees.

"In my mind, three thoughts competed for my attention. They traded turns stirring up worry. First was the yet unsettled solution to the crossing of the Cache, the White and finally the formidable Arkansas River. The first two didn't much concern me, but the Arkansas would be every bit as treacherous as the Mississippi had been. The next was the constant leak in my belly that might yet undo me. Finally was the recurring thought of my unburied bones lying bleached and scattered in the dirt, far from home. I feared falling dead from the saddle, or going to sleep, never to arise, with no one to bury me, or hear my dying words. It brought to mind the memory of the lost graves of fallen friend and foe that I had stood beside too often since jining the service.

"Riding through the hills late into the dark night, I found myself so weary as to be unable to go another step. I climbed down from Prince in a grove of oaks. Casting around in the gloom for a proper spot to roll out my blanket and rest a spell, I gladly came across a perfectly smooth, flat rock at the foot of a giant white oak. It inclined ever so slightly, making the base of the tree a perfect headboard. Kneeling to untie my bedroll, I unfurled the blankets on the cool slab. Tired as I was, not expecting to be there more than a couple hours before dawn found us, I let my pony stand in his saddle and tied him off by his bridle. I figured if someone was to come upon us, I could mount and ride out quickly. At least that was the excuse I made to myself for such slack cavalry discipline. But, my conscience didn't bother me long since no sooner had my head hit the blankets than I was sound asleep.

"The trouble with the dead is they don't always stay dead," Pappy continued, as we hauled yet another sow carcass into the steaming barrel above the fire. "That moonless night, my old friend T.A. Atkinson visited my dreams with startling clarity. He began, 'John, you know I ain't no superstitious lout, or a feller given to be easily surprised. But the more it goes along, the more convinced I becomes there really ain't all that much we can do about the circumstances of this here life. 'Cept'n for the occasional wrong turn made down some side trail so's to keep us a'thinkin' we're really holdin' the reins, our final journey has already been all laid out for us. It has many names...destiny, luck and fate bein' just a few of 'em. But whatsoever ye' prefer to call it, it has the same inevitable end, just as God wills it. Take for instance what's a'happening here and now. Never would you've thought of a more unlikely situation. Who'd've ever thought you'd be goin' home to marry my widow. It just goes to show ye', when it comes down to the really important things in life like lovin' a woman, or the friendship of a man, we really don't always know all that much about it after all. But soul, I gotta' tell ya,' you did make one fine horse soldier in your time. But now time's come to git yourself on home to Mary and the children, your warrin's finally done with. Good luck!' he concluded with a chuckle. With that, he looked up to heaven and was gone.

"Awakened by the next day's early light, I looked around to make sure the coast was clear before holstering the revolver from under my blanket. Sitting up slowly, a shooting pain in my gut jolted me awake better and quicker than any tin of coffee ever could've. I found that my body had stiffened-up. Tight as my muscles were from the brief rest, after long unrelenting months in the saddle, I dared not give them the good stretch they ached for, in fear of worsening the leak in my belly where it oozed just above the belt line. Using the great tree to rise gingerly to my pegs, I surveyed my bed. It was then in the first light that I found to my surprise and fright, I had spent the night atop an old grave. The long, flat stone at the roots of the mighty oak was tilted gently up at the base of the tree by years of growth since some person was long ago laid carefully there in the earth beneath it. Some soul had once't been buried there before the roots of the tree had spread through their grave, drawing nourishment from the corpse beneath it. I cast my eyes to heaven, looking through the leafy branches of the shady tree, silently asking the Lord if He meant some message for me in guiding my path to this place. I thought of the unknown ghost whose resting place I'd disturbed, hoping I hadn't offended it. And then I remembered the visit from T.A. and his cryptic, weighty words. What had he meant about Mary I wondered? I spoke an apology to the one whose bones I imagined interwoven within the roots beneath the stone slab.

"I slowly crawled up into the saddle, trying to put the fright of my discovery some distance behind us. The following days and nights were like a fevered dream as we forged ahead, angling southeasterly. Some unseen force like a guardian angel rested on my shoulder, somehow protecting us through it all. My body was a battleground, with this world and the netherworld fighting for my soul.

"I can't honestly tell you all the details of the journey after that point. I vaguely recall accidentally stumbling upon a band of Gypsies camped on the near bank of the L'Anguille River. Seeing our desperate state of affairs, they took me in, treating my wound with a poultice. They hid my gear and me in their wagons, whilst

349

Prince, never having known a brand, fit easily in amongst their equally gaunted livestock. They helped us in skirting enemy garrisons and patrols and the crossing of the much-impoverished regions and remaining river obstacles that yet lay before us. I can clearly remember but a couple things from that week. One bein' the words of their Gypsy queen Zelda. She was a conjuror, well practiced in the ancient art. Whilst pourin' various ingredients into an earthen urn, she said, 'Ye' might think it no matter the order ye' add contents into a vessel, but even the elements are territorial and ye' can't have 'em warrin' one with another'n, if'n ye' expect 'em to work well as one. It is sorely important the order ye' introduce 'em,' she concluded, squeezing at last even her own blood into the mix from a knife cut made to the thin web of flesh between the ring and middle fingers of her left hand. Then, whilst she read the lines in my palm, I lay weakly in her brightly painted wagon. She traced the lines in my hand as her eyes began to roll back in her head. Invoking the pure white magic of verse, she spoke these words...

'Before the anvil ye' beat the shoes and shod the feet of the devil's hooves.

Ye' bore the banner and blew the charge, whilst the red one crushed his foe so large.

Ye' are he cleft of the head, that for a time lay with the dead.

Then from Sheol ye' did arise, back to life by the riverside.

Your blade was wrought from Celtic steel, as ye' drove your steed on iron clad heels.

Your scourge was known from west to east, whilst ye' laid waste both man and beast.

Through rolling hills in sun and rain, in blood and fire ye' wrote your name.

Til your brother lost, his fate unknown, ye' set your heart on going home.

Then from the dead, ye' arose once't more, 'cross the river Styx, on the distant shore.

Never more to kill and maim, now ye' leave behind the death and pain.'

"With those words, she held my head and fed the bitter drink from the urn down my throat. Then I slept I know not how long.

"The only other memory still held so plain within my mind, is the sound of their haunting music that filled my unconscious, played with much skill and abandon on guitars, violins and mandolas, mixed with their songs and lilting laughter. After a few days in and out of delirium, I finally fully regained consciousness well within our own tenuous Confederate lines, less than fifty miles from my home. They had snuck me past the Federal garrisons, as I lay quietly hidden in the comfort of the Gypsy queen's painted wagon. I awoke with a powerful appetite that was quickly attended with the better part of a delicious pot of stew. My wound was dressed with white cotton strips and my strength was considerably renewed.

"In each of four pockets, Zelda placed amulets drawn on parchment. On each of them were seals, she explained, that were the same symbols employed by the ancient Israelites to invoke the laws of God's Own good magic. One was placed in either breast pocket and one in either hip pocket. These, she said whilst speaking another incantation, were not to be removed before our reaching home, for they would help protect us on the balance of our journey. Thanking the unfathomable kindness of our hosts with the Federal script still in my pockets, previously taken off dead and captured Yanks, Prince and I set out renewed for our final leg. When I asked Zelda's people for some caps and powder for my guns, I was told, 'Deprecate all violence now. Study only peace my friend and the Lord of all will bless ye.'

"Gypsies are said by most to be thieves, swindlers and grifters, criminals not to be trusted. But without the help of those wandering Bohemians, we would not now be here.

"With no ammo for the weapons at my side, we trudged ever westward through the steep hills, so similar to the approaches I remembered outside Fort Pillow. The biggest difference was this country was more gravel than sand. The forest was thick and heavily laden with all sort of vines draped from the branches. Once't more we feasted on wild fruit, the experience altogether ruining me to muscadines, for I've never ate 'em since. The ancient, high-pitched song of fresh-hatched cicada droned in the humid air. It was exceedingly hot and dry, leaving us longing for a cool stream in which to soak.

"Then from a pronounced promontory, we could see the tops of a tall cypress stand. We wound our way to the last rise where below slid a quiet little river, gurgling over moss-green, gravel shoals. But for the great discomfort of jostling in the saddle, we would have lunged galloping down the final steep slope to the inviting water. Instead, we gently negotiated the perpendicular drop. Next to the stream, on a high mud bank under the shade of overhanging willows, was two pair of shoes, stuffed with socks. From their size and style I gathered they belonged to young girls. I stepped down from Prince and led him into the cool, ankle-deep shallows. The gentle current made the water stand in cooling plumes about his ankles. I dropped his reins, leaving him to drink whilst I sat on the sandbar at water's edge. He lapped noisily, ears forward, tail switching, obviously enjoying the long awaited draught. Downstream in a deeper pool, two youngsters poked their heads up above the surface, inspecting the newcomers. We must have made a frightful sight, rough and wooly as we were, bristling with whiskers and weapons. Prince was road weary, streaked with sweat and dirt, with every rib showing beneath his drawn flesh. I appeared none better. But even beneath the layers of mud, blood and dust they surely recognized the remnant of the once't proud Confederate gray.

"I removed my boots and holey socks, rolling up my pant legs before wading into the current. Seeing the girls some fifty-yards downstream staring at us, I waved. Their hands quickly broke the still surface of the swimming hole to wave back. I admired the cool, shady surroundings and the clearness of the water that still remained largely untainted by spilt blood. I stood knee deep, my toes wiggling in the gravel. I dipped hands full of the sweet liquid to my lips and face, washing away the accumulated sweat and trail dust. I heard laughter from the other two occupants of the water and looked to see they had again returned to their carefree play, doing handstands in the chest deep coolness of the stream.

"After removing knife and gun, I sat down, clothes and all, easing up to my neck in the gentle current. I felt it wash over the dressing of the wound, at first stinging the hypersensitive flesh afore slowly soothing away the fiery pain. I gapped open my shirt and pulled down the bandage wrap, tenderly cleansing away the masticated food scraps from the hole, then letting the water continue to wash over it. After a bit, I felt tiny minnows nibbling the dead flesh at its edges. Prince and I listened and watched the children playing, as I soaked in the life-giving water. If I never made it to the old home place from there, I was finally back, within my own land, bathing in the Saline.

"I would spend one more night before reaching home. Late that afternoon, after leaving behind the banks of the Saline, again feeling weak and famished, we rode up on a secluded farmhouse, on a dim trail far off the main road. I was surprised to look up and see the little homestead, for the road we traveled revealed no sign of recent traffic. Before we could hide from the prying eyes of the house, we were hailed by a woman's excited voice. Stopping in our tracks as we turned to retrace our path, I saw a lady near my own age, burst from the front door of the structure and come running toward the yard gate. It soon became evident I'd been mistaken for another long absent veteran finally returned home. She called out 'Alec, oh Alec, you've come home to us!'

'No ma'am, I ain't Alec,' I said, sorry to dash her hopes as she reached the gate. The disappointment in her large, sad eyes was hard to bear, as she apologized. 'I'm so sorry sir, I thought you were my husband at last come home.'

'I am the one who's most sorry madam, for your disappointment. Please forgive me for lifting your hopes.'

'It's quite all right, sir. It's just we get so few travelers down our road and you sit a mount much the color our Alexander was riding when he and our two sons went off some two years thence.'

"Thinking I might know her family, I asked, 'What are their names ma'am?'

'My husband is Alexander McKinney. Our boys are David and William. They serve with the Ninth Arkansas Infantry. The last I heard from them, they were with General Lee in Virginia. But where are my manners, I'm Josephine McKinney. Please climb down and come in out of this hot sun.'

'No'm, I couldn't impose on you so. And I've miles to go to yet reach home.' But she insisted, calling her daughter to see to Prince. In my weakened condition, I was in no shape to argue. She noticed my discomfort on leaving the saddle and asked if I were injured. At that moment a biting pain near cut me into and I grabbed for the gatepost to steady myself. She rushed to prop me up, taking my arm around her shoulder and assisting me to the house. She helped me to a couch and fetched cool water, whilst instructing her daughter Martha, to lead Prince away to the shade of the barn, where he enjoyed a meal of fresh oats. The gracious lady had large, doe-like eyes and a pleasant, full mouth. A strawberry blonde, she was not what you'd call a beautiful woman, but striking in appearance nonetheless. Even in my weakened condition, I was stirred, feeling some unexplained kinship of spirit to her, bordering on attraction. But I reminded myself she was a married woman, the wife of a fellow brother-in-arms.

"The farm looked prosperous and well kept. There was no sign of slaves about the place. The rough calluses, on their hardened hands, told me who'd done the backbreaking tasks that keep a place in order. As I rested from the road, the daughter returned from the barn, saying Prince, too, was resting well. They brought warm, buttered bread and sliced ham. I relished the sustenance and the soft cushions under my head, soon lapsing into sleep. When I awoke late that evening, the lamps of the parlor burned with a gentle glow. The ladies were shuffling around in the kitchen, rattling plates and pans. The aroma of home cookin' filled the house. I gingerly arose from the divan and slowly made my way to the sounds of the women. 'Mr. Ledbetter, are you sure you ought to be up?' the daughter asked seeing me at the kitchen door. Mrs. McKinney came to my side, helping me to a chair at the table. They soon set bowls of heaping servings before me and pulled up their own chairs. They served my plate, then their own, before asking if I'd like to return grace. Not accustomed to praying out loud, I demurred. Then without further hesitation, Josephine said a simple prayer of thanks, ending with, 'Amen. Eat up!'

"Over the delicious meal, unlike I'd had since I couldn't remember, I told the ladies of our family home, only some twenty miles to the northwest. As tempting as it was, I was careful not to overeat because of the distress stretching would cause my injured stomach. They said they'd heard of the name Ledbetter, as I had McKinney. They'd settled in the region after moving there from Alabama around the same time we'd come from Tennessee. Mrs. McKinney told me the remarkable story of how, with her men away at war and the outcome of the conflict looking more inevitable, she'd shrewdly traded away their slaves and farm on the main Military Road, for this larger, undepleted acreage, much removed from the main thoroughfare. She had realized slaves would soon be liberated by invading Federals and that the thieving Yanks would regularly be recrossing in front of their former home, en route from their supply depot in Pine Bluff on the Arkansas, to resupply the garrison that had been occupying Camden on the Ouachita. Not wishing to see their wealth carried away with the Federal wagon trains, she'd relocated, parlaying the soon to be worthless labor stock and worn out dirt for a safe haven on new ground, far removed from the threat and prying eyes of marauding invaders.

"She further related how our local boys had recently driven off the invaders. One of many notable local battles had transpired between several Confederate units, including the reorganized Second Arkansas Cavalry and General Steele's invading Yankees, at a point on the Military Road roughly halfway between our two farms, at a crossroads near Henry Marks' gristmill. The two ladies had listened, in the mid-afternoon of April twentieth, to the distant rattle of musketry and the ominous rumble of cannon. A large train of four-hunert Federal wagons, full of stolen personal property, had been attacked and captured whilst traveling to Pine Bluff from Camden for reprovisioning. Just as it happened at distant Fort Pillow and but one day later, coloreds found under arms, as well as refugee slaves fleeing on the heels of the Union wagon train, were visited with fierce atrocities by the vengeful Confederates.

"After the bitter action, white folks came from as far west as Chidester all the way to the Marks home place, to reclaim their stolen furniture, clothes and paintings retrieved from the captured wagons. Most of their former slaves, along with their liberators, had been mercilessly laid waste.

"I enjoyed the company of the two ladies into the wee hours, whilst they redressed my wound, finally calling it a night sometime after twelve. We caught each other up on news of war and home. The fine company was a rarity for us all, not to be easily bid adieu. Daughter Evelyn had prepared her brother's bed for me earlier in the evening. We finally said goodnight before all retiring to a peaceful night's sleep, disturbed only by the hooting of owls and the lonesome cry of the whippoorwills.

"Rising late the next morning, I found the ladies had packed me a kerchief of goodies for the road. Mrs. McKinney, being a proven practical woman, had also taken the liberty to clean and recharge the cylinders of both my pistol and my carbine, warning me to avoid the busy roads through the country east of my home. Overwhelmed with gratitude for their kindness, I asked they send word to me if there was ever anything they needed. Mrs. McKinney told me before I rode out, 'When this mess is over with, come back and see us, I want you to meet Mr. McKinney and our lads when they get home.' Then with mixed sentiments of both sadness and excitement, I set out to cross the final miles to my long absent home.

"I learned some time later, Josephine's elder son David was severely wounded at Gettysburg and died after arriving home. Her husband Alexander and younger son William managed to survive the long war. She was said to have prayed adamantly for the salvation of William's rowdy soul everyday for the rest of his considerable life, she outliving him by a half-dozen years.

"Prince and I made a circuitous journey home, winding far into the Moro Creek bottoms, to approach from the more sparsely settled southwest. The long day in the saddle left me completely drained. Late that evening, under cover of a moonless night, I rode up to the weathered doorsteps, collapsing from the saddle into the dusty yard. I noted our old hound Buster was not there to greet me. I learned he, too, had suffered at the hands of Jayhawkers, being shot dead for severely biting one of the culprits. The date of our homecoming was September third. We'd been twelve days and nights coming from Memphis and nine hunert days away from home.

"When I come to next mornin', I was surprised to be staring up into the eyes of T.A.'s widow, Mary Atkinson. Being the daughter-in-law of the local physician, she came each day to the home of my aging parents to help my father with the care of my ailing mother. When I awoke, I recognized my old bed and the room I'd shared with William as a child. It's the same room you use now Polk," he said to me. "Before lapsing back into sleep, I told Pa, 'Take good care of Prince for he's served me well!'

"Mary stayed on to help with my care, as I fought for my life against the fierce fever that racked my body. Her father-in-law, T.A.'s father, Dr. Atkinson, came by and examined my wound, determining it was not septic, thanks, he said, most likely to the acid of the muscadines we'd so often dined on during our journey. I told him I attributed it as well to the poultice, white magic and dark medicine of the Gypsy queen. He further gladly informed me the wound had done no more damage than to puncture the outside of my belly and should continue to heal well.

"Doc Atkinson was hanged soon afterward for killin' another man in a fight over the feller's wife. He too now lies in Gum Grove Cemetery. I think the loss of his oldest boy, my friend T.A., was what drove him to it," he concluded before falling silent.

Reaching into his trouser pocket, he pulled out an item that stopped our labors. Shocked and dismayed, we stared in disbelief at the misshapen slug in his palm. He added, "After a few days home, this here bullet rolled out the wound. Within a few more days, the hole began to heal over as the fire in me belly slowly subsided. Having survived the long ordeal, I couldn't help but be happy to've again arrived home, even with so much trouble behind and more yet to come.

"I spent the next six months mostly hidden safely within the snug log walls, convalescing from my time at war. Prince, himself deeply battle scarred, fattened at pasture, whilst I ate only bland foods, avoiding all hot and cold drinks. I grew oh, so tired of cold coffee and warm beer whilst on the mend. Prince thereafter grew long in the tooth, living to the ripe old age of twenty-nine. Once't, many years after the war, when a well-dressed peddler come calling in our neighborhood, wearing a Union blue three-piece suit and ridin' a gelding, Prince charged the fence of his paddock, stomping and snortin' at the gate to get at the feller and his mount. We could only assume the old warhorse still had some fight left in him and was just then rarin' to get at the strangers dressed in the colors of past adversaries.

"We got word from William not long after my homecoming. He was held in prison at Camp Morton, Indiana. It was cold and hard, he said in his letter, but they had a kind warden who tried to take as good a care as was possible of his charges, given the limited resources at his disposal. He made the best of a bad situation and managed, himself, to survive the war.

"Mary and I grew closer over those long days and nights. The shouts of glee as her children played outside in the yard were sweet music to our ears. I no longer felt any obligation to the war effort when remembering T.A.'s mysterious words as he came to me in the fever-dream atop Crowley's Ridge. I did, however, yet feel obliged to my messmates, still giving their final sacrifice to the lost Cause. But I knew Mary and her children needed me far more than anyone else't ever could. I was proud just to have survived the whole affair.

"Bein' no solitary owl, I soon asked the Widow Atkinson to take me hand. I figured she'd be so grateful, what with the younguns to rear, she wouldn't raise a fuss for months to come. I finally screwed up my courage and suggested I haul her off to the parson. When I did, she took me into her hungry arms and crushed me to her breast. She accepted my offhand proposal and I won the hand of my nurse. She made me a fine wife and I tried to be a good father, husband and provider."

As we scraped the last of the hair from the hog hides in the evening's last twilight and placed their sectioned bodies in the tubs of salt, preparing to retire to the warmth of the indoor hearth, Pappy concluded his story.

"In the Reconstruction I learned to hire the blacks that come through our country, some with family in tow, some long since separated from all kin. From 'em, followin' my heart and my eye with harsh discrimination, I attempted to winnow out the shiftless from the worthy. That first season we had nothin' to offer the homeless wanderers but our sparse food, a warm spot in a dry shed to lay their heads and unending repairs in preparation for spring plantin'. After we made our first good crop, we furnished 'em credit, a snug little house and land of their own to till.

"One feller that worked long and faithful on the place was the very first hand I ever took in. His name was Earnest Lee. He come wanderin' up to the porch one evenin', lookin' for a cool drink of water. Introduced himself sayin' he'd been named Earnest for being an honest man and Lee in honor of the General. He was still just a single lad, stout as an ox, lookin' for a job workin' for food, or wages. We took him in and he and I worked side by side on the place over the comin' years. Together we picked, cut, skinned, notched and stacked the logs to build him a little house right cross the road there," he said, motioning to the cropper shack where it still stood under the shade of a great spreading oak. "He bein' strong as a mule, lifted the butt ends whilst I lifted the thinner ones when raising the pine poles into place. A genuine brotherhood was born of our common labors, toiling as we did, side by side.

"Being so prosperous as to have his own roof overhead, he soon married Nellie. Over the years Earnest and his family grew and prospered right long side our own. He was a fine hand, plenty handy about a farm," he said, thinking fondly of the friend he'd looked after and worked with for so long. Then he added, "Some like him, genuinely loved their work and were fine stewards of the land. Then there was a few I misjudged, that we took in, who made no connection to the Earth they worked. They'd be again gone some mornin' without a word, disappeared back into the same dark night from whence they'd come.

"With some amount of success however, I managed over time, to put several formerly displaced refugees on twenty-acre plots. With cooperation and coercion, we turned many good crops of corn, cotton and peanuts, shared on the halves, in a market booming after the secession of hostilities. I truly believe that due to the blessings of Providence and a Christian sense of fairness and justice, instilled in me by my own dear parents and the teachings of the Methodist Episcopal Church, we all prospered, with but few instances of conniving, those bein' mostly attributable to self-righteous, windbag stumpers, claiming it their call from God to educate the 'new nigra.' I've no problem with educatin' any man, woman, or child, but them scalawags weren't toutin' 'education', but rather inflammation! The average, northern opportunist seemed not to understand that former slaves, for the most part, had no real understandin' about the workings of free society. The interlopers would have had us vote, eat, sleep with and even marry the nigra! No nigras that I ever knew wanted such!

"I can't tell ye' how many freedmen lost their new homesteads, cause they didn't grasp the concept of mortgage, payin' property tax, or even how to manage a thing they'd never before had...money! They was much like'n to innocent children, as yet unschooled in the ways and workings of the world, and as such, taken advantage of by many unscrupulous white men, Southerner and Yankee alike!

"Those of our community, who never before the war owned slaves, when patient, tolerant and careful with instruction, fared far better after the emancipation than did most former pre-war slave holders. The 'croppers,' in time, helped make many of us into a sort of 'country gentleman,' freed of most labors, to pursue broader social and political interests. Some criticism of the reversed state of affairs came from the old-time planters, about our handling of the 'race problem.' Some former veterans had even missed bed sheets so badly during the long conflict, they took to wearin' 'em right regular in the Reconstruction period. Indeed, such a state of relations existed in the mercurial atmosphere of the antebellum south, that some form of order was required to belay the growing chaos. But, the new order was achieved by more than one means and we were as good to the new black residents of our neighborhood as they would allow," he said.

In conclusion, he added, "Several years after the war, I read in a newspaper, a quote from Lincoln. I'll be danged if'n I don't believe the South would've been better fixed should Booth not've kilt old Abe, cause the ole' feller plainly had some good common sense. Lincoln said, 'Ye' can't bring about prosperity by discouraging thrift. Nor can ye' strengthen the weak by weakening the strong. Ye' can't help the wage earner by pullin' down the wage payer. Ye' can't further the brotherhood of men by encouragin' class hatred. Ye' can't help the poor by destroyin' the rich. Ye' can't keep out a trouble when spendin' more than ye' make. Ye' can't build character, or courage by taking away men's initiative, or independence and ye' sure can't help men permanently by doin' for 'em what they ort to do for themselves."

After placing the last tub of salted meat in the smokehouse, the gathering broke up as we headed for our respective homes. The task was complete, with another year's worth of pork ready for curing

With the coming of spring, came one of our favorite holidays, Saint Patrick's Day. Being proud of our Scotch-Irish descent, this was always a special day in our family. Pappy's strength was fading with every passing sunset, but that crisp spring morning his sap seemed again on the rise, renewing, again for awhile, both his flesh and spirit. When I walked into his bedroom that day, I was surprised to see the old gentleman dressed out in the wool uniform that had lain hidden in the old trunk for as long as I could remember. The room was filled with the pungent aroma of mothballs that permeated its stained and faded gray fabric. On his head sat the once gray, leather-billed Confederate kepi with the very hole where he'd nearly been snuffed-out at Brice's Crossroads. He stood erect at attention and snapped a crisp salute, hand held to the brim of his cap, as the old saber rattled at his side. I saluted back.

Stuffed in the cracked, black-leather belt with the bullet-dented C.S. buckle, was the familiar Colt pistol. It was a sight I'll never forget. "Fetch me the Spencer from the trunk lad," he said. Stepping lively, I quickly returned with the lightweight carbine, that he stood by his side at 'parade rest.' "How do I look?" he asked.

"Fine Pappy, just fine! Like a real old soldier."

"I been a'thinkin' on attendin' the upcomin' reunion of Confederate veterans that's comin' to Little Rock this next May. I figure after all this time, there maybe ain't much worry left in association with my quitin' the service without leave the way I done those many years past. After all, what's done is done!" Although I was a bit surprised at his statement, it being in such complete contradiction to his standard policy since the war of avoiding all veterans' associations, I agreed that he was probably right and it would be mighty good for him to see all those fellow soldiers while there was yet opportunity.

"Yep," he said, "I reckon I might just do that, seein' how I ain't none too busy these days. I can take the train. I understand they're offering special rates to vets for the occasion. I do believe it'd be a plum shame to miss."

After a few minutes admiring his figure in the dresser mirror, he removed the gun, sword and coat, laying them across his bed, before standing the rifle in the corner and taking a seat in front of the morning's freshly kindled fire, still wearing the wrinkled, stained and smelly uniform trousers.

He began to speak. "Son, if you'll notice, you'll find that all things can be broken down into their components, so as to more deeply and readily understand their nature. The prism your teacher showed ye' in school, dissects white light into its seven separate components, revealing a beauty previously unseen in its clearer state. And through its more detailed appreciation, we grasp ideas before unknown about its fuller understanding. You'll find the same applies with all things. Such appreciation of our environment adds to the richness of our existence. Always remember that, watch careful and don't let ye'self be taken in by the pompous windbags of this world."

Looking intently at me, he said, "An eye that knows can see preceding loved ones in the face of his children and grandchildren. I see in you and your siblings the features of your great and great-great-grandparent's. I also see traits of their character in each of ye'. It touches me in a way I can't readily describe. You watch and you'll come to see it too. And always remember, nothing in this life is more important than your kin, perhaps second only to your heritage. Protect the honor of your family name, try never to bring any shame upon it."

Interrupting but briefly, I interjected, "It's had no shame I'm aware of."

Pausing to give me his kindest smile, I could see those simple words brought great joy to my old grandpappy. Then he continued. "After big brother Will and kid brother James Andrew returned home, we oft walked together in the evenings, three old soldiers recalling former glories. Will used to say, 'When we cross that final river, John, we won't have to worry 'bout Hell, for we did our hitch with the devil long ago.'

"Both my brothers applied for and received Confederate pensions and jined the Confederate veterans organization, Camp

Denson, formed in Bradley County on July fourth, 1895. For a long time I avoided both, as did I association with the Klan. Since never being lawfully discharged from the service, I never wished to call any attention to my incomplete military records. Though truth be known, I soon discovered that, for various reasons, almost no one's records were complete

"When my two brothers passed on with age, with no other men of our family left from those former days, I felt as if there was very little distance remaining between death's horizon and myself. It's a lonely feeling son, to be the last of your generation. But I'll tell ya' like my ole' grandpappy tolt' me, 'There's only one way to keep from growing old laddie…and that's to die young!' I've also come to know through my own experience though, that a fellow can live too long."

Then, after a pause, he added, "Son, when I'm gone, I want ye' to watch after Mammy. She'll need you boys to help her out." I didn't ask where he was going, thinking at the time he was referring to his new plans for a trip to attend the upcoming Veterans' reunion in Little Rock. I didn't realize until the next day what journey he'd actually been referring to.

He stood and reached in his watch pocket, handing me as a keepsake, the bullet that had come from the wound in his stomach. Like a similar bullet that had once lodged itself against General Forrest's spine and not unlike the tales related to me of his stint as a Confederate cavalryman, that slug had worked its way out, lest, like a sleeping dragon waiting to arise, it remained in Pappy's gut to some day render him a cripple.

With that, instead of returning the relics to their trunk where they'd lain hidden so long, he proudly hung them in a gun rack on the wall he'd prepared for the occasion. That done and his and Uncle Will's stories passed on complete, it was as if he somehow sensed his time had come. I could see a weight lifted from his shoulders as a peace descended on his soul. We spent the balance of the long day together, relishing one another's company. I bid him goodnight that evening, March seventeenth, 1911, as he retired early, alone to his bedroom to take his final rest. His spirit slipped away before the dawn. Next morning, when he didn't come to breakfast, Mammy found him passed quietly in his sleep. He'd crossed over and joined all those gone before. He died well, after a long, full life, with all his wits still about him and a loving family near at hand.

I suppose I must have known his days were numbered, but still found myself left with a great void in my young life at the loss of my father's own father. I felt like no more than a remnant, the proverbial vine without its branch. It hardly seemed fair at the time to come by such a great loss so suddenly, but I've been reminded many times since that there are worse ways to pass than peacefully in your sleep. And I'd been given in return a rich understanding of the man and his time. It pained me greatly to consider that we would never again in this life share our visits, but all he imparted to me made a long-lasting impression that I have since carried through all the walks of life I've known.

At the wake in his old house, I felt duty bound to stand stoic and vigilant like a good soldier at parade rest behind Mammy's rocker - a lanky, bucktoothed lad in an ill-fitting suit, solemn and ever present at her shoulder, perfectly silent, unsmiling and unteared throughout the course of the long evening, guarding faithfully like a statue over her quiet, dignified grief.

****

Two months after Pappy found his final resting place, some twelve-thousand surviving Confederate soldiers, joined in with one hundred six-thousand Arkansas citizens at the state capital to celebrate the twenty-first annual United Confederate Veterans Reunion, held in conjunction with the fiftieth anniversary of Fort Sumpter's shelling.

As a former Confederate State, Arkansas had seen hard fighting during the rebellion and remembered too well the devastation wrought of total war. During four years of the conflict, She had furnished forty-seven infantry regiments, seventeen cavalry units and thirteen artillery batteries, as well as filling the ranks of many other non-Arkansas regiments. Sixty thousand of the one million veterans from the state had been, like Uncle James Andrew, conscripts, forced into service against their will.

In honor and tribute to the old soldiers, Little Rock's City Park, located right next door to the old U.S. Arsenal, on the very ground where young David O. Dodd was hanged as a Confederate spy by the Union on January eighth, 1864, turned temporarily for the special occasion, into "Camp Robert Shaver."

In a tent city made of row on row of army surplus shelters, ten thousand of the visiting twelve thousand gray-haired, "gray backs" were temporarily housed in Spartan military fashion. For three special days they were roused each morning by the familiar notes of reveille, reliving together the experience of outdoor military camp life, while sharing their many reminiscences. Over the course of the seventy-two hour event, twenty-five hard-working cooks prepared nearly sixty-four thousand meals in the camp.

On the third and final day of the reunion, under a clear and sultry blue sky, one hundred fifty thousand excited Southerners, come from all corners of the former Confederate States, lined the streets, or filled the buildings and rooftops to watch the Grand Parade.

It began at the Old State House near to the river on Central and Markham. Former regiments and military musicians, many in uniform, marched through some twenty-five-city blocks. Many of the ex-soldiers in attendance were missing a leg or had an empty sleeve pinned to their waist. Row upon row of former troopers, including the surviving remnant of Forrest's Cavalry, proudly sat their well-groomed mounts. Accompanied by the clomping beat of their ironclad hooves on pavement, they turned out to be the most prominent feature of the martial spectacle.

Winding its way through the throngs of spectators, the route ended in front of the old Arsenal Headquarters Building in City Park, where a new statue was to be dedicated to the honor of the "Capital Guards." In February of 1861, the tiny Little Rock militia unit had barely averted the first shots of the Civil War from being fired in that city, when they stood between nearly ten thousand mostly south Arkansas frontiersmen, inflamed by Lincoln's national call-to-arms, who had rallied in the state capital with the intention of expelling the Union garrison then manning the U.S. Arsenal there. Instead, in a negotiated truce and under escort and protection of the small hometown militia force, the Federal soldiers marched unceremoniously out of the armory the short distance down to the riverside, where they quickly boarded packet boats and safely vacated the city. Peace, for the moment, was maintained and the war that was to soon come, would have to begin elsewhere. The same "Capital Guards" that had forestalled the onset of hostilities, were soon turned over by Arkansas Governor Henry Rector, to the command of the newly formed Confederate government. They were designated as Company A of the Sixth Arkansas Infantry. They were among the first to enter Confederate service from our state and fought to the very bitter end, being present at such epic battles as Shiloh, Perryville, Tunnel Hill, Ringgold Gap, Stones River, Murfreesboro, Chickamuaga, Atlanta and Franklin. Of the original one hundred thirty-four militia members sent into service from Little Rock, one hundred eighteen never returned to their home soil. They had been mostly professionals in their civilian walks.

At the ceremony crowning that day's festivities, twenty thousand roses were lauded over the life-size bronze statuary of a Confederate infantryman standing boldly, facing north, high above the crowd atop his tall white-granite pedestal. He yet stands vigilant before the Headquarters Building on the Arsenal grounds of what today we call MacArthur Park (in honor of the five-star general born there) as a reminder for us still of the selfless sacrifice once made by so many to that long-lost Cause.

At the close of that historic and special day, the veterans tearfully vacated the camp and in many cases, bid goodbye for the last time to their comrades-in-arms.

****

367

At his funeral in Gum Grove Cemetery, two months before the UCV Reunion, the parson concluded with a short poem over Pappy's open grave...

"He was a soldier once and young, and into the war was wholly flung.
Now the bugle call, the battle ball, again shall raise him never.
He fought and fell, he served us well, so his furlough lasts forever."

With sickening inevitability, the dark clouds of war were then already again gathering on the distant horizons of Europe.